HM

First published in Great Britain 2013
by Mills & Boon, an imprint of Harlequin (UK) Limited,
Eton House, 18-24 Paradise Road, Richmond, Surrey TW9 1SR

TO TAME THE PLAYBOY © by Harlequin Enterprises II B.V./S.à.r.l 2013

*The Playboy of Pengarroth Hall*, *A Night with the Society Playboy* and *Playboy Boss, Pregnancy of Passion* were published in Great Britain by Harlequin (UK) Limited.

*The Playboy of Pengarroth Hall* © Susanne James 2009
*A Night with the Society Playboy* © Ally Blake 2008
*Playboy Boss, Pregnancy of Passion* © Pamela Brooks 2009

ISBN: 978 0 263 90549 6
ebook ISBN: 978 1 472 00122 1

05-0413

Harlequin (UK) policy is to use papers that are natural, renewable and recyclable products and made from wood grown in sustainable forests. The logging and manufacturing processes conform to the legal environmental regulations of the country of origin.

Printed and bound in Spain
by Blackprint CPI, Barcelona

# THE PLAYBOY
# OF PENGARROTH HALL

## BY
## SUSANNE JAMES

**Susanne James** has enjoyed creative writing since childhood, completing her first—sadly unpublished—novel by the age of twelve. She has three grown-up children who were, and are, her pride and joy, and who all live happily in Oxfordshire with their families. She was always happy to put the needs of her family before her ambition to write seriously, although along the way some published articles for magazines and newspapers helped to keep the dream alive!

Susanne's big regret is that her beloved husband is no longer here to share the pleasure of her recent success. She now shares her life with Toffee, her young Cavalier King Charles spaniel, who decides when it's time to get up (early) and when a walk in the park is overdue!

For Kathie,
a true friend.

# CHAPTER ONE

THIS just had to be paradise, Fleur thought, as she trod her way carefully through the extensive grounds of Pengarroth Hall, her feet crunching through the undergrowth. A pale December sun filtering through the naked branches of the tall trees towering all around had not yet managed to thaw the dainty traces of frost glistening everywhere—but, if *this* was beautiful, what must spring and summer be like, with everything alive and in full leaf? the girl thought.

Finding the first gated entrance she'd come to locked, she had decided to walk, and had been going for some time before realizing that there had to be a more obvious route to the house than this. The path she'd started along had seemed established enough at first but had gradually petered out, but it was such a beautifully restful area in which to stroll, she'd decided to keep going just to enjoy being out of the car after her long drive from London and breathe in this fresh country air. She'd retrace her steps in a minute, she thought, and drive further on down the hill. Mia, the friend who'd invited her to spend Christmas here in the family home she shared with her brother, had been characteristically vague with her instructions.

"Just drive through the first big gate you come to," she'd said airily. "You can't miss it."

A little later, and with a painful stab of anxiety, Fleur recognized the familiar prickling at the back of her neck which usually heralded one of her bouts of exhaustion, and she kicked herself for being an idiot. She knew that if she wanted to stay well, she had to take care of herself, and she knew she had been overdoing it in the run-up to Christmas. They'd been working late at the laboratory for the last two weeks, and today's long drive to Cornwall hadn't helped. It would have been better to have waited until tomorrow, Christmas Eve, before leaving London, but Mia had persuaded her to come a day early.

"None of the other guests will have arrived, and my darling brother won't be there either, not until Christmas morning, so we'll have the house to ourselves," she'd enthused. "It'll be like old times in the dorm!" The two girls had been at the same boarding school and had remained firm friends ever since, though this was the first time Fleur had visited Pengarroth Hall.

Spotting a flat tree trunk just in front of her, Fleur sat down on it gingerly—she knew she wouldn't be able to stay there long because it was clearly very cold and damp, but it would do for her to rest there for just a few moments. She glanced at her watch—it was four o'clock already and starting to get dark—before closing her eyes briefly.

Suddenly, from out of nowhere and causing her to jump, a strong voice interrupted her thoughts.

'Good afternoon. Can I help you?'

The enquiry was brusque, with no hint of Christmas cheer about it, and Fleur looked up quickly, scrambling to her feet. She was confronted by a tall man wearing a mud-smeared wax jacket and heavy boots—and a rather forbidding expression on what was clearly a very handsome face. A shotgun hung over his shoulder. His eyes were darkly penetrating as they stared down at her, and she couldn't help feeling a tremor of apprehension—mixed with something else she was not going to acknowledge!— as she returned his gaze. Then she straightened her back, and she smiled—obviously this was the gamekeeper, or some other person employed at Pengarroth Hall.

'I don't need any help at all, thanks,' she said brightly. 'I've been enjoying a stroll in these wonderful woods, that's all.'

He didn't answer for a moment, unable to drag his gaze from the most delectable female features he'd seen in a long time. Then, 'Well, you are on private property. This area is not open for walkers. The public right of way is much further back up the hill,' he said bluntly. 'The notice is clearly marked.'

Fleur bristled at this show of pomposity. There was no need to be quite so horrible about it, even if she had been trespassing which, as an invited guest, was not the case. She attempted a thin smile, irritated with him now and not wanting to reveal that she was going to be staying at the house, or that she was a long-time friend of one of the owners.

'Oh, really?' she said. 'I really must be more careful where I put my size threes, mustn't I.' She glanced at the gun. 'Do you shoot trespassers?'

His firm mouth twisted slightly at the question, and he pushed a damp stray lock of dark hair back from his forehead. 'I'd better show you the way back in case you get lost. There are several different paths,' he said.

Fleur stared at him coldly. She could rely on her own brain and sense of direction, thank you. She certainly didn't want any favours from this surly individual. 'Don't bother yourself. I don't need any guidance, thank you,' she said tightly.

'Well, daylight will be gone soon,' he said. 'Please make your way back to the road.' He looked straight down into her cool green eyes before adding, 'This section of the grounds is being restored—blight damage to some of the trees has meant considerable replanting, and we don't want the new saplings to be disturbed by people tramping where they shouldn't.' Then he nodded briefly, turned around and walked away without another word.

Well, Fleur thought as she watched him disappearing through the gathering gloom, she'd give him ten out of ten for carrying out his duties. He'd certainly put *her* in her place. Say what you mean, and mean what you say—a man after her father's heart, that was for sure! She shook her head briefly as she thought of her parents—Helen and Philip—who were, unusually, spending Christmas in Boston this year. She couldn't remember a time when they'd not all spent the festive season together at home. But Professor Richardson, a renowned lecturer in mathematics, had seized an opportunity to mix business with pleasure, so the usual family plans had been changed.

She retraced her steps, making sure she was going the right way. It was obviously her own fault that she'd fallen foul of Mia's vague directions, and she'd known almost straight away that the path she'd chosen was not the one which would lead to the house. But she'd thoroughly enjoyed her stroll in the woods—shame that she'd had to meet up with the dour groundsman and spoil it.

It was now practically dark by the time she got back to the car. No wonder the gate had been locked—it was a wonder that they hadn't put coils of barbed wire all around it to keep everyone out!

Half a mile further down the hill, Pengarroth Hall came into view, and as Fleur approached she saw the gate which Mia had said she couldn't miss. It was wide open and inviting and, making her way slowly up the curving drive to the front door, she felt a rush of renewed pleasure at the thought of being somewhere different, with different people, for the holiday. Mia had said she'd invited several other friends along as well.

"The only one you'll have met before is Mandy,' Mia had said on the phone. 'Remember Mandy? She's a real laugh.'

Oh, I remember Mandy, Fleur had thought, a total man-eater, but yes, she'd be fun.

'All the others work with me at the office, but I promise not to allow any shop talk,' Mia had said. Mia was employed by a very successful PR company in London—a far cry from Fleur's research work in one of the city's teaching hospitals. Although their lives had taken such different paths since school and university days, they had never lost touch, and it was Mia's free and easy personal life, unconstrained by the wishes of demanding parents, that had caused Fleur many pangs of envy. Philip Richardson had had such plans for his only child—it had never occurred to him that she might have had some ambitions of her own. But, dutifully, Fleur had attained her science degree, as he'd directed, and was also careful not to introduce too many boyfriends to her parents. Not that her mother would have objected but, like Fleur, the woman was in thrall to the intellect and influence of the man in their lives, and both of them did their best not to cross him.

Now, in answer to the clanging of the ancient bell, the door was opened by a tall, rather straight-faced woman in her mid-fifties, Fleur guessed, but her broad smile was engaging enough as she introduced herself quickly.

'Oh, hello. I'm Pat—I'm housekeeper here,' she introduced herself.

'Hi, I'm Fleur Richardson.' Fleur smiled back.

'Yes, I was told you'd be the only one arriving today. Do come in. You obviously found us all right.' She stood aside as Fleur entered. 'Mia's washing her hair,' she added. 'I'll tell her you're here.'

As soon as she set foot in the place, Fleur knew that Pengarroth Hall was a home in every sense of the word. She was aware that the building was more than two hundred years old and had been owned by Mia's family for four generations, but it felt beautifully warm, cosy and welcoming. The entrance hall where she was standing was enhanced by a gigantic Christmas tree, glistening with tinsel, baubles and lights, standing at the foot of the wide staircase. In the corner was a huge grandfather clock, along the walls were a couple of low sofas, a well-worn table with some daily papers scattered about and in another corner on a low armchair a very old black Labrador snoozed, its grey-whiskered jaws and body almost lost amongst the squashy folds of an ancient blue velvet cushion. When it became aware that Fleur was standing there, the animal opened one eye, took a long deep breath, then went back to sleep. Fleur couldn't help smiling. How different all this was from her parents' well-kept mid-thirties house in Surrey—to say nothing of her own smart London flat. But she felt almost embraced by the atmosphere here, and knew she was going to love every minute of the holiday.

Just then, Mia appeared at the top of the stairs, wearing only her bra and pants, her head swathed in a large white towel.

'Hi-ya Fleur! Come on up—shan't be a jiff. Isn't this fun? I *love* Christmas!'

Happily, Fleur did as she was told, sitting on the edge of Mia's bed as Mia began rubbing her hair briskly.

'I hope you don't mind sharing my room,' Mia said breathlessly, 'and I'm asking the others to share as well.' She peered out from among the folds of the towel. 'It's not that there aren't enough rooms to go around in this place, of course, but I didn't like to give Pat all the extra work. And I know the boys won't mind sharing—you'll like them, Fleur. Gus and Tim are old friends in any case, and Rupert and Mat are really nice.' She draped the towel over the back of a chair and reached for her hairdryer.

'Of course I don't mind sharing,' Fleur said at once. 'It'll be like old times.' She paused. 'Your hair's grown so long, Mia. I've never seen it like that.'

Mia was strikingly tall, and her dark brown hair, reaching well below her shoulders, made her seem even taller. Her hazel eyes twinkled.

'Well, that's Mat's fault. He likes it this way,' she said, switching on the dryer.

Fleur raised her eyebrows. 'Oh? So Mat is—important—is he? The man of the moment?'

Mia smiled briefly. 'Sort of,' she said vaguely. 'We've been going out for a bit—nothing too heavy. In fact, I thought it wise to mix him up with others for Christmas—before we both get carried away.' She paused. 'What about you—anyone special on the scene?' She raised her voice slightly above the noise of the dryer.

'No, there isn't,' Fleur replied flatly. And probably never will be, she could have added, but didn't. Mia shot her an understanding glance, but said nothing. She knew that Fleur's father had always discouraged his daughter from having relationships. 'Don't waste your intelligence and education on marriage and children,' was his frequent advice to his daughter. 'There's plenty of time for that.'

'Well, let me remind you that next year we're both going to be twenty-seven,' Mia said, somewhat ruefully.

'Not that our biological clocks are running out exactly, but time does seem to be on wheels, doesn't it?' She switched off the dryer for a second and sighed. 'I love the idea of marriage and a family, but finding the right partner seems an impossible task. As soon as I get to know someone, really get to know how he ticks, I lose interest.' She gave a short laugh. 'It's obviously all *my* fault.' She waited a second before going on. 'Has there been anyone special since you and Leo split up?'

Fleur shrugged, looking away. 'No, not really. A few of us from work get together fairly regularly for drinks or a night out somewhere, but I always go home alone, like the good girl that I am.' Her lip curled slightly as she made that remark. Looking back on her time with Leo, when they'd meant so much to each other, she couldn't believe, now, that she'd allowed her father to come between them. But in the three years that had elapsed since that time, she'd come to realize that it had all been for the best, after all. Because she'd become utterly convinced that marriage was not for her. She would never risk being in the position which her mother had occupied all *her* life—to be subservient, having to fall in with every wish of her husband's. Although Fleur acknowledged that he was basically a good man, he had totally domineered his wife—and his daughter—because there was only one opinion that mattered: his own. And he could never accept that he might sometimes be wrong, or that others might be right. With her reasoning, analytical, intellect, Fleur know that it was fundamentally wrong for one human being—whoever he was—to always have his own way, and that she would never put up with that state of affairs.

She got up and went over to the window, gazing out across the garden and the woods beyond.

Mia, sensing her sudden sadness, said cheerfully,

'Well, unfortunately for the rest of us, when we were all young and innocent, you were the one that the guys all fancied, and we were very jealous, I can tell you. I don't know how you've managed to stay single for so long, Fleur Richardson, I really don't.'

It was true that Fleur had always been attractive to men, her dainty figure and heart-shaped face dominated by thickly lashed large green eyes crying out for attention and admiration. Plus those two other seductive characteristics—a high intelligence coupled with a teasingly vulnerable nature making men automatically feel protective towards her.

'Oh, there's nothing to it—staying single, I mean,' Fleur replied. 'Just keep your head down and go on working. There's always—*always*—stuff waiting to be done in the lab. Stuff that can't wait.' Besides,' she added, 'in my experience, men always seem to need to be in control all the time…and I want to be in control of my own life, thanks very much.'

'Some of them do,' Mia agreed, 'but there are ways of dealing with that. A little feminine cunning and you can often bring them around to your way of thinking.'

'Hmm,' Fleur said. 'If you say so. But I can do without the hassle. If I've only got myself to please, there's no emotional conflict. And I like a quiet life, I'm afraid.'

'Oh, there's going to be someone out there, somewhere, who'll change your mind one of these days,' Mia said, 'you mark my words.' Her shrewd eyes narrowed slightly as she glanced over at Fleur, and she thought how fragile the girl looked—fragile and pale. She also seemed to have lost weight, which she could not afford to do.

Fleur turned, shrugging. 'We'll see,' she said lightly. There was a pause. 'As a matter of fact, I've not been very well lately, Mia. I've completely lost my appetite and I'm tired all the time. The doctor mentioned "stress"—how I hate that word—but I have agreed to take a longer than normal Christmas break, so I'm not due back to work until mid-January.'

'Well, why not stay on longer here, then?' Mia said at once. 'All the others are going back the day after Boxing Day, but I'm not returning to London until the second of January… We'll have some lovely extra time together. It'll do you good to be here in the peace and quiet, and Pat will love looking after you, spoiling you. And if her cooking can't bring your appetite back to life, no one's can. You've not made other plans, have you? Haven't got to go back to the parents for some TLC?'

'No, I haven't promised anything,' Fleur said quickly. 'I…haven't said anything to them about not feeling well lately… I don't want any fuss…'

'Well then, stay here and relax. Read. Walk. Watch telly. Stay in bed till mid-morning if you like. No one to please but yourself—that is what you want, isn't it?'

'Sounds wonderful,' Fleur said slowly, 'but I couldn't outstay my welcome like that, Mia—I'd feel awful having someone to wait on me, prepare my meals…'

'I'm telling you—Pat will be ecstatic,' Mia assured her. 'It's a funny old life for her, really, looking after a big house that's got no one in it, sometimes for weeks on end.' She finished drying her hair and opened her wardrobe, peering inside. 'What to wear, what to wear,' she muttered to herself, before selecting jeans and a chunky woolen jumper. 'We must bring in all your stuff from the car,' she said over her shoulder, 'and then I'll leave you alone for an hour to settle in.' She smiled. 'It's going to be just the two of us until tomorrow evening, so we can have a good old gossipy natter.' She pulled her still damp hair free from the high neck of her jumper, and picked up her hairbrush. 'I only got home myself a couple of hours ago,' she added. 'Hasn't Pat made the tree look fantastic? That woman really is a treasure.'

'She doesn't live in all the time, then?' Fleur asked.

'Oh, no, only when one of us, or some friends, are here. She lives in one of the estate cottages with her mother, but the two of them make sure everything's OK while the house is unoccupied. My brother is regularly away, working for a law firm who engage him on a part-time basis—of course, he's the one in charge of the estate now that our parents aren't here any more.' Mia stopped brushing her hair for a second, biting her lip.

Fleur said quickly, 'It must be difficult for him, juggling work and the estate. I don't expect he thought he'd have to take over here quite so soon.'

'He certainly didn't. Neither of us did,' Mia said. 'For both our parents to die so unexpectedly, four years ago, before either of them had reached sixty, was a dreadful shock.'

'I know,' Fleur said sympathetically. She had never met Mia's parents, or her brother, but knew all about them from her friend.

'And it dropped Pengarroth Hall prematurely right into Seb's lap,' Mia said. 'He was only thirty, and enjoying his life in London—rather too much, in some people's opinion! But my playboy brother had to grow up some time—to the disappointment of the party crowd and his many lady friends. I don't think he was best pleased. Still—' she brightened up quickly, as Mia always did, whatever the circumstances '—he's got used to it. And it pleases Gran. She and Gramps loved Pengarroth Hall— where they lived too, of course, for most of their lives.'

'Goodness—is your grandmother still alive?' Fleur asked.

'You bet!' Mia said. 'And we both visit her often. As a matter of fact, I believe she was a bit of a girl-about-town in her youth, when she met my grandfather. And she still loves being in the big city, where she lives in the most amazing flat. She's in her mid-eighties now, but she's got a large circle of friends... They go to the theatre, out to meals, play bridge regularly. There's no stopping her. But she loves to think that Pengarroth Hall is still in the family. Worships Sebastian, of course. He's the golden boy.'

'She's not coming here for Christmas?' Fleur asked.

'We couldn't persuade her,' Mia replied. 'Especially when she knew there'd be a crowd of us in residence. Said she'd rather spend it with her own friends, and leave us to ours. She always spends a couple of months here in the summer, though.'

'She sounds a lot of fun,' Fleur said wistfully, thinking what a solitary sort of life she had led, with no siblings and never having known *her* grandparents, or any other family members.

'She's fantastic,' Mia said breezily. 'We love her to bits.'

Going downstairs to collect Fleur's belongings from the car, Mia stopped to pat the sleeping dog's head as they went by.

'Poor old Benson,' she said softly. 'He's so old now, snoozes most of the time, but Sebastian won't have another dog on the premises, not until Benson has popped his clogs. Says this is Benson's territory.' She rubbed the dog's nose with her forefinger. 'Anyway, Frank, our groundsman, has enough to do without having a young animal to train.'

Fleur made a face. 'I think I met Frank earlier,' she

said, 'and was roundly told off for trespassing. I came in at the wrong gate—the upper one—by mistake.'

'Oh, you mad woman!' Mia said. 'But I'm a bit scatty with directions so that was probably my fault. Why—what did he say?'

'More or less told me to clear off and to be more observant in future and follow appropriate signs.'

Mia giggled. 'He can be a bossy boots and rather short-tempered,' she said, 'but he's worth his weight in gold. Seb relies on him totally when he's not here. And of course when visitors come to shoot game in the autumn, Frank runs everything.'

Later, when she was alone, Fleur unpacked and, taking the hint from her friend, changed into jeans and a green jumper that did marvelous things for her eyes and brushed her hair back into a ponytail. Then she wiped off all her make-up before moisturizing her skin. It felt so good not to have to bother about looking immaculate and put aside her heels for the evening. She suddenly felt upbeat, looking forward to a cosy evening with one of her best friends. Then, slipping her bare feet into her Uggs, she left the room and went downstairs, almost colliding with Pat at the bottom.

'Oh, there you are,' the woman said. 'Mia's just dashed down the road to deliver some Christmas presents. Go into the sitting room—the one there on the left. I'll bring you some tea in a few minutes.'

Fleur wandered along the hallway to the room which had been indicated, going straight over to the huge fireplace, where some logs were burning brightly in the grate. This holiday had all the elements of a real Dickensian Christmas, she thought, feeling thrilled all over again that she was a guest here. The large room was comfortably—though not opulently—furnished, with sofas and armchairs, none of which were new. The carpet, though worn, felt soft under her feet and she kicked off her Uggs as she sat down on the armchair nearest to the fire. Leaning her head back contentedly, she closed her eyes. She could get used to this, she thought dreamily, this serenity, this feeling of well-being. Perhaps—perhaps she *could* allow herself to be persuaded to take Mia up on the offer to stay on for a while longer…just so long as she was certain she wouldn't be in anyone's way. Perhaps for an extra week, she thought, wiggling her bare toes in front of the flames, a delightful drowsiness beginning to seep over her.

After a few moments, something made her open her eyes and with a start she found herself staring up into the familiar face she'd seen before today. The groundsman stood there, wearing well-cut jeans and dark polo shirt, one hand thrust casually into his pocket. He was obviously very much at home here, Fleur thought instinctively. She smiled faintly.

'Oh…hello,' she said non-committally, nestling back down into the chair. 'We meet again.' She hoped he would feel a slight pang of conscience when he remembered his curt behaviour earlier, especially when it was obvious that she was a guest.

His eyes narrowed slightly as he took in her appearance, noting the willowy figure and unblemished skin devoid of artifice, but, before he could say a word, Mia breezed into the room—stopping short as she saw him standing there.

'Seb! What on earth are *you* doing here?'

'I do live here from time to time, remember,' he said, going towards her and giving her a bear hug. 'Hi, Mia.'

'Yes—but you said you wouldn't be home until

Christmas morning,' Mia protested. 'What made you change your mind?'

'It was changed for me—but I can't be bothered to explain,' he replied. 'Why—does it matter?'

'No, of course not. You just took me by surprise, that's all. And Pat didn't tell me, either.'

'Because she didn't know until half an hour ago. I didn't see her at lunch time when I arrived, and then I took myself off straight away to look around the estate while it was still light. It's Frank's day off today.' He paused. 'Still, I'm here now. Hope my presence hasn't ruined your plans too much.'

'Idiot,' Mia said fondly. 'Course not.' She went over to Fleur, whose colour had risen perceptibly, and who suddenly wanted to kick herself. This was not Frank the groundsman, this was Sebastian Conway! What a stupid assumption to have made!

'Have you two introduced yourselves?' Mia asked. 'Fleur—this is my gorgeous brother, and this, Sebastian, is one of my very best friends, Fleur Richardson.'

Fleur stood up then, slowly, wishing she could just disappear, but Sebastian came across and held out a strong hand, gripping hers firmly. He looked down at her, his thoughtful black eyes glinting in the firelight.

'We have met before, haven't we,' he murmured. Then, 'You really should have said who you were.'

Mia looked bewildered. 'What's going on?' she demanded.

Fleur looked at her helplessly. 'This was the man I thought was…Frank…' she began, and Mia burst out laughing.

'Oh, Seb! Fleur told me you were horrible to her, accusing her of trespassing! How could you?'

'If I'd known she was one of your guests, I would

have said nothing, but escorted her back to her car and directed her to the house,' he said. 'It's just that Frank is very protective of all the new saplings—for which I'm grateful to him—and I was out checking up on them when we…er…Fleur and I…came across each other.'

'Well, allow me to apologize for my earlier misde-meanour.' Fleur smiled, trying to sound more relaxed than she felt at that precise moment.

'And I offer mine for running you off,' he said equably.

Just then, Pat came in with a tray of tea. She smiled as she set the things down on a low table. 'It's great to have folk about the place for a change,' she exclaimed, standing back and looking from one to another happily. 'Supper will be ready in forty-five minutes,' she added as she left.

As the three of them sat drinking their tea and chat-ting, Fleur was painfully aware of Sebastian's long legs stretched out in front of him, of his powerful frame and strong features. This was a man to be reckoned with, she thought. A man used to getting his own way. A man who liked to be in control. Who would always *expect* to be in control.

And Sebastian, as he listened to his sister's high-spirited account of what she'd been up to since they'd last been together, was making judgements of his own. For once, this particular friend of Mia's—and he'd met a few—didn't fall into the normal category he'd come to expect. She wasn't lowering her eyes at him, or exhibit-ing the kind of come-on tactics that were all too famil-iar. She was undeniably very attractive—and, from her self-deprecating description of the research work she was engaged in, unusually clever. But she displayed an oddly distant attitude which he found disconcerting. She was not aloof exactly, but there was a wistful coolness about her that he confessed to finding distinctly intriguing. He stood up quickly and went across to the cabinet to pour some drinks.

## CHAPTER TWO

'THAT really was the best Christmas I've ever, ever had,' Fleur said as she and Mia helped Pat to clear up in the kitchen. Pat, with assistance from Beryl, her mother, had produced the most amazing food all over the holiday, and now, with everyone else having just departed, it was time to wind down from the festivities.

'I don't think I'll want another thing to eat—not until tomorrow, anyway!' Mia joked. 'You really are fantastic, Pat—thank you *so* much for all your hard work. I'm still dribbling after that goose!'

'Well, you know I always look forward to you and Sebastian being home,' Pat said, spreading some tea towels to dry, 'and all your friends were very appreciative. No one left anything on their plates, anyway,' she added. 'Always a good sign.'

Mia glanced at Fleur, thinking how easily she had fitted in with everyone else, and how she'd seemed to enjoy all the festive food—despite her apparent lack of appetite.

'Yes, everyone enjoyed themselves thoroughly,' Mia said. 'We might do it all over again next year!' She giggled. 'Mandy's such a naughty girl, though, isn't she? She told me that she'd intended seducing Sebastian this time—

she's tried before—hoping that the spirit of Christmas, or Christmas spirits, might make him fall for her charms.'

'Hmm, some hopes,' Pat snorted. 'Sebastian is much too clever for antics like that. And I don't blame him either.' Pat had known the family for too long not to feel quite comfortable about expressing her opinions. 'Especially in view of…you know…' Her voice trailed off.

'Yes, you're right, Pat. Poor old Seb…' Mia began, pulling out a chair to sit down.

'What's the matter with poor old Seb?' he demanded as he came into the kitchen.

'Oh, I was just saying how incorrigible Mandy is,' Mia said hurriedly. 'Flirting outrageously with all the guys—including you, Seb. Or didn't you even notice?'

Sebastian merely grinned at that, and Mia went on, 'Not that you showed your face much anyway; we hardly saw anything of you.'

It was true that he'd been rather conspicuous by his absence, Fleur thought as she glanced up at him briefly. He'd apparently spent Christmas Eve with friends in the area, not coming home until the small hours, but had joined them for the main Christmas Day meal and for supper again on Boxing Day. But he'd seemed to prefer leaving the eight of them to enjoy themselves without him—and Fleur couldn't blame him. They were all just that few years younger than him, and she'd noticed that sometimes their chatter and alcohol-fuelled banter had appeared to bore him. Her eyes narrowed briefly. He was sort of…mysterious…in a way, she thought. Certainly not your normal run-of-the-mill handsome bachelor. The only woman he seemed to have eyes for was his sister— who he clearly adored. But Fleur couldn't help wondering what he thought about *her*. She'd noticed him glance at her speculatively from time to time, but he didn't seem to like—or dislike—her. She was, after all, just another of his sister's friends, who he seemed to tolerate but, as Mia was entitled to invite whoever she wanted to, he'd have to put up with it.

By now, it was late afternoon and already darkening outside, and Fleur suddenly felt a need to get out into the open air. Although they'd all gone for short walks once or twice during the holiday—keeping strictly to the paths which Sebastian had recommended—most of the time had been spent eating, drinking, dozing, watching films and telling ghost stories.

'I'd love to go for a walk, Mia,' she said, looking down at her friend, who was lounging back in her chair lazily. 'Just for half an hour…can we?'

'Oh, Fleur…count me out!' Mia begged. 'Tramping about in soggy undergrowth is the last thing on *my* mind. But—hey, Seb will go with you—he'll protect you from all the wild animals out there. Won't you, Seb?'

Fleur felt a huge wave of embarrassment sweep over her. 'No! There's no need for that… It doesn't matter, really,' she said quickly. 'It's just me being silly. Forget it.'

'No need to forget it,' Sebastian said casually. 'But we must go now while there's still some light.' He glanced at her. He'd already observed her obvious stylish dress sense, and on Christmas evening, as they'd all sat around the candle-lit table, her simple black low-necked dress and the fine gold chain around her neck had, in his opinion, set her apart from everyone else. 'You'd better dress warmly—you brought some walking boots with you, I hope.'

Well, that sounded a bit headmasterly, Fleur thought, but still—presumably he had her best interests at heart.

'Oh, yes—Mia warned me that I'd need them,' she said. She went towards the door. 'I'll get a thicker sweater and a waterproof. Shan't be a minute.'

As soon as she'd gone, Mia said, 'Seb, I want you to do me a big, big favour—' and he interrupted.

'Not another one. What's it this time?'

'It's not for me, personally,' Mia replied. 'It's just that… well…Fleur is going to stay on for a bit—about ten days— after I've gone back. Pat has kindly agreed to look after her for me, so that's no problem…'

'It'll be a pleasure,' Pat said, as she finally emptied the dishwasher. 'I like your friend, Mia—she was always the first to offer to help us out.'

'What's it got to do with me?' Sebastian demanded.

'I want you to kind of…well…take her under your wing while she's here. You said you weren't going back to London until the end of the month, and…'

'What exactly does "taking her under my wing" involve?' Sebastian said resignedly.

'Oh, nothing much, you know…just be *nice*—be around to share the occasional meal with her, maybe show her the area, take her down to the pub…' She paused. 'I'm worried about her. She's lost weight since I last saw her, and I know she doesn't sleep too well. A bit of a holiday here will do her the world of good, but she will need some company now and again and you're just the man.'

'Now, look Mia…' Sebastian began.

She said at once, 'Oh, don't worry, Seb, it's not what *you're* thinking. I wouldn't dream of trying my hand at the matchmaking game. Never again. Not with you or anyone else. I've learned my lesson in *that* department.'

'I should think so too, and I'm very glad to hear it,' he said flatly. It had been another "best friend" of his sister's—she seemed to have so many—who, not so long ago, he'd become engaged to, which had turned out to be a total disaster. And since then he'd hardly looked at another woman, no longer seeming to need female company. Not in any serious sense. And that worried him slightly.

'In any case,' Mia went on, 'Fleur is not on the market, so you can relax. She's not interested in tying herself down to any man, so you're quite safe. I guarantee it.' She sighed. 'I feel so sorry for her, that's all. Despite all her outward success and although ostensibly she's a free woman, she seems sort of…trapped…as if she can't break free to be really happy. It must be dreadful to feel like that.' Mia made a face as she thought about it.

'Well, I don't mind being civil, if that's what you mean,' Sebastian said shortly, 'but don't expect me to provide non-stop entertainment for her, will you? I've got four weeks to catch up on things here before I'm due back in London, and I've got appointments in Truro with the surveyor and the accountant…but…' he paused '…yes, all right, I'll arrange to be here for some of the time to hold your friend's hand—if that's what you want.'

Mia smiled up at him. 'You don't need to go *that* far,' she said demurely, 'and Fleur won't thank you for getting close enough to hold her hand, either. Just be your darling self and keep her company now and then, that's all I'm asking. You'll be just the tonic I think she needs.'

Fleur, about to go back into the kitchen, had paused outside the door just long enough to overhear most of what had been said…and she froze, horrified. The last thing in the world she wanted was to be a burden to anyone—certainly not to the somewhat austere Sebastian! How could Mia put him—put them both—in such an awkward and embarrassing position? But what could be done about it now? She could hardly burst in and tell them she'd heard his reluctant reply to Mia's request—or even say that she'd changed her mind and wasn't going to stay after all. What excuse could she give? She'd already accepted the invitation, and Pat had been so touchingly pleased. Fleur bit her lip, feeling her cheeks flood with colour as she stood there. It was obvious that Sebastian saw her as an unwelcome intrusion into his busy life, and that was the last thing she'd envisaged when she'd accepted Mia's suggestion. Then common sense prevailed, and she took a deep breath. There was a simple way out of this, she thought. She'd stay a day or two after Mia had gone before inventing a telephone call telling her to return early. It could be about something important in the lab that needed her input. That was it—no need to panic, after all, she told herself.

She opened the door and went inside, and Sebastian clicked his fingers for the dog to get up from the floor.

'We'll take Benson with us,' he said, 'as we shan't be going too far. A short walk won't tire him too much.'

Outside, it was much colder than Fleur had thought, and she turned up the collar of her jacket. Sebastian glanced down at her briefly.

'We can always go back if you find you're not enjoying this,' he said casually.

'No, it's fine. I'd like to walk,' Fleur said, not looking at him. 'But…I'm perfectly all right by myself if you've things to do. I know this path because we all walked this way yesterday, and Benson will keep me company.'

'Oh, Mia would kill me if I abandoned you,' he said.

They walked in silence for a few minutes and, although it was certainly wet and soggy—as Mia had predicted— there was something magical about their surroundings… the magic Fleur had felt when she'd arrived at the beginning of her stay, and it made her say suddenly, 'It must be wonderful to be able to wander in these enchanted woods whenever you want to…' She hesitated. 'Mia told me that you work part-time in London, but…how often do you get down here? You must hate having to go back to town.'

He thought about that for a moment. Then, 'Sometimes I do,' he admitted, 'but, in any case, the time is coming when I shall have to part company with the firm I work for and live here permanently. It's getting more and more difficult to stretch myself between the two places.'

Something in his tone of voice made Fleur look up quickly. 'Will you mind that?' she asked quietly.

'I'm getting used to the idea,' he said. 'Of course, I knew it would come to an end one day, but I never expected it to happen quite so soon.' He paused. 'I've made a lot of friends in London that, with the best will in the world, I'll eventually lose touch with. It's inevitable. I'll be well and truly buried down here for keeps. I've just got to accept it.'

Neither of them spoke for a few moments. 'It's very annoying—to say the least—when your life is planned out for you,' Fleur began, and he interrupted.

'You sound as if you speak from experience,' he said, and she smiled up at him quickly.

'Well, in a way I do,' she said. 'Not that *I* have been given the responsibility of having to hold the reins of a large family estate, nothing like that, but…'

'Go on,' he said, wanting to know more.

'It's just that, well, I had my own plans for what I wanted to do with my life but my father had other ideas.' She paused. 'He persuaded me…' she didn't utter the more truthful word *insisted* '…that my true vocation was in the sciences, and that with my "exceptional brain"—his words, not mine—I had a duty to use it for the good of others. So that's why I'm in medical research.' She shook her head briefly. 'I enjoy the work—of course I do—it's fulfilling and very exciting when we make any sort of breakthrough. But such a lot of it is painstaking and repetitive and often very disappointing.' She looked up at him again. 'So there you are—that's my life sorted out for me. And I had such ideas of my own. Probably ridiculous when I really think about it.'

He grinned back at her and for the first time Fleur saw his heart-stopping smile, a smile enlivened by immaculate, strong white teeth. 'Go on—I'm waiting for the punchline,' he said.

Fleur sighed, looking away. 'I always imagined myself as an opera singer,' she said, almost apologetically. 'I realize that it was probably an impossible dream—the professional stage is overwhelmingly competitive, and luck is such a huge factor. But it would have been good to at least have tried.' She gave a short laugh. 'Not that luck is *my* second name—I mean, I never win *anything*, never win raffles or anything that relies on chance. Some people win things all the time.'

'Yes, they do,' he agreed. 'Actually, I do win things now and then.' He didn't bother to add that in the circles he mixed in he was constantly asked to purchase massively priced tickets for good causes and that he always obliged, very generously. Which probably increased his chances. 'But do go on,' he said. 'You've obviously had musical training?'

'Oh, yes—I *was* allowed that,' Fleur said, a slight trace of bitterness in her tone. 'I achieved all my grades up to the point where I should have gone on to gain higher qualifications…then the paternal foot was well and truly put down. So—' she sighed '—as you so rightly said, it's hard to do two things at once. In my case, impossible.' She shrugged. 'So I content myself with enjoying music at a distance, as a listener and a devoted member of numerous audiences. And singing along with my CDs. When I was still living at home, that was how I learned all the famous arias, making sure that my father was never around when I was doing it. He would *not* have approved!'

The tangible note of regret in her voice made Sebastian's brow crease slightly. That didn't sound fair, he thought. 'Well, in a way, our situations are not dissimilar,' he said. 'We've both ended up doing what others have decided we should. Although—' he smiled down at her again '—in my case it was the hand of fate that merely hastened my inevitable destiny.' He hesitated. 'But it's not too late for you, is it? You could change the course of things, couldn't you?'

Fleur chuckled. 'My father would *never* forgive me if I did that,' she exclaimed. 'And he would make me feel so guilty if I gave up my career to pursue such a dramatically different path. Which, in his view, would be a very flippant one. I mean, you don't save lives by singing songs, do you? He has no time for music and rarely listens to any. But my mother does—though she doesn't often play the piano any more because it disturbs my father when he's working.' She shook her head. 'No, it is much too late for me now, Sebastian.'

With a little jolt of surprise, Fleur realized that that was the first time she had called him by name…but the easy conversation had seemed to put them on a more comfortable footing.

By this time they'd walked on quite a bit further than Sebastian had intended, and he glanced at the dog, who was padding rather forlornly behind them.

'I think we ought to go back now,' he said. 'Benson's had enough and we shan't be able to see a thing in a minute, though I did bring my torch.'

Fleur smiled up at him. 'We don't want to tire Benson out, but I could carry on like this for hours!'

Yes, I believe she could, Sebastian thought. Even though she was obviously more used to being in town, Fleur had a definite affinity with the countryside, had picked her own way over the pits, humps and bumps of the terrain without any help from him. He hadn't once felt the need to put his hand under her elbow, or steady her as they'd made their way. Perhaps she wasn't as fragile as she looked.

When she knew that their walk was coming to an end, Fleur made a sudden decision—thanks to the rather unexpected familiarity which seemed to have developed between them. Keeping her eyes fixed firmly ahead, she said lightly, 'By the way, Sebastian, you needn't worry that I'm going to get in the way of your plans while I'm here.' She hesitated. 'And I'm…sorry…that Mia has put you in the unenviable position of being my "minder". But I assure you that I am very used to looking out for myself. I do it all the time, because I live alone.' Now she did look up to find his searching eyes—black and intense and clearly visible, even in the gloom—staring right into hers. 'It was wrong of Mia to expect anything from you where I'm concerned—anything at all—I certainly don't. It's extremely kind of you—of both of you—to invite me to stay, and I don't anticipate being bored. I can never remember being bored, in any situation,' she added. She smiled. 'I shall explore the area thoroughly, and lock it all into my memory so that when I get home I can relive it. And you must just…just pretend that I'm not here.'

Sebastian was ready to admit that it would be hard to follow *that* instruction! Fleur Richardson was the first woman for a very long time to excite his interest. But, although it was patently clear that the conversation with his sister had been overheard, it didn't worry him in the least. He was seldom embarrassed or fazed by anything any more.

'Isn't there a man at home who'll be gasping for your return?' he asked bluntly.

Fleur smiled at that. 'No,' she said simply. 'No, there isn't.'

His rather peremptory enquiry made Fleur feel that she could ask a similar question. What was sauce for the goose…

'And you?' she asked coolly. 'Don't you have a lady ready to be mistress of Pengarroth Hall?'

'Don't bother to ask,' he replied, his mouth tightening at the thought.

Just before they stepped into the pool of light shining from the house, they both automatically slowed in their tracks, as if neither of them wanted to bring this particular time to an end, and standing closer to her now, closer than he had during their walk, Sebastian looked down at her.

'I do have things to do during January,' he said, 'but I'm also due for some time off. So…as Mia has told me I must, it will give me great pleasure to spend some of it with you. And, because I always obey my sister's wishes, I will take you under my wing—and you must try and enjoy it. Because,' he said patiently, 'that's what Mia wants us to do.' He smiled down at her then, a crooked, knowing smile that made Fleur's knees tremble slightly.

Well, he seemed to have cleared the air without any difficulty, Fleur thought, feeling strangely relieved. He obviously believed in coming straight to the point in any situation. But, whatever he said, she'd make herself scarce most of the time she was at Pengarroth Hall. There was certainly no need for him to add *her* name to his list of commitments!

# CHAPTER THREE

MIA lay quite still, watching Fleur's sleeping form in the bed opposite her. Frowning momentarily, Mia wondered how her friend would really manage to enjoy herself when she, Mia, had returned to London. It would naturally feel very different at Pengarroth Hall without her, Mia realized, and although Sebastian had said he'd 'look after' Fleur—as much as his work would allow—would that be enough to keep her happily occupied? Not to mention the fact that Seb could be an unknown quantity at times.

As if she knew she was being watched, Fleur suddenly opened her eyes and smiled, turning to lie on her back and stretching her arms above her head. 'Morning,' she said sleepily.

'D'you know what the time is?' Mia enquired and, without waiting for a reply, added, 'It's gone ten-thirty.' But she was genuinely pleased that Fleur seemed so much more relaxed and was definitely sleeping better than when she'd first arrived.

Fleur sat up then, hugging her knees. 'Well, we were very late to bed, weren't we?' she said, yawning. 'I've never spent New Year's Eve in a country pub before, with everyone so friendly and singing along...' She paused. 'You and Sebastian knew almost everyone there.'

'Quite a few,' Mia agreed. 'Like us, some return home

for holidays and the festive season, so we meet up then. But it's all very uncomplicated and informal.'

'I thought it was great,' Fleur said appreciatively, 'and I've never been kissed by so many complete strangers in my life when the twelve o'clock chimes rang out!' She didn't bother to mention that Sebastian hadn't joined in with that part of the proceedings—not that *she* could see, anyway—he certainly had not kissed *her*! But, even in that large, milling crowd, he had stood head and shoulders above most of them and had looked very debonair, casually dressed, his black hair sleek and shining with health.

'Oh, that only happens on this one night of the year,' Mia said, 'when everyone goes a bit crazy. I wouldn't like you to have the wrong impression of our neighbours, or our lifestyles!' She threw back her duvet and went across to the window, drawing back the curtains. 'Oh, look—there's been a really heavy frost again…everything looks so pretty.' She paused. 'And there's my brother, with Benson.' She yawned loudly. 'Seb's always up and about at the crack of dawn—I wonder if he ever goes to bed at all.'

'You and Sebastian are very close, aren't you,' Fleur said enviously. 'I wish *I'd* had a brother—or a sister.'

'Hmm,' Mia said. 'Seb and I have always got on brilliantly, it's true, but I think the age gap between us sometimes makes him feel responsible for me. Too responsible. He has played the heavy-handed head of the house once or twice—which can be extremely annoying—and with which I am not well pleased, I can tell you.'

'Oh?' Fleur said, not altogether surprised. Even though Sebastian seemed very tolerant and affectionate towards Mia, she could imagine him playing the dominant male when he felt like it. 'Why—what happened?'

'Oh, it was over relationships, of course...I used to feel he was vetting my boyfriends all the time, but the big crunch came over Andrew... You remember Andy? You met him once or twice, didn't you... About four years ago, it was.'

'I did,' Fleur said at once. 'He was a real charmer, and I thought he was the one for you. I was staggered when that all fell apart.'

'Yes, well, it fell apart because my big brother found things out about him and confronted him about it...in my flat! It was the most embarrassing, hurtful night of my life!' She shuddered. 'In Seb's defence, he *had* tried several times to warn me, privately, but of course I wouldn't hear a word against Andy. Wouldn't believe it. So in the end the whole wretched business was brought right into my sitting room! And Andy couldn't deny any of it! I thought I was going to die at the time, but of course I didn't,' she added cheerfully.

'Another woman?' Fleur said, curiosity overcoming her normal reluctance to pry into other people's affairs.

'Oh, nothing as simple as *that*,' Mia said, reaching for her dressing gown. 'No, it turned out that Andy was engaged in financial skullduggery—big time. Sebastian had obviously decided to make some enquiries, and he dug out some real dirt, I can tell you. And I was as mad as hell that my brother had interfered in my life... I felt I should be allowed to make my own mistakes. But, of course, every single thing he'd found out about Andy proved to be true—and if I'd had my own way I might be visiting my husband in jail by now!' She grimaced. 'I am grateful to Seb—but I didn't see it quite like that at the time.' She turned to look at Fleur. 'And the last remark Andy made to me was that he'd make damned sure his next woman didn't have a hard-nosed, interfering lawyer for a brother!'

'Where's Andrew now?' Fleur wanted to know.

'Oh, disappeared to Spain or somewhere, I believe…no doubt carrying on his nefarious exercises undetected—for the moment. Seb never took it further—as he said, he's not a member of the police force. All he wanted was Andrew out of my life. And in that he was very successful indeed!'

Even though it had clearly been very fortunate for Mia that her boyfriend's activities had been exposed before it was too late, Fleur could readily understand how her friend would have felt. And it confirmed Fleur's impression of Sebastian. A force to be reckoned with and a force not easily deterred. Like someone else she knew!

'I am going to be very jealous thinking of you here, just lazing around,' Mia said, changing the subject. 'Though I do hope the days won't drag for you, Fleur.'

Fleur got out of bed as well then, and went across to join Mia. 'Don't give that a thought,' she said. 'I'm never bored. It'll be wonderful to just let each day take care of itself instead of trying to make every hour count.' She paused. 'The only thing is, I didn't bring enough clothes with me for an extended stay… I'll probably have to do some washing.'

'That shouldn't be a problem, and I know we're not the same size—*or* shape,' Mia said quickly, 'but help yourself to anything of mine, Fleur… Well, you'll be all right for skirts if my jeans don't fit. And sweaters galore, which remain here permanently. Anyway,' she added, 'no one dresses up down here. Just be warm and comfortable and forget about looking good. Not that *you* wouldn't look good, even in sackcloth and ashes!' She turned away. 'You go and shower first,' she said, flopping back down on her bed. 'Take your time—I told Pat we'd get our own breakfast and lunch today so that she could go home to her cottage for a few hours.' She smiled. 'And that's another thing I'll be picturing—you sitting down to Pat's glorious meals.'

'She's certainly a fantastic cook,' Fleur said. 'I shall be twice the size by the time I go home.'

'Hmm,' Mia said, thinking that even if she was, Fleur wouldn't ever reach *her* weight. But she was really pleased to see how relaxed she had become over the days. She looked less wan and more like the enthusiastic young woman she'd always been at school and university.

Neither of them spoke for a few moments as Fleur remained by the window, gazing out at the gardens below, her eyes searching the near and far distance… but Sebastian had gone.

The following morning, after Mia had left Pengarroth Hall, Fleur decided to explore the area outside the house and grounds. She had not yet seen anything like the full extent of the estate, but felt it would be a good move to go somewhere different today. She didn't want to keep bumping into Sebastian—whom she and Mia had seen very little of since New Year's Eve. He'd looked in on them briefly last evening, but hadn't joined them for supper. It was obvious that he was very preoccupied, and Fleur had seen him and Frank in the distance once or twice, clearly in deep discussion.

Fleur had persuaded Pat that she could easily manage to get her own breakfast and lunch every day, and that at most she need only concern herself with the day's main meal…and that was more for Sebastian's sake than her own.

'We'll see about that,' Pat had said 'I shall be popping

in and out, in any case, but it'll be useful to be with Mum a bit, because she's not too well at the moment. She's going to be eighty-five this year,' she added, 'so it's only to be expected if she has an off day sometimes.'

It was a clear, icy morning as Fleur set off along the winding drive, well wrapped up against the cold as Mia had instructed her, admitting to herself again that she hadn't felt as good and as energetic as this for ages. She also had to admit that she'd scarcely thought about work—or her parents—for the entire holiday. A change of scene, especially with Mia there, was what she'd obviously been needing after all, she thought, not those tablets the doctor had prescribed. Then she put her hand to her mouth, suddenly realizing she'd forgotten to take any for the last two days. Oh, well, she'd take one tomorrow.

Outside the huge gate, she stopped for a moment, wondering whether to go up the hill or down to the valley—the direction in which Sebastian had driven them to the pub the other night. Downhill sounded the better option, she thought, turning decisively and starting to make her way along the narrow, high-hedged road.

She'd hardly gone any distance when she heard a car approaching rapidly behind her and she instinctively stood back, well into the side. It wasn't a car—it was a Land Rover, with Sebastian at the wheel, and he immediately pulled up and spoke through the open window.

'Good morning. Want a lift? Do you know where you're going?' he asked.

Fleur smiled faintly—this was just what she was trying to avoid. 'No—on both counts, thanks,' she said. 'I'm just going to have a look around, sort of get my bearings.' She paused, conscious that he was staring unashamedly at her, right into her eyes, burrowing his way into her soul! She hoped he approved of the thick jacket of Mia's that she was wearing, with its fur-lined hood framing her face. But his expression remained as it always was—curiously unfathomable—and it had its usual effect so that she quickly tore her gaze away. 'What's at the bottom of this hill?' she asked, pointing ahead.

'Well, when you get there—and it's more than a mile—there are some houses, cottages, a couple of farms, a few shops, the village hall and the pub. Which you've already been in,' he said. 'Plus the river, of course—which is in full flood at the moment.' He paused. 'Why don't you hop in—I can at least give you a ride one way.'

Fleur hesitated, then, 'Oh, go on, then,' she said, slightly reluctantly. Her plan had been to give him a wide berth today, to keep clear of Pengarroth Hall and not be under his feet, but thanks to him, that plan had come unstuck straight away.

He leaned across and opened the passenger door, stretching out his hand to pull her up as she climbed aboard. His firm grasp enveloped her hand and she slammed the door quickly behind her, not looking across at him as he revved the engine. They set off down the hill at considerable speed and after a moment Fleur did turn her head. He was wearing heavy-duty gear, as before, she noted, though the sturdy fabric of his trousers couldn't disguise the strength of his firm thighs. But his hands, brown and lean as he held the steering wheel, were surprisingly smooth, the fingers long and sensitive. Which was hardly surprising, Fleur thought, because although today he could be mistaken for a farmer, he was a businessman, a lawyer. A man of many parts, and of obvious distinction. She sighed briefly. Why was she dissecting him like this? she asked herself. He was just another male person, the sort she came across all the time. But… no…that wasn't true, she acknowledged. She couldn't remember ever having been in the company of someone so outstandingly handsome, so out-of-your-mind gorgeous. The fact that he had an undoubtedly imperious streak was a bit of a turn-off—she remembered their first encounter!—and yet, who could blame him? He had a lot of responsibilities, both here and in London. A weak-minded individual wouldn't get very far. But he was obviously capable of other, much more likeable qualities—proved by his affection and care for Mia. On balance, Fleur thought wryly, she'd be very happy to have him for a brother.

'You're quiet,' he observed non-committally. 'Are you feeling OK?'

Fleur looked at him sharply. 'Why do you ask? I'm fine, thank you.'

'Oh, it was only that Mia hinted you'd been off colour lately, that's all. Though you look good to me,' he added, smiling briefly across at her.

Oh, Mia, really! Fleur thought. She didn't want her health discussed—certainly not with Sebastian. He probably thought he'd have to be on standby to ring the doctor in the middle of the night if she had a funny turn! She gave a short unnecessary cough. 'I've been suffering from a slight case of over-work, that's all,' she said lightly. 'This time away is already working wonders—plus Pat's wonderful meals, of course. So there's no need for you... for *anyone*...to worry about me.'

'I wasn't worried,' he said casually.

'That's all right, then,' she replied.

They reached the bottom of the hill and he pulled up and drew into the side of the road. 'I'm seeing someone at this farm here, for an hour,' he said, and Fleur shrugged inwardly. He didn't have to explain his whereabouts to her. 'There are plenty of good walks around for you to try,' he went on, 'and there are the shops, over there—though I think your money's safe enough!' He paused. 'If you find your way down to the river, be careful. It's very wet, and it'll be muddy. I don't want to have to come and fish you out.'

Fleur opened the door and got out, slamming it shut. 'I'll be fine,' she said. 'Thanks for the lift.'

She stood back as he drove off, and she watched him take a sharp turn left and disappear up a farm track.

She started walking along slowly, revelling in her surroundings and the almost traffic free road, and comparing it all with manic London and the frantically busy hospital she worked at. But could anyone be really happy here, all the time? she wondered. She remembered Sebastian's words, and his obvious regret that soon he would have to give up practising law, cut off that part of his life, presumably for ever. It was bound to be hard for him at first, she thought. Then she shrugged. Why was she concerned about him? They were his problems, not hers.

After strolling around for about an hour, Fleur's steps automatically took her along the public footpath towards the river. She could hear it before she saw it and, when she did, Sebastian had been right. It was brimful, and gurgling along happily. As if to complete the picture, a watery sun suddenly broke through the clouds, slanting its rays through the trees, and Fleur stopped. What a great picnic spot this must be in the summer. Yet did the locals ever really appreciate what was on their doorstep? she wondered.

She began treading carefully along the undulating path, her eyes riveted to the magnetic sight of the water bubbling along beside her, when, without any warning at all, and as if by an unseen force, both her feet shot from beneath her on the slimy undergrowth and she landed full-length with a thud, ending with a slithery slide, her hands flailing helplessly about as they tried to find something to hold on to.

She lay there for a few seconds, wondering how she was going to get up. She'd have to be careful—everywhere around her was wet and there was plenty of potential for further disaster—though thankfully she was well away from the water's edge.

She saw that she was generously smeared with mud, which she foolishly transferred to her face as she wiped her now running nose with the back of her hand, and she groaned. Whatever must she look like? Staring down at herself helplessly, she saw that Mia's jacket was plastered all down one side, and on the front, and she knew that somehow she must get back to Pengarroth Hall before anyone saw her. And, to achieve that, there was that long trek back up the hill first…

Gingerly, she moved on to her side and grasped a convenient piece of log, which allowed her some support as she got to her feet, very relieved that she didn't seem to have hurt herself. The only thing hurt was her pride! What an idiotic thing to have happened, she scolded herself crossly—and she had nothing with her to try and repair the damage, either. She'd only come with a couple of tissues and a ten pound note in her pocket, which were no help at all. It was very unlike her not to be better equipped—she usually never went *anywhere* without her precious handbag, which always contained all the essentials. In fact, without it she almost felt undressed.

Now, she turned and began climbing upwards on to a higher path away from the water, her eyes intent on watching where she was treading, when Sebastian's deep voice made her look up quickly. He stood a few feet away, his hands in his pockets, the merest semblance of that crooked smile playing lightly on his lips.

'Oh…dear *me*…' was all he said, as he looked her up and down, and Fleur gritted her teeth, feeling overwhelmingly awkward. As she climbed closer to him, he put out a hand to pull her up beside him, and as he did they came perilously close to a bear hug! He held her to him for a few seconds before releasing her and staring at her from head to foot, as if lazily assessing the damage.

'You obviously took a little tumble,' he said, and Fleur's eyes narrowed slightly. The man was laughing at her, she thought, irritated.

'Well observed,' she said coolly. 'But I avoided a swim.'

'You're not hurt…?' he asked, and now the dark eyes were serious, the hint of amusement no longer there.

'Absolutely not. I'm fine. If a little sticky,' she replied, flapping her hands together and making it worse.

'Well, then, let's get you cleaned up,' he said purposefully, in a way which left no room for argument. 'They'll sort you out at the Black Horse.'

'Oh, but I'd better go home…I mean, back to Pengarroth Hall…' Fleur began. 'I thought…'

'And *I* thought we might as well have some lunch at the pub first,' he interrupted. 'They do good food—I know you enjoyed New Year's Eve, didn't you?' He glanced down at her again, and suddenly his heart missed a beat—or two! Although her somewhat crestfallen face was liberally smeared with mud, it did nothing to detract from her overt desirability—a characteristic he'd tried to dismiss since the very first moment he'd seen her…and Sebastian Conway almost stopped in his tracks. *What* was that word which had slipped, almost unnoticed, into his stream of consciousness? *Desire?* That had disappeared, along with

Davina's departure, a long time ago. Had this small, unassuming, mud-smeared woman, dressed in unglamorous winter wear, woken up his libido? He swallowed, a surge of pleasure—or was it relief that he wasn't dead after all?—coursing through him, and he looked away from her. Because if she gazed at him once more, with those beautiful, expressive sad eyes, he wouldn't be responsible for his actions!

He walked slightly away from her as they reached the lane, and he cleared his throat. 'I do think that a glass of wine and a spot of lunch will do you good, Fleur. The slightest fall can be a shock to the system. And, anyway, I'm hungry,' he added.

Fleur didn't bother to reply. He'd decided that they were going to eat at the pub, and that was what would happen, even though she would have much preferred to go back to Pengarroth Hall. But still, on reflection, it would get lunch out of the way, she thought. Pat was not coming back until it was time to prepare the evening meal, so she might just as well fall in with his wishes and eat here, now.

As soon as they set foot inside the pub, Joy, the landlady, took one look at Fleur and sized up the situation at once. 'Oh, my good lor',' she said in her lilting Cornish way. 'Just look at you!'

Fleur smiled apologetically. 'I was taking a walk—or rather a slide—by the river,' she began.

Sebastian cut in. 'Fleur would appreciate the use of your toilet facilities to get cleaned up, Joy,' he said, 'and then I think we'd like some lunch, please, plus a good bottle of red.'

There were, as yet, only a few customers drinking at the bar, and the woman beckoned to Fleur to follow her. 'I'll get you a decent towel, dear,' she said. 'There are only paper ones in there.' She smiled at Sebastian, handing him a menu. 'And you can be looking at this, Sebastian.'

Alone, Fleur sighed briefly. *Why* did she have to fall down and make such a fool of herself? She took off the jacket, examining it closely. All that mud would hopefully brush off when it was dry, she thought, putting it over the back of a chair for a moment, and noting that her jeans were relatively unscathed. She stared at her reflection in the rather dingy mirror and groaned. She had nothing with her to restore some of her confidence—no blusher, no lipstick, not even a comb to run through her hair, which she'd left loose that morning.

Sitting at a table by the roaring log fire in the bar, Sebastian half-stood as Fleur came back to join him, and he pulled out a chair for her. 'You look better,' he said casually. Then, 'Are you really sure there was no physical damage, Fleur?'

She smiled up at him quickly, shaking her head. 'Quite sure, thanks,' she replied.

While he'd been supposedly studying the menu, Sebastian's thoughts had been more occupied with what *could* have happened to Fleur, down there by herself. She could have badly sprained—or even broken—an ankle, and been lying there for goodness knew how long if he hadn't decided to try and find her. And it had only been a last-minute thought as he'd left the farm that had prompted him to check whether she was still around. He shuddered slightly, reminding himself that he'd actually not intended to go back to the house until much later on—so, if Fleur hadn't returned, it could easily have been dark before anyone had realized she was missing.

He'd handed her the menu and, after studying it for a moment, she gave it back and looked up at him, properly.

'I'm really sorry if I've…interrupted…your day,' she murmured.

Her bewitchingly long eyelashes were still wet from washing her face, and he noticed again the way she had of sometimes blinking in a kind of slow motion…which he admitted to finding strangely titillating. At this moment, she was totally unadorned, he thought, her face rather pale and her unusually untidy, loosely flowing, wavy hair touching her shoulders.

'You're not interrupting anything,' he lied. 'Stop worrying. And I've ordered red wine because I've noticed that's what you seem to prefer…'

Fleur couldn't help feeling surprised at the remark. She wouldn't have thought he cared enough about her—or any of Mia's friends—to be that observant. She bent forward slightly to warm her hands by the fire. 'I don't ever drink at lunch time,' she said, 'but I could be persuaded to make an exception—under certain circumstances. Thank you, Sebastian. Just one glass will be perfect.'

He grinned at her now, and she was aware again of his startlingly white teeth, which seemed to light up his rather serious bronzed features. 'And, as I'm driving, I'd better follow suit.' He paused. 'Joy will keep the bottle safe for us. We'll finish it another time.'

Fleur was about to say—*Look, there doesn't have to be another time—you don't have to do this, Sebastian. I'm all right by myself*…but she didn't. Because after that first stab of embarrassment when he'd turned up by the river, she'd been grateful of his presence and his company.

Suddenly, he bent forward too and took one of her hands in his, looking down intently. 'Look, you *have* hurt yourself, Fleur,' he said, almost accusingly. 'See—there's quite a bad graze here on your knuckles… Didn't you see it, feel it?'

'A bit,' Fleur conceded. 'But it's nothing, Sebastian, really. No blood. So, no blood, no tears. My father's maxim all my life.'

He said nothing, but didn't let go of her hand, gently tracing the affected part with his forefinger, and Fleur couldn't help liking the sensation it gave her!

Just then, Joy appeared with the wine, and she glanced down, her quick eyes taking in the scene. Sebastian Conway had not had a woman with him for far too long, in her opinion. And this one was obviously someone special. Even with all the hubbub on New Year's Eve she'd noticed her amongst Mia's crowd. And she'd also noticed Sebastian's eyes following her every move. Well, about time, the woman thought.

# CHAPTER FOUR

'This is always the worst bit of Christmas,' Pat said, from her lofty position on top of the stepladder as she handed down the last of the decorations to Fleur.

'Yes, it is rather sad—the ending of something you've really enjoyed,' Fleur agreed, kneeling down to coil all the fairy lights into a large box. 'But time goes by so quickly, it'll soon be happening all over again.'

Just then, Sebastian came in and glanced at the two women. 'Hi there,' he said briefly. Then, 'Good—putting all the junk away and getting back to normality.'

'Oh *you*, Sebastian!' Pat exclaimed. 'Talk about not being in the spirit of the season!'

Still intent on her task, Fleur glanced quickly up at Sebastian and their eyes met for the fleetest of seconds. He was dressed, as usual, in outdoor gear, and his hair was tousled and wet from the early morning rain.

'I could murder a black coffee,' he said. 'Can I get us all some?'

'No, you cannot,' Pat said firmly, as she climbed carefully down from the ladder. 'I'll do that, Sebastian, if you'll be so kind as to take this tree outside.'

'My pleasure,' he said at once, as Pat left the room.

Fleur finished putting the lights away, then closed the box carefully and got to her feet.

Sebastian said, 'How've you been doing, Fleur, over the last few days?' He was feeling somewhat guilty because he'd seen hardly anything of her since her fall, not only because he'd had to be elsewhere, but because he was determined to avoid—as much as he could—any emotional entanglements, and he was honest enough to admit that Fleur could, if only she knew it, change his mind on the matter. When they'd sat together in the pub the other lunch time, two whole hours had passed like five minutes... He'd found her an engaging conversationalist, unpretentious without being coy, and with firm opinions which, though freely expressed, were never combative. And, as she'd become thoroughly relaxed in front of the fire, her face had glowed, enlivened by her eyes glistening in the light from the flickering flames. At the point when he'd reached for her hand and held it for those few moments—ostensibly to make sure she wasn't really hurt—a sudden warmth had coursed through *him*, too. But with that sensation had come a wariness of being entrapped again. Easier to start than to stop, he'd reminded himself cynically. Hadn't he always considered himself an astute judge of human nature—didn't his profession hang on that premise?

So how could he possibly have been blinded to the essential components of Davina's nature? He'd learned the truth eventually—fortunately before he'd made her his wife. But it had been a close run thing, the possibility of their union becoming the subject of much discussion, both at work and down here. The news of their split had travelled fast too, and his independent, rather private nature had resented the publicity bitterly. Not that all the facts of the debacle had ever generally been known, which was somehow worse because what people didn't know they made up. And the locals who'd been expecting a glitzy wedding to talk about had had to go away empty-handed. The lesson, for him, had been a hard one, and there would never be a next time. That much he'd promised himself.

Besides, was there a twenty-first century woman alive who'd be prepared to incarcerate herself down here in the wet Cornish countryside for the rest of her life? He very much doubted that! Today's women were different. They didn't want to be tied to someone else's expectations and demands. It might work for the first few months, or a year, but after that the novelty would soon wear off. No, he had set his singular course straight ahead, with no distracting turnings. Here, pretty much alone, was where he was to spend his days. And he knew that that was the best possible thing for him, and for Pengarroth Hall. It would have to be a child of Mia's who, eventually, took charge of the estate. Even if the name died out, the blood line would almost certainly continue.

'Oh, I've been having a great time, thanks,' Fleur replied cheerfully, in answer to his question. 'I've had the chance to really explore the area, and I've finally stopped getting lost every time I leave Pengarroth Hall. All the locals are so friendly…they love to stop for a chat. I feel as though I'm becoming part of the scenery!'

'Hmm,' Sebastian said briefly. No doubt tongues were beginning to wag already, he thought. He'd been aware of the landlady at the Black Horse darting them knowing glances from time to time. He cleared his throat. 'I'm sorry I haven't been around for a while,' he said, 'but I knew I was going to be caught up…'

'Please—there's no need to apologize,' Fleur said quickly, 'and…'

'No, perhaps not,' he said, 'but I did promise Mia that I'd be able to sort of…'

'You shouldn't have promised Mia *anything*—and she

shouldn't have asked!' Fleur said, her colour rising, and angry again that Mia had taken it upon herself to interfere. Perhaps now was the time to invent that phone call, she thought, and go back home. 'If I'd thought,' she went on more calmly, 'that you—or anyone—were going to feel responsible for me, I'd have refused the invitation in the first place. I told you, I'm used to being alone, and I like it! I *like* doing my own thing without the constraints of having to fall in with other people's wishes.' She paused, looking up at him, her face flushed. 'Please—for heaven's sake—pretend I'm not here!'

He half-smiled as he looked down at her, resisting the temptation to cup her chin in his hands and place his lips on hers. How could he—or anyone—pretend this woman wasn't here? Even Pat, who had been known to show her disapproval of one or two of Mia's friends, seemed to genuinely like Fleur.

'OK,' he said easily, 'but first, you can guide this tree outside for me… We'll have to use the side door to the garden. Here, put these on.' He handed her his gloves, then went across and with surprisingly little effort heaved the tree out of its pot and leaned it towards Fleur, who immediately took it by a bough near the top and helped him guide it out of the hall, appreciating the gloves which protected her hands from the prickly pine needles.

'Coffee's ready,' Pat called out and, after they'd deposited the tree outside, Fleur and Sebastian joined her in the kitchen. Benson was stretched out in front of the warm stove and Fleur automatically bent down to pet him.

'I suppose Benson's tired from his walk?' she said, glancing up at Sebastian.

'No, because he hasn't had one yet,' Sebastian replied. 'I couldn't persuade him to accompany me earlier. And I'm seeing Frank up at the top end of the estate this morning, so this lazy dog will have to wait until later on for his stroll.'

'Oh, can I take him?' Fleur asked eagerly. 'I know the places we're allowed to go. Will he come with me?...I haven't been out myself yet, anyway.'

'I'm sure he'd love to go with you,' Sebastian replied, taking his mug of coffee from Pat.

The three of them sat there for a few minutes making light conversation, then Sebastian got up decisively. 'I must go,' he said, then turned to look at Fleur. 'I'm going into Truro tomorrow morning—would you like to come? And you too, Pat,' he added as an afterthought. 'I know how you women like shopping.'

'It's kind of you to offer, Sebastian,' Pat said firmly, 'but I've lots of things to do and, besides, I want to be with Mum as much as possible. But Fleur will enjoy Truro— there's lots to see, apart from the shops.' She threw a shrewd glance at the two of them as she spoke. Sebastian had always been a bit of a dark horse where women were concerned, but she could definitely feel something in the air every time she caught him looking at Fleur. So *she* wasn't going to play gooseberry, thank you very much. Her expression softened as she looked at Sebastian. He was a good man, and a fantastic employer—as his parents had been—never over-demanding and always apprecia- tive. And, although he had a bit of a short fuse at times, it was usually justified; he had a very keen sense of right and wrong. She knew Frank worshipped him, would do anything for him, and now Frank's son, Martin, always a bit of a tear-away, had come to work on the estate as well. And Sebastian had seen the youngster's potential as a carpenter and was paying for him to go part-time to college to learn the trade properly. But Fleur...this young woman...she could be just the one for Sebastian,

Pat thought. She was different from other hopefuls who'd turned up occasionally at Pengarroth Hall… She seemed to sort of fit in with the atmosphere of the place, and to really enjoy being here and wandering about by herself. And she wasn't always looking at herself in the mirror, either.

'Oh, fine,' Sebastian said casually. 'How about you, Fleur? I promise there's enough to keep you interested while I'm seeing the accountant.'

She looked up at him. 'Are you sure it won't be rather inconvenient, thinking about me when you've got other more important things on your mind?' she asked.

He was just about to reply when Fleur's mobile rang, and she paused to answer it. It was Mia.

'Hi, Mia! Yes…fine, absolutely fine! Having a great time…and feeling great, too.' She smiled as she listened to her friend's exuberant tones. 'Oh, poor you, having to work so hard…but it'll be the same for me in just over a week…unless I'm called back earlier,' she added quickly, giving herself the option of cutting her stay short—and of letting Sebastian hear it. There was another pause, then, 'Yes, he's standing right here by my side. Do you want a word?'

She passed the phone up to Sebastian and listened as he and Mia exchanged the usual pleasantries. Then, 'Yes, you know that I always do as you tell me, and I'm taking Fleur into Truro tomorrow so that she can have a look around while I'm with the accountant and the solicitor. What? Oh, yes, we might do that as well… OK, OK, I'll pass you back. Be good.'

Fleur raised her eyebrows. *She* hadn't said she'd go with him—he was assuming that she would. But then, why not? she thought. She knew Truro wasn't that far away, and they'd only be gone for the morning…there'd still be plenty of day left for Sebastian after that, without having to think about her.

She watched his retreating back, then took their mugs over to the sink.

'Now, you leave those things to me, dear,' Pat said, thinking how pretty Fleur looked in her huge cream chunky sweater, her golden hair loose around her face. 'And, by the way, Mum says why don't you come up to the cottage for afternoon tea one day? Then you can bring back the novels she promised to lend you.'

'That would be great, Pat—thanks,' Fleur said. Pat's mother had been at the house for almost the whole of the three festive days, helping out, and she and Fleur had chatted, among other things, about their favourite authors. And when Fleur had said she was into romantic novels at the moment and had finished the one she'd brought with her, the older woman had offered to lend some of hers.

'Well, then, come up with me the day after tomorrow,' Pat said now, 'if you're going with Sebastian to Truro tomorrow.'

'I didn't say I was,' Fleur corrected. 'He did.' She smiled. 'But yes, I will go because I've never been to the city before—it is a city, isn't it, with a lovely cathedral? I mustn't pass up the opportunity to visit it.'

'You don't know Cornwall?' Pat asked curiously as she started slicing thick pieces of gammon from a delicious-looking joint for their lunch.

'No, not really,' Fleur said. 'My father preferred Scotland and the Lakes, so we always went there when I was young. And in more recent years when I've been on holiday, it's to foreign countries with friends.' She paused. 'I must be the only person in the whole world who doesn't particularly look forward to going away. I'm much happier at home. But I have to, because that's what everyone does.' She watched Pat's deft handling of the carving knife, the pink ham glistening with succulence, making her mouth water even though it was a couple of hours before she'd be eating any. 'And thank your mother so much for the offer. She's an interesting lady, and I'd love to come to tea.'

Pat smiled, pleased. 'And I know she'll love it too,' she said. 'She doesn't see that many people any more and I think she's a bit lonely sometimes. See, even when Mia or Sebastian are away, I'm here most days, checking up, cleaning up, doing the odd bit of decorating where I see it's needed. And the kitchen garden round at the back is my domain too. Not that I do much to it this time of year,' she added.

Fleur stood up. 'I think I'll take Benson now. The weather seems reasonably fine, so maybe it's the best time of day to go.'

'You do that,' Pat said, giving the dog a gentle nudge with her toe. 'Get up, you lazy hound,' she said affectionately.

'What happens to him when you're not around?' Fleur wanted to know.

'Oh, he stays with Mum or me. Or Frank has him. He's well looked after. Up until a couple of years ago, Sebastian would take him back to London with him, but that proved impractical, and the dog pined a bit for home and hearth, I think.'

'Oh, well, then, Benson and I are of like mind.' Fleur smiled.

Pat finished what she was doing, then wrapped the remainder of the joint in cling film and put it in the fridge. 'Now, I'll prepare the lunch for one o'clock,' she said. 'Sebastian said he might be a bit later than that, but it'll all keep. And I'll take some of this on up and have mine with Mum.'

Fleur looked over at the bustling housekeeper as she spoke, hoping that Sebastian and Mia knew how lucky they were to have such devoted people to look after them and their property, whether they were here or not. Such staff would be hard to find in London. Everything here seemed so efficient, yet so easy-going.

Fleur took her warm jacket from the hook on the back door where she'd noticed that Sebastian always kept his, then called to Benson to follow her. And, surprisingly, the dog immediately got up and padded after her.

'See you later, Pat,' she called as they went outside. They set off, soon leaving the house behind them as they began treading up the soggy paths, the dog happy to lead the way, stopping and sniffing every few yards.

Thinking about it, Fleur still didn't know whether to say she'd been called back to the hospital or not… It was rather difficult now that she was going to Truro tomorrow, and to tea with Pat and her mother the day after. Which meant that there were only going to be five days left, in any case. She shrugged to herself. She'd see how things panned out. If she got the slightest suspicion that she was being a burden to Sebastian, or—perish the thought—that he was bored with her unasked-for company, she'd be gone within the hour. Until then no reason not to go with the flow, she told herself.

After half an hour or so of gentle strolling, she called out to the dog, who was investigating a scrubby bush. 'Have you had enough, Benson?' she called. 'Shall we turn back now? Good boy. Come on.'

The animal emerged reluctantly from whatever had held his interest, but continued on without even looking around at Fleur, who followed on behind him. Well, he was obviously enjoying himself, she thought.

And then, as usual and without much warning, a fine rain began again. She called out, more decisively this time, 'Come back, Benson…come *on*. We must go home now.' But, staying where he was, the dog merely turned and looked back soulfully at her.

Fleur sighed briefly. Pat had told her to take the lead, just in case, and now she went forward to attach it to the dog's collar. And, as if making a decision of his own, Benson sat down on the wet ground and refused to budge.

Fleur frowned, giving the lead a little pull. 'Come on, there's a good boy. We've had a lovely walk and it's time to go back. Come on, up you get.'

But the dog had other ideas, and after a few pointless moments of trying to persuade him, Fleur began to feel slightly worried. What if Benson refused to come home at all? He was much too heavy for her to pick up and carry. And if she went back alone, what would Sebastian's reaction be? She realized that the dog probably could make his own way home without any help from her, but that wasn't the point, and she couldn't take it for granted.

She crouched down by the dog. 'Well, have a little rest and then come with me, Benson, *please*,' she begged. She suddenly remembered that she had some mints in her pocket—maybe she could entice him with one of those. Getting up, she moved a few feet away and crackled the sweet paper between her fingers.

'Come and see, Benson. See what I've got,' she said cajolingly but, apart from a slight twitch of his nose, the dog expressed not the slightest interest.

'OK, then, we'll play it your way,' Fleur said. 'I'm going back now. See you later. Goodbye, Benson!' She turned away and started walking back in the direction they'd come, in the hope that the dog would follow her. But, as she turned to glance back, she could see that he hadn't moved an inch. He was not coming, and that was that.

Now Fleur was really exasperated. What now? she asked herself. She could not go home minus the dog; that would make her look silly. Glancing at her watch, she was horrified to see that it was almost one-thirty—they'd been gone far longer than she'd thought, or than she'd intended. But both she and her canine companion had been enjoying their walk so much that the time had slipped by. She shrugged. There was nothing else for it, she'd have to just wait and sit it out until Benson made up his mind to come home.

Feeling completely inadequate, she leaned against a tree for a few moments, then sat down on a piece of log a foot or two away from the dog. With her chin in her hands, she stared pensively at him and, hardly blinking, Benson stared back.

By now, the rain had become a steady downpour and both she and Benson were looking distinctly the worse for wear. Fleur had scarcely noticed that her hood had slipped off, or that her hair was hanging in wet ringlets around her face. 'No one warned me that you were a difficult creature, Benson,' she said sorrowfully. 'What on earth am I to do with you?'

'And what on earth am I to do with *you*?' Sebastian's voice intervened and, with an unmistakable sense of relief, Fleur saw him striding towards them. He stopped and looked down at her. 'What's going on?' he said. 'Pat's gone on home, but she did tell you she'd arranged lunch for one o'clock—didn't she?'

Fleur didn't bother to get to her feet, but nodded

towards Benson, who was viewing them both pensively. 'Ask him,' she said. 'He just refused to get up. I couldn't leave him here, could I?' She sighed. 'I must be rubbish at handling dogs.'

Sebastian cocked one slightly amused eyebrow, then clicked his fingers. 'Come, Benson,' he said masterfully, and at once the dog got to his feet and padded over to lick his hand.

Fleur could hardly believe it! The naughty animal, she thought. He'd seemed rooted to that spot, yet two words from Sebastian and he'd obeyed at once. 'Obviously it's his master's voice that he responds to,' she said sniffily, getting up and falling into step with Sebastian as they began to make their way home.

'No, I think the fact was he was enjoying your company so much, he didn't want the walk to end,' Sebastian said generously, glancing down at her. She was soaking wet, her hair looking as if she had just come out of the shower, and he smiled faintly to himself. Not many of the women he'd known had shown such stalwart tendencies, usually running for cover at the first brush with the elements. But Fleur seemed to almost revel in being wet and untidy.

It took another half an hour to get back, with Benson now trotting quite happily ahead. 'I don't believe that dog,' Fleur said. 'Look at him. What did I do wrong?'

'Nothing,' Sebastian replied. 'I expect he just felt like a lie down, that's all—you had gone quite a way—much further than I usually take him nowadays.'

Fleur looked up quickly. 'Oh, dear…I hope we didn't overdo it…I mean, I don't want to be the cause of any trouble…'

'Shut up,' Sebastian said cheerfully. 'The dog's fine.

The only one suffering any discomfort is me, because you've kept me waiting for my lunch.'

'Well, why didn't you go on and have it without me?' Fleur began.

'What, knowing that my dog and my…er…*charge*… were missing, believed lost?'

Fleur decided to ignore the word he'd used because she knew he was teasing her.

Back at the house, she had a quick wash, then took her place opposite Sebastian at the kitchen table. He had placed the ham and pickles and the piping hot, gloriously brown jacket potatoes in front of them, and soon they were both tucking into it all, while Benson lay flat out on the floor, snoring.

Without asking her whether she wanted any, Sebastian filled Fleur's glass with water from the jug, before taking some for himself. She was glad that there was no wine on offer because, as she'd already told him, she seldom drank alcohol during the day. That must have made her sound terribly goody-goody, she thought, because most of her friends had no problem with having a glass or two at lunch time. But she didn't care what Sebastian Conway thought of her, anyway—about anything at all—she'd always made a point of never altering her principles to suit others, and she wasn't about to start now.

Finishing his lunch, he asked mildly, 'What are you going to do with yourself this afternoon?' He realized that it wasn't a polite enquiry, but he was curious and admitted that he would much rather spend the rest of the day with Fleur than helping Frank. But suddenly the phone on the wall rang and he stood up to take the call. It was Pat and, after listening for a few moments and glancing across at Fleur, he said, 'No, you must stay with her, Pat… That's no problem. For heaven's sake, we can cope alone, sort ourselves out.' There was a pause. 'Sorry? Oh, yes… of course. I found them…up Middle Hill. Yes, right up there. Soaking wet, with Benson having gone on strike. He didn't want to come home, apparently. But they're both here, safe and well, and we've just enjoyed the lunch— thanks, Pat.' Another pause. 'Absolutely not—you stay with Beryl. We'll be fine.' He listened again, then, 'OK, got it. And it's best you don't come back tonight at all— your mother needs you more than we do just now. See what the doctor says, and we'll see you tomorrow some time, when the panic's over. OK? Cheers, Pat.'

He replaced the receiver. 'Pat's mother has just had another of her angina attacks, so I've told her that we can look after ourselves for twenty-four hours.'

'Of course we can,' Fleur said at once.

'And apparently we're having steak for our supper— they're in the 'fridge, along with mushrooms and tomatoes and stuff…' He eyed her hopefully. 'Can you cook? I'm not the greatest,' he added.

'Well, then, you'd better leave it all to me,' Fleur said, realizing how quickly she and her host had become so… so comfortable with each other, with no pressure, no emotional vibes cutting into the warmly pleasant atmosphere they seemed to be enjoying. Well, what else did she expect? He was Mia's brother. She had always loved her friend…and she was beginning to love him, as well…in a purely brotherly way, naturally, she assured herself. 'Not that I shall hope to come up to Pat's standards,' she went on, 'but beggars can't be choosers. It's me or nothing.'

He treated her to one of his rather enigmatic smiles. 'You'll do nicely,' he murmured.

She took their empty plates over to the sink, thinking that he needn't concern himself. She'd always enjoyed cooking, and she knew she could produce a meal to satisfy anyone. And she'd bet anything that he'd like his steak cooked rare.

He turned to go. 'Right, I'll be back up the top with Frank for the rest of the day.' He paused. 'You don't envisage wearing my dog's paws out again, do you?'

'No. I shall be having a long, hot bath and washing my hair.' She made a slight grimace, knowing that she must be looking totally scruffy after the morning's drenching. 'After which, I might watch a DVD, and then think about our supper.'

He stopped to look down at her, suddenly feeling a wave of pleasure sweep through him. It would be rather good to think of coming home to Fleur after a heavy day outside, he thought, for them to share a meal and just sit and relax and chat. And to have her here, all to himself, at Pengarroth Hall. As he dwelt on that for a second or two, and despite his avowed intention to watch it where women were concerned, a ripple of anticipation coursed through his veins and stopped him in his tracks. It had been a long time since he'd experienced these sensual instincts. The need to be with a woman, close enough to touch, and it had taken this rather unusual friend of Mia's to make him realize how much he'd missed it!

## CHAPTER FIVE

'WELL, *that* was a surprise,' Sebastian said as he and Fleur were relaxing in the sitting room after supper. 'Eleven out of ten for the way you did my steak, Fleur—thanks.'

He glanced across at her as he spoke. Curled up as she was on the sofa, with her knees drawn up comfortably and her eyes closed, she looked ridiculously at ease.

'I'll take that as a compliment, rather than an insult, if you mean that you were surprised I didn't ruin that wonderful meat,' Fleur said drowsily.

When he'd returned late in the afternoon, he'd lit the fire and now the logs were crackling and hissing in the flames. With the lamps turned down low, the room was swathed in a gentle, soothing light, adding to the contented atmosphere which both of them were very much aware of. Sitting opposite her in one of the huge armchairs, he was wearing chinos and a light open-neck sports shirt, his bare feet thrust into loafers, his long legs stretched out in front of him.

He was quietly amazed at how totally comfortable he felt in Fleur's company—as if he'd known her for ages. She was certainly the only woman he'd ever met who didn't send out the usual signals that he was accustomed to receiving—the telling eye contact or suggestive comment, or any kind of simple gesture that told him she might fancy him. He thought she seemed to quite *like* him, but nothing more than that—and that pleased him. Because it made it easier for him to keep her emotionally at arm's length. Neither of them—certainly not him—were interested in having a meaningful relationship with anyone, so that obviously explained why there was no tension, he thought. He smiled faintly to himself. The only slight problem was that she was so attractive… It would have helped if he could have looked at her dispassionately, but there was no hope of that. Still, soon they'd be going their separate ways and he doubted that he'd ever see her again. All of their lives, his and Mia's and their respective friends, were so busy these days, it was difficult for any of them to get together.

He'd brought in the half-empty bottle of wine they'd shared the evening before, and now he leaned forward to refill their glasses, glancing across at her. He didn't want her to go to sleep—which she seemed in imminent danger of doing—he wanted her to talk to him, wanted to hear some more of her opinions.

'I take it you've no objection to helping me out with the remains of this?' he enquired.

Still not moving, she opened her eyes lazily. 'All right, but please make it a small one,' she murmured. 'I don't have a very strong head for alcohol, but it was delicious.'

She watched his strong, completely steady, tanned hand pour the ruby liquid. He placed the bottle down on the small, low table in front of them with a gentle thud. 'Good. That's a dead one,' he said. 'But there's plenty more we can open if you feel like living dangerously.'

She smiled back at him. 'No, thanks. But I won't say no to a coffee. I'll go out and make some in a minute.'

He drank some wine, then leaned back, twirling the

glass in his fingers. 'No, you stay there. You look so comfortable, it would be a crime to disturb you. I'll make the coffee, since you did everything else.'

There was silence for a few moments, then, 'You said your parents were holidaying in Boston,' he said. 'Have you heard from them?'

'Oh, yes, they rang me on New Year's Day with the usual good wishes… Well, my father hoped I'd have another successful, fulfilling and productive year ahead, but my mother's greetings centred more on fun and happiness.' She smiled faintly. 'She's desperate for me to provide her with a grandchild, drops hints all the time— when my father's not around—but it's never likely to happen, I'm afraid. I've never actually said that to her, of course, because it sounds rather cruel, but I fear she hopes in vain.'

Sebastian looked at her seriously for a moment. 'You don't like kids?' he said.

'Of course I like children,' Fleur replied at once. 'What I don't relish is having to hand my life over to their father, to become anonymous.' She shook her head quickly. Her mother was a beautiful, gifted woman and had become like a silent, wistful bird in a cage—or so it seemed to Fleur. There was no way she was going to suffer the same fate, to be controlled by a man. Her father had done enough already to utterly convince her of that.

Sebastian didn't need any further explanation. Fleur's deep-rooted resentment about certain influences in her life had tarnished the natural inclination most women had for matrimonial commitment and child-bearing. He stared at her thoughtfully. What a waste, he mused. She was clearly an intelligent woman, who'd produce beautiful children.

After a few moments he left the room, returning with

the coffee things on a tray, which he set down on the table.

'Sugar and cream for madam,' he said briefly, passing them to her, and pouring himself a black coffee. Fleur leaned forward, not surprised that he'd obviously noted what she liked, without having to ask. He was that kind of man.

Stirring her drink slowly, she said, 'Soon this will all be a distant memory.' She smiled up at him briefly. 'I've kept a diary so that I can refer back.'

'Well, you can always come and visit again,' he said casually. 'Whether Mia's here or not. It's good for the house to be used, and Pat's always around… You'd be more than welcome, any time.' That was a first, he thought—telling one of his sister's friends to make herself at home! He paused. 'You'd love it when all the spring flowers are in bloom…. Our bluebell woods are something else—in fact, we have a bluebell event every year, the first weekend in May. Everyone around comes to admire our carpets of blue, and we lay on a bit of a tea in the garden and the kids are invited to pick primroses to take home.'

Fleur's eyes sparkled as she listened to the picture he had just painted. 'How fantastic!' she exclaimed. 'I *love* bluebells—not to pick, of course, because they don't last once they leave the ground, but they're always such a magical sight.' She paused. 'I'd *love* to see it—perhaps one day, if Mia's coming down, we could drive here together.'

'It doesn't matter whether Mia's coming or not,' he repeated. 'Though she usually does put in an appearance. I always make a point of being here because it's the only occasion when anyone and everyone is welcome to explore the estate…and it's good for community spirit, that sort of thing. I'm often glad of local help to give Frank a hand from time to time, so it's in my interests to be convivial now and then.'

They fell silent for a few moments, then Fleur said suddenly, 'On Christmas Eve, when the others were all here, everyone started telling ghost stories, and Mia said that…'

'Oh, she told you about our supernatural presence, did she?' he asked good-humouredly. 'Well, it's kept many a guest entertained after dinner.'

'But—there isn't *really* a ghost, is there?' Fleur said, keeping her voice totally expressionless, even though her pulse had quickened at the thought. 'I thought she was pulling our legs.'

'None of *us* have seen him, certainly,' Sebastian replied easily. 'But there are accounts of others having had the experience.' He drank from his mug, then looked over at her. 'Why, that sort of thing doesn't bother you, does it? You don't believe such nonsense?'

'Of course not,' Fleur said loftily. 'I'm a scientist. I only believe what I can see or prove. And, to my knowledge, no one has yet proved the existence of such beings, have they? I mean, they may *believe* they've seen certain things, but that's not the same thing as actually seeing or touching—with others there to corroborate, is it? It's just all in the mind. Still,' she added, 'tell me more. Because Mia had hardly started telling us when Mandy nearly had hysterics at the thought, so she had to stop.'

Sebastian leaned back, his hands behind his head. 'Well, our ghost is apparently a well-dressed middle-aged man who wears a top hat. He's been seen walking along the upstairs landing, hangs around a bit as if he's waiting for someone to join him, then walks straight out through the wall at the end.'

Fleur gave a slightly sardonic smile. 'How bizarre.' She paused. 'Who's supposed to have seen him, anyway?'

'One of our forebears made a note of it a hundred years ago—it's quoted briefly in the official documents,' Sebastian replied. 'Since then two others have declared they've witnessed it. One was a young lad, the tea boy, who was boiling a kettle upstairs to make some drinks for the decorators my parents had employed to do some work. Someone must have said something to him about our ghost and the lad swore he saw it do the disappearing trick through the wall. Anyway, he dropped the kettle and fled out of the house, refusing to come back in.' Sebastian chortled at the thought. 'But then there's also…'

'Who else has seen it?' Fleur interrupted eagerly.

'Beryl, Pat's mother, swears she's seen it too, twice— when she's been upstairs cleaning.'

Fleur caught her breath. '*Beryl's* seen it?' she said. 'Really?' This was different. The woman was a practical no-nonsense character and, in Fleur's opinion, not likely to make up things about seeing visions.

'Yep. So she insists,' Sebastian said cheerfully. 'But she has no problem with it at all. Says that as long as the chap doesn't give her any aggro or get under her feet, she's quite happy to see him now and again.' He chuckled. 'Mind you, I have to say that Beryl's private remedy for any ailment she might be suffering from is a rather good elderberry wine she makes. And I'm pretty certain that she enjoys a daily dose—which might explain things—not that I've ever seen her the worse for wear.'

'Well, so Mia *wasn't* having us on, then,' Fleur said slowly. She sat back and feigned a yawn, feeling unde-niably uncomfortable. What she had just said about not believing in the supernatural wasn't entirely true because, in spite of her training, she knew there were still certain things which seemed to have no rational explanation. Phenomena whose secrets were yet to be revealed... Of course, it would all become clear one day, she was sure of that. There were so many more curtains to push back in order to find the truth behind the myriad unanswered questions.

'My mother would find your ghost absolutely fascinating,' she said, looking across at Sebastian. She paused. 'She is what you would call a...spiritual person, with a very open mind. Though of course my father scoffs at anything which isn't firmly rooted in proven fact.'

'And you agree with him, obviously,' Sebastian said.

After a second's thought, she replied, 'Yes. Of course.'

'What about horoscopes—you don't read them either?' he persisted. 'I know that Mia does—it's the first page she turns to when I see her with a magazine. And she's totally unashamed to admit it. She'll say things like, "Oh, good, someone special is going to enter my life this week," or "Hurrah—I'm coming into unexpected money!"'

Fleur smiled across at him. 'And what about you—where do you stand on all this?' she enquired.

'I never read women's mags, that's for sure,' he replied, 'and I've never read my horoscope either, though Mia has often insisted on looking up my sign and telling me what's in store for me in the imminent future.'

Neither of them spoke for a few moments, then Fleur got up, stretching her arms above her head. 'I really must go to bed now,' she said. ' I think I had too much supper, and too much wine...' She bent to pick up the tray. 'I'll just clear this up first.' She glanced across at him. 'When do you want me to be ready in the morning? I mean...you said you've appointments in Truro...'

He stifled a yawn too then, and got slowly to his feet.

'We should leave at nine.' He smiled. 'Do you want an early morning call?'

'That won't be necessary,' Fleur replied. 'I always wake up with the birds.' Though she had to admit that almost since her first day here she'd slept like a log, not rousing until much later than usual. The stress she'd been experiencing for the last few months, which had been the cause of disturbed nights and early waking, seemed to have vanished.

'I'll say goodnight, then, Sebastian,' she said, turning to go.

'Goodnight, Fleur—sleep well,' he added.

Up in her room, Fleur undressed quickly and, after a quick wash and cleaning her teeth, she burrowed beneath her duvet. Glancing over to the other single bed, she wished that Mia was still there. It had been very comfortable, the two of them together, nattering away about everything—old times, new plans—until one or other had been the first to fall asleep. Now, the room seemed very still with only her own breathing to keep her company. She'd heard Sebastian come upstairs and pass her room, had listened to his firm tread receding for several moments. She didn't know which bedroom he occupied, only that it seemed to be away at the far end of the wide landing.

Sighing briefly, she snuggled down.

And that night Fleur dreamed, her subconscious mind teeming with thoughts, events, voices, memories and feelings… For several hours, she tossed and turned restlessly. In her dreams, she and her mother were having one of their discussions about other-worldly things, about Helen's inexplicable forebodings, which often turned out to have some verity, about the second sense which she seemed to possess, about the angels that she implicitly believed were all around… And then, without any warning, and with a huge wave of anxiety sweeping over her, Fleur sat bolt upright, her forehead spangled with perspiration. Because she was no longer alone! She could see him—he *did* exist! The ghost of Pengarroth Hall, his top hat firmly on his head, was right there in her room, and he was walking slowly towards her! Pulling the duvet right up around her shoulders, she opened her mouth to say something, to cry out, to tell it to go away and leave her alone! But no words would come! Her tongue had stuck fast to her dry mouth, rendering her impotent and helpless… She was his prisoner and she was trapped with no means of escape. With her shaking knees drawn up to her chin, her eyes huge with fright, she watched him come nearer and nearer all the time, and suddenly…suddenly… amazingly…she recognized him… It was her father—her *father* was here! But how…why? She could make out the familiar features, the determined expression, the permanently puckered brow, and at last Fleur did find her voice and she screamed, *'No! Go away! You shouldn't be here! Leave me alone—leave me alone!'* But the figure kept on walking and Fleur kept on screaming a high-pitched, frantic scream until, cowering now, she could almost feel him, he was so close… Suddenly the door burst open and Sebastian stood there, a look of shocked disbelief on his face.

'Fleur… *Fleur!* What the hell is it?' He strode right over to the bed and, without a second's hesitation, she sprang up into a kneeling position and clutched him feverishly around his neck, almost bowling him over in her desperation to feel him near her. And with that human contact, feeling the comforting warmth of his bare chest against her flimsily clad form, she burst into tears. Helpless, hopeless tears. Tears partly of shock, partly of relief—and partly of release. She could not remember the last time she'd cried—it must have been years and years ago, and she sobbed unashamedly.

Sebastian let her cry, saying not another word, but now sitting down on the bed with her, his arms wrapped around her, his chin resting on the top of her head.

'I saw him…I did see him,' she gasped tremulously between sobs, and he held her even closer to him.

'Hush, Fleur…it's OK…you're OK. I'm here…' he murmured.

Afterwards, she couldn't recall how long they'd stayed like that, but eventually her tears began to lessen and she raised her eyes to look up at him. And then, as if it were the obvious, natural sequence of events, his mouth came down upon her lips—lips that were parted with the effort of trying to breathe normally after her anguished weeping. And the moist warmth of that brief union sent thrilling waves coursing down her spine… She didn't pull away, she didn't *want* to pull away because, in a kind of wonder, she found herself glowing in this intimate contact, Sebastian's overt masculinity making her feel desired, wanted, protected…but not overpowered. Not threatened in any way. And, as her terror finally died, she stayed quite still in his arms, not wanting him to leave her. Amazingly, she felt no embarrassment that they had kissed like that, no shyness that she had felt his body harden against her, had felt the muscles of his broad shoulders tense against her fingers as she'd clutched him to her.

Eventually, reluctantly, he drew away and said softly, 'Fleur, you did not see anything… You've just had a horrible dream, that's all, and I'm really sorry that I told you about the wretched ghost… It was a silly thing to do, just before going to bed.' He gazed down at her for a long moment… Her brief nightwear exposed her slight shoulders and the cleft of her smooth breasts, her hair tangled and damp. Gently, he pulled a lock of it away from her forehead, smoothing his fingers across her cheek for a second. Then, reaching across, he took a tissue from a box on the bedside table and carefully wiped away her tears.

Fully awake—and aware—now, Fleur suddenly became very conscious that he was clad only in dark boxer shorts, conscious of the black hair on his bare chest, of his broad, muscular thighs, and she shivered briefly. Was this part of the dream, would she wake up in a minute and find him gone? But she knew it was no fantasy… His throbbing body, melding with hers, was no figment of her imagination.

After a moment of trying to control his own heightened awareness, he murmured, 'Do you want me to stay?' He paused, feeling a surging, burgeoning hope that she would say yes.

But, after a second's hesitation, she replied, 'No…no, there's no need, thank you…I'm fine now, really. And I'm so sorry.' She swallowed, taking the damp tissue from him and dabbing at her eyes. 'Of course you're right, Sebastian. I was dreaming. How could it possibly have been anything else? But I'm sorry I disturbed you, sorry that you had to come and…and sort me out…'

He smiled briefly, releasing her gently, and got up straight away and went over to the door, glancing back at the crestfallen woman half-kneeling, half-crouching on the bed. 'Can I make you a warm drink, Fleur? Something to help you get back to sleep?' he said quietly.

She returned his smile, beginning to feel calm and more in possession of her self-control. 'No, thanks. I'll have a glass of water and take one of my tablets,' she said.

'I'll…I'll sleep now, Sebastian. And I really do apologize for being such an idiot.'

He nodded at that, going out and closing the door softly behind him.

On his way back to his own room, he was aware that his nerves had quickened dangerously, making him feel frustrated and edgy, and he cursed under his breath. It would have only taken one word from her to make him slide into that bed beside her and take and hold her in his arms, and make tender, unhurried love to her until dawn broke. How had she managed that? Would he really have succumbed that easily? There may not have been any ghost about, but she'd certainly cast a spell on him!

He went into his own room and shut the door, leaning against it for a second. Thank heavens she'd turned down his offer to spend the rest of the night with her. He must have been out of his mind to suggest it. He went across to the window and stared out moodily into the darkness for a moment. He'd thought he was impervious to the lure of beautiful, vulnerable women—but obviously not. Well, it had been a timely warning to keep his distance! And especially with this one, and for whom his restless body still ached. Would he *never* learn?

# CHAPTER SIX

FLEUR stood for several moments, staring at the small bottle of tablets in her hand. She knew she wasn't going to take any—because she didn't want her mind to become even slightly numbed, or hazy, about what had just happened. She wanted the memory, the sensation of Sebastian's mouth hard on hers to stay with her for as long as possible. She wanted to feel his strong arms around her, she wanted the manly fragrance of him to linger in her nostrils.

She glanced at herself in the bathroom mirror—what a sight she looked. Her face was pale and tear-stained, her hair a tangled mess of damp waves, yet that hadn't seemed to matter to Sebastian. She knew that he had wanted her just now—even looking like this—he had wanted her badly, and it had taken all her common sense and control to deny him. And to deny herself, she admitted. Because for those few moments her need had been as acute as his. How had she managed to send him away?

She frowned slightly… What a bizarre thing to have happened, she thought…that their 'ghost' should have suddenly taken on her father's face… What on earth was that all about? Then she shrugged. That was the thing with dreams and nightmares. They *were* bizarre, and had no rhyme or reason.

She filled a glass with water and drank freely. She knew very well how she had managed to resist Sebastian. Even though he had been so kind and thoughtful…and gentle…she knew him to be yet another powerful man, an important man whose self-worth was never in doubt, used to giving orders and to being in command. To having things his way. The very sort she didn't want to become involved with, to have any meaningful relationship with. And, anyway, something he'd once said had made it clear that he wasn't the committing sort either. So that was all right then, she thought. His philosophy would undoubtedly be to enjoy any fleeting moment of passion and pass on unhindered.

Slowly, she climbed back into bed. Tomorrow was another day, and tonight's little episode must be forgotten, ignored, as quickly as possible. She was sorry that she'd accepted his offer of a trip to Truro, but when he was otherwise engaged she'd invent the phone call asking her to return to London. It was safer to get back, to get away from Pengarroth Hall.

She did, finally, drift off to sleep and this time her dreams were pure luxury. Sebastian was there all the time beside her, cradling her in his arms, caressing her in a way that no one had ever done before. It was comforting, it was calm…it was exquisite.

When she woke up, she felt refreshed and resolute. That ridiculous nightmare had resulted in her behaving in an unbelievable way. She'd allowed Sebastian—her host, after all, and Mia's brother—to kiss her passionately, in very intimate circumstances. What they'd been wearing had left nothing to the imagination!

She showered and put on jeans and the silver-grey sloppy sweater which her mother had given her for Christmas. Then she brushed her hair up into a knot on top, touched up her face lightly with blusher and a hint of eye-shadow, and went downstairs.

She could hear Sebastian already in the kitchen and as she opened the door she felt her heart lurch inexplicably. Upstairs, she'd felt so confident of herself, of her feelings, of her determination, so sure that she could appear as if nothing special had gone on last night, and now her legs felt as if they belonged to someone else.

He was at the stove with his back to her as she entered, and he immediately turned to face her, fleeting admiration in his eyes as he took in her appearance. But then his expression changed almost immediately and, clearing his throat, he turned back to making the coffee. 'Morning,' he said briefly. 'Did you manage to sleep OK—eventually?'

'Yes, thank you, I had a good night in the end.' She went over to the fridge. 'Would you like me to cook you something—eggs poached, boiled or fried?' she asked casually, as if she was asking the question of just anyone rather than the man who could have seduced her last night if he'd wanted to.

He put the lid firmly on the percolator, then took it across to the table, where he had already laid two mugs and plates. 'No, I seldom eat breakfast,' he said, pulling out a chair to sit down, 'but you carry on if you want to.'

'Just some toast will be fine for me,' she said. She paused. 'Shall I make some for you as well?'

'Go on, then. I'll keep you company,' he replied.

Making enough for both of them, she brought it over to the table, together with some butter and a jar of home-made honey, then sat down opposite him. Raising her eyes briefly, she said matter-of-factly, 'I really must apologize for last night, Sebastian. I don't know what came over me.'

She paused to butter the toast carefully. 'I'm very sorry that you were disturbed.'

He was about to say, *I wasn't sorry...not a bit.* How could any red-blooded male feel regret at being allowed to kiss a delectable woman in the middle of the night? Then he thought better of it. It was different today—totally, utterly different. She was cool, composed, almost indifferent towards him. He wondered whether she remembered that he'd held her so closely, that she'd given him her lips so willingly. Perhaps that, too, by now had become part of her dreaming, he thought.

'There's absolutely no need to apologize,' he said smoothly. 'If I'd waited for just a few more moments, you'd have recovered by yourself, and there would have been no need for me to...intrude...on your privacy. But...' he paused '...when I heard you calling out, I did feel that I should at least enquire. The comfort of our guests is always paramount at Pengarroth Hall.'

His remarks were neatly put, Fleur had to give him that. He *might* have said, *When I heard you screaming your head off, I thought you were being murdered.* Or something like it.

'The strange thing is, I don't think I usually have nightmares,' she said, 'but, as I sleep alone, there's no one who could confirm that.' She shook her head briefly. 'But last night that ghost seemed so very real... How the mind can play stupid tricks sometimes.' She pretended to giggle, to be amused, but there had been nothing amusing about the effect it had had on her. She had been utterly terrified. Still, there was no need to prolong the experience by going on and on about it. She decided to change the subject. 'So, you have meetings today,' she said, biting into her slice of toast. 'Do you expect to have lengthy discussions?'

'Oh, I shouldn't be too long,' he said, 'but it's always hard to tell. I fully expect to be able to pick you up in time for some lunch.' He picked up his mug. 'We've got some literature hanging about somewhere, about Truro—I know there's plenty to keep you interested there while I'm gone.' He glanced over to her as he drank his coffee. He couldn't believe that their physical encounter last night was being totally disregarded today. As if it had never happened. When anything so stirringly emotional as that had taken place, it was usual for those involved to acknowledge that it had happened—by a word or a gesture. But…that was good, wasn't it? he asked himself. It fitted in with his plans exactly as he wanted it to. He wanted to forget the feel of Fleur's body enveloped in his. Wanted to forget the tide of feeling which had hit him with the force of a tsunami as he'd claimed her sweet, moist lips. And she was clearly of the same mind because the emotional distance between them now was vast—and obvious. It was clearly going to be the host/guest relationship from now on. So—that was good…wasn't it?

'Yes, I noticed the leaflets about Truro on the table in the hall,' she said, 'and, from what I could see, I don't expect to have time to fit it all in. Quite apart from visiting the cathedral and the museum—and all the shops, of course—I just like wandering around places I don't know, walking along the alleys and side streets, getting a feel of how a place ticks. I even like peeping in at people's windows,' she admitted. She smiled across at him quickly. 'So please don't give me a thought, or worry that I may be at a loose end. I assure you, I shan't be.'

'OK, that's fine,' he said casually. 'But I'll ring you on your mobile as soon as the meeting's over, and come and pick you up, wherever you happen to be.' He paused. 'There are plenty of coffee houses for you to refresh yourself, but we'll have some lunch at a rather special place later.' He threw her a glance. 'Mia instructed me on the phone that I must take you there, so I'd better do as she says.'

Fleur stirred some cream into her coffee thoughtfully for a moment. 'You don't have to do that, Sebastian— really you don't. Why waste any more time in Truro?' She hoped she wasn't sounding offhand or ungrateful, but it still rankled with her that Mia had more or less put him in a corner, to 'look after' her. She was quite all right on her own—as she'd tried to convince him before.

'Oh, we might as well have lunch before we head back,' he said casually. 'I'll be hungry, even if you aren't. And, by the way,' he added, 'Pat rang earlier—her mother's much better, apparently, so she'll be back to take up the reins again tonight.' He paused. 'I did tell her that we were managing OK on our own, but she's very possessive of her position here, and I didn't want to make her feel unnecessary, or unwanted…so I didn't try and persuade her to stay at their cottage for a bit longer. Anyway, that means you won't be on supper duty tonight.'

Fleur looked across at him as he spoke. Despite his overtly purposeful nature, and undoubtedly rather imperious streak at times, he was always thoughtful. Even if on their very first encounter he'd made her feel as small as a five penny piece. But she must forget that, she told herself. First impressions, though often valid, did not tell the whole story. As had been proved!

She suddenly remembered the dog. 'Where's Benson?' she asked.

'Oh, Frank's got him.' Sebastian poured himself another coffee. 'And then Pat'll be here later on.'

Soon they were ready to leave and, going outside, Fleur saw that Sebastian had brought his car around to the front door. It was the latest BMW model, a hazy, sensuous blue-grey, and she smiled up at him as he opened the passenger door for her. 'This is…rather…beautiful,' she said. 'A slightly more elevated specimen than my own car,' she added. She'd not seen her car since arriving—Sebastian had parked it for her in the garages, which were obviously around the back somewhere.

'Your car is a very sensible size,' he said, 'especially if you don't need to use the motorways too much. Perfect for London.'

For only the second time since she'd been here, the sun started to break warily through the grey skies and, as Sebastian drove smoothly along the drive, Fleur's spirits rose with every turn of the wheels. She loved a day out, to go somewhere different, and in spite of her misgivings about Sebastian—as well as her own deep-seated feelings—being with this outstandingly-good looking, elegant man certainly put the icing on the cake! She gave him a sidelong glance. He was dressed formally in a sharp suit, plain shirt and knotted tie—the perfect picture of British masculinity, she thought. And his rugged profile, hinting at just an element of harshness, seemed to confirm her view of him as possessing a many-layered personality. Then she amended her thoughts slightly. No, not harsh, she decided…just faintly mysterious, as though no human being would ever be able to reach the real man, to get to the very heart and soul of him. She turned to look steadily ahead.

It took less than an hour to get to Truro and, after they'd exchanged mobile numbers, Sebastian pulled into the car park of the offices he was visiting. 'As soon as I'm done,' he said, glancing across at her, 'I'll ring and come and find you.' He smiled slowly at her as she got out. 'Have fun,' he murmured.

* * *

For the next hour or so, Fleur strolled through the streets, lapping up the atmosphere of the ancient city. Even in early January, there were plenty of tourists about. She soon came upon the County District Offices, and the new Crown Courts, wondering idly whether Sebastian had ever had to flex his professional muscles there. But it was the cathedral that dominated the city centre as it gazed down authoritatively on the Georgian streets that meandered and weaved their way through the city.

Wandering on she came to the two covered markets which were thriving and busy as they set out to encourage early shoppers, but it was Lemon Quay's Creation Centre that Fleur knew would absorb her interest. It was a fascinating arcade, housing specialist shops which were calling out to be explored. This was a holiday experience she certainly hadn't known she'd be enjoying—spending time at the shops! With her head on one side thoughtfully, she assessed the well-dressed windows, wondering whether to buy anything. She seldom shopped much in London, not unless she really needed something, so just wandering about and not having to worry about what time it was added to her sense of freedom and well-being.

In the end, she bought a dainty silver bracelet to take back to her mother, and some unusual embossed notepaper for herself, then decided that she would get something for Pat and Beryl as well. But what? she wondered. She didn't know either woman well enough to know their tastes. She'd have to go on thinking, and hope for inspiration.

She stopped for a few minutes for coffee in one of the small restaurants before deciding to go into the cathedral. Although she knew it to be one of the newest in the country—work only starting on it in 1880—that did not detract from its powerful grandeur or sense of history, its towers and spires dominating everything around it.

Just before she decided to go in, her mobile rang. 'I'm finished here,' Sebastian said. 'Where are you?'

'About to go into the cathedral.'

'OK. I'll come in and find you.'

As soon as she set foot inside, Fleur was struck by how large and wide it was, its slender pillars and tiers of pointed arches automatically making her look upwards to the vaulted roof. There were other visitors looking around too, and presently Fleur trod quietly along the nave, musing at how many sacred buildings like this there must be around the world, places of sanctuary and worship. And, for a reason she couldn't explain, a huge lump formed in her throat. But it was the sudden magical music from the organ as it spilled out and filled every corner of the building with its awesome sound that took Fleur's breath right away. That majestic instrument of praise echoed and re-echoed around, so that every single stone and pillar might hear the timeless messages of hope, solace and inspiration.

She decided to sit down for a few moments, closing her eyes and conscious that a solitary tear was drifting slowly down her cheek. Followed by one or two more.

And then…Sebastian moved in to sit quietly beside her and, without saying a word, he touched her arm gently. Quickly opening her eyes, she saw that he was offering her his handkerchief and she took it from him, touching her face with it briefly. He looked down at her quizzically.

'These places can get to you, can't they?' he said unexpectedly.

'Oh…they make you feel so small, so insignificant, so…pointless, somehow,' she replied with a small smile.

He was still looking at her, and his expression had softened as she spoke. 'I think it's high time I bought you some lunch. Come on. You've done enough soliloquizing.'

He took her arm and drew her to her feet. 'I've had a very successful morning,' he whispered cheerfully. 'All problems laid to rest.'

She smiled up at him quickly, glad to be brought back down to earth. 'Oh, that's great,' she said, automatically thinking that whatever the 'problems' were, they would undoubtedly have been solved to his advantage. It would take a very strong person—whoever he was—to get the better of Sebastian Conway.

'We're going to eat at a very special inn—one that my sister and I have visited several times,' he said, as they arrived outside, 'but we mustn't overdo it because Pat's cooking for us later, remember.'

And it *was* special, Fleur thought as they entered. It had a robust atmosphere but it was obviously a well-run and welcoming place. They found a convenient corner table by a window and, while Sebastian was ordering some drinks at the bar, Fleur gazed outside at the busy streets, the comings and goings of passers-by. She felt almost dizzy with contentment as she glanced over at Sebastian's lean, athletic figure, the handsome head held high, and suddenly he glanced back at *her* and their eyes met in a way that she would remember for a long time. Then he came back with a lemonade for her and a lager for himself, and handed her the menu.

'I recommend the crab sandwiches,' he said, 'which are very generous and served with an amazing salad… but if you want anything cooked, then the steak and beer pie is equally wonderful, though somewhat filling.'

Fleur smiled up at him. 'Crab sandwiches will suit me very well,' she said happily.

When the food came, it was absolutely delicious and after she'd finished it Fleur unashamedly ran a forefinger around her plate to mop up the last bit of the dressing. 'Yummy,' she said softly, looking up at him gratefully. 'Thank you.'

*Yummy* was a word he might have used to describe *her*, he thought. Why did she look so good in everything she wore, and why did those soft eyes with that occasional lazy blink affect him every time…? For crying out loud, this was a Monday morning in early January, he'd just sat through nearly three hours of an important business meeting, and yet all that was consuming his interest was the beautiful woman sitting opposite him. He pulled himself together. She was going home next week, and she'd be out of his life. Why waste his feelings on a ship that would pass in the night? Or waste his feelings on *any* woman? He'd already made his mind up about that—and he seldom, if ever, changed his mind about important issues. It was not in his nature.

After their meal they wandered back to the car and Sebastian drove them home—much more slowly than he would have done if he had been alone. He'd enjoyed himself much, much more than he could have imagined. Enjoyed being with Fleur. And when he'd thrown out the invitation to take her with him to Truro, he'd only really done it to satisfy Mia.

'Oh, I forgot something! Can you…is there…?' Fleur interrupted his thoughts.

He turned and looked at her briefly. 'Why—what is it? What have you forgotten?'

She tutted to herself, irritated. 'I wanted to buy some little gift for Pat—and her mother,' she said. 'Going into the cathedral pushed everything else out of my mind. I meant to do it later. They've both been so kind to me,' she added.

'No worries,' he said easily. 'Do you know what you want to buy?'

'Haven't a clue,' she admitted.

'Well, we'll be passing a very good garden centre in a mile or so, and they've got splendid little gifts.' He smiled faintly. 'Beryl will very much appreciate a bottle of dry sherry, so don't worry about her. There's plenty of the stuff at home and you can have one of our bottles. And I'm sure you'll see something for Pat.'

Stopping at the garden centre, a very pretty hand-painted ceramic watering can, mainly for indoor plants, was decided upon and, as the assistant wrapped it carefully in tissue, Fleur looked up at Sebastian. 'If Pat never actually uses this, it'll look lovely as an ornament, won't it?' she said.

'Oh, she'll use it,' he said. 'Pat likes nice things around her. She's a wizard with anything that grows. And she'll like it especially because you've given it to her.'

As they neared Pengarroth Hall, Fleur suddenly thought of something else she'd forgotten! To tell him of the non-existent phone call asking her to come back early... She'd been so enjoying herself, it had completely slipped her mind. It would seem odd to mention it now, she thought. Never mind—she'd invent the message for later on, when she and Sebastian had been apart for a while.

When they got home, Pat was already back in harness in the kitchen and, after staying around for a few minutes to make enquiries about Beryl, Fleur went upstairs to her room. She realized that she was feeling quite tired and, with the last of the daylight filtering in through the curtains, she lay down on the bed and closed her eyes. Just for a few minutes, she thought. Well, she was on holiday, wasn't she, and being lazy was allowed.

It was the ringing of the doorbell which woke her a whole two hours later, she saw, as she glanced at the bedside clock. It was pitch-black outside and she'd been asleep for two hours! She hadn't heard that bell since the arrival of Mia's friends on Christmas Eve. Not many visitors came to Pengarroth Hall, obviously.

She jumped out of bed quickly, deciding that today she'd have a long, leisurely bath rather than a shower.

For a full half hour she luxuriated thoughtfully in the expensive bubbles. She'd had quite long enough to make up her mind that she was definitely going home the day after tomorrow. She did not want the feelings she had about her host to trouble her common sense for a moment longer... She needed to get back to work! But first, if Beryl really was well enough to receive visitors, she'd go up to their cottage for afternoon tea tomorrow, as they'd arranged. Pat had reminded her about it when they'd come back earlier. But after that, it would be Goodbye Pengarroth Hall!

Fleur smiled to herself as she brushed out her freshly-shampooed hair in long sweeping strokes, feeling bright and light-hearted. Apart from last night's ridiculous episode, she'd slept brilliantly the whole time she'd been here, and eaten even more so, thanks to the hospitality of Pat and her host. Her host! How could she ever think of Sebastian as that, now? He would have to rank as one of her friends, surely—a friend she would keep in casual contact with, and perhaps meet up with once a year—or once every two years! She knew the saying that 'absence makes the heart grow fonder', but she also knew that absence from anyone, or anything, would eventually dull the appetite to the point where it was no longer important, no longer needed. And that was exactly what must happen here. She liked Sebastian, a lot—she may even have fallen in love with him, just a little, she acknowledged ruefully—but she was also too wary of his type to endanger her future. Her future was already mapped out. And it did not include the Sebastian Conways of this world.

As this was to be her penultimate evening here, she decided to make an effort in the dress department, choosing the only skirt she'd brought with her—a three-quarter length swirly number in midnight-blue. It went perfectly with her fine, loose pearly top, especially when she pulled her hair back into a French pleat. She looked at herself in the mirror, hoping that she hadn't overdone it, because she knew it was a glamorous ensemble. Then she shrugged. So what? Anyway, it was too much trouble to take it all off and jump into yet another pair of trousers—either her own or Mia's. Have the courage to stick to your first decisions, she told herself. Stop dithering.

Faintly in the distance she'd heard voices and as she came down the wide staircase she saw Sebastian standing in the hall talking to another man. Fleur hesitated for a second, wondering whether to turn and go back to her room, or to go on down and be introduced to the newcomer. She didn't have long to make up her mind, because both men looked up and watched her descend gracefully. It was the expression on Sebastian's face that made her catch her breath, and he came forward at once.

'Ah, Fleur…meet an old friend of mine, Rudolph Malone… We've been fairly close neighbours for yonks, haven't we, Rudy? And this…this is Fleur—one of Mia's cohorts, Rudy.'

The man came towards Fleur with his rather pale, podgy hand outstretched in greeting. 'Well, well…you never fail to surprise me, Sebastian,' he said. 'Where did you find this one, may I ask? You must let me know your source of supply!'

He was rather a short individual, Fleur noted, with indeterminate brown hair and a face which was dominated by rather thick lips. She supposed that he wasn't that bad-looking but, comparing him to the god-like Sebastian, he didn't have much of a chance. She let him hold her hand for longer than was necessary, before pulling away and smiling up uncertainly.

'I told you, *I* didn't find Fleur—she's a friend of Mia's. And staying for a short holiday before she heads back to London and a very exacting position in the field of medical research,' Sebastian replied.

'Well, well,' Rudy said again. 'How convenient that *you* happen to be here as well, old chap. You said that Mia had already returned?'

'I did. She has,' Sebastian replied, almost rudely, Fleur thought. She saw that his expression had darkened considerably in the last few moments—perhaps this man wasn't liked here, she thought. So what was he doing here?

As if in answer to her unspoken question, Sebastian said, 'Rudy works in London too, Fleur, and he's also having a break at home.' He paused, as if regretting the next thing he was going to say. 'And, since we haven't seen each other for a couple of years—well, not to chat to anyway—he's going to stay and have supper with us this evening.'

'Aren't I the lucky one,' Rudy murmured. 'I shall insist on being allowed to sit very close to your charming visitor, Sebastian. You won't deny me, will you?'

The man hadn't taken his eyes off Fleur from the moment he'd seen her, and suddenly she felt uneasy... She'd met his slimy sort before—the sort she avoided at all costs.

Pat called from the kitchen, 'Supper's ready—I've laid up in the dining room.' Fleur knew that Pat would have been pleased to do that because she jumped at every opportunity to do things properly, and together the three of them strolled along the passageway and took their places at the table. Fleur couldn't help admiring everything— the shining cutlery and glassware, the single decorative candle and a sweet arrangement of holly leaves and berries and Christmas roses in a small bowl in the centre. Yes, Pat *would* love that watering can, Fleur thought.

The meal was delicious, marred only for Fleur by Rudy's proximity to her. He seemed gifted at being able to make their knees, their thighs, touch occasionally, and she tried not to shudder each time he did it. He hadn't waited to be asked where he should sit, but had plonked himself down on the chair next to her, half-turning so that he could look into her eyes.

'I know the sort of food that gets served up in this place,' he said, 'but the only feast I'll need is to look at my charming neighbour. That will be food enough!'

'Shut up, Rudy,' Sebastian said. 'Turn it off, for Pete's sake.' He looked over at Fleur. 'Rudy inhabits the theatrical world,' he said. 'As if you needed telling.'

Fleur wished fervently that she'd decided to dress more casually. All the daft compliments which were being thrown at her were making her feel awkward, and she hated being admired by the absurd man sitting next to her. Once or twice she caught Sebastian's eye, but the usual rather intimate look she'd become used to him sending her didn't seem to be there. He looked as uncomfortable as she was feeling, a coldness in his expression making her feel unsure of herself.

Sebastian admitted to feeling absolutely furious that he'd been more or less obliged to invite Rudolph Malone to supper. Why hadn't he just offered the man a drink and sent him on his way? Why should this lovely day have to be spoilt by an intruder—an intruder who was making one pass after another at Fleur? If he hadn't been so quick with his offer of hospitality, it needn't have happened. He speared a morsel of meat savagely with his fork. Good grief—was he *jealous*? Jealous that he was having to share Fleur with another man, even for one evening? What the hell was going on?

# CHAPTER SEVEN

THE following morning, Fleur woke up later than usual. At midnight, she'd eventually excused herself but had not been able to get to sleep. Rudolph Malone's rather annoying voice—not to mention his persistent and unwelcome flattery—had stayed in her mind like a record that had become stuck in the groove. She couldn't imagine how on earth he could possibly be a friend of Sebastian's, but as they were long-time neighbours she supposed it was a social obligation to offer hospitality now and then.

She frowned briefly as she showered and got dressed. Sebastian had seemed distinctly on edge a few times during the evening…she'd noticed a look on his face that was undeniably dark and moody. After all, she thought, as she brushed out her hair and began working it quickly into one long plait, if he really disliked Rudolph Malone's company that much, why ask the man to supper? He could have made some excuse, surely? She bit her lip. She'd found Sebastian's overt coolness a touch embarrassing. It had made her feel awkward, though she wasn't really surprised, not when she thought about it. Her host was the type who didn't suffer fools gladly, and it seemed obvious to her that Rudy fell quite easily into that category. She stopped what she was doing for a moment and stared at herself in the mirror. The two men could not have been more different, she thought. Rudy was smooth-tongued, his languid gaze as he'd kept on studying her unashamedly making her cringe, his touchy-feely mannerisms distinctly offensive. While Sebastian… Well, Sebastian was something else entirely…

Then she coloured up, remembering the way his lips had found hers a couple of nights ago, the way he'd practically wrapped himself around her so closely she'd actually been aware of his heart hammering against her breast. But…had it *really* happened? Because neither of them had referred to it since, which was so incredibly odd. Then she shrugged. Who cared, anyway? She was going home tomorrow. It was time to move away, move on. With no emotional complications.

Anyway, she thought, as she went towards the door, a kiss was no big deal, surely—didn't mean a thing. She paused for a second before going down the stairs. Liar, she thought. That had been no simple kiss. Sebastian Conway—no doubt highly experienced in the art—had filled her whole body with such intense longing he could have taken her that night with no effort at all. And she felt ashamed to admit it. If she'd said yes, instead of no to him staying, what would that have done to her long-term plans? Because one-night stands were not for her, and never had been. If she and Sebastian had been lovers that night—as she'd known he'd wanted them to be—it would have been merely a passing pleasure to him. But not for her. It would have meant far more to her than that. Yes, it was certainly time to go home.

When she went into the kitchen, she was surprised to see Sebastian there. It was gone nine-thirty—he always breakfasted far earlier than this. He was sitting at the table, turning the pages of a daily newspaper casually, his mug of coffee untouched. He barely looked up as she came in.

'Morning, Sebastian,' she said brightly, glancing down to see that her place had already been laid at the table.

'Morning...er...Fleur...' he replied, almost as if he'd forgotten her name! When he did look up, his eyes were totally impassive as they met hers. 'I trust you slept well?' he said briefly.

Fleur's heart sank for a moment. This was not the same man who'd driven her to Truro, who'd bought her that delicious lunch, who'd sat with her for those few brief minutes in the cathedral and so thoughtfully handed her his handkerchief to dry her tears. This was another man, someone else, someone unknowable and mysterious—and not particularly friendly!

'Pat's gone down to the shops,' he added, without looking at her. 'She'll be back mid-morning, so she says, and then you're expected up at the cottage for tea, I believe.' He paused. 'Coffee's just been brewed, by the way.'

Fleur swallowed. What had happened to make him so cool with her? she asked herself. He was in a funny mood and it certainly wasn't her imagination. She sat down opposite him and began pouring out her drink.

'It looks as if I have to go back tomorrow, Sebastian,' she said. 'I've just received a call from the lab. There's a flap on about something that needs everyone there.' She reached for the cream. How easily that complete lie had slipped from her lips. It hadn't even made her blush. 'So my holiday is going to be cut short, I'm afraid,' she added. 'But I've had a great time, and I feel rested and fully restored.' She paused. 'I hope I haven't been too much of a nuisance.'

'Isn't that out of order,' he said abruptly, 'telling you to return early? Surely everyone needs a decent break to really unwind—especially in your particular field.' He drank from his mug. 'Can't you tell them that if you stay until next week, as you'd intended, you'll be in a better state of health so that they get their pound of flesh when you do return?'

Fleur was surprised at that. She'd have thought he'd have been delighted to see the back of her!

'Sadly, a couple of people are off sick,' she said. 'So they didn't have any option but to call in the rest of us.' Another lie, she thought. Well, wasn't it the case that one little lie led to another and another until you couldn't stop?

There was silence for a few moments while he finished what he'd been reading. Then, again without looking at her, he said, 'Well, what did you think of Rudy?'

Fleur hesitated. 'I…well, he's rather…outspoken, isn't he?' she replied slowly. She'd better be careful because the man was Sebastian's friend. It wouldn't do to express herself too freely.

'If you mean he's rather full of himself, then I would certainly go along with that,' he said flatly.

Fleur shrugged. 'He's in the theatre, so you said. I believe they're all a bit like that. Goes with the territory.'

'Did you…find him attractive?' was the next question, which caught Fleur right off guard.

She frowned briefly. 'I didn't think about him in those terms,' she said.

'Oh, come off it. All you women size us men up and down, make instant assessments, don't you?' he persisted. 'Viewing the potential candidate to progress the human race… All way back in the subconscious, of course, but I believe it to be a substantial fact.'

'I can't speak for others,' Fleur said calmly. 'I certainly didn't find him…interesting…if that answers your question.'

'Oh, well, I just thought you two were getting on rather well, that's all,' he went on. 'You seemed to be hanging on to his every word, giving him all the attention, which he was clearly lapping up. It saved me from having to entertain the man,' he added. 'You did that all by yourself.'

Right, Fleur thought. If he wanted a battle, she was up for it.

'He was a guest in the house, Sebastian,' she said coldly, 'as *I* am. And if I had thrown the evil glances at him that *you* did, I would have failed to discharge my duty in that capacity. So if you really want me to give you my honest opinion of the gentleman, here it is. I thought he was the most revolting little creep that I've met in a long time, curling his ankle around mine like some disgusting worm. Would you like me to have slapped his face, demanded an apology, and then run from the room? Well, sorry to disappoint, but I'm not combative by nature. I prefer to avoid trouble if possible. And, incidentally, it was *your* feelings that were uppermost in my mind. It would have been embarrassing for you if I'd made a scene. So, to answer your enquiry, I did not find him attractive, not one bit. And, as for that squeaky little giggle of his, I'm sure that's a condition he could get treatment for.' She paused, her face flushed. 'The man is a complete buffoon,' she finished.

He closed his newspaper with a flourish and stood up. 'I think I've got the message,' he said, 'but you acted out the part very well. So perhaps I should thank you for that. He left almost as soon as you'd gone to bed, by the way, so clearly he thought there wasn't anything else worth staying for.' He turned away to fetch his jacket from the hook. 'I'll be away for the rest of the day, so…

enjoy your…last one,' he added, going out and closing the door.

When he'd gone, Fleur sat back, completely confused. What on earth was all that about? she asked herself. The man was a peculiar mixture, there was no doubt about that. Often kind and considerate…even beguiling…but today he was like a quarrelsome child. And, this morning, undeniably irritable. Perhaps he and his 'friend' had drunk too much last night. Perhaps that was it. There was no other reason that she could think of. Then she made a face to herself. Let him get on with it. This time tomorrow she'd be well out of here.

Pat returned later on in the morning and Fleur was really pleased to see her, to see her open, friendly, un-complicated face. Sebastian's attitude earlier had upset her more than she wanted to admit, and it was comforting to have the older woman around.

'I'm roasting a little duckling for tonight, for you and Sebastian,' Pat said. 'He's very partial to game, so that'll please him.'

'Hmm,' Fleur said non-committally. The fact was, Sebastian Conway had always been a spoiled brat, she thought. Brought up to expect the best of everything, and getting it, thanks to his heritage.

'Are you happy enough with bread and cheese and some soup, now, Fleur?' Pat asked, 'or do you fancy something else?'

'Bread and cheese will be absolutely perfect, thanks, Pat,' Fleur replied, smiling at the woman gratefully. She paused. 'I'm going to miss you terribly when I go home tomorrow…'

'Oh, but you're not going until next week, are you?' Pat said, turning to look at Fleur, her face crestfallen.

'Sorry—no, I've got to go back early,' Fleur replied.

'Duty calls. But—' she smiled '—I've had the most super time, and most of it is thanks to you. You've treated me like one of the family, like a queen in fact, and my own cooking is going to seem pretty ordinary after yours.'

'Well, well, that's a disappointment,' Pat said. 'It's been lovely having you around, Fleur. Makes such a difference being with another woman, someone young to chat to.' She sighed. 'Mum and I do all right, and we love our lives here, but it can be lonely, and the best times are when the family are here, and bring their guests. Then the place comes alive. Still—' she turned back to what she'd been doing '—we mustn't grumble. We feel very privileged to work at Pengarroth Hall.'

Presently, they sat together at the kitchen table enjoying the lunch—a simple meal which, in Pat's hands, seemed to turn into a banquet. Especially as it began with a piping hot bowl of homemade curried parsnip soup.

'I hope I've left enough room for the duckling,' Fleur said, sitting back.

'Mum's making some lovely saffron buns and a potato cake for our tea first!' Pat exclaimed. 'She's so looking forward to you coming up to the cottage.'

Fleur groaned inwardly. She'd momentarily forgotten about the afternoon tea appointment! But, if it killed her, she'd eat some of Beryl's home-made cakes!

At three o'clock, with Pat leading the way along the wooded paths, they went up to the cottage and Fleur was surprised at how soon they arrived. 'It doesn't take you too long then, Pat, to come down to the house?' she asked. 'Which is just as well, seeing you have to do it so frequently.'

'Oh, my, no, dear,' Pat said. 'Doesn't take any time at all, especially when you know the way, like I do. It takes Mum a bit longer, but then, she only comes to the house when I need a bit of extra help. There are other cottages on the estate, which are rented out, but ours is the nearest—for obvious reasons.'

As they pushed open the door, the smell of fresh baking greeted them and Fleur sniffed the air like a hungry child. 'Oh…I wish I hadn't eaten so much lunch, Pat!'

The woman grinned, calling up the narrow staircase, 'Mum? We've arrived. Are you decent?' She turned to Fleur. 'Mum has a rest after lunch every day.'

'Of course,' Fleur said. 'Is she really all right, Pat—to have me up here, I mean… Has she recovered?'

'Perfectly,' Pat assured her. 'She gets these funny turns fairly regularly, but they soon pass. And she's been looking forward to your visit—insisted on baking the cakes. I could have done it, but no, she's the one in charge here.'

Just then Beryl appeared, wearing a pretty pink jumper and navy skirt, with her almost-white hair brushed up into a knot.

'You look nice, Beryl,' Fleur said.

'Well, we don't often have visitors,' the woman replied. 'Now, let me have your jacket and scarf and you sit there—kettle's already boiled.'

The modest-sized room was simply furnished but cosy and immaculate, the small dining table laid with a white lace cloth and rose-patterned china. Fleur leaned back and looked around her admiringly. 'This is the sort of room you'd see in a child's picture book,' she said, looking up at Beryl. 'So…appealing…and lovely.'

'Old fashioned, you mean,' Pat said good-naturedly. 'But it's how we like it, don't we, Mum?'

Beryl poured boiling water into the pot, then brought the plates of cakes over to the table. 'Now, dear, have you ever tasted potato cake—the real thing, I mean? Like we make down this way?'

Fleur studied the plate she was being shown, on which was a rather flat-shaped cake, criss-crossed on the slightly browned top and dusted with sugar. 'I don't think so,' she replied, her mouth already watering. 'How's it made, Beryl?'

'Easy,' Beryl said. 'Cooked, mashed potatoes, big spoonful of fresh beef suet and the same of sugar, all mixed up by hand, add a few currants, shape it up on a baking sheet, mark it out so it's easy to serve, and let it cook slowly for about an hour. Eat it hot. Like this.' And, with the deft use of a sharp knife, she lifted a generous piece onto Fleur's plate and stood back. 'Try it,' she said.

Fleur did—and it was delicious. Her obvious enjoyment naturally pleased Beryl, and for the next half an hour all three women tucked into it, their teacups being refilled regularly.

'Now, how about a saffron bun—have you ever had saffron buns?' Beryl said, really getting into entertainment mode, but Fleur shook her head regretfully.

'Honestly, Beryl, I've had three slices of potato cake! I couldn't eat another mouthful!'

'Well, have a rest and come back in a minute,' Beryl said happily. 'I've looked out those two books we were talking about the other day, by the way.'

'Oh, I don't think I'll be here long enough to read them,' Fleur said. 'I'm going home tomorrow, Beryl—a bit earlier than I originally thought.'

'Well, take them with you, dear, and you can bring them back next time you're here.'

There won't be a next time, Fleur thought, but instead she said, 'I can't thank you both enough for all you've done to make me so welcome…I've never had a holiday like this, and I've loved every minute of it.' Bending down, she reached for her bag and took out the tissue-wrapped bottle of sherry which Sebastian had left out for her. 'This is just a little thank you, Beryl—and don't drink it all at once!'

'Oh, my goodness—thank you so much,' the woman replied, 'but you shouldn't have, you know. You've been a rather special guest—it's been a pleasure to look after you. Not that I've done much, but I know *Pat's* enjoyed your company.' She hesitated, then added rather slyly, 'To say nothing of our lord and master.'

Fleur looked away at that, then reached for her gift for Pat. 'And I hope you'll find a use for this, Pat.'

Pat unwrapped the watering can, holding it up to admire it. 'It...it's beautiful, Fleur,' she said. She paused. 'Of course I'll use it. And I shall always treasure it.'

No one spoke for a few minutes after that, and Fleur wondered whether it was time to go back.

'You've done Sebastian the world of good, Fleur. We've not seen him so...so relaxed in a long time,' Pat said, breaking the silence. 'And both Mum and I think that it's because *you're* here. He obviously likes you a lot and it's good to see him happy again—especially after what happened.'

Fleur had coloured up at the words, but admitted to being curious as to what Pat was talking about. 'What did happen?' she asked.

'Oh, don't you know—hasn't Mia told you?'

'Told me what?'

'Well, Sebastian was going to be married to one of Mia's friends—well, actually, Mia hadn't known her for that long but she introduced her to Sebastian and he fell for her. Hook, line and sinker. He never tended to bring girlfriends down here—though he had plenty of them, I believe, and he was considered a bit of a playboy when he was younger. Anyway, we all got excited when this one turned up—Davina, her name was. She looked like something out of a fashion magazine—and actually I quite liked her. She was friendly enough. But obviously something pretty disastrous must have happened because, out of the blue, they finished, everything was cancelled. And, after that, Sebastian didn't come home for a while— he left everything here for Frank and the others to deal with. Most unlike him. Anyway, it became a taboo subject very quickly and no one ever refers to it now. But Mum and I think it's high time he found someone else—and we think that you'd be just the one for him, Fleur.' She sat back with the satisfied air of someone who had just made a profound and world-changing statement.

Fleur gave a slightly hysterical giggle and covered her mouth with her hand. 'You must be joking!' she exclaimed. 'My goodness, Sebastian has been a very kind host, I can't deny that, but I assure you that's all he is. I know neither of us is looking for a relationship…I'm very dedicated to my work…but though I'm flattered that you place me in the elevated position as a possible partner for him, I don't think he would share your enthusiasm. In fact, I'm sure he wouldn't,' she added, remembering the morning's conversation.

'Well, that's where you're wrong,' Pat said flatly. 'I know the bloke, have known him all his life, and I've seen the way he looks at you.' She shook her head briefly. 'Mum and I have been chatting and we think it would be fantastic if you could bring him out of his shell again, bring him back to how he used to be. When that woman departed—whatever the reason was—it took the life right out of him.' She shrugged. 'Anyway, we can't do anything about it, but we just wanted you to know what *we* think. We think he's fallen in love with you, and that's all there is to it. And it would be wonderful for Pengarroth Hall to have someone like you around permanently.'

Fleur smiled at the two women. 'Beryl—Pat—you've been reading too many of those romantic novels,' she said. 'Life—real life—isn't like that. Sebastian and I only met a few weeks ago; he doesn't know me, and I don't know him. But thank you for all the nice things you've said—and I'm sure that someone will eventually be the right one for him. It's just not me, I'm afraid.'

No more was said after that and presently, after Fleur had thanked Beryl again for her hospitality, she and Pat made their way back down to the house so that Pat could prepare the evening meal.

'I hope you don't think we spoke out of turn, Fleur,' Pat said as they reached the house. 'You know—about you and Sebastian…what we were hoping…'

Fleur smiled quickly. 'Of course I don't, Pat,' she said. 'I thought it was rather sweet of you to be so concerned for Sebastian's well-being. He's…very lucky to have such concerned friends. And he *will* meet someone soon, I'm sure. Just give him time.'

As Sebastian showered and changed in time for supper, he felt angry with himself, at his undeniable disappointment that Fleur was going home tomorrow. He'd planned one or two things they could do, places he could show her, because she was such an easy woman to please. When Mia had asked him to 'look after' her, he hadn't realized how much he was going to enjoy it!

He put on light trousers and a black open-neck shirt and brushed out his thick hair vigorously, wondering how *she* would be looking this evening. Then he stopped what he was doing, his expression closing in. They'd had quite a spat this morning, and he knew it was all his fault.

Unable to stop himself, he'd done it deliberately. Because he'd known very well that she had not found Rudolph Malone attractive. He was beginning to know her well enough to sense what she was feeling. And she had behaved impeccably—naturally. He wouldn't have expected anything less.

No, what had disturbed him that morning when he'd awoken, had been the memory of how she'd looked as she'd stood, poised, at the head of the stairs, coming down to meet Rudy. She had not taken the trouble to dress herself up like that before and, far from admiring her spectacular appearance, he had been filled with an unexpected dread. Because it was so reminiscent of how Davina had always put in an appearance. Asking to be admired, to be the centre of attention. And this did not fit Fleur's personality one bit. He knew that very well— yet he could not rid himself of the sense of distaste he'd experienced in seeing her like that. It was an unpleasant sense of déjà vu that he could have done without.

Then he shook himself angrily. She was going home tomorrow and a good thing too. He had his life to get on with.

# CHAPTER EIGHT

AT ABOUT eleven o'clock the next morning, Fleur made her final preparations to go home. Sebastian had already left the house, but not before wishing her a casual goodbye and a safe journey, adding a slightly non-committal invitation to come and visit again some time. He had already brought her car around to the front entrance, and put her case in the boot.

Now, she gave one last look around the bedroom to make sure that she'd not left anything behind, then zipped up her hand luggage, slung her bag over her shoulder and went downstairs. Pat was in the kitchen and Fleur was aware of the tangibly sad atmosphere which prevailed. She bent down to smooth the head of the sleeping dog.

'I shall miss you, Benson,' she said softly. 'Even if you did disobey me the other day.'

'Not as much as we're going to miss *you*,' Pat sniffed.

They made their final goodbyes, with Fleur making vague promises to come back to Pengarroth Hall some time in the near future—though she knew that that was not likely to happen. She felt in her bones that her time here should have a final line drawn under it, and that now she should get back to the safety of work.

She smiled faintly as she passed the big gate at the

top end of the estate—the one she'd mistaken for the main entrance, remembering Sebastian's reaction when he'd spotted her sitting there in the semi-darkness. And, automatically, her mind did a rerun of everything that had happened since and her smile deepened. She had had a great time, as she'd told them all, but she finally admitted that the towering influence over the holiday had been that of her reluctant host.

Pausing for a moment at the crossroads before joining the B road which would eventually lead her to the motorway, Fleur made a face to herself as she thought about Sebastian. He hadn't been reluctant at all, she decided, or, if he had been, he'd covered it up very well, because after his initial antipathy to Mia's request that he should look after Fleur, he appeared to have warmed to the task with every day that had passed. If he'd wanted to avoid her, he could have done it easily enough. And, although she had deliberately tried to shut out of her mind all the things which Pat had said yesterday, the woman's remarks would keep floating back into her consciousness. To imagine, even for a second, that Sebastian fancied her was too ridiculous for words! He was clearly not looking for another emotional relationship—he'd made that abundantly clear during one of their early minor discussions on the subject, and, even if he was, there'd be a plentiful selection of women in the elevated life he led from which to choose. *She* would not be top of his list, that was for sure. Then, having hardened those thoughts in her mind, Fleur experienced the familiar tingle of sensuousness when she remembered what had happened a few nights ago in her bedroom...how she'd clung to him and, more importantly, how he'd responded. *Did* he fancy her? Or had that been the automatic, passing reaction which any red-blooded male might have made in those circumstances?

She shrugged. It was difficult to tell but, anyway, it was too late now. That incident had passed like water under a bridge, and neither of them had alluded to it since.

As she drove swiftly along the smooth, well-maintained road, her mind flipped to the time they'd spent together in Truro. They had both enjoyed their time together there—*she* had certainly enjoyed experiencing the city and then, when he'd joined her in the cathedral, his attitude had been so…so special. It had been a simple, yet magical day and he had been so considerate, so warm, and there seemed to have been that certain thread of familiarity between them which only a couple—a devoted couple—might expect to enjoy.

Irritated with herself for dwelling on things—things which were now of the past—she put on a CD and let the music of one of the Verdi operas swell around her like a comforting tide, filling her mind with its beauty.

The traffic began to thicken as she sped along, hampered largely by various delivery trucks and milk and petrol tankers, but as the distance between herself and Pengarroth Hall—and its owner—lengthened, Fleur felt distinct relief, a lightening of her mood. She was glad she'd decided to invent the excuse to go home early—because, right there in the centre of all her other thoughts, was the uncomfortable memory of Sebastian's behaviour yesterday morning at breakfast. His suggestion that she had given Rudolph Malone undue attention, or that she had been making up to him, had upset her more than she wanted to admit. It was an offensive, preposterous suggestion, but it was Sebastian's manner which had been the worst part. He had been almost aggressive—accusing—and she had given him no reason to be either.

Fleur's lips set in a tight line. That little episode had been a demonstration of the real Sebastian, she thought with a trace of bitterness. He had obviously felt an unusual lack of control in that particular scenario, and he hadn't liked it. She shrugged. Well, was she surprised? He fitted perfectly into the mould of men to avoid.

Working up in the top fields with Frank as they stood listing and marking the trees needing attention, Sebastian felt moody and annoyed with himself. He'd deliberately left the house early because he hadn't wanted to stand there in the drive and wave goodbye to Fleur. And he just didn't understand that, didn't understand himself. Didn't understand the minor agony he was going through.

She was just another female. Yes, she was gorgeous to look at, but he'd met plenty like that, and yes, she was highly intelligent, but his law firm had its fair share of bright females. So what was the big problem? The problem was that he felt thwarted. He had expected her—wanted her—to be staying for several more days and instead she'd gone with barely twenty four hours' notice. It had seemed to him an unduly hasty departure. Especially as he'd made plans to entertain her—as Mia had asked him to—and he'd looked forward to it. He knew he was being petty-minded and he could kick himself for his feelings, his folly. But, unfortunately for him, he'd been drawn to Fleur—drawn to her like a pin to a magnet—from almost the first moment he'd set eyes on her. He knew he should resist these impulses, because it was safer, in his own best interests to remain emotionally unshackled...wasn't it? So why wasn't he pleased that she'd gone? He kicked idly at a clod of earth beneath his boot. The damnable thing was that he knew she wasn't in the least interested in *him*—and that only fired his longing to have her, to have his own way. He knew it to be one of the frailties— or strengths—of his character that when anything was denied him he didn't rest until he'd succeeded in getting it. And now she'd gone and he somehow didn't think it would be easy to entice her back to Pengarroth Hall.

'So what do you reckon about this one then, Sebastian?' Frank asked for the third time, and Sebastian looked back at the man quickly.

'Sorry, Frank—what did you say?'

'This one.' Frank tapped a tree trunk with his stick. 'I think it should probably come down.'

'Yes. Yes, I agree,' Sebastian said vaguely, and the older man stared at him, his shrewd eyes narrowing slightly.

'What the 'ell were you thinking about just then?' he asked. 'You were miles away.'

'Um…sorry, Frank,' Sebastian muttered, thinking that he'd been about fifty miles away, which was where she'd be by now.

Much later, back at home, Fleur made herself a large mug of tea and started to unpack. As she pulled everything out of her case, she realized that she'd brought one of Mia's tracksuit pants with her by mistake. She shrugged—it didn't matter because she'd be sure to meet up with her friend again soon. And Mia would expect a blow-by-blow account of everything she'd done at Pengarroth Hall. She paused for a second, her mind going backwards again. One thing she would *not* be describing was her ghostly nightmare. She must try and pretend that had never happened—and she was certain that Sebastian would never bring the subject up. Least said, soonest mended, she thought.

As she took the last of her things from the case, she suddenly spotted Sebastian's handkerchief—the one he'd so thoughtfully passed to her in the cathedral—nestling in amongst her tights. What was it doing there? And why hadn't she given it back to him straight away, or given it to Pat to go into the laundry? She bit her lip. Well, she'd give that to Mia as well, when she saw her, she thought. There'd be no need for any explanations. But, as she picked up the handkerchief, she held it to her nose for a second. It could only belong to Sebastian, she thought... It had his distinctive smell—a mixture of aftershave or cologne and the pervasive fresh, sweet scent of country air and leaves and bracken. She stared across to her window, where the only sight she could see was the tall brick wall of the building next door... *Why* had she come home early? she thought. She could still be there in Cornwall, she and Benson could go for a gentle stroll before she sat down with Sebastian to one of Pat's mouth-watering meals! No regrets, she told herself crossly. She'd made the right decision.

She switched on the television to distract herself, then stood back and looked around her with some distaste. The flat needed a good clean, she thought. It was time to roll up her sleeves and get stuck in. Energetic housework had been the time-honoured way she'd found usually lifted her from any feelings of ennui. She had to confess that for several weeks before Christmas when they'd been so busy at work, and had then gone on to one or two festive gatherings afterwards, she'd not spent much time at home at all. Certainly not enough to move furniture about and do some cleaning and polishing. Counting the weekend, she still had six days left before her holiday was finally over, so that ought to be long enough to bring the place back up to standard. She'd begin tomorrow.

She was about to unwrap the small packet of ham she'd bought for her supper from the deli nearby when the phone rang. It was Mia.

'What are you doing at home?' Mia demanded 'You should still be on holiday!'

Fleur hesitated for only a second... She just could not go on with this deception, not with her friend, anyway. Although she *would* have to manipulate the truth, just a tad.

'Oh hi, Mia. How...how did you know I was back?' she asked—but thinking that there could only be one answer to that.

'I rang home to talk to you, and was told by Pat that you'd been called back to work. Honestly, what a pain.'

Fleur took a deep breath. 'Mia—look, I'll come clean. The lab hasn't been in touch at all. It was just that I thought...I got the impression that...'

'What? Don't tell me Sebastian was being difficult...'

'Oh, no, no, of course not,' Fleur replied quickly, 'but I did think that I might be outstaying my welcome. He's very, very busy with everything, and I began to think I was in the way...' The words petered out as she tried to give a rational explanation. 'And Pat has put in so much effort on my behalf—I've never eaten meals like it in my life.' She patted her waistline as she spoke. 'But it was a wonderful break, Mia, thanks to your kind offer that I should stay, and I felt so well the whole time. In fact, I've had to keep reminding myself to take those tablets.'

'I think you were probably over-sensitive, Fleur, because Pat couldn't stop going on about how much she liked you,' Mia said. 'Now, tell me everything. I hope Sebastian showed you around the area, took you one or two places...'

'Sebastian was extremely kind,' Fleur began carefully, sitting on the arm of her sofa and preparing herself for a long discourse. Mia liked all the details in Technicolor.

After making plans to meet up next week, they were

about to ring off when Fleur said casually, 'By the way, Mia, don't tell Sebastian, you know, that I came back because I felt in the way… It's best that he thinks I'm indispensable at work.'

'OK,' Mia replied cheerfully, though thinking that she'd jolly well find out what her brother had said, or done, to give Fleur the impression she was in the way.

Much later, curled up comfortably in her dressing gown, Fleur rang her parents. Philip answered the phone and his pleasure on hearing his daughter's voice was tangible.

'*Hello* there, Fleur! Well, my word, you *are* having a good break, aren't you, dear? All raring to go back to work, I expect? What? Oh, yes, Mum and I are fine, enjoyed Boston, but it's good to be back in harness. Holidays are fine but too much of it addles the brain.'

Fleur let him go on, interspersing everything he had to say with casual remarks of her own about Cornwall. 'Is Mum there?' she asked.

'No, she's gone next door. New grandchild staying there, I believe.' He sighed, clearly mystified as to why anyone should be interested in babies. 'When she's stopped drooling, I'll get her to ring you, OK? Thanks for the call, and all the best. Let's hope for a successful year for all of us.'

Fleur snapped the phone shut, smiling faintly. Dad'll never change, she thought—and anyway, would she really want him to? At least he was consistent—and he was never unkind. Everyone had their faults, but no one was all bad, she mused.

She decided to go to bed. She'd had a lengthy drive and the day had seemed incredibly long. Snuggling under her duvet, she lay there staring up at the ceiling for a moment… It felt quite strange to be back home amongst her own things and she realized how quickly she'd settled into Pengarroth Hall—she'd felt at home there straight away. She wondered whether Pat was still there, or whether she'd returned to her cottage to be with Beryl. That potato cake had been absolutely scrummy, Fleur thought sleepily—she'd have a go at doing that herself one of these days. What was the recipe again… flour and suet and sugar and…?'

With a start, she was brought back from almost-sleep by the ringing of her phone and she sat up quickly. Glancing at the clock, she saw that it was eleven o'clock and she frowned—her mother wouldn't ring at this hour because Philip always said that telephone calls from, or to, anyone should cease after nine p.m., other than in emergencies.

'Hello?' she said sleepily—and the voice that answered sent a rush of pleasure right through her.

'Oh, good—you're home, safe and sound,' Sebastian said. 'Good journey?'

'No problems to speak of,' Fleur replied, smiling. It was so good to hear him.

'I haven't disturbed you, have I?' he said. 'You weren't asleep?'

'No,' she replied truthfully, 'I wasn't asleep—though I am in bed.'

There was a pause after that, and Fleur imagined him lounging there alone, probably in the sitting room, fingering a glass of red wine or a whisky. And Sebastian pictured Fleur's graceful, feminine curves as she lay in bed, pictured her hair spread out on the pillow, imagined the creamy smoothness of her skin.

He cleared his throat. 'Actually, I've been talking to my sister, so I knew you were home,' he went on. He would like to have said that he'd wanted to hear her voice—but didn't think that was a good idea. 'But I thought I'd ring anyway,' he added.

'I'm glad you did, because now I can thank you again for my holiday, Sebastian,' Fleur said. 'I…I did love every minute of it.' Well, not quite every minute, she thought, but most of them. 'I think Pengarroth Hall and the surroundings are just…idyllic,' she went on, 'and if I were in your shoes, I'd be counting the days before living there permanently.'

He ignored that last remark because it only reminded him of the distance which would soon separate him from the city life he enjoyed, from the people he was close to… And from any chance he might have found to spend time with this woman—a woman who had slipped so effortlessly into his life and to such significant effect! He still had difficulty in believing it because *vulnerable* was not a word he'd ever use to describe himself.

'Oh, we were happy to have you stay…Pat's gone into a sulk because it's only me here now.' He paused. 'And you don't need to thank me—it was all Mia's idea, anyway.'

Fleur froze at that last remark, feeling an uncomfortable chill run through her. Yes, of course it had been Mia's idea that she should prolong her holiday—plus the fact that he should spare some of his valuable time to act out the genial host. Let there not be any doubt about *that*! she thought. She bit her lip, wondering what to say after that.

'Oh, by the way, I very stupidly forgot to give you back your handkerchief—the one you lent me when we were in Truro? I'll let Mia have it when we get together next week.'

'Oh, yes…I remember,' he said casually. 'But don't worry about it, Fleur, I've got others.'

For some unaccountable reason, neither of them wanted

to be the one to hang up first, and Sebastian said seriously, 'Don't let them harass you at work, Fleur. I don't want all that rest and relaxation to be swallowed up now, and ruined by undue pressure.'

Fleur was frankly amazed at his genuine concern. Did he really care whether she was hassled or not? She swallowed and said quickly, 'No, I promise to do only my fair share, and to be sensible, not to stay on too long after hours.'

'Well, I hope you mean it,' he said firmly. It had been noticeable how well she'd begun to appear after the first day or so at Pengarroth Hall, how that winsome, wistful, rather tired look had been replaced by a healthy glow to her cheeks, by a tantalizing sparkle in her large eyes. Cornish air had obviously suited her, he thought.

She stifled a yawn. 'Well, I suppose I'd better go to sleep,' she said softly. 'I know it'll be a busy day tomorrow.' She crossed her fingers as she said it. Yes, she *would* be busy—cleaning her flat!

He paused before answering. 'Yes, of course. So...I'll be back in town myself in about ten days...and I'll be seeing Mia at some point. Perhaps we could all get together for a drink.'

'Perhaps.' Fleur smiled. 'Goodnight, then, Sebastian.'

As he rang off, Sebastian stared moodily into the dying embers of the fire. More than anything in the world at that precise moment, he wanted to be somewhere else. And he knew where that was. He wanted to be with Fleur, wanted to be holding her close to him, to mould her body to his, to possess her...fully...and all his senses rushed at him as he remembered the feel of her mouth on his when they'd kissed the other night. But he didn't think she'd given it another thought...there'd been no look, no word, not the slightest sign that it had had the impact on her that it had on him. She liked men—oh, yes, he was sure that she liked men. She just didn't want to be…how could he put it…cornered by anyone in particular. She wanted to be a beautiful *Mary Celeste*, sailing alone.

He stood up, kicking aside a footstool irritably. There was not the remotest chance that the relationship he wasn't sure he wanted would ever come to anything. The best thing for him would be to try and forget that he'd ever met Fleur. But how the devil was he going to do that?

# CHAPTER NINE

IN HER kitchen on the Saturday evening ten days later, Fleur stood rather precariously on her short stepladder and started to paint the ceiling, wielding the large brush back and forth vigorously.

Having used up some of her holiday, plus more time since, in spring-cleaning the flat, she'd come to the conclusion that the kitchen had gone beyond needing a mere clean-up—it needed redecorating. And, once she'd made up her mind that that was what she was going to do, she'd lost no time in buying everything that was needed. She'd decided that this time the walls would be the palest green—which would suit the oak cabinets—with the skirtings and other woodwork gloss white. And when she'd completed the job, she thought, straining her head back and looking upwards at the rather challenging area to be done, she'd have a great time purchasing some new stuff—towels and tea towels, and maybe replacing some of her china as well. All to blend in. She felt the definite need to inject something new, something original, something to kick-start the new year.

She'd been welcomed back to work with open arms by her colleagues, who'd all said how well she looked and teased her that she'd put on weight, and soon it felt to Fleur that Pengarroth Hall and her time there was becoming a distant memory. But lives were built on memories, she thought now, and she had so many locked away into hers…things she would never, ever forget.

Bending to dip her brush carefully into the paint pot, her thoughts were of Sebastian—as they seemed so often to be—and she was glad she'd not heard anything from him since his phone call. Time was already passing so rapidly, and it was only time which would help her to push him further and further away from her, so that he stopped being the first thing on her mind each morning when she woke and the last thought each night before going to sleep. But it wasn't just him, Sebastian Conway, she tried to convince herself. It was Pengarroth Hall and its atmosphere, it was Pat and Beryl's friendship, and the clear, melting Cornish air. As her thoughts ran on, she grimaced slightly as she remembered Rudolph Malone's visit. His appearance on the scene had been the one thing—apart from Sebastian's reaction to it—to mar the perfect holiday. Then she shrugged. Who cared, anyway? She'd never come face to face with that silly man again.

She was about three-quarters of the way through the area to be painted when the doorbell sounded, and its unexpected intrusion almost made Fleur drop the brush. She paused, frowning. Who would call on her without ringing first? she asked herself. And at nearly nine o'clock on a Saturday night? She put down the brush and began to climb down from the ladder cautiously but, before she could get to the door, the bell rang again—twice in quick succession.

'OK, OK, hang on a minute…' she called. 'I'm just coming.'

As she went into the hall, she glanced at herself in the long mirror—heavens, what a sight she looked! She was wearing the oversized and stained decorator's apron—an old one of her father's—which she always used, and had tied her hair up in a knot with a tatty scarf to keep it in place and to protect her hair from any white splashes. The only make-up she had on was a big smudge of ceiling white on one cheek—which was also on her hands, she noticed, rubbing them down the apron hurriedly.

Going forward quickly, she peered into the security peephole—and gasped in surprise and a certain degree of horror. *Sebastian*, she thought—*what on earth?*

She opened the door and they both stood there for a moment without saying a word, Sebastian looking at her up and down, a curious expression on his face.

'Oh—I've obviously come at a bad time,' he began, and Fleur cut in at once, standing aside. Well, how could she be offhand or unwelcoming—even if she was in no fit state to receive guests?

'It's all right, Sebastian, come in,' she said quickly. 'Though you'll have to take me as you find me,' she added.

He entered, but stood there, just taking in her appearance for several seconds and there was absolutely nothing Fleur could do to make herself look anything other than grubby and unattractive. But, as he stared down at her, Sebastian's only thought was how utterly seductive she looked… There was something so appealing in the hastily drawn-back hair, the untidy scarf, the careless dabs of white on her skin. He could as easily have swept her up into his arms and covered her mouth with kisses as on those other times when, immaculately turned out, she had stirred his desire. He couldn't help fleetingly remembering the time she'd stood at the top of the staircase looking like a society darling—he knew which picture he would want to keep close to his heart.

'I won't ask you what you're up to, because I can

see for myself,' he said casually, following her into the sitting room. 'I didn't realize you were a painter and decorator.'

'It's my kitchen,' she explained. 'I decided that it was some time since it had had a makeover—and a new year seems appropriate to change things a bit, don't you think?'

He was wearing well-cut trousers, a purple shirt, open at the neck, and an expensive long dark coat—and, not for the first time, Fleur found herself admiring the casual elegance which seemed to personify the man. But she was also aware of the tiny flecks of grey beginning to show a little more in his hair. Today he did look the seven years older than her, she thought impulsively.

There was a distinct sense of awkwardness between them—they both felt it—and Fleur went on hurriedly, 'So…you're obviously back in London now, Sebastian… When do you expect to return to Pengarroth Hall? And do sit down,' she added, indicating one of the armchairs. 'Can I offer you a drink—something to eat?' Help, she thought, what have I said? It wouldn't be easy to produce anything in her kitchen at the moment.

He didn't sit, but came towards her slowly and for a moment Fleur thought he was going to take her in his arms…then…

'Fleur…' The word was almost choked out, and involuntarily she put out a hand.

'What…what is it, Sebastian?'

There was a long pause while he struggled to utter the words. 'It's Benson…he died two days ago.' He waited before going on. ' We…we buried him in the grounds yesterday.'

'Oh, *no*—*Benson*!' Fleur covered her face in her hands, hot tears springing to her eyes. 'What…?'

'Of course, none of us should have been surprised,' Sebastian said quietly. 'He was a very old dog, but I can barely remember a time when he wasn't there. He...he seemed to be his usual self in the morning,' he went on, 'then suddenly he couldn't get up from the floor and just looked at us as if he was trying to tell us what was the matter. But, before we could even call the vet, he lay his head down on my knees and... and was gone. In a couple of minutes. At least we were all there to say goodbye.' Sebastian swallowed hard before going on. 'But it's hit us all badly—Pat's been in tears ever since, and Frank's going around with a perpetual scowl on his face.'

It was obvious that Sebastian was terribly upset—and trying hard not to sound too sentimental—and, without thinking what she was doing, Fleur went across and put her arms around his neck, burying her head in his shoulder.

'Poor, dear Benson,' she whispered. 'I wish I'd been there as well, I wish I'd been there to hold him.'

'Yes, I wish you had,' Sebastian said. 'Benson loved you, Fleur, we could all tell. That was why he wouldn't come back home with you on that walk. He wanted you to stay out there with him in the woods.'

A stifled sob left Fleur's lips at his words, and she looked up into Sebastian's face. 'That dog would never have known anything but love and comfort,' she said, 'and, from what you say, he didn't suffer, did he? Not even at the end?'

'No. We don't think so,' Sebastian replied.

'So...he was lucky, wasn't he—lucky to have all of you for his whole life. There are many animals who don't have that kind of luck.'

They stood there still locked together, and Sebastian said, 'I'm sorry to have intruded on you like this, but I just couldn't bring myself to ring you with the news…I wanted to tell you, face to face…because I knew you'd be upset, too.'

Fleur tried hard to stem her tears, and Sebastian put his hand in his pocket and gave her his handkerchief.

'Here,' he said, 'have another one. I told you I had plenty.'

In spite of everything, they both managed to smile at his words. Fleur took the handkerchief and blew her nose and wiped her eyes, sighing heavily. 'Oh, dear,' she said. 'I don't feel like doing any more painting tonight. In fact, I don't feel like doing anything at all.' She blew her nose again. 'I hate bad news,' she said.

'I know, and I'm sorry,' Sebastian said quickly, pulling her into him even more closely. 'I just wanted someone to be miserable with, and you were the first one I thought of. Sorry.'

'Is that a compliment?' Fleur asked, beginning to recover, and thinking that she'd shed more tears since knowing Sebastian than she'd allowed herself in half a lifetime. It had to be those tablets, she thought. She'd take the last few, and that would be it. It was not like her to give way so easily… She'd always been taught that undue emotion portrayed a weakness of character.

'I hope you will take it as such,' he replied. 'I haven't even told Mia yet.'

Fleur looked at him quickly. Well, it *was* a compliment, she thought, to have been put first in these circumstances, and it made her feel ridiculously important…and…special. She went over to the small cabinet in which she kept her modest supply of alcohol.

'I think we both need a drink,' she said, looking across at him. 'I do have some whisky, Sebastian, or would you prefer wine?'

'What I'd really appreciate is a good strong cup of tea,' he said unexpectedly. 'If you can actually produce one—in the present state of your kitchen, I mean?'

Fleur smiled quickly. 'Yes, I can definitely manage a cup of tea,' she said lightly, 'and there's an unopened packet of chocolate digestives to go with it, as well. But I'd better clean myself up a bit first.'

He followed her into the kitchen and looked around him speculatively. 'Look,' he said, 'you're halfway through the ceiling—and you're making a good job of it too—it seems a shame to leave it.' He shrugged off his coat, and looked down at her. 'Let me finish it for you while you make the tea.'

'Oh, honestly, Sebastian…I don't want to put you to any trouble. I can do it tomorrow…'

'No, we'll finish it now,' he said firmly. 'It's not good to leave your post in the middle of a job. If you'll let me have the use of that somewhat roomy apron, I can do it in half an hour. And I think the tea can wait.' He grinned down at her. 'Come on, no arguments. It'll do me good to do something positive.'

Fleur understood exactly where he was coming from with that remark and, without another word, she untied the massive apron and handed it to him. 'This is certainly more your size than mine,' she said. 'And I must admit that my neck was beginning to ache, looking upwards all the time. It was taking longer than I thought it would.'

'So it's just as well that I turned up,' he said reasonably. 'It's an ill wind that blows nobody any good. Isn't that what they say?'

Fleur watched as he set to with the brush, and was impressed with how quickly he was covering the area. 'If I'd known you were going to arrive, I would have waited so that you could have done it all,' she joked.

'I should have let you know,' he said apologetically, glancing down at her briefly, 'but it was only as I was nearing town that I made up my mind to try my luck and see if you were in.' He dipped the brush into the pot again and resumed painting.

'How...how did you know where I lived, anyway?' Fleur asked curiously.

'All your details were written down on the pad in the kitchen—you obviously gave them to Pat, because they were in her handwriting,' he said casually.

'Oh, yes—of course,' Fleur said. 'I remember now. She wants us to keep in touch—which is what I want too, of course.'

In less than forty minutes the job was complete, and Sebastian surveyed his handiwork critically. 'I think that'll do,' he said, 'and if you see any bits I've missed—white on white is always difficult, especially in artificial light—I'll drop back and touch it up.' He put the lid firmly back on the pot and went across to the sink to wash the brush and, as Fleur watched him for a second, she thought how surreal it was that he should be here, painting her ceiling, when she hadn't expected to see him ever again—or, at least, not for a very long time.

He finished what he was doing and turned, looking down at her as he took off the apron. 'I've gone off the idea of tea,' he said. 'A glass of your whisky would be much appreciated—if it's still on offer.'

Fleur smiled up at him. 'Of course it is,' she said, 'and then I'll prepare us some supper—unless you're going on somewhere?'

He shook his head briefly. 'No, I've got no plans,' he said.

'Then I'll wave my magic wand and get us something to eat—though it won't be up to Pat's standard, I'm afraid,' she said, going over to the drinks cabinet, and Sebastian sat down in the armchair with his whisky while Fleur went into the kitchen.

'I'm doing us cheese omelettes—or you could have ham,' she called. 'Which do you want?'

'Cheese will be fine,' he replied. Then, 'Can I help?'

She smiled to herself. 'No, I think I can manage this all by myself,' she said, 'but I'll let you make the coffee later.'

It was surprising how quickly they'd both managed to step back from thinking about poor, dear Benson, Fleur thought, reminding herself again how blessed routine and activity helped to dull pain—at least temporarily. It would take Sebastian—and the others—some time to come to terms with not having the lovely animal around, but at least for the moment Sebastian seemed less upset, though she had to swallow a lump in her own throat as she remembered the dog's soulful eyes looking up at her. And she couldn't help feeling an enormous sense of privilege that *she* had been chosen to be told the news. Even before Mia.

It was getting on for eleven o'clock by the time they sat down, with a tray each on their laps, and enjoyed the soft, buttery omelettes and thinly sliced brown bread.

'I think Pat would say you have done us proud,' Sebastian said as he mopped up the last of his supper with a piece of crust, then put down his knife and fork. 'That was actually quite fantastic,' he added. 'And I hadn't eaten since lunch.'

'It probably seemed fantastic because you were hungry,' Fleur said, 'and so was I.' She took his tray, then went back into the kitchen to put the kettle on. And almost at once he was by her side, standing behind her, with his hands lightly on her waist, before sliding them gently to rest on her hips—for just a moment… She had difficulty in not shivering in pleasure at his touch. Instinctively, she turned away and indicated the coffee things on the shelf.

'There you are,' she said lightly. 'Your turn.'

With the television flickering in the corner, they drank their coffee on the sofa in what Fleur could only think of as companionable ease, with neither of them feeling the need to make unnecessary conversation. Then Sebastian glanced around him.

'You have a very…cosy…place here, Fleur,' he said casually. 'It has your taste stamped all over it, if I may say so.'

Fleur smiled at that. 'I've been here for three years,' she said, 'and the first thing I did was change things as much as I could without actually knocking down walls. My father helped me decorate, but I chose everything myself. It's lovely to own something for one's self, isn't it, and not have to worry about what other people think, or want.' She paused. 'I particularly like my bedroom—it's the largest room and it looks over the park at the back. I just *have* to see grass and trees—foliage of any kind, really—because it helps me ignore the hustle and bustle and brick walls at the front. I see children playing in the park sometimes, and people walking their dogs. I can make believe that I'm in the country somewhere.' She stopped abruptly, wondering whether she should have mentioned dogs, but Sebastian nodded in agreement.

'Yes, it's amazing what a few acres of grassland can do for people. I did bring Benson back to town with me occasionally, a few years ago, but it didn't really work out. He was much happier at home.' He drank from his cup. 'And that's where he is now,' he added.

Neither spoke for a few moments after that, then

Sebastian said, 'When I went into the bathroom to wash my hands, your bedroom door was open…and I agree with you. It is a lovely room, with a big window, which must act as a kind of picture frame for the view outside.' He turned his head and looked at her steadily, not bothering to add how enticing he'd found the sight of her king-size bed with the luxurious pillows and immaculate covers. In fact, he wouldn't mind sliding beneath that duvet with her now, he thought… She was wearing a sort of clingy soft grey dress which just hinted at the curvaceous figure beneath, and she'd done her hair in two bunches, which fell casually around her neck and shoulders. He shrugged inwardly. He knew there'd be no invitation from her to spend the night here, he was sure of that.

He put his empty cup down on the small table in front of them and began to get up reluctantly. 'I suppose I'd better be going,' he said, and she looked up, treating him to one of those languid eye movements which always made the muscles of his neck twitch.

'It's past midnight,' she said coolly. 'You…you're more than welcome to stay, Sebastian.'

That was the last thing he'd expected her to say, and his heart rate went up a notch! 'Um…well…my car's parked along the street and it'll only take half an hour or so to get home,' he began, and she shrugged, getting up as well.

'It's up to you. I feel I owe you bed and board—it'll be my way of saying thank you for doing the ceiling,' she said. 'And I always have bacon and eggs for breakfast on Sundays.'

At that precise moment the telephone rang and Fleur's expression changed at once to one of immediate concern. Frowning, she looked up at Sebastian, her eyebrows raised, then went over to answer it. And, before she had chance to say anything, Mia's voice could be heard by both of them.

'Fleur? Oh, Fleur—I haven't got you out of bed, have I?'

'No, Mia—of course not… What is it? What's the matter?'

'It's Mat! We've split up—just now. Oh, Fleur, it was horrible! We had the grandmother of all rows and he's… he's…' There was the sound of much sniffing and nose-blowing '…he slammed his way out of the flat as if I had something contagious! Honestly, he is being so un-reasonable! And I'm sorry to ring you at this hour, but I couldn't go to bed, go to sleep, without telling *someone*! Why does this always happen, Fleur? I'm beginning to think that I shall never have a lasting relationship with anyone, *ever*!'

In spite of her friend's obvious distress, Fleur couldn't help smiling. Mia was always exuberant—whatever the circumstances—and she knew that this time next week she and Mat would probably have made up. 'Oh dear,' she said sympathetically, 'and I thought you were getting on so well at Christmas…'

'We *were*. It was all going brilliantly, but you're right, Fleur—men always have to be in control. Although I don't usually agree with your mantra, I do now. It's what *they* want all the time; their ideas are the only ones that count…' She blew her nose loudly again, and by now Fleur had made appropriate signs to Sebastian to give him some idea what was going on. Covering the mouthpiece with her hand, she whispered, 'Shall I tell her you're here?'

He grinned and whispered back, 'Why not?'

After listening to a few more frenzied outbursts from

Mia, Fleur said gently, 'Look, there's someone else you might like to talk to, Mia…Sebastian's here.'

For a moment there was dead silence, then Mia said, '*Seb's* there? What's going on? I thought he wasn't coming back to London until next week.'

'Perhaps you'd better speak to him and let him explain,' Fleur said, handing the phone over.

'Hi, Sis. What's it this time?' Sebastian's reasonable voice seemed to calm Mia down slightly as she put him in the picture, and he smiled faintly at Fleur as he listened.

After several more minutes of pouring her heart out, Mia said, 'But…why are you over at Fleur's place? Is something the matter? No one tells me *anything*!'

'Look, it's rather a long story, and I think we'd better meet up,' he began, and Mia interrupted.

'Oh, yes, please. Will you come over and have lunch at my place tomorrow? Please say you will. I can't bear Sundays on my own—and make Fleur come too… I'm desperate to see you—to see you both…'

After arrangements were made for lunch at Mia's flat tomorrow, Sebastian hung up the phone. Fleur said, 'Well, never a dull moment with your family.' She smiled, then stretched her arms above her head, yawning. 'I *must* get to bed—and it's pointless you going home now, Sebastian— if you're having lunch with Mia tomorrow—because her flat is miles away from your place, whereas it's quite convenient to get to from here. So—' she smiled up at him sleepily, turning to go into her room '—I'll give you pillows and a spare duvet in a minute, and then I'll show you how that sofa turns into a very comfortable extra bed.'

# CHAPTER TEN

WHEN she woke up the following morning it took Fleur a moment to remember exactly what had happened last night... Was Sebastian really here and sleeping in her sitting room? Then she sat up quickly. Yes, it was no dream, she assured herself. He *had* turned up last night, had painted her kitchen ceiling—and spent the night on the sofa bed. Though she had not heard a sound from him after they'd wished each other goodnight.

She threw back the duvet and reached for her dressing gown, going into the bathroom. She'd better wash and get dressed quickly so that he could have a shower, she thought. There were plenty of toiletries he could make use of, but no shaving kit. Then she shrugged. That was his problem, not hers.

When she emerged from her bedroom, she was faintly astonished to see the sofa bed returned to normal and no sign of Sebastian. She stood still, looking around her as if expecting him to materialize... *Had* she dreamed it, after all? she asked herself stupidly, knowing full well that she had not. But there was not a sign of him anywhere, and no note.

Slowly, she went into the kitchen feeling suddenly dispirited. She couldn't imagine why he'd disappeared, but the emptiness she felt made her feel forlorn. Then she made a face—for heaven's sake, don't let the man get to you like this, she scolded herself. He'd obviously had a good reason to leave the flat, but so what? She'd go on to Mia's by herself, and whether he turned up or not didn't matter. She glanced up at the ceiling—it did look great, even in the rather poor wintry light coming in the window and, as far as she could see, no spot had been missed. So he needn't bother to come back to do any patching up.

Just then, she heard her front door open and close and, going out quickly into the hallway, she saw Sebastian standing there, two large paper bags in his hand.

'Good morning, Fleur,' he said, looking down at her quizzically. 'Found your house keys on the hall table to let myself back in, in case you still hadn't surfaced, and thought if *I* didn't do something about breakfast, we'd never get to Mia's place.' He went past her into the kitchen, put the things on a shelf and switched on the kettle. 'I know you said you always cook bacon and eggs on Sundays, but I thought there wouldn't be enough time today…so I've bought hot croissants and fresh rolls instead. That's a super deli you've got next door, by the way.'

Fleur felt a rush of pleasure seep through her that he hadn't gone off somewhere without saying anything. She hadn't really thought he would be that rude, but he was something of an unknown quantity and she didn't know him well enough to be sure. She gazed up at him. There was dark stubble on his unshaven features, which might have given him a slightly menacing appearance—until she remembered his reaction at losing Benson. Whatever else he might be, he was not menacing. She smiled quickly.

'I'm sorry I woke up so late—and thanks for getting the breakfast,' she said. 'Besides, Mia's lunches are always very generous so we'd better get there with an appetite.'

'Just what I thought,' he replied, pouring the water onto the coffee grounds in the percolator and reaching for two mugs. He glanced upwards briefly. 'Ceiling's OK,' he said. 'I don't think I missed any bits.'

'The ceiling's perfect,' Fleur said. She paused. 'I didn't want to ask Dad to help me this time… I wanted to do it by myself. But I'm really glad *you* turned up.' She stopped herself from saying any more… This wasn't good, she thought. They were getting too close and she knew that neither of them would appreciate it.

While Sebastian went into the bathroom to shower and freshen up, Fleur busied herself with putting out plates and butter, and they were soon seated once again in the sitting room, munching away at the deliciously fresh food he had bought.

'Did you manage to sleep all right?' she asked, leaning forward to refill their mugs. 'Everyone who's spent a night on that sofa bed declares it to be very comfortable.'

He looked across at her as she spoke. She was wearing well-fitting white trousers and a black figure-hugging jumper, her hair tied back in a ponytail. She had hardly any make-up on, her skin exhibiting that healthy glow he'd come to admire so much, and had put on a pair of white gold hoop earrings which dangled prettily and caught the light as she moved.

He cleared his throat. 'You don't need to apologize for the sofa bed,' he said easily. 'I slept like a log, and it has my full recommendation.' He was going to add that he hoped he'd be invited to use it again, but that wasn't what he meant. To hell with the sofa bed—he'd like to try the king-size in her bedroom, he thought. Preferably with her in it. His expression darkened briefly. Mia had warned him that Fleur was not one for emotional relationships—and Fleur had confirmed it herself. And neither was she the sort to indulge in passionate short-lived flings, either. Any plan he might have had in that direction seemed hopeless.

He stared thoughtfully into his coffee mug. He had thought he'd found the one for him when he'd met Davina—and he'd been proved horribly wrong. Yet his feelings for Fleur were on another planet entirely, and he wanted to kick himself. It was just that she was someone he wanted to be with—all the time. Not only because she was so enticingly beautiful but because she was so…so… ordinary. No, not ordinary. She was unspoilt, uncompli- cated, unsophisticated, undemanding. The sort of woman he'd dreamed of finding, who might one day agree to share his life at Pengarroth Hall. But he knew that was an impossible thought. She was not the marrying kind, and certainly didn't want children. He shrugged inwardly. He knew plenty of women whom he could easily persuade to be his wife—but he didn't want any of them. He wanted just one—the one who obviously didn't want him.

The Sunday morning traffic was blissfully light and it only took half an hour to reach Mia's flat. Sebastian was able to park the car right outside, and Fleur was surprised at that—until Sebastian explained.

'Mia always arranges to park her car somewhere else,' he said, 'when she knows I'm coming—which is thought- ful of her. Otherwise we might have had a fair walk.'

Fleur had been to the imposing building several times before, but it never failed to impress her. The marble- pillared entrance announced the grandeur of what would once have been the residence of a wealthy family, but which had been turned into four spacious flats. She knew that the whole place was owned by the Conway estate, with Mia living in one of the flats and the others rented out—mostly to friends or acquaintances.

Sebastian gave a quick ring on the bell before opening the door with his own key, then ushered Fleur in front of him as they made their way along the wide, richly carpeted hallway. The discreet chandeliers above their heads threw a welcoming light as they went up the stairs and, before they could reach Mia's door, she appeared, leaning over the gleaming mahogany banister to greet them.

'Oh, good—you've timed it just right,' she enthused. 'I'm *so* glad to see you both.'

Despite her distress of the night before, Mia seemed to have recovered enough to be her usual bubbly self and Fleur thought—not for the first time—what a joy people like her were. Whatever happened, she always seemed to bounce back cheerfully.

'Now, first things first,' Mia said, as she poured some wine into three glasses and handed them around. 'What on earth were you doing at Fleur's place so late on a Saturday night, may I ask?' she demanded. 'It was only after I rang off that I realized I didn't have the faintest idea what that was all about.'

Sebastian looked sober for a moment before he spoke. 'I don't really know what I was doing there myself,' he admitted. 'But I wanted to tell Fleur something…something which I knew would upset her, and I didn't want to use the phone.'

Mia was mystified. 'Well,' she said impatiently, 'what was it?'

'Benson died a couple of days ago, Mia,' he began, 'and…'

'Oh, *no*!' Mia was aghast at the news 'What happened…how…did he go?'

'Very peacefully,' Sebastian said slowly, 'with his head in my lap. He was just tired, that's all. There was no pain.'

There were a few moments' silence while Mia absorbed the news.

'Of course, I wanted you to know too,' Sebastian went on quickly, 'but because Fleur had been at the house for some time, Benson had got used to her being there—she did make a lot of fuss of him and he liked that. They'd become firm friends, I think, and it seemed right that I should tell her face to face.' He paused. 'They had quite a relationship going in the end.'

For once, Mia seemed deflated—but it wasn't long before she recovered. 'Well…we all knew Benson's days were numbered,' she said, 'and his walks were beginning to get shorter and shorter, weren't they?' She glanced at Sebastian. 'You'll have to get a replacement, Seb. I don't think Frank—or Pat—will survive without a dog in the place.'

'There's time for that,' he replied shortly.

Fleur decided to lighten the atmosphere. 'Whatever you're cooking, Mia, it smells fantastic,' she said. 'I'm very glad I didn't cook bacon and eggs for us this morning.'

Mia was quick to pick up on that remark. 'Oh, you stayed the night, then Seb—well, well.' Her mischievous eyes twinkled as she looked from one to the other.

'I was offered the opportunity to sleep on Fleur's extremely comfortable sofa bed, to save me driving home, then having to come back again to pick her up before we came on to your place,' Sebastian explained smoothly.

'Hmm,' Mia said enigmatically, and Fleur looked across at her friend.

'I was only being polite, Mia,' she said. 'It seemed the right thing to do, especially as Sebastian had just painted my kitchen ceiling for me.'

'Painted your what?' Mia turned to Sebastian. 'I can find one or two things for you to do here if you're ever at a loose end,' she teased, 'though I don't think that any of my ceilings would have quite the appeal for you that Fleur's obviously had.'

Sebastian stood up to offer the wine around. 'Why don't we talk about you and your love life, Mia?' he said easily. 'Come on, out with it.'

'Oh, that can wait until we've eaten,' Mia said airily. 'I've cooked a piece of beef—which I would be glad if you would now come and carve please, Seb—and the roast potatoes and Yorkshire puddings are done to a turn.'

With her mouth already watering, Fleur took her place at the table and soon they were tucking into a meal which could almost have compared with Pat's.

'This is wonderful, Mia,' Fleur said, helping herself to more of the buttery carrots which Sebastian was offering around.

'Oh, I've learned everything from Pat,' Mia said. 'She's always happy to pass on her knowledge to anyone who'll listen.'

It was not until they were finishing the last of the apple tart and custard that Sebastian brought the conversation round to Mia again as he leaned back in his chair. 'Now then, what went on last night between you and your latest?' he said, and Fleur glanced at him quickly. His question sounded like that which a lawyer might ask of a client, she thought—brisk and to the point. Although the relationship between Sebastian and his sister was clearly a very loving one, she did wonder whether Mia was slightly in awe of him—especially because he was that much older than her.

'Oh, I don't know,' Mia said, pushing her plate away and leaning her elbows on the table. 'Everything was going well, and I thought that this time I'd found someone I could tolerate for the next forty years...but lately he has seemed...different...somehow. Always wants the last word. Always thinks he's right. And very determined about certain things.' She paused. 'And last night—we'd seen a good film, had supper, and then he started nagging me about something. And guess what—when I told him to go, if that's how he felt about me—he did. *Go*, I mean. Just marched out with not another word.'

'Well, if you told him to go, then it's not surprising that he did,' Sebastian said briefly. 'What else did you expect?'

Mia stared across at him. 'I did *not* expect him to go, Seb! I did not expect that at all. I expected him to stay and be reasonable. To try and see my point of view for once.'

Sebastian shrugged. 'I don't understand females,' he said. 'If a woman showed me the door, I'd be gone without a backward glance.'

'What exactly is it that you don't agree about, Mia?' Fleur asked gently. 'Is there a particular sticking point that gives rise to a lot of other silly arguments?'

Mia thought about that for a moment. 'He accuses me of being over-adventurous, of always having mad ideas...I mean...I want...I'd *love* to do a parachute jump...' She paused. 'But he's more cautious than me, and doesn't want

me to do it. Says life's too short to take unnecessary risks.'
She hesitated. 'I suppose you can understand it because
his best friend was killed doing one a year or so ago.'

'Then you certainly *can* understand it,' Sebastian said
firmly, 'and doesn't it tell you something, Mia? That the
man cares enough for you that he doesn't want you to
come to any harm? He *could* say, *Carry on and good luck*,
but he wants you in one piece, presumably so that you can
spend a lot more time together.' He shook his head as he
looked across at his sister. 'When are you going to grow
up and settle down, Mia? I seem to remember spending
most of your teenage years—and afterwards—catching
you as you fell out of trees, or into rivers.' He put his
napkin down and stood up. 'Anyway, I'm with Mat, who
I thought was a pretty sound bloke, by the way. I'd prefer
you not to go jumping out of aeroplanes just for the fun
of it. Because—' he looked down at her seriously for a
second '—it's up to you to provide the next generation
for Pengarroth Hall—that's the least you can do in return
for all the privileges that come with the dynasty.'

Mia pretended to sulk. 'Well, *thanks* for your support, Seb. And anyway, what about you?' she said. 'Why
can't *you* do something about making sure the line
continues?'

'I've decided to leave that bit to you,' he said, going
over to look out of the window. 'I've already planned to
give up what's left of my life to run the place as efficiently
as it's been done for generations. That's enough to be
thinking about. The baby business is yours.'

'Well, that's all right then,' Mia said sarcastically. But
it was obvious that chatting about her love life with the
others had allowed her to see things in a different light.
'Anyway, Mat did ring me this morning—with a sort of
apology,' she conceded. 'So I'll forgive him.' She smiled

cheerfully. 'He *can* be a darling,' she said, 'and as long as he lets me win some of the arguments, I expect we'll end up together.'

'Winning half of the time is a perfectly reasonable expectation,' Sebastian said. 'Give and take. Win some, lose some. It's called being reasonable.'

He's back in lawyer mode again, Fleur thought.

Later, they sat there in the beautifully furnished room, lazily reading the Sunday newspapers.

'By the way, Mia, the law event is the Saturday after next—remember I told you about it? It's a bit earlier than usual,' Sebastian remarked.

Mia stood up to consult her calendar. 'Oh, dear, I *had* forgotten, Seb.' She ran her finger down the page. ' Sorry, but it's out of the question, I'm afraid. Big do at work. Can't possibly miss it.' She looked across at Fleur. 'But Fleur might be able to go with you…'

Fleur coloured up at the words. Mia was at it again—making arrangements for other people.

Sebastian said, '*Would* you be free on that day, Fleur? It's something I just have to attend every year and it's… useful to have a companion.'

'What he means is it helps to keep predators at bay,' Mia said, grinning. She looked down at Fleur, who was still sitting at the table. 'You'd love it, Fleur—it's always in a splendid hotel, great dinner, entertainment…and usually goodie bags for all the ladies.'

'Well, I'll have to see what…' Fleur began hesitantly, getting her diary out of her bag. Quick, make up something, she told herself—but make it sound genuine. She turned the pages of the little book—but the date was completely free. And, when she looked up, she saw that Sebastian was gazing at her with that inscrutable expression which defied any excuses she might come up with. 'I can probably go with you...' she began slowly.

'There you are, then. That's settled.' Mia beamed as she went towards the kitchen. 'I'll fill the dishwasher and Seb can make the coffee. He makes great coffee,' she said over her shoulder to Fleur.

Much later, after they'd had coffee with Mia, Fleur and Sebastian made their way back to her flat, Fleur desperately trying to find a way of saying something about the impending law dinner without sounding negative.

'Are you sure you want me to come with you to the law dinner, Sebastian?' she asked as casually as she could, gazing out of the side window. 'I'm afraid Mia has a gift for putting you in awkward situations—she's done it before, hasn't she? Aren't there lots of lovely lawyers who'd be pleased to accompany you?'

He didn't even look at her as he replied. 'There are. But I don't want them to accompany me, thanks very much. I see quite enough of them without sharing my Saturday evenings with them.' He paused at the last set of traffic lights before they reached their destination. 'I'm glad Mia suggested you come, Fleur. I can't think of anyone who'd fill the vacancy with more grace.' Now he did look at her, and his eyes were glistening darkly. 'Don't worry about it. Having to suffer my company can be a small payment for painting your ceiling.'

They pulled away again and, when they reached her flat, he turned off the engine and looked down at her. 'When do you want me to come and finish it all—the glossing, I mean? You don't want the job hanging around, do you?'

'Oh, there's no need for you to come back and do anything, Sebastian—I can manage that all right. But... thanks for the offer.' She hesitated. 'Would you like to come in for a…drink?' she asked, though thinking that *she* didn't want anything else to eat or drink until at least tomorrow.

'No, thanks, I'll be on my way,' he said. He got out of the car and came around to open her door. 'Well, have a good week—and don't overdo it, will you.'

She smiled up at him quickly. 'Thanks for your concern, Sebastian. I'm sure I'll survive whatever they throw at me.'

She watched him pull away swiftly and stood for a moment before going inside. She had very mixed feelings about her date with Sebastian…. very mixed feelings about him full stop. The thing was, she knew that she was in love with the man, but didn't want to be. Being heavily involved wasn't how she'd imagined her life to ever be. With anyone—anyone at all.

She let herself into the flat and threw her bag down on the sofa before going over to look out of her bedroom window. It was already dark outside, the lamps of the park throwing their yellow glow across the trees and bushes, illuminating the few people still strolling around. If she tried really hard, she could imagine that she was back at Pengarroth Hall, back amongst the scenery, the greenery, might even be able to smell the damp earth, the leaves, the freedom.

Then she turned away decisively. She must stop this daydreaming, she told herself. And she must never go back to Pengarroth Hall. It was safer to stay here, for this was where she belonged, not there. And if Sebastian did get in touch with her again—before the dinner date she'd agreed to—she'd make an excuse, any excuse, not to meet up until then. Distance was the safest thing.

She smiled faintly as she took off her coat. You'd be proud of me, Dad, she thought. Resist all interruptions to worthwhile plans—wasn't that what he always said? It wasn't her fault that Sebastian had turned up last night, or that Mia had invited them to lunch, or that she had been more or less forced to accept the law date with him. None of that was her fault. But not to worry. She'd be careful not to step too far out of line.

# CHAPTER ELEVEN

SITTING pensively in front of the mirror in her bedroom as she smoothed body lotion along her neck and shoulders, Fleur anticipated the evening ahead with some misgivings. The night of the law dinner had come all too quickly. She'd tried to put it from her mind.

Two weeks had passed since she and Sebastian had had Sunday lunch with Mia, and during that time Fleur had done her best not to think of him. This had been helped considerably by the fact that there'd been a particularly absorbing project at work, no one leaving the laboratory until eight o'clock for several days running, so that by the time she eventually got home and prepared herself a meal, bed and sleep were all that mattered.

She frowned slightly as her thoughts ran on. Sebastian, too, must have obviously been very occupied, because the only contact he'd made had been one message left on her answering machine, hoping that she was OK, and also that the rest of the painting in her kitchen had gone well. She made a face to herself as she remembered that bit—she'd not had the chance, nor the inclination, to complete the job. It would have to wait until things quietened down at the lab.

Anyway, as far as this evening was concerned, she knew that the only reason she'd been invited to the event was to act as a decoy for Sebastian. To protect him—how had Mia put it?—from predatory females. Well, that was fine by her. She'd play the part, no problem. And knowing that that was the sole point of her being there would help her to enjoy herself, with no underlying emotional pressures. Her expression cleared. It could prove to be a rather special game of make-believe, she thought, with her and Sebastian the only ones in on the plot. And, afterwards, he could go on his merry way and leave her to go on hers.

His secretary had phoned the night before to explain that he had arranged to send a cab for her at seven o'clock, and exactly on time her doorbell sounded. Picking up her pearl coloured faux fur wrap and a clutch bag, she left the flat and went downstairs. A uniformed chauffeur stood there with the car door already open and, feeling as if she were about to go to a command performance, Fleur picked up the hem of her skirt and got in. Well, that was what this was, she thought—a command performance—though she doubted whether there'd be any red carpet waiting for her.

It took less than half an hour to reach the grand London hotel and, as they pulled up, an official doorman came forward to hand her out of the car. Inside, the brightly-lit and luxurious entrance was thronging with people in full evening dress, and for a second Fleur felt like turning around and running away. She wasn't used to this kind of thing, she thought, and although there had obviously been a few special occasions in her life where everyone had dressed up, they had been few and far between. And they were certainly not her preferred way of spending an evening. But…she'd agreed to come so she'd better make the best of it.

Almost immediately, Sebastian was at her side and

as Fleur looked up at him she felt a tremor run right through her. He looked suave, immaculate—and painfully desirable—in a beautifully-cut dinner suit, his hair dark and glossy—and slightly in need of a cut, she thought instinctively, but it suited him like that—and, as usual, with the advantage of his height, he stood head and shoulders above everyone else around. She was aware again of the cut of his jaw, the strength of his shoulders, and as he stood there now, totally relaxed among people he knew and who knew him, she could almost feel the powerful awesomeness which seemed to radiate from him. He smiled down at her, taking her arm and leading her towards the cloakroom.

'Do you want to leave your wrap?' he asked. 'I can assure you that you'll be warm enough in the function room, but perhaps you'd rather hang on to it?'

'No, I'll leave it,' Fleur said.

'Then I'll wait here for you.'

After leaving her wrap with the attendant, Fleur went into the adjoining powder room to take a last look at herself in the mirror. There were several other women there, touching up their make-up, and she could hear the conversation of a few of them who were standing around by the door.

'Well, no one's seen him with anyone,' someone said, 'not for a long time.'

'Doesn't he usually bring his sister?' someone else enquired. 'I liked her—she's a really friendly, bubbly girl.'

'Not like him, then,' was the next remark, and everyone laughed.

'Oh, he's all right,' another one said, 'when you get to know him. Personally, I *like* the strong, silent type. I wouldn't throw him out of bed, that's for sure.'

'Dream on,' said the first girl. 'Anyway, he'll be out of our lives soon, and the place won't seem the same without him. He's going down to the family pile in Cornwall, apparently, to run their estate.' She sighed heavily. 'What a waste of a man—to bury him down there amongst all those pixies and pasties!'

Everyone laughed again as they opened the door to leave, and the parting remark which Fleur heard was, 'Anyway, he's definitely not the marrying kind—not any more.'

'Shh,' someone warned quietly, 'he's standing there outside.'

Fleur stood rooted to the spot. It had been clear to her from the outset that the women had been discussing Sebastian and, although nothing really derogatory had been said, it had made her feel uncomfortable—and defensive—to hear him talked about. And it was also completely understandable why he should not want to come to this function alone, she thought—not if he wanted to avoid unwanted attention.

She left the room and went across to join him. She was going to enjoy carrying out her mission tonight, she thought, and she'd make a good job of it. She'd give those women something to talk about!

Now that he could see her properly, Sebastian made no secret of the fact that he was almost bowled over by her appearance.

'I've never seen you in that colour before,' he murmured slowly, staring down at her. 'It…it really suits you, Fleur.'

'I've only got three good occasion dresses,' she admitted, 'and at first I'd decided to wear my black one, but then I thought everyone would be wearing black. So…' she smiled up at him '…I thought I'd be different.'

The dress was a flame-red, slinky, full-length number, scoop-necked to reveal the slenderness of her neck and shoulders, and the skirt was slit up one side to reveal just enough thigh to be teasingly-seductive as she moved. He noticed that she was wearing slightly more make-up than usual, with the addition of a slick of eye liner and some smoky shadow, and her hair was centre-parted with a lustrous chignon coiled expertly at the back. Her only jewellery seemed to be the same white gold hoop earrings he'd seen on her before, but the whole package was breathtaking—and he knew there'd be plenty of eyes on both of them during the evening. Could this be the next Mrs Sebastian Conway, they'd all be asking themselves, against all the odds? Well, he'd answer that—not a chance. Not because he wasn't interested in her—but because he knew that she wasn't interested in *him*. Charming she certainly was—especially at this moment because he was aware that she'd tucked her small hand into his arm, an unusual act of familiarity on her part. But charm by itself did not equate to feeling anything about someone, he knew that. It was merely a superficial pleasantry. He sighed briefly to himself. He'd better concentrate on this evening—an occasion he usually dreaded rather than looked forward to—and on making sure that Fleur enjoyed herself. He glanced down at her, at the top of her head, at her shining golden hair as they made their way through the crowd... He somehow didn't think it was the sort of event which would appeal to her much, either. In fact, he knew very well where she'd rather be at this moment—tramping through all that wet undergrowth at Pengarroth Hall!

In the crowded reception area, wine was handed around freely and dozens of different conversations soon filled the huge room, everyone talking loudly in order to be heard.

Sebastian introduced Fleur to several people—whose names she knew she'd forget almost immediately. But everyone was chatty and friendly and she smiled happily, thinking what a good thing it was that she was not here as a romantic partner of the man standing so possessively beside her. Because it meant that she could relax totally, without worrying about emotions and feelings. She was here for a practical reason—to ward off unwanted admirers—and just as well, she thought, because she couldn't help noticing the covetous glances directed at Sebastian from time to time. He certainly did need protecting, and there were many attractive, beautifully dressed women he could choose from. But, for a change, she was to be *his* 'minder'—and she was going to make the most of it.

At the signal, they all went into the massive dining room and took their places at one of the round tables, each set for ten people. There were four men and six women on theirs and as they sat down Fleur looked up at Sebastian and smiled provocatively. Let those females without escorts be in no doubt that he was spoken for! And he smiled back, taking her hand and squeezing it gently. He obviously intended to play his part, too!

'Are you OK?' he asked out of the corner of his mouth. 'It's not so good being somewhere among complete strangers, is it…not knowing anyone.'

'But I know you—and that's all that matters,' she replied softly, holding him captive once more with that hesitant, lazy lowering of her eyelids.

Almost at once the small band on the stage began to play in the background, and Fleur automatically tapped her feet in time to the rhythm. She was *glad* she was here—with Sebastian.

It was obviously a very rich gathering, with a mixed age group, she thought, looking around her as the meal was being served. Fleur could only imagine what the tickets for the event must have cost, because success, and the affluence that went with it, was tangible.

'This is one of our main fund-raising events, and I'm glad so many have supported it this evening,' Sebastian told her, as if reading her thoughts. He stopped speaking for a moment while a waiter filled their glasses with sparkling wine. 'We engage an appropriate firm to arrange everything, and they always seem to come up with something special to swell the funds. Last year we did fantastically well—after dinner they set up a mock horse-racing game and everyone gambled.' He drank from his glass. 'We never know what they've planned until the night, but it's usually great fun.'

The man sitting next to Fleur turned towards her for a moment. 'And what do you do in your working life, Fleur?' he enquired politely. 'No, let me guess. You're a famous model…'

Fleur smiled quickly, giving the man brief details in answer to his question, and he was clearly impressed. 'Makes a change from what many of us in this room do all day,' he said. He paused, glancing surreptitiously across at Sebastian, who was talking to the woman on his other side. 'Have you…have you known Sebastian long?' he asked curiously.

'Long enough,' she replied obliquely. Let the man make what he liked of that remark! Poor Sebastian, she thought. His personal life was obviously a matter of great interest to his colleagues. And she could guess how much he must hate it.

The food was good and well-served and after dinner the grand auction began—this year's special event. It got going quickly and with great enthusiasm, and Fleur was amazed at the value of everything. The list of desirable items went on and on, and bidding was fast and furious. Fleur's breath was almost taken away by the speed of everything in the hands of the professional auctioneer, and also by the totals being achieved. She looked up at Sebastian.

'I've never seen anything like this,' she said over the noise in the room, and he smiled at her, obviously pleased at how much money was being raised.

'At this rate, we're going to beat last year's total,' he said, and she realized how genuine his concern was for the charity they were supporting.

The atmosphere in the room had become more and more hectic and excitable, and Fleur's head had begun to spin slightly as her wineglass was regularly refilled. But the expensive alcohol and the food had the effect of totally relaxing her, making her feel almost on another planet as she took in everything that was going on around her. She was overwhelmingly conscious of Sebastian's closeness to her, of how he occasionally leaned forward towards her, putting his arm around her shoulders and drawing her in to him in almost a bear hug as he bid for something enthusiastically.

Finally, everything had been spoken for, with cheques and bank notes being hurriedly counted, and the MC took the microphone.

'Now then, ladies and gents,' he said. 'Tonight, as a somewhat novel slant to the proceedings, I'm going to ask for a volunteer from each table to come up and sing for us. Sing along with the band, I mean—anything you like—and I shall ask the rest of you to bid the money you think each singer is worth.'

A gale of whooping and laughter greeted his words, followed by shrieks, protests and arguments as people tried to cajole others to volunteer.

Fleur sat back languidly and looked around her at the rest of the table. One of the women would be only too happy to do it, she thought. They'd certainly all been very noisy so far during the evening, if that was anything to go by. But, surprisingly, there was a flat refusal from each one.

'You can count me out,' the tall brunette opposite said. 'Not my scene, thanks.' She looked across at the man sitting next to Fleur. 'How about you, Tom? Music's your thing, isn't it?'

'It is,' he agreed, 'but I only sing in the bath these days.'

Sebastian decided to take charge of proceedings. 'Look, it's only a laugh,' he said reasonably. 'You're not auditioning for the West End. Come on—one of you has to do it.'

'How about you having a go?' someone said. 'I propose Sebastian!'

'Not a chance,' he replied. 'But one of you simply *must*—we can't be the only table not to take part. Come *on*…'

'Oh, dear, Sebastian has spoken,' one of the women said, her words slurring slightly, 'and we all know what *that* can mean…'

Suddenly, as if someone else was speaking for her, Fleur said calmly, 'I'll do it, if you want me to, Sebastian.'

Afterwards, she would never know what had made her volunteer, but the look of relief on Sebastian's face was reward enough.

As the organizers had known, hearing unwilling victims make themselves conspicuous in this way was an inspired idea, and soon there was huge applause and ribald encouragement from the room as each singer took part, all of them crooning lustily to the latest pop number, and with hearty support from the band.

Sebastian's table was the last one to take part, and slowly Fleur got up from her chair, watched with mixed feelings by the other women. Sebastian stood as well and, with his arm held protectively around her waist, he led her up to the stage.

Going across to the keyboard player, Fleur said, almost apologetically, 'I don't really sing pop...but...do you know Mancini's *Moon River*?'

The man smiled up at her. 'Course I do,' he said. 'Lovely number.' And at once he played the introduction to the well-known song.

Feeling again as if she wasn't here at all, but drifting along several feet in the air, Fleur began the first notes of the sad, nostalgic tune, with its evocative lyrics. Almost at once the room fell silent as she sang, with no one calling out or shifting in their seats.... *'Moon River, wider than a mile, I'm crossing you in style, some day...'* her voice, pure and note perfect, echoed wistfully around the room *'...we're after the same rainbow's end, waiting round the bend, my huckleberry friend, moon river...and me.'*

As the last notes died away, there was a complete hush, apart from someone blowing their nose quietly as the wistfulness of the number touched a nerve. This was unexpected, unlike anything else that had been sung, and it had the effect of stunning everyone into momentary silence. But not for long. The reception Fleur got was huge, with some people getting to their feet and shouting for an encore, but at once Sebastian held out his hand to help her off the stage before leading her back to the table.

The money raised exceeded every expectation. Each singer had to stand up to be recognized again as people

shouted their bids from all around the room and when
Fleur got to her feet the bidding reached a crescendo.

Sebastian leaned towards her to whisper in her ear. 'I
think you can safely say you were the hit of the evening,
Fleur. And you certainly earned your dinner. Very many
thanks for stepping in.' He paused. 'You were…fantastic.'
He paused. 'I was…so proud of you.'

Fleur sipped again at her glass, thinking—did I really
do that? What came over me? And she realized that it was
the first time she'd sung in public for years. And it had
seemed such a natural thing for her to do.

Soon, that part of the evening was over and the dancing
began, and immediately Sebastian stood up.

'Come on,' he said, as Fleur stood as well, 'it takes
someone to start the ball rolling,' and immediately he
took her in his arms and together they went onto the dance
floor. And as they swayed there together, with Sebastian's
arms supporting her firmly, Fleur felt as if this definitely
was all a dream. She looked up at him and he gazed into
her eyes and suddenly, remembering that she had a job to
do, and that they were being watched by more than one
or two, she closed her eyes and raised her lips, inviting
him to kiss her. He seized the opportunity at once, closing
his mouth over her parted lips and holding her captive for
several mind-numbing seconds. Suddenly Fleur wasn't
acting a part any longer—she was engaged in something
far more realistic, far more subtle, far more true to herself.
She was doing—allowing Sebastian to do—something
which she'd been subconsciously yearning for, and the
enormity of that silent admission was almost too much for
her. This wasn't the way things were meant to be! Getting
involved, getting cornered, how would it all end?

He seemed to sense her sudden tenseness and looked
down at her as she pulled away from him. 'What is it?

Are you OK?' he asked, not letting her go, still holding her body against his.

'I'm fine,' she answered shakily. 'Just a bit warm, that's all.'

'Then we'll sit down,' he said, leading her by the hand over to the side of the room, where there were some chairs.

Fleur knew she was trembling and, to cover her confusion, she said, 'Well, how am I doing? Am I succeeding in my task for tonight?'

He stared down at her for a second, not understanding what she meant. 'Your task?'

'Am I providing sufficient armour for you against all the women lusting for you, Sebastian? Am I heading them off? Have they got the message?'

Now he did understand her and his expression darkened, his eyes glittering and thoughtful. 'I think I can say that you are fulfilling all the criteria in every particular,' he said slowly. 'And I'm sure I'm the object of much envy amongst my colleagues.' He paused, turning to face her and taking her hand in his. 'But, despite what you may think, you are not here because Mia left you no option, Fleur, but because I wanted you to be here. I wanted your company. I…I wanted *you*…I hope you'll believe that.'

And, looking at him longingly, Fleur did believe that. Because she wanted to believe it. And because she knew that Sebastian Conway did not make such statements lightly. But it did nothing to solve her long-standing problem—that she intended never to tread the same path as her mother had done all her life. Yet where did love, and passion, and physical need come in that plan? Those finer feelings were beginning to become vital components in an existence which had seemed so straightforward and clear-cut before she'd set foot in Pengarroth Hall. Where was she to go from here? she asked herself desperately.

## CHAPTER TWELVE

'FLEUR? Hi! Hope I haven't got you out of bed...I just had to ring and find out how you enjoyed last night. Was it fantastic?'

Fleur, still mooning around in her dressing gown sipping a cup of coffee, smiled briefly. She might have known that Mia would want all the details—because she couldn't rid herself of the suspicion that her friend was trying her hand at matchmaking.

'Hi, Mia—yes, it was a very grand affair, and I think a lot of money was raised.'

Mia sighed impatiently. 'Never mind about all that—what did you wear? I bet you looked stunning—and how about my brother? Was he in a "Seb" mood or a "Sebastian Conway" mood?'

'I wore my red dress,' Fleur replied, 'which I don't think you can have seen because I've only worn it once before...' She paused. 'And Sebastian was...' How was she going to put this? Was she going to say that he was the most drop-dead gorgeous man in the room and that he'd been utterly attentive towards her—attentive and charming and so desirable that she'd wanted him to kiss her. Had *invited* him to kiss her right there in the middle of the dance floor with everyone watching! She couldn't possibly say all that—especially as this morning she felt somehow dejected and confused.

'Sebastian was exemplary in every way,' she said neatly.

'What time did it finish?' Mia wanted to know.

'Oh, about one o'clock,' Fleur replied 'Sebastian came home with me in the cab, and then dropped me off.'

There was a pause. 'He didn't spend the night on the sofa bed, then?' Mia asked mischievously.

'He certainly did not,' Fleur replied. 'What made you think that?'

'Oh, just a feeling I had...' Mia said obliquely, then decided not to pursue that train of thought. She knew very well that Fleur was sensitive on the matter of relationships, but she also knew her brother well enough to realize that he liked Fleur—liked her a lot. In fact, she could have put it more strongly than that but thought she wouldn't tempt fate by assuming anything. 'Anyway, I *knew* you'd enjoy yourself—Seb knows how to give a woman a good time,' she said lightly.

They chatted casually for a while, making plans to meet later in the week before hanging up. It was only a few minutes later when the phone rang again. Fleur paused before picking it up... She knew who it would be this time.

'Morning, Fleur. I hope you slept better than I did.'

Sebastian certainly did sound gruff-voiced today, she thought. But that would be the effect of rather too much alcohol. 'I slept well, thanks,' she said. 'In fact, I'm not even up and dressed yet and I feel very lazy.'

There was a pause for a moment, then Sebastian said, 'I just wanted to thank you for...accompanying...me last night, Fleur. I hope you enjoyed yourself.' Well, he knew very well that she'd enjoyed herself—and *he'd* loved every minute of being by her side. And when, unbelievably, she'd stood up on the stage and sung that beautiful song, she had captivated many other hearts beside his own. It had seemed to put the crowning glory on his thoughts about her, demonstrating her gentleness and inherent goodness. She was the sort of woman whom any man would feel happy to trust with his future—qualities which he'd been quick to recognize almost from the moment he'd met her. He knew without a shadow of a doubt that, somehow, he had to convince her that she might be able to commit herself to him without all the nagging doubts and anxieties she clearly had about the opposite sex—her fear of being controlled and manipulated. But he knew he had to be careful. One wrong move too soon, and he'd lose her—it would be like trying to catch a dainty butterfly without crushing a wing, he thought. But he was determined to do it. Determined to succeed.

'I did enjoy myself—very much, thank you, Sebastian,' she replied. 'I…I only hope that making something of an exhibition of myself on stage didn't embarrass you,' she added.

'Not a chance, and I was very impressed. You…you've got a lovely voice, Fleur.'

'Well, anyway, I didn't notice any unwelcome females throwing themselves at you, so at least I must have been of some practical value,' she said.

'I wish you wouldn't think of it like that,' Sebastian said, his voice harsh for a second. 'I told you—I *wanted* you there. And I'm quite able to look out for myself, in any case. I don't need that kind of protection from another human being.'

Fleur was quick to notice the change in his tone. How could anyone think that he wasn't master of the situation—whatever it might happen to be?

'Actually,' he went on, changing the subject, 'I know you said you haven't finished painting your kitchen yet.' He paused. 'How about this afternoon…or maybe one evening in the week? I'm not too busy for a few days, as it happens.'

Fleur sighed inwardly. She knew she could not put him off with any old excuse, and it *was* good of him to offer. She'd better agree, and get it over with. Even if she *had* made up her mind that she wasn't going to see him again.

'I don't think I could face it today, Sebastian,' she said, 'but…next Saturday seems a better option…if you're sure you don't mind.'

'If I minded, I wouldn't be offering,' he said flatly, 'and next Saturday's fine by me too.'

After she'd put the phone down, Fleur stood for a moment, looking out of her bedroom window. She knew it was not going to be easy to keep him at arm's length, even though she told herself that that was the best thing to do. It was hard to be negative and choosy where Sebastian Conway was concerned, especially as she was honest enough to admit that for the first time in several years she felt a growing excitement inside, a feeling of anticipation—a feeling that life had a lot more to offer.

She went into the bathroom and switched on the shower. It was only six days before next Saturday…

'Something smells good,' Sebastian said appreciatively as he followed Fleur into the sitting room. 'See—I've come well prepared this time, brought my own brushes in case yours aren't suitable.'

It was the following Saturday afternoon, and Fleur had already prepared and cooked a curry for them to eat later. She felt that the least she could do was to offer him supper, and it would be easy to heat the curry up and boil some rice later. She smiled at him.

'I hope you like curry,' she said. 'The one I make is a special recipe given to me by an Indian lady I work with.'

'I like anything—and I certainly like curry.' He went into the kitchen to look around and assess everything. 'I approve of the colour you've chosen,' he said as he examined the pots of paint, 'and the white gloss will look good against it.' He shrugged off his jacket, taking the grimy apron from Fleur, and set to work at once.

'I think decorating is quite a therapeutic occupation,' he said, glancing down at her from the ladder. 'I don't do much of it at Pengarroth Hall, because we usually employ people, and Pat's jolly good at it and often insists on doing the honours.' He stretched upwards, drawing the brush firmly along the expanse of the wall. 'But when I'm living there permanently, I'll have more time. There'll be all sorts of things I'll be able to help out with.'

Fleur went out, leaving him to it—well, he'd get on quicker if she wasn't there, she thought, when suddenly she heard his mobile ring.

'Answer that, Fleur,' Sebastian called. 'The phone's in my coat pocket.'

'Hello, this is Sebastian Conway's number…' Fleur said obediently.

The female voice which answered was quiet and well-modulated, and its owner was obviously surprised not to hear Sebastian. 'Oh…is…is Sebastian there?' There was a moment's hesitation. 'This is his grandmother speaking.'

Sebastian had come into the sitting room, wiping his hands, and he took the phone from Fleur. 'Rose…how lovely to hear from you! How are you…?' There was a pause, then, 'As a matter of fact, I'm doing some decorating for someone at the moment. I was up a ladder when you rang.' He smiled briefly as he listened, then, 'Oh… it's someone called Fleur…Fleur Richardson…she's been staying at Pengarroth Hall recently…yes…no… She's actually a friend of Mia's. Yes…another friend of Mia's. I don't think you've ever met.' He raised his eyes at Fleur apologetically, but didn't interrupt his grandmother again as she continued speaking. Then, 'Oh…yes, I see. Well…' he glanced at his watch '…I could come over later— maybe about six… What? I don't know…I'll ask her but… just a minute…' He put his hand over the mouthpiece. 'My grandmother is begging me to go over to her flat later on because she's got someone staying with her who needs some advice about something.' He frowned briefly. 'I don't like to refuse because the man has been a good friend to our family, and his time's limited because apparently he's flying back to Australia tomorrow.'

'Then you must go,' Fleur said at once. 'The painting can wait, Sebastian. There are more important things in life.'

'Yes, but I've been instructed to bring you as well,' Sebastian said and, as she went to decline, added, 'Please say you'll come, Fleur…'

Fleur hesitated, but only for a moment. 'Oh, go on, then,' she said. 'If you really want me to.' Well, how could she have refused? Sebastian already knew that she was not going anywhere that night.

He raised his thumb at her briefly, telling his grandmother that they'd be there later on, then switched off the phone.

'Really, there's no need for me to be involved,' Fleur said. 'It's you they want to see, Sebastian…'

'On the contrary. As soon as my grandmother knew

I was with a young woman, that was it. She insisted that you come too, says she needs livening up. And when Rose has spoken, everyone obeys!' He smiled across at her. 'Actually, you'd like her, Fleur. She's a real character… and…she meant a great deal to me at a certain point in my life.'

'Mia has often spoken to me about her,' Fleur said. 'I always felt quite envious because I never knew my grandparents.'

'Well, I'll be delighted to introduce you to mine. Well, to one of them,' Sebastian said, going back into the kitchen and taking up the paintbrush again. 'Rose is in a class all of her own.'

Fleur watched as the elderly lady leaned forward to pour some sherry into two glasses, before handing one to her and sitting down opposite.

'Now, my dear,' Rose said without preamble. 'With the two men out of the way in the other room talking business, you must tell me all about yourself. You're a friend of Mia's, I understand, rather than a friend of Sebastian's, I mean?'

Fleur smiled inwardly. The significance of the remark was not lost on her. It was obvious that Rose thought there might be more to this than met the eye. But it was impossible not to warm to the old lady. She was a handsome, tall and elegant woman, her abundant silver-grey hair swept on top in a knot, and with her slender figure, immaculate make-up and pearl nail polish she reminded Fleur of one of the veteran actresses regularly seen in television dramas. She was wearing a cashmere dress in the softest lavender, and on her feet were smart high-heeled black patent leather shoes. The complete picture of a well-to-do lady, Fleur thought.

'I suppose I'm a friend of them both,' she replied in answer to Rose's question, 'though of course I've known Mia a lot longer because we were at school together.' She sipped from her glass. 'I was very kindly invited to stay at Pengarroth Hall for Christmas, and for a while after that…and Sebastian was there as well, so we do know each other a little better now…'

Rose nodded, her clear blue eyes fixed thoughtfully on Fleur, and although this might normally have made the girl feel uncomfortable, somehow it didn't. She couldn't help feeling perfectly at ease.

'Tell me what you do…where you live, Fleur. And you must forgive me for my questioning…but other people's lives are so much more interesting than one's own, don't you think? Especially when one is older.'

Fleur found herself explaining everything about herself, surprised at how uninhibited she was feeling. She wasn't usually this relaxed with strangers.

'So you see,' she concluded at last, 'Mia and I go back a long way, and she is the best friend anyone could have. I value her friendship so much.'

'And how did you get on with my grandson? I know he can be…difficult…sometimes.' Rose's question demanded an answer! 'I worry about him a little.'

'Sebastian has been very kind to me,' Fleur said at once. 'I was made extremely welcome in Cornwall, and I think they've got the most beautiful estate. And Pat, too, was lovely to me. I had a great time.'

Rose sighed briefly and leaned back in her chair for a moment. 'It's just that Sebastian is sometimes misjudged by people who don't know him, and I want him to be happy. To be understood. I want people to like him—because he deserves to be liked.'

'I don't think that *I* find him difficult to understand,' Fleur began.

Rose went on, 'He was always a complete mystery to his parents, you know, because he *was* a bit wild in his younger days.' She paused. 'But he was—and I'm sure still is—very idealistic, and could never see why some people appear to have so much of this world's goods, and others not. He disliked the idea of inherited wealth, you see. Then, just when he left university, he disappeared—for two whole months! Can you believe it? Nearly drove his mother potty! He left a note saying that they weren't to worry, that he was perfectly all right, but that he needed to be by himself to think things over.' Rose took another sip from her glass, while Fleur listened with growing interest. Yes, Sebastian *was* a complex character, she thought.

'Where…where did he go…where had he been?' she asked tentatively.

'No one ever knew exactly,' Rose said, 'but he told us afterwards that he'd been sleeping rough. Here, there and everywhere. Wanted to see for himself what it really meant to have nothing. To have to live by your wits. And that's apparently what happened, and I don't suppose it did him any harm because when he came back he finished his law education and settled down. Mind you, my dear—' Rose leaned forward conspiratorially '—I don't think he imagined he'd have the running of Pengarroth Hall quite so soon…terrible shock that his parents—my son and his wife—died so unexpectedly.' She sighed, looking pensive for a moment, and Fleur admitted to suddenly feeling sad for Sebastian. To have so much, yet not to be free.

'Sebastian and I have always been close,' Rose went on, 'because we seem to tick in much the same way.' She paused. 'When my husband and I got married and he first took me to live at Pengarroth Hall I thought I'd die at the very thought of it! The idea of being lady of the manor didn't appeal at all!' She looked rueful for a moment. 'I'm a city girl at heart and, although I did learn to appreciate all the beauty of the place, London was where I yearned to be for much of the time. Isn't that a dreadful thing to say? Most people would much prefer the country life. And I know Sebastian feels resentful sometimes, at the lot which has fallen on him.'

Just then, Sebastian and the visitor emerged from the other room and, presently after a few more minutes' chatting, Sebastian took Fleur by the arm, looking at his grandmother fondly.

'I'm sorry we can't join you for supper, Rose,' he said, 'because someone has already prepared a meal for us, and we can't disappoint them. But—' he paused, looking down at Fleur for a second '—I promise to bring Fleur back to see you soon.'

'Please do, Sebastian,' Rose said. 'We've had a lovely chat, Fleur and I, and you know how much I need you young things to keep *me* feeling young. And I want to hear all about the Christmas festivities at Pengarroth Hall. Mia told me some of it on the phone, but I'm sure there's lots I haven't heard!'

Driving back to her flat, Sebastian glanced across at Fleur. 'You're subdued,' he said and, when she didn't answer, added, 'What did you think of Rose?'

'I think she is absolutely lovely,' Fleur replied. 'Why don't you call her Grandmother, by the way?'

He waited a second before answering. 'Because I don't often think of her as that,' he said slowly. 'She's always been someone I could talk to—as a friend rather than a relation—and, anyway, I think Rose suits her perfectly. I think she has to be the most glamorous granny in the world.' He drummed his fingers on the steering wheel as they waited for the traffic lights to turn green. 'I hope my little fib about going on somewhere for supper was OK with you.' He turned to glance across at her. 'But I couldn't bear the thought of that curry going to waste.' He didn't add that he couldn't bear the thought of sharing her with others for a moment longer.

Fleur smiled without looking back at him. 'Of course it was OK with me,' she said. 'Anyway, there's the painting to finish.'

It was much too late to do any more painting that night and presently when they'd eaten their supper and shared half a bottle of wine, Sebastian stood up. He was not going to put Fleur in the position of inviting him to stay the night on the sofa bed again, because he had the distinct feeling that the cards were beginning to fall in his favour. It was just a feeling, he told himself, but it would do for now. And caution was advisable!

He held out his hands, taking both of hers and pulling her up towards him. 'I must go, Fleur,' he said softly. 'But I'll be back tomorrow and finish that kitchen if it kills me.'

'I don't want you to do anything that might kill you,' she replied, 'because…' She didn't go on, she couldn't go on, because now his lips were fusing with hers, the warmth of their bodies melding until it felt as if they were one person sharing an exhilarating thrill of passionate longing. Her lips were parted, her white teeth gleaming in the subdued light, and Fleur suddenly felt a terrifying thrill that her principles, her determination, were at risk of being blown away. She let him hold her there like that, not wanting to pull away, not wanting this to stop.

But it did. And it was Sebastian who stopped it.

'I must go, Fleur,' he repeated softly. 'But I'll be back tomorrow. Early.'

She closed the door behind him, waiting until she heard his car pull away from the street before going back inside and throwing herself down on the sofa. She was trembling all over with suppressed desire, and this self-knowledge both delighted and shocked her. After a few moments, her heart-rate lessened and she began to calm down. She knew very well that if Sebastian had asked to share her bed that night, she would have agreed with not a moment's hesitation. And she didn't know whether to laugh or cry!

# CHAPTER THIRTEEN

THE next day—without any further interruptions—Sebastian made short work of what remained to be done in Fleur's kitchen. Finally, at about four o'clock, he stood back and viewed his handiwork complacently.

'Well, although I say it myself, that looks pretty good to me,' he said.

'And I second that,' Fleur said as, with her arms folded, she stood in the doorway admiring his efforts. 'See what happens when you turn up unexpectedly? You didn't know what you would be letting yourself in for, did you?'

He glanced across at her as he began putting everything away. 'As I said, I rather enjoy decorating—in small doses.' He replaced the lid firmly on one of the paint tins. 'But I think I'm going to be ready for some supper later.'

Fleur had prepared some filled rolls for their lunch and she had to admit that she, too, would enjoy something a bit more exciting. 'We'll walk to the little Italian place around the corner—I think you'll like it,' she said.

After Sebastian had showered and put on the fresh shirt he'd brought with him, they sat together with a drink in their hands. Fleur looked across at him apologetically.

'Before we eat, Sebastian, I feel the desperate need for a walk amongst some trees—but you needn't come,' she said. 'There aren't many evenings when I don't have a stroll in the park—whatever the weather. And there wasn't a chance yesterday, was there?'

'Of course I'll come,' Sebastian said at once, his eyes narrowing briefly. Perhaps out there amongst the natural surroundings which she so obviously loved, he would find the opportunity to ask her a rather important question—something which had been on his mind for some time.

They made their way to the entrance of the park and Sebastian pushed open the big iron gate. A light rain had begun to fall and it was almost dark, the overhead lights already throwing their guiding beams along the winding paths as they strolled along. Fleur looked up at him.

'I must have walked the length and breadth of this place hundreds of times,' she said. 'It's my bolt-hole in times of stress and strain!'

He gazed back down at her. The hood of her jacket had slipped from her head and now there were dozens of tiny rain droplets glistening amongst the waves of her hair. At that moment he could easily have said, *Well, if you would agree to come and live with me in Cornwall, you could have as many walks as you like, each and every day.* But he was still unsure of Fleur, unsure of what her reaction would be, and he knew he must tread carefully. In spite of their passionate embrace last night, in spite of the delectable sensation of her moist lips on his, almost inviting him to seduce her, he felt undeniably wary. It was a new experience for him—because she was unlike any other woman he had ever met, and he would have to use a little cunning if he was to get his own way. Which he knew he was going to, in the end. He cleared his throat.

'I've been meaning to…to ask you something, Fleur,' he began hesitantly, and she looked up at him again quickly, sensing that this was something important! But how important?

'Oh…what's that?' she asked lightly, looking away.

'Of course…I don't expect an answer straight away,' he said quickly, 'because you'll naturally need time to think it over…but it's something I've had on my mind ever since I met you.' He paused, and Fleur's heart jumped in her chest like a nervous kitten. He was going to ask her to marry him! Heaven help her—what was she going to say? Wasn't he just the sort of man—insanely desirable though he was—that she'd promised herself to avoid at all costs? His whole personality shouted importance, determination, authority! Yet, above all that, she knew that she was helplessly in love with him—in love with him so much that her need, her longing for him was becoming a physical pain. She tried to breathe steadily, to calm herself so that when she was forced to respond to his proposal her voice would be steady.

'I don't think you can guess what I'm going to say,' he went on, 'but it would mean a great deal to me if you would agree.'

'Well,' Fleur replied carefully, 'until I know what it is, I can't promise anything, can I…?'

Would he go down on one knee on the wet grass? Somehow she didn't think so!

'I've had a brilliant idea for an event at Pengarroth Hall, which I think would go down well with everyone in the area,' he said, 'and which would be very profitable. But I need someone like you to help me make it work.'

Fleur stared at him uncomprehendingly. What was this all about? He wasn't asking her to marry him, after all! How could she have *thought* such a thing? He wasn't the marrying kind and never would be! She swallowed hard and kept walking—just a small step in front of him. To say that she felt as if she were standing on the edge of a big hole, about to fall right down to the bottom, would be putting it mildly! Serve her right—her stupid imagination had led her horribly astray! She tried to suppress a painful lump in her throat. 'Go on,' she said quietly, feeling almost limp with disappointment.

'I want to stage a summer musical extravaganza in the grounds. There's a perfect spot for it beyond the kitchen garden at the back of the house. It's a kind of natural auditorium, with a raised area perfect for a stage. These summer spectaculars are being done all over the country at the moment, and the money raised for charity can be fantastic! I'd want a full orchestra, singers, a real production with lighting and amplification—and of course I've got a huge advantage in knowing Rudy.' He paused, looking down at her, but Fleur had fixed her gaze straight ahead.

'What…what has he to do with it?' she asked. 'And, more importantly, what's it to do with *me*?'

'Because I'd want *you* to be the star attraction, of course,' he said in a way that suggested she should have known that straight away. 'You'd be perfect, Fleur. You look wonderful, you've got natural stage presence…and your voice, well, people couldn't stop talking about you after your performance at the dinner.' He stopped walking now and, taking her arm, turned her towards him, forcing her to look up. 'What do you think of the idea? Will you back me? Because I couldn't do it without you. I don't think I'd want to do it without you.'

Fleur's throat was so dry she couldn't even swallow and she was feeling so let down, so ridiculous, she could hardly bring herself to answer.

'And…Rudy Malone…?' she asked, the thought of ever having to meet the man again filling her with disgust.

'Rudy will be ecstatic about it,' Sebastian said at once. 'I know he can be a pain in some circumstances, but he's amazing at what he does. His London productions are always brilliant—he frequently gets awards. I'll only have to say the word and then leave the rest to him.'

For a moment, Fleur felt angry—and disillusioned. How could Sebastian ask this of her—especially after the way his friend had behaved at Christmas. It was unthinkable that she was going to go along with it… And it seemed to her that Sebastian was obsessed with raising money for charity. It seemed to be the main thing on his mind. Probably helps his conscience deal with his own wealth, she thought. Well, he could find someone else to sing for him!

They walked on in silence for a few moments, Fleur having difficulty in not bursting into tears. If she'd been given this opportunity by anyone else, at another time, she thought—the chance to do some real singing, to actually perform those famous arias that she knew so well with a proper orchestra—she'd have jumped at it! But this scenario was different—and it was cruel! If she agreed, it would mean being in close proximity with a man she detested—and also with the man whom she'd come to love, but who clearly didn't love her. It was an impossible, hopeless proposition.

'I'm not sure that I could find the time, Sebastian,' she said slowly. 'These things can't be thrown together any old how. There would have to be countless rehearsals, total commitment. I do have my work to think about.' She paused to pick up a small branch that had fallen across the path. 'But it was kind of you to think of me,' she added. 'I'm sure you'll be able to find someone else only too ready to step in.'

Now he stopped her again, and this time his arms were

around her waist so that she was forced to look up into his face. 'I'm not being kind,' he said gruffly. 'I'm being practical.' He paused. 'And I think I know the real reason you won't do it… It's Rudy, isn't it, Fleur? You're afraid he'll be a nuisance.'

Fleur had difficulty restraining her impatience. He didn't have a clue! she thought. But he'd given her the perfect excuse. Because she could hardly say, *No, Sebastian, it's you. You're the problem. And I must not be near to you, ever again. Knowing you has put me in a dangerous situation—a situation that I don't really know how to handle. Prolonging our association into the summer will only make things worse—much worse. How could I bear it, knowing that I mean nothing to you? I'm just someone who you enjoy kissing now and again.*

She sighed. 'Yes, it is Rudy Malone,' she lied. 'I would not willingly spend even half an hour in his company—unless I had police protection.' She tried to smile, and suddenly Sebastian could bear it no longer. What had made him use this cheap trick? he asked himself. Even though his ambition to stage a musical event on the estate was genuine enough. Why didn't he ask the woman to marry him, and be done with it? Why did he feel the need to get round her like this?

He was holding her close to him and the warmth of her body mingled with his own, filling him with a surging tide of emotion. 'You wouldn't need police protection, Fleur,' he said softly. 'My protection is all you'll need. That's a promise.'

She frowned slightly, beginning to regain something of her composure now that her position was clear. He could say what he liked, but this would be the last time that she and Sebastian Conway would hold each other close, she thought. She would not see him again, whatever Mia said or did. This was it. And it was good to have come to that decision. Her other life—the life she'd led before she'd met him—was so simple. So uncomplicated. Just the way she wanted it.

'But you couldn't—wouldn't—be there all the time,' she said slowly. 'How could you be? Your own life is as full as mine.'

Unable to stop himself for another second, he bent his head and claimed her lips—and she made no effort to stop him. Her open eyes were wide and misty, and he pulled away slightly, raising his hand and tracing the tender curve of her cheek with his finger. Then he held her again in a close embrace, resting his chin on the top of her head for a moment. 'If you will agree to another minor proposition of mine,' he murmured, 'I give you my word that you'll have all the protection you'll ever need.'

Mystified, Fleur eased away from him and looked up. And, before she could respond, she heard the words she'd lost all hope of ever hearing.

'Will you marry me, Fleur?' His voice was husky, deep with meaning. 'I'm asking you to be my wife. To come and live with me in Cornwall, for ever…' He trailed off, not wanting to hear her refusal, and for the second time in the last half hour Fleur felt her knees tremble, felt her whole body go limp. Only now it wasn't disillusionment that was the cause, but an overwhelming feeling that her heart was about to take flight and leave her body altogether! He *did* want her… He'd just said so! But…there was something he *hadn't* said, something which she'd never heard her father once say to her mother, in all the years they'd been together. And if Sebastian didn't say it, couldn't say it, then she knew what her answer would be.

'Why do you want me to marry you, Sebastian?' she

said coolly. 'Is it because Mia would like it…or because it's obvious that I do love Pengarroth Hall and all the people who work there, and would obviously fit in very well. Or perhaps you think I'd be a suitable person to provide an heir to take your place one day? Which is it, I wonder, Sebastian?'

He'd listened without interrupting her and now his face appeared drawn, almost sculpted in the dim light as he listened to her thoughtfully.

'It's none of those things,' he said. He paused, and Fleur waited breathlessly for what might—or might not—come. 'It's because I love you,' and his tone of voice left her in no doubt that he meant it—really meant it. 'I have loved you for as long as I've known you, Fleur. I can't help it if you don't believe me, but that's the truth.'

Oh but she did believe it! Fleur's arms went around his neck and she pulled him towards her, nestling her face in his neck, loving that same manly fragrance that inflamed her every time he came near her. 'Then…I will marry you,' she whispered. 'I will marry you, Sebastian.'

With a huge shudder he tightened his grasp of her until the breath nearly left her body. 'I can't believe it,' he murmured, burying his face in her hair. 'I didn't dare think you'd agree…especially when I knew how you felt about the male sex.' He lifted her face and kissed her again gently. 'And I don't know what you feel about nuptial agreements, but this is my side of the bargain. I give you my solemn promise that your life will always be under your own control. Anyway, I'm going to have enough to think about without butting in on your hopes and dreams…'

Fleur looked up at him, at the sensuous mouth, the firm chin, the wide forehead with those faint worry lines between his dark, mesmerizing eyes. 'I've got the strangest feeling that my hopes and dreams are going to be exactly the same as yours,' she said.

With their arms around each other's waists like two children, they walked along the deserted paths, not wanting these magical moments to pass. But Fleur knew that she must know something...that, if she didn't, it would be between them for the rest of their lives. But how would he take it? She glanced up at him.

'Sebastian...' She paused. 'Tell me about Davina...'

'Ah, yes, Davina,' he said without hesitation. 'You've obviously been told about her.'

'All I've heard—from Mia, and from Pat—is that you were nearly married to her and then suddenly it was all off. Why, Sebastian? What happened?' If he was offended at her curiosity, then it was too bad. This was something she *had* to know about because it had obviously been an overwhelmingly upsetting occurrence at the time— upsetting for others beside himself.

'When I met Davina,' he said, 'I was impressed with her vitality, her enthusiasm for the business she ran—and, of course, she was also very...attractive.' He paused. 'She had made something of herself despite having had no special advantages—no family background or support. And I admired that.' He waited before going on. 'But she was always very evasive about what she actually did. She told me at first that she ran a dress agency, and I believed her. Supposedly selling second-hand designer clothes. I'm not into ladies' fashions so it was unknown territory to me. Well, we were weeks away from the wedding when one of my colleagues—who I introduced Davina to—informed me that he had...availed...himself of her services a few months earlier. Said he thought I really ought to know about it. It turned out that she was running a very successful escort agency—and her fees for her own personal services were exorbitant.' Sebastian cleared his throat, obviously hating having to recall that time. 'My colleague was able to give me plenty of details…'

Fleur didn't look at him as he spoke. What an unbelievable discovery for him to have made—about a woman whom he had loved.

As if reading her thoughts, he went on, 'But, luckily for me, I was able to recover from the blow almost immediately—which rather suggests that my feelings for Davina must have been somewhat superficial. I admit that I was taken in by her, but her dishonesty about it all was harder to bear than knowing that she was happy to sell herself to any man who was prepared to pay.' He waited before going on, then looked down at Fleur solemnly. 'I want a wife who is prepared to be mine, and mine alone,' he said. 'It's one area where I do not believe in sharing.'

'I've no idea what my parents are going to think,' Fleur said as they drew up outside the family home in Sebastian's car.

'I rather hope they'll be pleased for us,' Sebastian said mildly. 'Surely they didn't expect that their beautiful daughter would stay single for ever?'

Fleur thought—never mind what *they* might have expected—her present situation had come as a surprise—a very happy and exciting surprise—to her! She could still hardly believe that Sebastian had asked her to be his wife—or that she had accepted. But when they'd rung Mia to tell her, the phone had almost exploded with her reaction.

'I knew it, I just *knew* it!' she'd cried. 'We'd all hoped for it—Pat and Beryl and Gran—we've been sending hopeful messages to the stars! When's the wedding—and what am I going to wear?'

In spite of Fleur's misgivings, Philip and Helen received the news with obvious pleasure, although Philip was slightly more guarded in his enthusiasm.

'Well, no doubt you can come to some arrangement with the hospital, to continue your research on a part-time basis,' he said. 'That sort of thing is done a lot nowadays, so as not to waste valuable people and their education. It should be simple enough.'

Fleur and Sebastian exchanged glances, and Sebastian said at once, 'I think Fleur will know exactly what's best, Philip. We can trust her to do the right thing.'

Helen's eyes had not stopped shining since she'd heard the news, and she held her daughter's hands tightly. 'I'm so pleased for you, darling,' she said softly. 'I can only hope that you will be as happy as Daddy and I have been.'

Fleur stared at her mother for a moment and thought that perhaps she'd been wrong all the time. Perhaps her mother had been happy after all. Happy to love and care for the man she'd married, whatever his failings. She shrugged inwardly. It was wrong to judge other people's lives when you didn't really know all the facts, she thought.

It was as they were driving back to her flat that Fleur's hand suddenly went to her throat anxiously, and she looked across at Sebastian.

'Sebastian—there's just one thing… It's something I really cannot agree to, so we'd better sort it out now, straight away…' she began.

Sebastian nearly swerved off the road at her words, but he recovered quickly. 'What…what the hell is that?' he demanded. 'You…you're not changing your mind…?'

'No, no of course not!' Fleur smiled across at him reassuringly. 'It's about the wedding…'

'What about the wedding?'

'Well, I know that… I know your family expects grand affairs and big celebrations and everything but…but I honestly could not bear it. Can we…can we just have a small ceremony, Sebastian—and maybe a party later? When it's all gone quiet? I don't want a fuss. I really couldn't stand it.'

Sebastian blew through his teeth in relief. 'I was wondering what on earth you were going to say,' he replied. 'And I agree with you entirely, Fleur.' He put his hand on her knee and held it there. 'The only people at our wedding are going to be you and me, of course, your parents, and Mia and Rose. And can Pat and Beryl—and Frank—come too? Would you agree to them all being there? I'd hate to leave any of them out—they'd be so hurt.'

Fleur felt a rush of pleasure at his words. He was such a softie, she thought. 'I'd want them there too,' she said. 'All of them. That would be just perfect.'

Two weeks later they drove back to Cornwall and were met at the door by Pat, who immediately burst into tears and threw her arms around Fleur.

'Since you rang with the news we've hardly slept a wink!' she exclaimed. 'We're so happy, Fleur.' She looked up at Sebastian. 'And you're a lucky chap, Sebastian.'

He grinned down at her. 'Don't you think I know that, Pat?'

Later that evening, hand in hand, Fleur and Sebastian walked slowly along the well-loved wooded paths of Pengarroth Hall. And it was raining.

'I'm beginning to smell spring in the air,' Fleur said happily. 'It'll be wonderful to be here when it's warm and sunny—just as wonderful as it is when it's cold and dismal!'

Sebastian put his arm around her waist. 'There's something I want you to see,' he said quietly, and in a few moments they came to a spot which Fleur immediately recognized. 'Oh, this is where…' she began, for this was where Benson had lain down and refused to obey her. The tree trunk she had sat down on as she'd waited for the dog to get up was still in the same place…

And there, on a small mound in the turf, stood a neatly carved wooden cross with one word burned into it. 'Benson' was all it said, and Fleur stopped in her tracks as if she'd been struck by lightning, her hand going to her mouth.

'Young Martin—Frank's son—made this for Benson,' Sebastian said. 'He's going to be a fine carpenter one day.' He paused. 'And he's made a good job of this, hasn't he?'

Fleur had difficulty in speaking, but after a moment she said, 'It's beautiful, really beautiful, Sebastian. Just like the beautiful dog who's resting here.'

The quiet family wedding was held on the first day of spring, and exactly nine months later Alexander Sebastian Philip Conway was born at Pengarroth Hall, with Pat happily assisting the doctor while Sebastian held his wife's hand tightly. And although Sebastian had been undeniably proud to hold his baby in his arms for a few moments, his main focus had been on Fleur as she lay on the huge bed, her hair spread out in soft damp waves on the pillows, her eyes moist and glistening.

'I didn't know what real happiness was until I met you,' he whispered in her ear. 'Or what it could mean, until I saw our baby being born.'

Fleur squeezed his hand. 'Do you think he'll like us?' she said.

'I know he'll like *you*,' Sebastian replied. 'How could he help himself?'

A few days later, Philip and Helen came to see their first grandchild and, with Mia there as well, they all sat downstairs in silent admiration as the baby was passed from one to the other. And the bouquets of flowers kept coming and coming until the house was filled with colour and perfume.

'Who's that one from?' Fleur asked as Sebastian took yet another bouquet from Pat as she brought it into the sitting room. He examined the label and smiled, looking across at his wife.

'It's from Rudy, Fleur. He says, "Many congrats and I've booked the last week of August next year for our first production."' He passed the flowers back to Pat. 'I told you there'd be no stopping him,' he added.

'This is one of the very best days of my entire life,' Helen said softly. It was her turn to hold the baby. 'An unforgettable day. All my dreams have come true.'

But it was Philip's reaction which astonished Fleur. He seemed besotted with his first grandchild, couldn't stop gazing down at the sleeping child and saying things like 'What a grand little chap,' and 'Do you think he looks a bit like me, Helen…his nose, I mean?'

At which point Mia had interrupted firmly, 'I think his nose is *exactly* like mine…'

But then Philip said, 'I wonder if Alexander is going to conquer the world some day, to help push scientific knowledge forward a step or two…or maybe he'll become a famous lawyer whose services everyone wants.' He glanced across at Sebastian for a second, before adding, 'I wonder what life has in store for you, Alexander.'

Sebastian went over to sit next to Fleur, slipping his arm around her shoulders for a second. 'Whatever it is, Philip, he'll make the best of it, like we all must do. But it'll be up to him, and it'll be his choice—with, I hope, a little guidance from his parents,' he added.

And Fleur, snuggling into Sebastian and looking around the room at all the people she loved best in the world, thought that wherever paradise eventually turned out to be, at this moment it was very definitely right here, on earth.

# A NIGHT WITH
# THE SOCIETY PLAYBOY

BY
**ALLY BLAKE**

When **Ally Blake** was a little girl, she made a wish that when she turned twenty-six she would marry an Italian two years older than herself. After it actually came true, she realized she was onto something with these wish things. So, next she wished that she could make a living spending her days in her pajamas, eating M&Ms and drinking scads of coffee while using her formative experiences of wallowing in teenage crushes and romantic movies to create love stories of her own.

The fact that she is now able to spend her spare time searching the internet for pictures of handsome guys for research purposes is merely a bonus! Come along and visit her website at www.allyblake.com.

To my urban family, Chris Sheree,
Tom and Ben Breasley: the ones
who have made my time away from home
feel like home.

# CHAPTER ONE

'WILL you, Damien Halliburton, take Chelsea London to be your lawful wedded wife?'

The minister's words blurred into one long onerous drone as Caleb, acting as best man to his mate and business partner, fidgeted inside his tux, stifled a yawn, and pretended as best he could to pay attention.

'I do,' Damien said, his voice deep and true, his eyes all for his admittedly scrumptious new bride.

Though he couldn't deny that Damien had seemed happier since Chelsea appeared on the scene, Caleb had long since decided that that kind of indiscriminate happiness was for chumps. Not only was it fleeting, once gone it invariably took a little piece of you with it.

And Caleb liked himself and all his pieces. Quite a bit in fact.

He enjoyed his privileged life. He adored the pursuits that came with it: tennis, sailing, golf, drinks at the club. The capacity to spend the occasional weekend basking on a private beach somewhere didn't go astray.

And he thrived on his work. He took great pleasure in doing whatever it took to land ostensibly ungettable clients for Keppler, Jones and Morgenstern day traders. Others in the biz thought him ruthless in his tunnel-visioned pursuit of the big fish. But the simple fact was he'd always found it too easy to make people say yes.

He'd been told by a former weekend getaway companion it had everything to do with a distracting glint in his eyes. It blinded people to the fact that he never switched off, he was always, always silently working out a way to come out on top.

To her credit it had taken him several seconds to realise she hadn't meant it as a compliment, or in fact a come-on, and by that stage she'd walked out his door never to darken it again.

Caleb glanced across the altar and caught the eye of Kensey, a bridesmaid, who also happened to be Chelsea's older sister. She was dark where Chelsea was fair, and he had always preferred brunettes.

He glinted for all he was worth.

Kensey's eyes grew wide before she flipped her left ring finger at him from beneath her bouquet. A gold wedding band flashed his way.

His smile only widened as he offered a shrug by way of apology, but as he moved his gaze away the smile twisted into a grimace. Was the whole damn world getting married?

He gave himself a mental pat on the back for deciding not to bring a date to this thing. Weddings stirred up all sorts of irrational emotions in people. He'd seen it before. Perfectly level-headed gents cut down by a giddy mix of floral scents, blinding amounts of pink satin, and over-indulgence in cake frosting.

Finding that scrunching his toes in his shoes wasn't proving distracting enough to keep him from yawning again, Caleb looked over the extensive crowd that filled the elegant city church.

He called upon his well-tuned affluence radar to decide which unsuspecting guest would be signing on the dotted line as a client by the end of the night.

The groom's divorced, but friendly, parents sat in the front row weeping all over one another. If they didn't end up renewing their vows by the end of the month he'd eat his shoes. But they were already Damien's clients so they didn't count.

His own parents, the estimable Gilchrists, a couple who had taken the 'till death' part of their own wedding vows so seriously he wouldn't be surprised if they one day throttled one another, had naturally wangled the next best seat in the house: row two, on the aisle. They were no doubt the filthy-richest pair in the room, but they had never forgotten the year he'd lost all his pocket money running a secret Spring Racing betting ring while in middle school and thus wouldn't part with a cent of their precious dough. Talk about the ungettable get.

Damien's Aunt Gladys gave him a little finger wave from the fifth row. Caleb winked back and she all but fainted on the spot. He knew without a doubt she would have given him a perfume-scented cheque within five minutes of him courting her. But where was the thrill in that?

Masses of other faces he'd never seen and never particularly wanted to again soon passed him by in a Technicolor blur.

Until his brain slowly caught up with his eyes and he realised halfway down on the left side he'd passed over a swathe of long brunette waves, the immobilising combo of soft blue eyes fringed by impossibly long dark lashes, and the kind of soft, sweet, wide, pink mouth any sane man would kill for. Would die for.

*Ava…*

Her name launched itself smack bang in the centre of his unsuspecting consciousness from somewhere deep inside like a guided missile gone astray.

His eyes retraced their journey over the colourful crowd,

sweeping across row after row, even though he knew it couldn't have been her.

Well, logically it *could*. She *was* Damien's sister. But the groom had never once mentioned his sister was coming home from Boston for the wedding and for the first time in nearly a decade. If he had it was not the kind of crumb of information that would slip Caleb's mind.

But he saw nothing but a sea of unfamiliar faces, none of which made his stomach clench as hers did. Or more precisely as hers had. *Once upon a time in a galaxy far, far away...*

The last time he'd laid eyes on her he'd been a twenty-two-year-old business school graduate who'd been perfectly happy to bank on his family name to get where he was going. While she'd been a nineteen-year-old humanities wunderkind prepared to go to the far end of the earth to find a place where nobody knew her family name.

They'd been friends since high school, combatants just as long, and lovers for just one night, the day before she'd left to take up a scholarship at Harvard, the first of several top-class schools she'd flitted between since, and never looked back.

Never written a postcard, nor a letter, nor an email. No carrier pigeons had been employed by her, nor telephones rung on his behalf.

He frowned and curled his toes into his new black leather shoes until they hurt. He'd searched every pew and couldn't find the brunette waves, the smoky blue eyes, or the wide pink mouth. He must have imagined her after all. Great hulking fool he had always been when Ava Halliburton had been the subject of discussion...

'Caleb?'

Caleb looked at the groom blankly as a ripple of laughter washed over the crowd.

'You're on, buddy,' Damien said.

'On what exactly?'

'The ring?' Damien said, loaded smile playing about his mouth telling Caleb it wasn't the first time he'd been called.

'Right,' Caleb said. 'Apologies. I was a million miles away.'

*And a million years ago.*

'Not the kind of thing I want to hear right now.' Damien's smile didn't slip a millimetre but Caleb had known the guy long enough to know his patience was thinning.

Caleb slid a finger into a tiny side pocket of his waistcoat and pulled out a skinny white gold band encrusted with diamonds. He summarily dropped it into Damien's upturned palm lest it rub some of its unwelcome romance upon him.

From there the wedding zoomed to a brisk conclusion.

The kiss was the best part. Damien grabbed Chelsea around the waist, dipped her halfway to the floor and planted one on her that had the two-hundred-strong crowd whooping it up in the aisles.

*That's my boy,* Caleb thought, glad his friend wasn't becoming a complete sap now that he was locked down.

Caleb followed the couple down the aisle, arm in arm with Chelsea's sister, who he could see out of the corner of his eye was grinning at him. He feigned boredom as he stared blankly towards the bright light of a video camera at the end of the aisle.

'I was afraid you might be about to faint on us there for a moment,' Kensey said.

He let his mouth kick into half-smile. 'Me? Faint? Simply not in me, honey.'

'So you're a fan of big white weddings, then?'

'Nowhere I'd rather be on a Saturday night.'

'Really? Must have been the way the light was hitting your cheeks that made you look like someone had walked over your grave.'

'Must have been,' Caleb said.

Though he couldn't help but look to the left in search of a pair of pretty sky-blue eyes and long dark hair.

Damn fool.

After a good long hour of photographs taken around the iconic Brighton beach huts, Caleb finally stepped out of his limo in front of the Halliburtons' house at the upper end of Stonnington Drive.

He stretched his arms overhead, let out an accompanying groan, and once the other groomsmen, Chelsea's brother-in-law and one of Damien's cousins, had moved on through into the house, he let his gaze swing straight to the second-floor window, third from the right.

Ava's bedroom window.

Between two beats of his heart he went from thirty-two-year-old man of enviable experience to twenty again, riddled with wild hormones and unable to help watching the sway of cream curtains flapping gently at the window, wondering if Ava was up there sleeping, studying, getting dressed, getting undressed...

Today the window was closed. No lights were on. His mind eased.

His hormones were another matter.

He jogged around the side of the massive house, hoping the exercise might relieve some of the tension he'd carried with him from the church.

The Halliburtons' manicured back lawn had been over-taken by two massive white brightly lit marquees. They draped languidly across the yard like decadent Bedouin tents. A ten-metre gap between them left a makeshift cork dance floor open beneath the stars. Fat pale purple bows were wrapped around the two-hundred-odd antique bronze chairs and the round tables were heavy with white roses, crystal glasses and gleaming silver cutlery.

He reminded himself not to stand directly below any of the dozen chandeliers. He was no engineer but he couldn't for the life of him figure out how the outrageous things wouldn't bring the whole deal crashing down upon their heads.

He took a deep breath, tucked his hands into his tuxedo trouser pockets and sauntered inside, familiarising himself with all exits, making instant friends with a passing waiter so he'd get first look in at the hors d'oeuvres, before making a beeline for the nearest bar.

He ordered something heavy and straight up. The burning liquid had barely touched his lips when an all too familiar female voice from behind him said, 'Caleb Gilchrist, as I live and breathe.'

His glass clinked against his teeth as he swallowed more than was entirely sensible on an empty stomach.

'Well, if it isn't little Ava Halliburton. In the flesh,' he said as he turned, a nonchalant smile already planted steadfastly upon his face.

And, oh, what a choice of flesh.

Her long dark hair hung from a centre part just as it had when she was nineteen, and it was still, oh, so sexily mussed, as though she'd spent hours running agitated fingers through it. Her blue eyes were luminous in a round face that had always made her look younger than she was. A naturally wide smile hovered cautiously upon her mouth and her cheeks were flushed.

The champagne glass between her fingers exposed finger-nails bitten to the quick. She wore a shapeless, sleeveless dark pink lace dress that stopped square below her knees. It was offbeat, slightly too big and not quite formal enough for the occasion.

She hadn't changed a bit.

A distant relative of some sort appeared from nowhere to capture Ava's attention. She shot Caleb a quick 'I'm sorry' with her eyes before she turned towards much pinching of cheeks and 'I knew you when you were this big' remarks.

Caleb took a step away, towards the bar, where he put down his glass and gladly took the reprieve.

Ava Halliburton. It had been some time since that name had made him curl his fingernails into his palms.

At twenty-two, confused and smitten, and only hours after the most raw, tender, surprising night of his young life, he'd followed her to the airport, and five minutes before she was due to check in and fool that he was he'd asked her to stay for him.

And he'd been serious. In that crazy moment he'd been prepared to throw away the thought of ever being with another woman if he'd been able to have just her.

Because in her warm, willing arms he'd thought for the first time in his young life he'd truly glimpsed happiness.

Yep, happiness, that old chestnut.

And it had taken her about, ooh, half a second to refuse and take flight.

He braced himself to suffer the onrush of unbearable frustration he'd associated with her memory for a long time after she'd left him standing there in the middle of the airport terminal.

But the onslaught never came.

While she looked as if she'd stepped out of her high-school yearbook, the intervening years had changed him so much he was a different man. For one thing he was far less easily moved by things like loveliness and sweetness and sky-blue bedroom eyes.

If he were in the mood for romanticising things he might think *she'd* made him immune to all that, made him seek out the company of women who didn't have a chance in hell of touching him in that way. But he wasn't in such a mood. Therefore he decided that in the past ten years he'd been lucky to experience enough lovely, enough sweet, enough feminine eyes of every colour not to be so impacted as he had been by her, and by her leaving, ever again.

That was until Ava's spare hand, the one not swirling champagne hypnotically in its flute, reached up to finger a strip of thin brown leather at her neck.

A long thin strip of brown leather. One that looked a heck of a lot like one that once upon a time had accommodated a chunky wooden locket he'd given her as a birthday gift.

He'd put his photograph inside as a joke. She'd left it in there. For years.

The last time he'd seen the locket was on that night, the one night they'd spent together. Lying bundled up in a pile of clean towels and thermal blankets in a suspended shell of a canoe in the Melbourne University boat shed on a cold winter's night, basking in one another's afterglow, he'd opened it. Seen his picture. And his future. Or so he'd thought.

The idea that she might have yet to remove it dug in its claws and refused to be displaced.

Caleb's eyes remained riveted to the fingers playing with the leather strap. It lifted gently away from her creamy décolletage and then slid back against her. He wondered if the leather had been warmed by all that soft female skin.

The tips of his fingers began to tingle.

He followed the line of the necklace to find it dipped beneath the V of Ava's dress. There was no way of knowing what she kept there now, nestled between her breasts.

He allowed himself a moment to ponder the thought. Especially since in the past ten years little Ava Halliburton had filled out a little more than he'd initially realised. Even though he knew it a self-destructive thought he sent up a small prayer of thanks to the god who decided such things.

The cousin thrice removed moved on and Ava turned back to Caleb, remnant smile lingering upon her wide mouth. Suddenly her necklace didn't hold anywhere near as much fascination as those lips, which at some point in the conversation with Cousin Whoever had been moistened.

Caleb tipped back onto his heels. If he'd thought his fingertips were tingly they had nothing on his bottom lip. He dragged his upper teeth over it to stave off the sense memory lingering thereupon.

'It was a beautiful ceremony, don't you think?' Ava asked, turning side on, stealing away her leather strap, the V of her dress and her lips from his gaze as her eyes roved lazily over the noisily expanding crowd.

She was playing it beautifully cool, was she? Well, she'd just met the master of cool. *Ready yourself for a chill, kiddo…*

'Gorgeous,' he said, his tone glacial.

'And have you ever seen such stars?'

'When I have looked up. Sure.'

'It's such a perfect night for an outdoor reception.' Her nose screwed up. 'Though it will rain.'

'Do you have a barometer tucked somewhere beneath your dress?'

Her mouth twitched. 'Don't need one. The patch of cloud to the east. That's cumulonimbus cloud, the bringer of rain. But it won't come till late tonight. My parents wouldn't have had it any other way.' She leaned in ever so slightly and lowered her voice as she said, 'And did you get a load of the chandeliers?'

'You mean the insurance nightmare,' he shot back.

'Yes!' she said, turning to face him, grinning and pointing at his chest. 'That's just what I was thinking. They are a *Phantom of the Opera* intermission just waiting to happen.'

He laughed. True, it was only a soft cough kind of laugh, but it was a definite departure from cool.

Who was he trying to kid? He'd never been cool around this piece of work. What was the point? She could speak several different languages but the nuances of plain Australian cool went straight over her head.

Caleb straightened his shoulders until he felt a slightly uncomfortable warmth seep into his muscles, but it was enough to get him to start to relax. Relaxed was usually his permanent state. He never had to try this hard.

He turned his right knee toward her and leaned in. 'Let's hope for the wedding planner's sake it doesn't rain or your mother will no doubt refuse to pay while your father will hole himself up in his office for a month glad for the excuse to do so.'

Rather than getting a grin for his efforts, Ava's answering smile was toothless, and brief. The continuous swirling of champagne was also a good sign she wasn't feeling as bright and breezy as she was making out.

She was working as hard at this conversation as he was.

He looked away lest she figure him out as easily.

And where was the waiter with the hors d'oeuvres when he needed him?

## CHAPTER TWO

'I'M REALLY glad I bumped into you tonight before things get too crazy,' Ava said.

'How crazy do you think they plan on getting?' Caleb asked.

'The DJ is a cousin of mine.'

'Right. So if he knows any music produced later than nineteen eighty-five we should be very much surprised.'

Ava smiled. Looked away. Looked back. 'Damien told me you were in New York late last year.'

That was some segue, he thought. 'That I was. It was a business trip. In and out.'

'I can't believe you never came out to visit. It's a forty-minute flight to Boston.'

'And a half-day spent at JFK. Time prohibitive.'

She nodded. Locked eyes. Swallowed. There was a husky note to her voice when she said, 'I missed you, you know.'

And just like that, with the faintest whisper of vulnerability, Ava turned Caleb's stoic resistance to putty. His tingling nerves burst into action, stinging the length of his fingers until he ached to reach out and touch her arm. To run his thumb over that full bottom lip. To hook a finger beneath that leather strap and slide its hidden secrets and regrets into the light.

Bad news. Little Ava Halliburton was nothing but bad news and it would pay to remember it. Just to hit the point home, through the pocket of his trousers he grabbed a pinch of leg hair and gave it a nice painful tug.

After her words had long since begun to fade into the noise around them, Ava cleared her throat and looked down at her shoes. 'I missed all of you guys. Heaps. Seeing everyone today really hit home how long I've been gone. My cousin the DJ was eight when I left and now…'

'Now he knows how to work a CD stacker like nobody's business.'

'Exactly.'

She glanced up at him from beneath those impossible eyelashes. He'd always thought them her best feature. But now they were running a pretty close tie with those wide smooth lips. He bit the inside of his cheek in penance.

Then said, 'It's nice to see you finally managed to peel yourself away from lectures and study groups for your brother's big day.'

A glint sparked within her sky-blue eyes and her lips widened, creating soft pink apples in her cheeks. Heaven help him.

'And just as nice to see you are no less of a buffoon than you always were. I can't believe Damo had to ask for the ring no less than three times. It will be *the* story they'll bring up every wedding anniversary for ever more.'

He gave a short bow. 'I aim to please.'

'Mmm,' she said, her eyes all too easily leaving his as she surveyed the room. 'I remember now you always were the kind of guy who liked to steal the limelight.'

She remembered *now*? How flattering. He said, 'While you always preferred to run from attention as though it might burn.'

The glint in her eyes flickered. Ever so slightly. But enough he knew he'd scored a hit. It felt less satisfying than he'd thought it would.

She brought her champagne glass to her lips and his obedient eyes followed. And then he saw that her left ring finger was clean and clear.

The last he'd heard she was meant to be living with a professor double her age or some such tale. It was one of many such tales he'd heard over the years, stories of inappropriate and much older men, of subsequent broken hearts and consequential school transfers from one side of the world to the other.

He wondered if running into Ava's 'plus one' was going to be his after-dinner surprise. He pictured some obscenely tall, grey-haired type with small glasses and a vocabulary built to keep ne'er-do-wells like him in their place.

At least by the look of things either the guy was a dud and hadn't given the poor girl the appropriate bling, or she was, in fact, as yet, still single.

He was a torn man deciding which was the more deserved outcome.

When he looked up she was watching him. More than just watching him—her eyes were roving slowly and carefully over every inch of his face.

When she noticed he had noticed, she smiled. 'I can see some things have changed. You never had stubble before.'

She reached out a hand but it stopped just millimetres short of touching him, the backs of her knuckles grazing nothing but air as she traced the contours of his face.

'It didn't occur to you to shave for the occasion,' she said.

Caleb took the opportunity to run his fingers over his stubble; the sting of short, sharp hair against skin was beautifully distracting to his other senses, which were on overload.

All that soft familiar hair, soft female skin, soft clouds of perfume he couldn't identify but knew he'd never forget;

those soft pink lips he'd kissed for the last time only moments before she'd walked away... Taking any naivety he might once have had with her.

'Nah,' he drawled, letting his hand drop to toy with his crystal-cut glass. 'I'm a rogue now, didn't you know? If I shaved I'd be unrecognisable.'

'Right. Wouldn't want to disappoint your public.'

The side of his mouth twitched into a smile despite itself. 'I've never been known to disappoint before.'

And where in the past she might have frowned, knowing there was a double entendre in there somewhere, and then blushed as she figured it out, this time her eyes slid back to lock with his.

She gave him a small smile to match his own. Then nodded, almost imperceptibly. Perhaps little Ava Halliburton had found time in her busy pencil-sharpening schedule to grow up after all.

'Be careful,' he said. 'You'll be on the business end of lots of pointing and staring and frowning if you stand next to me for too long. Your reputation will never be the same again.'

'I'll live.'

Caleb adjusted his stance as everything south of his thyroid felt fuel injected.

Before he had the chance to find out just how grown up she might yet be, she disregarded him in favour of looking up.

He tipped his head to see what was so great up there to find the stars were out in force, twinkling majestically through the gap between the two large swathes of white gauzy fabric that hung over the night.

Beside him Ava sighed. 'Did you know Galileo died in sixteen forty-two, the year of Isaac Newton's birth?'

Caleb grinned. Any other woman might have made a big

deal about the romance of the stars and the moon and the colour-tinted cake frosting… But not Ava. For all their history, and for all the niggling discomfort he felt not quite knowing where they stood with one another now, he couldn't deny she was one of a kind.

He leant his backside against the bar and crossed one ankle atop the other and asked, 'So how *is* school?'

After a few last lingering moments gazing at the dark sky, she dragged her eyes back to him. 'School's fine.'

'And what's your major? I can never keep up.'

'I'm nearing the end of my doctorate in Social Anthropology.'

'Meaning next time we see one another I'll have to call you Dr Halliburton? Marvellous.'

She didn't answer, just gave an indecipherable smile.

'And what does a doctorate in Social Anthropology entail exactly?'

'My paper is on consumption, gender and economic status among Manhattan adolescents.'

'Buying patterns of New York kids?' he asked.

Her smile was flat. 'It's not quite that simple. It's a study of ethnicity, family structure, peer pressure, needs versus desires, and identity.'

Spin it however she pleased, after her fancy-schmancy degree was finished little Ava Halliburton would be wanted by any American company that bought and sold goods and had a clue. Clever girl.

'So that answers my next question. You are still teacher's pet.'

Some unnamed emotion flashed across her eyes like quicksilver, but she lifted her chin and it was gone. 'If your memory stretches back far enough I'm sure you'll remember I was never the teacher's pet. I ask far too many obnoxious questions, which I've since discovered nobody really likes.'

Caleb laughed through his nose. And at the same time he felt muscles stretching that hadn't been used in years. Jousting muscles.

For a guy who had things come all too easily to him all his life, Ava Halliburton had always been hard work. She'd never backed down from an argument. Never given an inch when she could take a mile. She was a challenge. And there was nothing Caleb liked sinking his teeth into more.

*Down, boy.*

'Have you seen your parents yet?' he asked.

She glanced down at her drink. 'I've so far managed to avoid that little reunion.'

He didn't half blame her. Since her parents' divorce she and her father had barely spoken, and her mother, though a delight to sit next to at a dinner party, was a Stonnington Drive cliché: ten per cent plastic, ninety per cent self-absorbed, and the last kind of creature who should ever have been allowed to be in charge of nurturing another living soul.

'And how are yours?' she asked. 'Merv and Marion still as surly as ever?'

'My mother has taken up pole-dancing.'

Ava's jaw dropped while her bright eyes danced. 'She has not!'

'That she has. Her doctor suggested it would be good for her blood pressure. As to my dad's blood pressure? I'd put money on the fact she gave that little to no thought whatsoever.'

Ava ducked her chin and smiled into her drink. When she looked back at him her head was cocked, that wide warm smile of hers was out in force, and Caleb felt the years just slip away.

'Are you staying here?' he asked, when the real question he wanted answered was would she be staying long.

'Hotel,' she said, shaking her head, thick dark hair cascading over her shoulders.

Caleb shoved his hands deep into his trouser pockets to stop from reaching out and brushing her hair back so that he could better see her face. She did always have such a charming face.

She glanced up towards the big house perched magnificently atop the great lawn. 'You know this is the first time I've set foot in this place in near on ten years.'

Nine years and four months. Caleb gritted his teeth until his jaw hurt, hating the fact that he knew that.

He'd lived more, bigger, harder, better in those nine years and four months than most men lived in a lifetime, yet the fact that Ava had not seen a day of it still left an indent somewhere deep beneath his ribs.

Out of the corner of his eye Caleb saw Damien waving frantically at him from the other side of the marquee. He was miming taking a photograph.

'Then I reckon you have a lot of catching up to do with a lot of people,' he said. 'I should stop monopolising your time.'

He squared his shoulders and took a step backwards, disentangling himself from the heady mix of cloying memories and Ava's faint but memorable scent. 'And it seems my best-man duties have barely begun. Are you sticking around?'

'Until the death,' she said, raising her glass to him.

'Fine. If I don't see you again before you go, it's been swell.'

'The swellest.' She smiled serenely, not giving away any kind of clue as to whether 'until the death' meant she was flying out at midnight or if she was back to stay.

Caleb shook his head to stop the ridiculous guessing games. It mattered to him not a lick either way.

He'd seen her. He'd talked. He'd been within touching

distance. And he'd survived. He'd more than survived. He'd remained blissfully untouched.

Well, as untouched as a man in the company of a beautiful woman could ever hope to be.

He leaned in to give her a kiss on the cheek. She lifted her face to him, a small smile lighting her features.

In the moment before his lips touched her cheek he felt as if he'd been smacked across the back of the head with a mallet as the close up image of long dark eyelashes fluttering against warm golden skin covered in the palest smattering of tiny freckles stamped itself upon his consciousness…

*Waxing his boat late one evening. A sound. The scrape of a shoe on concrete. Turning. Ava, a shadow in the doorway. Tears glistening on those same cheeks.*

*And then the kiss. Their first kiss. Their first everything.*

*Her slim pale arms in the air, so trusting, as he slid her Greenpeace-emblazoned T-shirt over her head. The depth of feeling in her large eyes as she unclasped her bra. All that beautiful pale skin revealed just for him. Only for him.*

*Ava…*

Once again her name shot through him, though this time it came to him like the first summer breeze: surreptitious, lingering, and a herald of delights yet to come.

He closed his eyes, rested his lips upon her cheek for the barest amount of time and did his best not to breathe through his nose. But the second it occurred to him he couldn't help himself.

With his first breath she smelled faintly of soap, of powdered make-up and of orange blossoms.

With his second he got schoolroom chalk, old library books,

and the fresh-cut grass at that spot by the Yarra where they'd gone every day one summer holiday to play backyard cricket.

And finally, most strongly, miles of freshly vacuumed carpet beneath his feet as he'd stood in Melbourne Airport's International Terminal, completely stunned to realise that she was really leaving him behind and leaving his broken heart trampled beneath her feet.

He pulled away and the delicious scent of powder and orange blossoms returned, leaving him wanting more.

And for a man who wanted for nothing, that was something. His was a life of wealth and success, of fast cars and fast women. Of the best of everything money could pay for. It was a life lived loud and hard, no apologies to anyone.

He should have thanked her. His drive, his detachment, his determination to win at all costs had sprung from the ashes of that long-ago day.

Ava Halliburton had made a man of him.

Yet as Caleb turned his back on her he hoped she had an airline ticket burning a hole in her purse.

Ava stood alone in the middle of the big white puffy wedding marquee, her heart pounding so loudly in her ears she was surprised she'd heard a word Caleb had said.

Coming home had been nerve-racking enough knowing she was set to confront those in her immediate family whom she hadn't spoken to in a long time. So she'd deliberately put Caleb to the back of her mind.

Caleb Gilchrist. The boy she'd hero-worshipped since she was fourteen. The boy who'd always pulled her plaits, had coined the nickname Avocado, which had stuck all through high school. Her brother's best friend. The devil on her shoulder. The thorn in her side.

Her first.

It was a good thirty seconds before she realised she was still watching him walk away.

She bit her lip and looked around her, sure that the strange guilty pleasure of it was written all over her face. But once she was sure nobody gave a hoot about the practical stranger in their midst, her eyes slid back to him.

The years had been good to him. Better than good. They'd given him shoulders a tailor would kill to dress. A mien of haughty condescension that oozed power and privilege. He wore his tuxedo with such authority and ease he could have given James Bond a run for his money.

He now had a jaw that she'd barely been able to keep from tracing. His ash-brown hair was cut short, hiding any evidence of its natural curl. And his dark hazel eyes, which had always been fuelled by a mischievous glint, were now lit by a very different fire. Confidence? Experience? Or a play-by-play photographic memory of their night together?

She closed her eyes tight on the reminiscence.

All that had been a long, long time ago. Eons. A lifetime. Yet a funny kind of energy skidded down her bare arms.

When she opened her eyes, she watched him chat with someone she didn't know. He smiled his killer smile and her chest tightened.

And she wasn't even a woman who was usually struck by so much obvious male beauty any more. She liked men who were…seasoned. Men whose suits bore elbow patches rather than designer labels. Men whose beards had grown in rather than men whose stubble made them appear downright wicked.

Her current man was of a generation that meant it had been some time since he'd had the kind of knockout rear view that made a girl happy to see him walk away.

*Her man?* Ha! For a moment she'd forgotten she was now

all alone in the world with no man to speak of. In fact, she wasn't sure she'd ever had a man in her life long enough to call him her man. Lucky for her she was smart enough to know why.

If her mother had been less interested in where she lived, how she dressed, and who knew about it, then she and her father would never have separated, their divorce would not have been as vicious and unexpected, and Ava would have gone out into the world feeling more safe, more secure, and less likely to run from every situation in which she felt herself getting sucked into any scenario even vaguely resembling a relationship.

Feeling like a wallflower, and one in need of a therapist if she didn't get her head sorted and fast, Ava began a slow weave through the space, hoping she at least looked as if she knew where she was going.

She smiled benignly at others she didn't know. People obviously important in her brother's life. It made her more than a little sad that she'd spent so much time away, and less than sure she'd made the right move in coming back.

To Stonnington Drive. A row of thirty homes, no more, but a stronghold all the same. It was the last bastion of the pro-vincial old-fashioned good life to be found in what was now a relatively cosmopolitan city.

Stonnington Drive men wore suits long after they'd retired from high-powered jobs in the city. Stonnington Drive women believed in gin, tennis, and boarding school for the kids.

Ava believed it a suffocating, pulverising existence. The pressure to keep up with the Joneses, and the Gilchrists for that matter, had broken down her parents' marriage in the most vociferous, public, ravaging way. The run-on effect had left her searching for guidance wherever she could find it. And every day she'd been away from the place she'd thanked her lucky stars she'd managed to get out when she had.

For who knew at nineteen how strong one's principles really were? Another year there, another reason to stay, who knew…?

She glanced over to her brother to find Caleb had joined him. Damien had survived their childhood and made good. But he'd been older. Stronger. Luckier.

The two men put arms around one another as they ducked heads and talked. Best friends, even after all these years. As close as brothers. Closer even, considering her father had always treated Caleb like the second son he'd never had.

No wonder.

He was the perfect by-product of his upbringing: rich, good-looking, arrogant, lackadaisical. So she ought to have felt ambivalent in his company, despite their friendship all those years ago.

So why, now, couldn't she shake him off?

Because this place was insidious. It had a way of drawing people in with its luxury and its easy living and never letting them go. She felt her back teeth grinding and had to click her jaw open wide in order not to let it bother her.

Damien wrapped his arms around his bride and herded her towards the photographer, who was standing by a massive ice sculpture of a mobile phone. Ava felt a twinge of remorse that she had no idea what circumstances had led to what must have been some kind of crazy in joke in her brother's life.

Damien and Chelsea began to kiss, and didn't let up. It was so sweet. So romantic. Her stomach twisted. She had to look away.

A pair of hazel eyes snagged hers. Caleb again.

Guests' heads bobbed between them cutting off her view, but every few seconds that hot hazel gaze sliced through the air, unreadable at that distance, yet aimed directly at her.

She hadn't needed his earlier warning to take heed where he was concerned. It had taken no more than a second in his company to see that, just as she'd changed over the years, the boy she'd known, in all his varied incarnations, was no more.

There was apathy in his overly relaxed stance, arrogance in the angle of his chin, and the glimmer of barely restrained sensuality radiating from those disarming hazel eyes.

And despite the distance, despite the string quartet playing the perfectly respectable 'Clair de Lune', and despite the two-hundred-odd elegant party guests chatting up a storm between them, under his watch she began to feel warm and restless all at once.

She ought to have looked away. To have let her eyes slide past his as though she hadn't even noticed.

But after the month she'd had, having a man who looked like Caleb Gilchrist looking at her as if she were some kind of exotic dish he'd once tasted, and now was deciding if he wanted to go back for seconds, was like an elixir. Like a balm to the great gaping wound in her own self-worth she was trying her best to conquer.

She cocked her head in question. A leisurely smile lit his eyes. The heat of it leapt across the marquee and burned her cheeks.

She hadn't heard from him in nearly ten years. Yet she'd often wondered if he thought of that night fondly or with regret, or if he thought of it at all. Right then her question was answered; her old friend was not reminiscing about pulling her plaits.

Her heart responded, thumping hard and steady against her ribs, making her feel soft and breathless and interesting, not the great big loser with bad judgement in her past and big trouble in her future who'd jumped on the plane in Boston because spending time with her unhinged family had felt like the lesser of two evils compared with the situation awaiting her back at Harvard.

He made her feel as if her blood were so much lemonade. Always had. And it was the exact kind of feeling she needed right now.

She licked her suddenly dry lips and Caleb's smile grew until she could see a pair of pointy incisors. It was the slow, easy, sure smile of a predator who knew exactly what his prey was thinking. Ava was almost glad somebody did as right then she had no idea.

The hand holding the champagne glass shook ever so slightly. Enough so she sought out a table and placed the half-empty flute out of reach.

She turned away, ran her damp palms down the sides of her dress, spotted a gap in the crowd and went for it.

She hit the edge of the lavish white marquee and kept on walking, as fast as her low heels would carry her through the lush grass. She lifted her skirt, jogged up the steps at the rear of her parents' house and slipped inside.

And while everything outside had steadily made her feel as if she'd stepped into the Twilight Zone, inside the house was like déjà vu.

The walls were still panelled white below, pale striped wallpaper above, the floor still shiny blonde wood. Moonlight spilled in from discreetly angled skylights in the three-storey-high ceiling.

Memories swarmed over her, good and bad. But at least at last, for the first time since she'd left American soil the day before, she felt as if she was able to breathe again.

Coming home, even if only for a few days before she had to return to Harvard to front the Academic Review Committee, was the right decision.

Home was surely the only place to come to sort out her head, and her mess of a life, because this was where it had been all screwed up in the first place. It hadn't occurred to her that Caleb Gilchrist might play a starring role in the sorting. But if that's the way the fates wanted to play it, then who was she to argue?

# CHAPTER THREE

CALEB glanced towards the big house. He'd last seen Ava heading that way. And any kind of conversation with her would be preferable to the one he was having right now.

Damien, Chelsea, Kensey and her husband Greg were talking about window treatments. Seriously, fifteen straight minutes of Caleb's life had been spent listening to the advantages of curtains versus wooden blinds.

Enough was enough. If he didn't get out of there and soon he might develop a tic. He'd already twitched every time the word 'shrinkage' had been uttered.

He clapped a hand on Damien's shoulder. And he bit down hard.

Damien ducked out of his grasp and turned with a frown. 'Whoa, buddy, you aiming to lame me just before my honeymoon?'

Caleb said, 'Did I mention I just ran into your sister?'

Damien had the good grace to look sheepish. 'You've seen Ava.'

'Unless you have another sister I didn't know about. Of course I've seen Ava! I know you have just had the biggest wedding this town has ever seen, but it was still pretty likely I'd notice your long-lost sister had made an appearance. It didn't occur to you to give me some kind of heads up?'

Damien slid Chelsea's champagne from her grasp, took a gulp, then his nose screwed up as the bubbles tickled his throat. He slid the glass back into her grip and she just kept on talking to her sister without noticing a thing. 'I don't know why I did that.'

'I do. You're avoiding the topic at hand.'

'Which was…?'

'The prodigal daughter has returned.'

'Right. Well, the truth is I wasn't sure if she was coming.'

Caleb left a big gaping hole of silent disbelief between them.

'It's true,' Damien said. 'She wasn't sure she could get away from school. She's smack bang in the middle of her doctorate, you know.'

'Yeah,' Caleb said. 'So I heard.'

'Well, then, what's the big deal? You had to assume she'd been invited.'

'Not good enough,' Caleb said, still finding it hard to simmer down. Especially after that long hot look he and the woman of the hour had shared across the crowded room. He hadn't imagined it. The electricity between them could have shorted out the dozen Swiss designed watches in between.

'Fine,' Damien said. 'The truth is, after what you told me I didn't want to get your hopes up. That afternoon at the bar just before I proposed to Chelsea—'

Caleb held up a hand to stop his friend from saying any more. He remembered full well what he'd admitted to Damien in a unseemly fit of empathy brought on by a mix of hay fever medication, a week of late nights covering for his love-struck business partner, and a rearing of the ugly head of some random lone romantic gene life hadn't yet managed to quash.

He hadn't thought it wise to tell his best friend that he and the guy's sister had done the horizontal tango in a canoe in the University of Melbourne boat shed the day before she'd fled the country. But he had admitted that he'd had feelings for her a long, long time ago.

In case Caleb was feeling particularly forgetful Damien added, 'If not for my screwball parents setting such a bad example of what a real relationship should be like you and I could be related.'

Caleb's hand moved close enough to Damien's mouth he had to lean back away from it. 'Thanks for the recap.'

Damien grinned. 'Any time. So how did the big reunion go? Did violins play, hearts dance, angels weep?'

'It was peachy. Not exactly as exciting as root canal, but more fun than test cricket.'

Damien's eyes narrowed. 'Like that, is it?'

Caleb smiled; no teeth, no humour.

'I go on my honeymoon in three days' time. Between now and then I'm going to need you around and I'm going to want her around. So promise me you'll play nice.'

Caleb took a stuffed mushroom from a passing waiter and said nothing.

'It's taken some kind of convincing to make my new bride believe not all families are as screwed up as hers. I don't need you two going at each other as you always did and spoiling the illusion for me, all right?'

Instead of dignifying Damien's comments with a response Caleb stared at a point in the middle of his forehead, turned up the volume of his voice and asked, 'Are you wearing make-up?'

Damien's chin dropped and his eyebrows disappeared under his dark fringe. 'Are you kidding me?'

At her husband's raised voice Chelsea stopped talking and turned to join their little gathering. Kensey formed the last edge of the circle. And both women turned to look hard at Damien.

Caleb popped the mushroom in his mouth, grinned at his

friend and walked away. Out of the marquee and towards the house.

'Play nice!' Damien called out from behind him. 'For my sake, play nice.'

Caleb gave a small wave over his shoulder and made no promises.

Caleb rounded the corner of the Halliburtons' large foyer and found Ava sitting on the winding staircase, her legs drawn up to her chest, her arms wrapped around her knees, her ankles turned so that the toes of her silver Mary-Janes kissed.

Even though she had an empty stubby of beer dangling from one hand she couldn't have looked more like a little kid dressed up in her elder's finery if she'd tried.

When she saw him there she smiled.

'Hi,' she said, tilting the beer his way.

'Hi,' he said, pulling up short and tucking his hands into his trouser pockets.

Her smile, if anything, widened. And if she was any other woman, he would have thought by the coquettish look in her eyes the bottle in her hand swinging back and forth meant she was contemplating replacing one vice for another.

'We have to stop meeting like this,' she said.

'Ten years and not a word. Now twice in ten minutes. If I didn't know better, Ms Halliburton, I would think you were following me.'

'Hey, I was here first.'

'So you were.'

He smiled. She smiled some more. It was all far too civilised. It couldn't last.

'Any particular reason you've chosen to snub the festivities?' he asked.

Her soft mouth slowly grew wider and wider until her face

was all about killer cheekbones and eye sparkles, and Caleb decided it best not to say anything remotely nice or amusing in the hopes she'd save that debilitating smile of hers for someone else.

'I'm hiding,' she said.

'From whom?'

'Family, basically.'

'Right. So have you caught up with your father yet?'

She bit her lip and looked straight through him for several seconds before blurting out, 'Aunt Gladys. I'm mainly hiding from Aunt Gladys. She's cornered me three times already with the aim of setting me up with her nephew Jonah. The fact that Jonah is also my cousin seems to have escaped her.'

'That's a tad alarming, even for Aunt Gladys.'

'I'll say. I figure if I stay out of sight she'll find some other poor sap to coerce.'

'Sounds like a plan.'

Caleb wondered why she hadn't just told Aunt Gladys she was with someone. The image of the lanky grey-bearded professor, who no doubt thanked his lucky stars daily for whichever man in her past had sent her into the arms of someone of his ilk, popped unwittingly into his mind. He mentally stuck out his foot and smiled inwardly as the figure tripped over his large shoes and fell face flat on the floor.

After that diverting little thought he figured now seemed as good a time as any to find out what the situation was.

'You didn't think to bring a date along to ward off randy family members?' he asked. 'Just in case I run into Aunt Gladys I'd love to be fully informed so that I can help you out any way I can.'

Ava blinked and her eyes suddenly seemed darker. 'I only arrived this morning. Not much time to rustle up a date. There was a guy washing windows at an intersection on the way from the airport. If only I'd been more on the ball.'

'If only.'

If only she would give him a straight answer.

Maybe what she needed was a straight question.

'So where's this professor of yours Damien told me so little about? Back at the hotel? Past his bedtime? Or did he not want to give up his nightly malted milk by the fire with his cat at his feet to come across the pond?'

'Yep,' she said, not looking at him. 'Something like that.'

She lifted herself off the step and wobbled a tad. Caleb wondered if that had been her first beer.

'So,' she said, head down, hair falling in a waterfall over her face as she scuffed her shoe against the step, 'which of the bevy of beautiful blondes out there under the stars is your arm candy for the evening?'

'Who says I have any interest in arm candy?'

She lifted her chin, her mouth twisted as she pinned him with her trademark flat, discerning, too-smart-for-her-own-good gaze. 'There is such a thing as email, you know. And from what I hear from those who've used said email to tell me things about home, these days you're a regular hound dog.'

Caleb laughed. The sudden explosive release of tension was such a surprise he let it rumble through him a good deal longer than he'd normally bother.

And it felt good. Really good.

It was enough to make him glad he'd sought her out again. For one thing she didn't seem to have an inordinate interest in Roman blinds. And for another he was definitely enjoying her attempt at being sassy. She honestly had no idea she looked as if butter wouldn't melt in her mouth.

'And what makes you think you can trust such stories?' he asked.

'The source.'

He glanced her way, eyebrow raised.

'My brother.'

Caleb laughed again. 'You can't be quoting your brother, I'm sure.' Damien would have used far less ambiguous language.

'I am,' she said. 'Or I think I am. He may have put things another way and I simply extrapolated that meaning. So you're not a hound dog?'

The minx actually looked disappointed.

'Honey, I'm not sure any man has been a "hound dog" since the nineteen fifties.'

'But—'

'But I understand your meaning. And he was quite wrong. I'm perfectly discriminating,' he said with a devilish smile.

'How's that? No blondes after Labour Day?'

'I said I was discriminating, not an imbecile.'

This time Ava laughed. Her eyes brightened, her hair shimmied, and those lips… Damn, but she was one gorgeous creature.

Caleb's extremities stirred as he wondered how long it might take for butter to melt anywhere else on her body.

'So anyway,' Ava said, before he could sink too deeply into that fantasy, 'I was thinking of heading up to my old bedroom for a nose around. See if my mother turned it into an aquarium, or a gift-wrapping room, or a yoga studio. What do you reckon?'

'Knowing your mother I'd say…trophy room.'

Ava clicked her fingers. 'Right. Of course it is. So, do you want to come see if you're right?'

Caleb waited for the other shoe to drop, but she merely blinked at him, all ingenuous blue eyes.

Ava was inviting him up to her old bedroom.

It didn't mean what the sudden surge of adrenalin through-out his body indicated it meant. Or did it?

Only one way to find out for sure…

He placed his right foot on the bottom step and leaned in towards her, thus crowding her personal space to the point where he could see flecks of silver and navy in her irises.

And he waited for her to lean away. Or frown. Or run as she had run before.

But she didn't move an inch. She just blinked back at him until he could tell that an extensive array of wheels whirred madly in her head.

Every look, every move, every word that had come out of her mouth had been entirely deliberate. She knew exactly what she was doing. She'd done it all before…

*Her arms in the air, so trusting, as he slid her Greenpeace-emblazoned T-shirt over her head. Her small hands tugging his T-shirt from his jeans. Her soft hands sliding around his waist…*

Caleb's temperature began to soar.

Ava reached out and ran a hand over the carved sphere balanced on the end of the banister and said, 'You coming?'

He had never in his life wanted to be an inanimate lump of wood more. He waved a hand up the stairs. 'After you.'

Damien had asked him to play nice, after all.

Damien…

He shunted that particular name from his mind. This had nothing to do with his best friend and business partner. Nothing to do with the guy who'd taken him in and made him feel a part of a family the moment he'd realised Caleb's own family were as warm as a meat locker.

It never had. And it seemed it never would.

Ava gave a little curtsy, ducked her chin and smiled before jogging upstairs without looking back. It wasn't until she was halfway up that he came to his senses and followed.

She didn't even glance at the several other doors they passed, she just kept walking until they hit the third door from the end. It was closed. Her chest lifted and dropped before she grabbed the handle, turned and opened the door.

'Was I right?' Caleb asked.

She shot him a quick glance, and the smile that lit her face was as stunning as it was surprised. 'Not even close.' And in she went, leaving the door open for him to join her.

If he'd thought his body temperature was adversely affected by her before, now it was skyrocketing far too quickly out of his control for his liking.

One of the many things Caleb liked about himself was the fact that he was never out of control. Whether entertaining clients at a gentlemen's club, risking millions of dollars on one single stock market trade, or in the presence of a beautiful woman, he never let himself forget where he was and what *he* wanted from the situation.

All he could think to account for his current state was that he had not one single clue what he wanted from Ava Halliburton…

*Her soft hands sliding around his waist. Her warm lips opening up beneath his. Her cool, naked body wrapped around him. The two of them joining. Sultry, hushed, tender joining. And all the pressure and hope and expectation that sat upon his shoulders each and every day stilled…*

He shook his head to shatter the avalanche of memories overcrowding common sense.

*You are two old friends,* he told himself. *This has nothing to do with the last twenty-four hours you spent together; it has everything to do with the several years before that. Or the ten years since. You are both simply being pleasant. Re-*

*forging ancient ties. For Damien's sake. Damien your business partner and best friend.*

Ava poked her head back out the door and curled a saucy finger at him, then disappeared back into that which Caleb had once seen as the promised land.

If he truly believed they were simply being pleasant he was some kind of fool. And if he gave in to the invitation in Ava Halliburton's sultry blue eyes then he was an even greater fool. On a thousand different levels.

Nevertheless he turned the corner and followed her into the bedroom. Her bedroom. Kept neat and tidy and exactly as it had looked the day she left.

There Ava's bonhomie faltered. She glanced from him to the bed, which stood out like an albatross in the middle of the near wall. Then she shot to the other side of the room to open the bay windows, putting as much distance between them as she could.

Once the breath of cool night air took some of the edge off the heat simmering like a mirage between them, she relaxed again. And soon became engrossed in the hundred-odd books filling her childhood bookcase.

Caleb sauntered over to her dressing table, picked up a powder brush and sniffed. The scent was overwhelmingly familiar. Powdered make-up and orange blossoms.

It brought back a dozen memories. A hundred moments. It was sweet. Clean. And irresistible. It was her.

No other woman in the world smelt quite like that. Like innocence and loveliness and spring and whimsy. He'd been with enough of the female population to be quite sure. Not that he'd been keeping score.

He put the brush back where he found it and turned to find Ava picking out a book, opening the first page and beginning to read. He knew the rest of the world, including him, had slipped away the instant the first word on the page had sunk into her consciousness. She'd always been that way. Wholly engaged. Greedy for knowledge. Smartest in the room by a Melbourne mile.

He ambled away from the dressing table, sparing a longer glance at the frilly pink bed taking up the bulk of the room before his gaze shifted back to her, and he wondered how close he might be able to get before she remembered he was even in the room.

Her bedroom. Alone. With her. And that cruel, sweet, intoxicating scent.

She grabbed a hunk of hair, twisted it into a knot and held it atop her head and he wondered if he sank his nose into the skin below her right ear whether she might feel as soft and sexy as she looked.

The longer he spent watching her, the more he realised that he'd been kidding himself. The tousled, gangly dilettante of years past was no more.

Arcing smile lines book-ended the corners of her soft pink mouth and the frown lines above the bridge of her nose never completely went away. While the best curves now curved all the more, overall her figure had fined down as the last of her puppy fat had been eaten away by cold winters of the northern hemisphere.

And where the old Ava had curved self-consciously into herself, this Ava stood straight, shoulders back, hip cocked, sure of herself in a way Caleb wasn't certain he wanted to identify.

The Ava he'd known so briefly and lost so quickly all those years before had been exceedingly smart, but mostly a scared and stubborn girl.

This Ava was all woman.

Music from the marquee below filtered up through the night and wafted into the room. Shuffling cymbals, a moody piano, and a breathy male voice singing of foolish lovers.

She looked up from her book, blinked, stared for a moment through the bay windows, then smiled a sad smile. A smile heavy with experience. Innocence and whimsy suddenly didn't belong anywhere near the airless atmosphere of her bedroom.

Caleb realised his heart was thumping far too loudly in his chest for comfort.

'I love this song,' Ava said, her voice unnaturally husky.

She turned from the waist and looked his way, her smile soft and warm, her eyes hooded dreamily as she looked him in the eye with half her attention on the hazy melody echoing across the lawn.

Caleb didn't look away. He couldn't. Hell, he didn't want to. He simply let himself drink in the sight of her. Those piercing blue eyes. That fringe of sooty lashes. The heavy dark hair cascading over her shoulders.

Until that moment, Caleb didn't even know there was such a thing as perfect shoulders. Hers were lean, shapely, pale as porcelain with curves and crevices in all the best places.

She sucked her wide lips between her teeth, looked down at her hands, only then remembered the book she was holding, and furrowed her brow ever so slightly. She shut the book with a loud snap, then reached around to slide it back into place on the bookshelf, angling her head so that Caleb realised that her neck was pretty damned near perfect too.

He was so mesmerised by all that beautiful pale skin glowing in the moonlight spilling through the bay windows, along with the obscenely romantic music, that he didn't realise she was walking towards him until the scent of orange blossoms made his nostrils flare like a stallion in heat.

'Don't you love this song?' she asked.

Song? There was a song playing?

There must have been. She was swinging her hips, her chin was tilted down so that she was looking up at him from beneath her lashes, a small smile playing about her mouth. The music slowly wound its way back into his consciousness.

She held her hands towards him, palms up. 'Dance with me. For old times' sake.'

He'd been around the traps long enough to know that a dance wasn't all she was after. One of them had to be level-headed. What a great pity it had to be him.

'Ava,' he began.

But she held a finger to her lips and swayed up to him, taking one stiff hand and placing it in hers, then taking the other and winding it around her waist until it rested on her back.

If he moved his little finger an inch it would meet the curve of her buttocks.

Caleb closed his eyes and prayed for forgiveness.

That was the last time in some time that he thought of anyone else bar the woman in his arms.

# CHAPTER FOUR

THE slow beat of the music was seductive. But Caleb still fought against giving in to the undermining scent and softness assailing him.

As was her nature Ava led. Or at least she tried to.

As was his nature Caleb couldn't let her. Mentally cursing himself as he did it, he slid his arm far enough around her that she was pressed bodily against him.

After he'd spent an excruciating minute trying his best to keep his steadily building desire from spilling over into anything slipperier than just dancing, Ava tipped her head back and looked into his eyes.

'Hi,' she said.

'Hello again,' he returned.

'This is nice.'

Nice? She thought the vertical foreplay they were so casually indulging in was *nice*? He thought it was pretty much akin to madness!

'We could do this downstairs, you know,' he suggested. 'Where there is an actual dance floor just for this precise purpose. Under the stars you were so taken with earlier.'

Ava screwed up her nose. 'I hate dancing in public. I have two left feet.'

True, Caleb hadn't been taking all that much notice of her feet until that point, what with all of her other parts vying for his attention.

His voice was a good note lower when he said, 'You're not doing a bad job of it right now.'

Ava snuggled closer until all of her soft bits curved all too neatly against his hard bits, and he had to grit his teeth to stop throwing her over his shoulder and carrying her to the bed and ravaging her senseless.

'Neither are you,' she said brightly, oblivious to the volcano building inside him. 'Have you had lessons?'

'Dance lessons?' Caleb cringed. There he was feeling like Valentino and she saw Fred Astaire. 'Ah, no. I was born with unparalleled natural grace.'

'Were you, now?' Her smile was sultry as all get out and Caleb was almost undone.

'Just shut up and dance, will you?'

'Yes, sir.'

He pulled her closer so that her head rested against his chest. Her hair slithered against the bottom of his chin, but at least he didn't have to look down into those smoky eyes, or be within kissing distance of those heaven-sent lips.

The song came to an end. The echoing cheer of a happy crowd seeped into the room from the party below and finally they stopped swaying.

The honourable thing to do would be to extricate himself from Ava's arms, to bow out of whatever game she was playing and leave her room, get back to his best-man duties and keep his hands and every other part of his anatomy well enough away from the groom's sister.

But Caleb didn't do any of that.

If anyone at that wedding had the notion that he might be an honourable man, they had another think coming. True, he

didn't lie, cheat or steal, but he did push the boundaries of re-
spectability on a daily basis.

If he knew a client had a penchant for wet T-shirt contests
he would and had found the best Melbourne had to offer if that
was what it took to get them to choose him over any other firm.
He'd dated women, and the next week dated their room-mate.
He risked millions of dollars of other people's money every
day and did so without flinching.

Because he had a burning desire to win. To get what he
wanted. To never again hear the word no and let it break him
down to his very essence. Even though he knew he could build
himself up again. He'd done it before. It just hadn't been all
that much fun.

As to what he wanted in that precise moment? There was
one thing he was not going to deny himself…

He pulled away. Ava's head lolled back and when she
looked up at him her eyes were drowsy and dark, her lids
heavy, her everything as sexy as hell.

'I've been itching to do this all night,' he said.

Her eyes widened, her view focused and she swallowed.
Hard.

Caleb let go of her hand. Hers fluttered to rest against his
shoulder with the delicacy of butterfly wings.

His free hand stole around her neck, his thumb running
slowly along her clavicle.

Her breath caught. Her breasts pressed against his chest. Her
pupils grew so large there was barely a speck of blue left within.

He gently slid his fingers beneath the leather strap, slowly
lifting it off her neck and from beneath her dress until the
pendant it held peeked over the top.

The locket.

The locket he'd bought her for her sixteenth birthday.

She was still wearing it.

Caleb didn't know whether he ought to feel uncomfortable or wholeheartedly smug.

He stared at the clasp, visualising opening it to see if the picture of him winking at the camera still held pride of place within. But going that next step would have given too much away. More even than he wanted to admit to himself.

He was rather glad that he had suddenly found other more pressing things to concentrate on.

Like how warm the skin of her neck felt beneath his knuckles.

Like the fact that her breaths were coming harder and faster, pressing her torso closer and closer to his.

Like the small crease at the edge of her lips that was just begging to be kissed.

He let the pendant go until it swung between them; cool, closed and jammed full of memories. Memories that did not span any of the past ten years. Because she had left. Without looking back.

*She's all grown up,* he reminded himself. *She's no longer the innocent who came to you looking for deliverance all those years ago.*

But just as he knew he was made of stern enough stuff to rise again after any setback, he also knew it was in her nature to run when the going got tough. It would pay to remember that. He had few serious qualms about seeing where she was going with this little seduction scene of hers but emotional detachment was paramount.

Then he looked into her eyes.

She was smiling. The little vamp knew exactly what he was thinking.

He raised an eyebrow in question. She did the same just as her hand slid around the back of his neck, kneading the tops of his shoulders until he felt like purring.

Another song started up. This time the slow, easy, lazy

strum of an electric guitar. Echoing, rumbling, bass deep notes vibrating through his bones.

The thumb of her other hand stroked the inside of his palm with such dexterity he felt it in the backs of his knees.

And just when Caleb thought things couldn't get any better Ava pulled him close and she kissed him. Open mouth. Exploring tongue. Eyes closed tight. Body pressed hard against his.

*Ava…*

It took about a second and a half of half-hearted resistance before he joined in boots and all.

She tasted like lemon meringue pie and spring sunshine. Her hair beneath his hands felt like silk tumbling through his fingers. And the faint mewling sounds she made as he kissed her were to the tempo of his heart like a shot of epinephrine.

The kiss lasted thirty seconds at most, yet he'd never felt more turned on his whole life. She felt like a woman, she kissed like a woman, and it only made him hunger for her like a man.

When she pulled away her eyes were dark, unreadable. However, she was smiling and that was enough for him. He bent to kiss her again but she turned her head.

It seemed Ava had ideas of her own. She slid a finger into his bow tie and gave it a little tug. The back of his neck stiffened instinctively in response and her smile only widened. Whatever game it was that they were playing was getting more complicated. The rules were smudging as the furtive fun overtook rationality.

He couldn't walk away now. Especially when it was either this or choosing which he preferred: sphere-ended curtain rods or fleur-de-lis.

Sure, as if that made a lick of difference. If a chorus line of half-naked dancing girls appeared out the window at that moment he wouldn't have cared.

Ava tucked her tongue between her teeth as she concentrated on sliding his bow tie undone. It fell apart in her hands. He didn't blame it. The buttons of his shirt were next. Pop. Pop. Pop.

And then her hands delved into the gap in his shirt to perform long, languorous strokes across the skin of his chest. Sliding around his waist. Scraping down his back.

Academically Caleb liked the idea of a woman seducing him rather than the other way around as much as the next guy would. But being there with Ava had nothing to do with academics. Not for him anyway.

This was a dangerous game she'd started and he had every intention of showing her just how dangerous he could be. He was far too jaded now for her to ever affect him the way she once had, but he had every intention of blowing her mind.

And for that to happen it was time for him to take charge.

He spun her on the spot until her back was tucked in against him. She lost balance. He steadied her. Listened as her sharp breaths split the silence, a soundtrack to the burgeoning desire running thick and fast between them.

He waited until she softened and leaned into him. Pliant. Willing. His to guide.

Her ready supplication to his will brought back a flurry of memories of their first time. Sweet, soulful, gentle memories.

He shut them down.

If she wanted sweet and soulful tonight she'd come to the wrong place. She'd worn the wrong dress. She'd kissed the wrong man.

He slowly, slowly brushed aside the swathe of hair from her neck and pushed the strap of her dress aside, revelling in the faint tremors distinguishing her next breaths as he exhaled against her skin.

Then he sank his teeth into the tendon joining her perfect shoulder with her perfect neck. The most insanely delicious taste exploded on his tongue. Like fresh milk and hot skin and potential.

He bit down again, this time closing his eyes to all other sensations as he tasted her with his tongue. Oh, God, she was as smooth as honey and cream and milk chocolate and all things bad and decadent.

Had she tasted this good the first time? If so, how could he possibly have forgotten?

With every slow nip and lick of her shoulder she sank further against him as though her knees were about to give way.

Her hands quivered against his thighs before taking purchase. Clinging to him. Making his every muscle contract and ache for more.

An inch closer to his zipper and she would have felt exactly how turned on he was.

He bit her earlobe and she groaned. He wrapped his hand in her hair and tugged her head back to get better access and her mouth fell open with desire.

Her reactions were all instinct and honesty. Nothing held back. It was intoxicating. She was enchanting. He was fast forgetting how cynical he was about such things.

And they'd barely begun.

He had no doubt a lesser man than he would have been apprehensive about living up to the intensity of the heat between them. Lucky for him, and even luckier for her, he was not a lesser man.

He traced the edge of her dress with a searching hand. He found her zip and slowly, agonisingly slowly, slid it open. The sound grated against his nerves like fingernails down a blackboard.

The fabric flapped aside revealing even more pale, perfect skin and shoulder blades right up there with her shoulders and neck.

It was then he realised she wasn't wearing a bra. A sound something along the lines of 'Phwoar' escaped his lips before instinct kicked back in.

The backs of his knuckles caressed her naked back. The bumps of her spine. The scar where she'd cut herself on an overhanging tree branch when hiding out by the fifth tee of the nearby golf course as a kid.

The past and the present slammed together so fast he could barely remember what the word detachment meant.

As though she'd sensed his hesitation, Ava turned her head, pressed a hand against his cheek and drew his lips back to hers. The kiss was sweet, gentle, slow, almost innocent and at the same time erotic as all get out.

*Oh, to hell with it,* he thought. *What the lady wants…*

She twisted in his arms, and he shucked the dress from her shoulders. A trail of goose bumps following in the wake of his touch.

Her responsiveness was astounding. She made him feel as if every touch was a caress. Every look a proclamation of desire. But he remained in control. He always did.

She stepped away, her dark eyes locked to his as her dress snagged on her hips. And all semblance of control flew out the window.

The Ava he once knew tangled with the changes that nearly ten years had made. Her lean, mean, girlish figure now curved delicately in and out in all the right places.

Caleb felt himself turning blind with lust.

As he drank in the sight of her she tossed her hair. But not with arrogance. Her fists clenched and unclenched at her sides. Her trembling was no longer purely a measure of simple pleasure.

Again her vulnerability snagged him. For a moment he tried to second-guess why she wanted this.

But then he remembered why he wanted it. She was woman. He was man. Period.

He looked back into her eyes, made sure she was hooked, then he gave her the full-glint treatment. 'Tell me I'm not dreaming.'

She slowly shook her head, a small smile tickling at the corner of her luscious mouth. 'You're not dreaming.'

'Then what the hell am I waiting for?'

He took two steps towards her, slid a hand into her hair and kissed her. Her breasts pressed against his naked chest. She slid her hands into his short hair and closed her eyes.

His vision blurred until all he could think about was skin and pink and visions of what else lay beneath what suddenly seemed like way too much dress for comfort. Her softness and sweetness was almost unbearable. Almost.

He kept his head as he backed her up against the bed. Her knees hit the mattress. She fell backwards. He landed beside her.

He was still lucid when he kissed his way down her body, taking his time to get to know every glorious turn of her breasts before moving down to her belly.

When her hands gripped the pink floral bedspread as he took the edge of her dress between his teeth and began pulling it past her hips his self-control remained in check. But only just.

The edge of her pants peeked back at him. White. Lace. Tempting. Taunting. His nostrils flared, blowing hot air across her lower belly, and she jerked towards him.

And for the first time in his life he found himself trying to keep up with the pure sexuality of a woman rather than the other way around.

When he touched her it was as though he were being touched. When he kissed her belly he felt liquid fire in his own belly. The scorching heat that surged through him as he slid a hand beneath her skirt and caressed her velvet-soft skin was irrational.

He was still fully clothed, for Pete's sake. Yet he was aroused to the point of agony.

The scrap of lace keeping her from his touch was laughable. He teased the edge with a feather-light caress and her eyes closed tight.

But he wanted her to know exactly who was putting her through this. 'Ava, open your eyes.'

They fluttered open. Took their time focusing. His pulse throbbed through his body as he waited for the catch in her breath, the surrender in her eyes, the acknowledgement in her smile that she was ready for the night of her life.

But they never came.

Instead she said, 'The average bed is home to over six billion dust mites.'

'No worries,' he said with a diabolical grin. 'You can be on top.'

Her throat worked. Several small frown lines appeared above her nose and then her hands pressed gently against his chest, the international sign for 'stop'.

Something had shifted within her. She was no longer the willing participant, and even less the instigator she had been mere moments earlier. Heck, she was so susceptible two more minutes and he would have had her spiralling into oblivion.

*Two more minutes*. Never before had so little time seemed so close. Yet so far away.

He slid his hand back into the light, pressed himself away from her, knowing the only way to think straight was to get his hands off all that gorgeous warm skin.

When he looked into her eyes instead of wildly passionate she suddenly looked panicked.

She might as well have doused him in a bucket of iced water for how quickly the haze of lust shrouding his judgement dissipated.

He moved so that no part of her touched any part of him. And she couldn't have hurried to disentangle herself from him faster.

By the time she sat upright on the edge of the bed her dress was held to her chest, her hair a mess, her knees clenched.

He ran a fast hand through his hair, reached out to her, then pulled his hand back to his side.

He was a selfish beast at the best of times, thus not any good at making other people feel better. Unless she could be assuaged with a flip remark, indulgence in more of what they had been doing, the inside news on a good trade, or a member's key to any of the top private clubs in town, he wasn't the guy for this.

'Ava, honey,' he said, his voice hoarse and stilted, 'are you okay?'

Her distant eyes lingered on his open shirt before she held up a hand, and said, 'I just need a minute.'

A minute? Boy, was she cool when she needed to be.

He buttoned the bottom two buttons of his shirt with thick fingers as he shot to his feet and paced to the far side of the room and back again and tried to figure out how he'd ended up there. With Ava. Rebuffed. Again.

His voice was cool as a suburban pool in winter when he asked, 'What was that all about, then?'

She shook her pretty head. 'Nothing.'

He pointed at the half-open bedroom door. 'Sweetheart, you bringing me up here and jumping my bones while there are two-hundred-odd people including your family just outside and after not seeing me for ten years is not nothing.'

She looked up at him. Glared, more like. But that was fine. It was much better to be on the end of that kind of expression than the self-loathing he'd seen in her eyes earlier.

'I didn't!' she said. 'I just needed… You wouldn't understand.'

'Try me.'

She bit her lips.

He ran a hand across the back of his neck, which felt hot and itchy. That was the feel of his self-protect mechanism finally whirring back to life.

'Ava, speak now or for ever hold your peace.'

'I… Just thanks, okay? It was just what I needed.'

Well. He'd wanted a straight answer, hadn't he?

# CHAPTER FIVE

'JUST what you needed?' Caleb repeated, sounding as dumb-founded as he felt. 'Is foreplay the latest craze in jet-lag cures?'

'Maybe it should be,' she shot back.

'Ava,' he warned.

Her brows flattened, her mouth twisted. Then she shook her shoulders like an actor in the wings after a particularly difficult stage performance. 'It's just,' she began, 'the past month has been just so humiliating I can't even… Taylor and I broke up. So I left. And now I'm here. And I barely knew a soul out there under the marquee, which was only more depressing, as it only made me wonder why I came back. But then there you were…'

Her voice petered out. And no wonder.

She'd been using him. From the get go.

'Taylor?' he managed.

'My boyfriend. Ex-boyfriend.'

'The professor.'

Her mouth dropped open and she made true eye contact with him for the first time in an age. 'How did you—?'

'I am in contact with your family even if you're not.'

'Right. Of course you are.' When she looked back at him her eyes were luminous. 'We're cool, right?'

Cool? *Cool?*

'Sure,' he said cool dripping from his every word. 'Why be a best man unless you're guaranteed a tumble with the desperate, beer-soaked sister of the groom on the rebound?'

She threw her hands in the air with such gusto his tirade stopped at his throat. That same throat swelled shut when he saw actual tears glimmering in her eyes.

'I'm sorry, all right?' she said. 'Are you happy now?'

'Deliriously. You?'

'Oh, yeah. Beyond belief. My life is so-o-o peachy keen. You want to know why he dumped me? My so-called partner was offered a position on the Academic Review Committee, the committee charged with monitoring the progress of students attempting higher degrees. And with my doctorate in the pipeline he saw our situation as an ethical clash.'

Her bottom lip began to quiver and Caleb dug his toes into his shoes to stop himself from moving a muscle in her general direction.

And then she said, 'He chose the school over me.'

The parallel was priceless. Surely there was some kind of cosmic balance at play after the way she'd left him standing in the airport, but though the opportunity was ripe, and though he was feeling pretty darned indignant, he couldn't make himself say it.

When did he become so soft? When Ava Halliburton butted her pretty face back in his life, that was when.

'Damo's wedding must have felt like auspicious timing, then. What better a chance than to come home to lick your wounds?' he offered, hoping she might deny it, might still have some other reason up her sleeve for the sudden sexpot act. Like that he was simply irresistible.

But she looked up at him with a small smile on her face and nodded, as if the fact that he figured her out so easily was a good thing.

Well, damn her. Damn her and her perfect shoulders and her soft lips and the spell that she could still cast over him even though he knew damn well better than to fall for it.

He scratched the sudden itch at the back of his neck. Being around her, the move was becoming quite a habit.

'And then when you saw me coming you must have thought all your luck had come at once. You thought, Old Caleb's good for a quick roll. He's been there and done that and sold the rights to the T-shirt. He'd be the perfect means to getting my groove back.'

'No!'

'No?' he said, his voice dropping, no longer able to control his infuriation. 'You didn't think I'd be good for a quick roll? A slow roll, perhaps. A take-our-time-and-savour-every-second-as-we-take-all-night roll. Rolls so many and varied you'd wake up tomorrow unable to remember Professor Egghead's name. If you'd given me enough time I promise I could have surpassed your expectations back there.'

He waved an arm in the direction of the bed, which was messed up just enough anyone looking in would be in no doubt of what had happened. A spark relit the warmth in his veins and he realised how much he wanted her still.

Ava swallowed hard and looked up at him with those big blue eyes. Eyes that all too recently had been feverish with desire were now careful. She sniffed. And just looked at him. As if she were seeing him for the first time.

And though her hands were now wringing, and though her bottom lashes were still spiky with unshed tears, there was knowledge in her gaze. Pure, stark, feminine insight.

She saw right through him.

Her gaze dropped to the open neck of his shirt. She took one slow, shallow breath, then licked her lips. As though she

Ava zipped her dress, ran a finger around the edges of her lips to fix her lipstick, tidied her hair and tried to ignore the sounds behind her.

But it was no use. Each noise only served as a reminder of the fact that she'd just tried to re-enact a night a long time ago when making love with Caleb had made everything in her life crystal clear.

Yet this time when she'd come to him looking for clarity, or even a little comfort, she had failed dismally.

And no wonder. The funny, sharp boy she'd always had a little crush on had become some kind of beautiful, which had caused her fuzzy synapses to snap.

The slide of buttons slipping through the button holes of Caleb's snowy white shirt reminded her of how strong and solid he'd felt beneath her hands. The rustle of tucking his shirt back into the beltline of his tuxedo trousers reminded her how liberating it had felt to tug them out in the first place.

She swallowed hard. Closed her eyes. And tried to think about something else…

*Sliding open the door of the university boat shed, looking for her brother to tell him that the next day she might well be leaving to take up the full scholarship to Harvard she'd been offered.*

*Finding Caleb instead, alone in the half-darkness, waxing the hull of his row boat. Long-sleeved T-shirt rolled up to his elbows and clinging to muscles she hadn't ever realised he had.*

*Eyes dark as he'd turned and seen her there. Eyes narrowed as he'd realised she was upset. And the flash of awareness she'd felt as he'd taken her in his arms to comfort her.*

*Raining kisses over her face, taking away her tears. Feeling such certainty, such trust as he'd lifted her arms above her head and rid her of her T-shirt.*

wasn't nearly done with toying with him for her ow
tional needs.

He was pretty sure she had no idea the power of the s.
she was giving off. They were too pure. Too artless. An
was obviously feeling too mixed up and raw.

He knew then that if he took three long strides to her s.
and gathered her in his arms there would be no more waitin.
The girl, the *woman* he'd wanted again for as long as he coul
remember would willingly be his all night long.

But a girl like Ava always came with strings. Far too
many strings.

A burst of screeching laughter split the loaded silence,
followed by stomping footsteps, and it was obvious that
another pair of party guests had the same idea they'd had and
were looking for an empty room in which to finish the thought.

That was enough to pull Caleb from his daze. He smart-
ened up. Found his nerve. Packaged the whole evening into
a tight ball and filed it deep down inside himself in the folder
marked 'bad experiences best buried'.

'Come on, Doc,' he said. 'Let's get back to the party. I have
a pretty speech to make before the night is out and no doubt
Aunt Gladys has sent out a search party for you by now.'

Ava nodded. Straightened her back. Squared her shoulders
Stood. Smoothed her dress.

She looked his way. A flicker of guilt now etched acro
her beautiful face. Uh-uh. Oh, no.

Caleb was no longer going to allow himself to be mo
by her. Not in any way, shape or form.

If that day at the airport nine years and four months e
had set him on the life's path of living big, living we
living alone, then this disaster of an evening had seal

Big, bad, shrewd, imperturbable Caleb Gilchrist w
Kicking butt and taking names.

\* \* \*

*The power surging through her as she'd unclasped her bra and felt his eyes on her. The revelation. The power.*

*Touching, caressing, all that warm, damp skin and those hard, lean limbs. The moment of pain when they'd first come together. But he'd been so careful, so gentle, yet so sure, the pain had soon been lost in the waves of pleasure so extraordinary she had been completely swept away…*

Ava's body still thrummed every place he'd touched. Everywhere he'd kissed. Every other spot his warm breath had caressed.

She opened her eyes and stared at a blank spot on the wall. Was that what she'd been seeking from him again? The kind of pleasure that would make her forget her life for a brief while? If so, was that really such a lot to ask of a guy like Caleb Hound Dog Gilchrist?

She shook her head, shutting out the sense memories. She was a 'boyfriend' girl, not 'affair' girl or 'one-night stand' girl. The length of time it had taken her to get over Caleb after the first time proved that.

The first time together there had been a moment as she'd lain in his arms when he'd played with her locket, smiled at his picture still therein. In that moment if he'd asked her to stay, rather than as an afterthought at the airport the next day, her whole life to this point would have been different. Harvard would have been forgotten. She would never have travelled and studied at several of the world's top universities. She never would have experienced different cultures and different men and been able to create a realm of knowledge from which to gain perspective on life.

At best they might have stayed together, married and bought a house near their parents. And she would have become one of *them*. The dreaded Stonnington Drive wives.

At worst she would have had to watch the boy she worshipped move on to someone cooler, prettier, easier to love.

Either way she would have been the unhappiest woman on the planet.

But he'd dropped the locket back to her chest and thus let her go. He'd given her release. And the courage to spread her wings.

Caleb Gilchrist had been a pain in her behind her whole adolescence. He'd been her first crush just as long. He'd been her greatest awakening, sexual and otherwise.

And now? Now he was all shoulders, and a perfectly etched jaw line and a rear view for the ages. He wasn't as easygoing about the whole 'friends with benefits' thing as his reputation had made her hope he'd be. And the resultant embarrassment was quite simply the cherry on the top of what had been the worst month of her life.

'Ava,' Caleb said, his thick dark voice carrying to her across the room.

She turned to find him looking immaculate. Sleek. Unruffled, as if he'd been in this exact situation a hundred times before.

When she'd imagined him over the years he usually came dressed in jeans, a T-shirt, likely with a tear in the collar, and a baseball cap to hide his adorable ash-brown curls—the epitome of trust-fund-baby cool. That Caleb she'd been able to mock, to joke with, to like.

This Caleb was beyond her experience, varied as it had been. He was too strong, too cool, too sure of himself. She was pretty sure any teasing would bounce off him like a penny off a well-made bed.

Why hadn't she realised all that before she'd enticed him up here with half-baked hopes he'd be happy enough to do whatever it took to make her feel halfway desirable again?

His brow furrowed for a moment, and his mouth jerked at the corners.

*So, so beautiful…*

She ducked her chin. The fact that he'd even kissed her back meant she'd got what she'd come for. Enough was enough.

'So,' he said.

'So,' she said.

'They'll be serving dessert soon enough. Bacio Bacio's cinnamon gelato is the second reason I agreed to do this gig.'

Ava's mouth twisted into a half-smile that surprised even her. 'Plain vanilla is the world's favourite flavour of ice cream, making up twenty-nine per cent of all sales,' she found herself blabbing.

'Thank goodness you went to all those fancy schools.'

'I read that on the back of a packet of ice-cream cones.'

Laughter lit his eyes even if he didn't let it out. 'Shall we?' he asked, holding out his hand.

She had no idea what she'd done to be lucky enough not to be treated as if she were some misguided harpy. She opened her mouth to tell him so, then decided it would be best not to push her luck.

She put her hand in his. Such a large hand. It enveloped hers in warmth. And made her feel as if she wasn't as alone as she had felt an hour earlier.

If only she had realised that was all she'd needed before she'd invited him up here. Hmm. Deep down inside, in places she wasn't likely to tell another living soul about, she was actually rather glad she hadn't.

He tugged her towards the door.

'Wait,' she said, tugging back.

His altered expression told her his cool was waning.

'I am really sorry,' Ava said.

'Yeah,' Caleb said. 'So am I.'

They headed out the door and down the stairs in silence.

A tall silver-haired man walked past the bottom of the staircase. Ava's Mary-Janes squeaked on the carpeted stairs.

'Stop. Wait,' she whispered. 'It's my father.'

Caleb didn't even falter. 'Then you'd better get your game face on.'

*Oh, no…*

'Ralph,' Caleb called out as he dragged her onwards. 'How's it hanging?'

Ava saw her father's face light up before he'd even looked up the stairs.

'It's hanging just fine, son.'

He turned with an easy smile, winking at Caleb. Winking. Ava was pretty sure she hadn't seen her father wink since she was a little kid.

And then he saw her. If the refrigerator lost power, the sudden chill in Ralph Halliburton's face would still have kept the vodka happy.

'Ava,' he said. His voice gruff.

'Hi, Dad.'

He glanced between the two of them, then up the stairs, then back again. Her stomach sank so fast she felt it land somewhere in the vicinity of her ankles. And she felt a sudden need to check that her dress wasn't hooked into her undies.

When her father said not another word, Caleb leapt in. 'Having a good time tonight, Ralph?'

'Lovely time, thanks, Caleb. And you?'

'The mini quiches were an anticlimax, but apart from that the evening has been illuminating.'

Ava felt a tingle of alarm trickle down her spine. She crushed Caleb's hand, but he seemed not to even notice.

'Taking notes, are you, son?' Ralph asked.

'Wouldn't dream of it, sir.'

'Hmm. Shouldn't you be out there helping Damien do whatever it is he still has to do before this long night is over?'

Caleb smiled. 'Shouldn't you?'

'The father of the groom is obsolete. At least the father of the bride has a role, even if it is giving up his child.'

Ava's teeth clenched as she waited for him to acknowledge her in some way, but his stoic gaze didn't move.

This time Caleb squeezed her hand. The sense of warmth and safety he infused in her slowly returned. Making his sudden sideswipe all that much more perturbing.

'Poor fellow,' Caleb said. 'Then we'll just have to get this daughter of yours married off so you don't feel so obsolete. Though since she just so recently lost *another* boyfriend on the trail to becoming a sociologist, or a philosopher, or archaeologist, or whatever it is she's studying this week, I'm not sure what we are to do.'

Ava could do nothing but glare at Caleb. He smiled benignly at her as though she were the bride atop a wedding cake, but she saw the gleam in his eye.

She was *not* forgiven for what had happened in her bedroom. Far from it. Caleb had every intention of making her pay. For starting something? Or for stopping it?

The urge to kick him in the back of the knee and run was tempered by the lingering imprint of his lips upon her body.

'Oh, I don't mind not having a starring role in the play so much any more, Caleb,' her father said. 'It gives me more time to read the paper.'

'Then you are a luckier man than me.'

Pleasantries exhausted, Ralph Halliburton's eyes scooted back to Ava. 'I wasn't sure you'd made your flight.'

'It came in really early this morning and I knew you guys

would be really busy with the wedding and all so I went to a hotel.'

He nodded. Barely. 'Then I'll have someone sent to pick up your things and bring them back here.' It wasn't a question.

Ava thought about defying him. She really did. Anything to get a reaction from him. Any reaction. But in the end it only would have caused more friction and there was enough in the air to light a city. 'That would be great, Dad. Thanks.'

He smiled at Caleb, then reached out and shook the guy's hand. While he hadn't offered her a smile, a hug, a kiss on the cheek. Nothing. After ten years.

'See you kids later,' he said before walking away.

When it was just the two of them again Ava began to shake. 'What the hell was that all about? Marrying me off? Are you mad?'

'Mad? Me? Never. Happy about being the only one here who seems to have a clue *why* you're here? No, not that either.'

'And why's that?'

'Let's shelve this.'

'No,' she said, holding her ground. 'You've got something you're dying to say, so say it.'

'Fine. You've run away from your problems. Again. It's what you do.'

'Hardly.'

'My mistake. So you came back to quench the decade-long desire to have me again. I know I'm good, but that's given my ego a nice massage.'

'Get over yourself.'

'Maybe later. Right now I thought it best to keep your dad busy with a little inane conversation to give you time to come up with another reason that won't break your family's heart, is all. I was doing you a favour.'

'Well, don't do me any more.'

'Fine.'

'Fine.' Ava made to huff away, but it was only then that she realised they were still holding hands.

'Let me go, Caleb,' she said between gritted teeth.

He did so with such speed she rocked on the step.

'Sweetheart, I let you go a long time ago,' he said, giving her one last long look before he slid his hands into his trouser pockets, skipped down the last two steps and ambled away, whistling.

The bastard.

Ooh, she ached to… What? Hit him? Kick him? Humiliate him? Drag him back upstairs and finish what they'd started, once and for all?

'Ava!'

She closed her eyes tight and sent a few choice words to the gods for giving her such a perfect welcome home.

Then she turned towards the shrill voice with a smile plastered across her face. 'Yes, Aunt Gladys?'

Some time after three the next morning Ava sat on the frilly pink banquette below the window of her bedroom, wide awake.

Through the window she watched the wedding organisers pack while inside she relived the events of the past few weeks that had led her back home.

Taylor not thinking twice before taking the job on the Academic Review Committee. Coming home for the first time in almost ten years to a father who would barely look her in the eye. And, last but not least, the reckless and ultimately botched seduction of her brother's best friend in this very room.

She'd been looking for love in all the wrong places her whole life. Which was ridiculous. Her doctorate was in social anthropology; cultural development. Yet for an otherwise pretty bright woman she sure was eight kinds of dumb when it came to relationships with the men in her life.

Take Caleb. Once, years ago, he had given her everything he'd had to give on the one night when she'd so needed to have it. And tonight she'd thrown that back in his face, using him as she might have a gigolo, or a faceless man in a dark bar. As a means to feel desired again.

The moment the last marquee peg was packed away and the last van had driven off, the heavens finally opened, washing hard and fast buckets of rain over the Halliburtons' garden.

It was almost as though the clouds had crossed their legs until the coast was clear. Not so surprising. Nothing ever really went wrong for those who belonged on Stonnington Drive.

Her parents divorced, throwing her idyllic childhood into disarray. Yet now according to Damien they were best friends, which only served to throw her relationship barometer out of whack. Since she'd left, Caleb's life had gone from strength to strength. Even Marion Gilchrist, who must have been near sixty years old, had taken up pole-dancing and not yet broken a limb. And it never rained here on important days.

She wrapped her arms around her knees, her fingers catching on the frayed holes in the knees of her old, faded red flannel pyjama pants. And the raindrops sliding down her windowpane did little to mask the matching tears running down Ava's face, only proving she'd never really belonged here and never would.

# CHAPTER SIX

SUNDAY morning Caleb got out of the car and tetchily slammed the door behind him. He stomped around to the Halliburtons' back entrance, knowing the terrace door would be open.

Sunday mornings in spring on Stonnington Drive meant tennis on the private courts, or golf at the private course that butted up against their backyards, or, for the really enthusiastic, laps of the pool. But in every house they meant a never-ending parade of food on the terrace from morning till night.

Caleb jogged up the back steps, grabbed a berry Danish from the fully laden table and headed through the open French doors and into the kitchen.

'Caleb, darling,' Rachel Halliburton, Ava and Damien's society queen of a mother, said as she passed by with an air kiss, her left hand grasping what looked very much like a Bloody Mary.

At eight in the morning that might have been shocking in any other house on any other street, but not here. His grumps dissipated a very little as he revelled in the idea that the rest of the world had no idea of the lifestyle they were missing.

'What are you doing here so bright and early?' she asked. 'Did you stay at your parents' house last night?'

'Ah, no. The king-sized bed in my apartment was enough to send me to my apartment last night. I'm here now for best-man duties. Damien insisted I attend the opening of the gifts. I'm hoping to pilfer a couple of the better ones to teach him a lesson.'

'Lovely. Lovely,' she said distractedly as she retied the lace on her new white tennis shoes.

Ralph Halliburton came in with a rolled-up broadsheet newspaper tucked under his arm. He patted his wife on her tennis-skirt-covered behind before making a beeline for the gigantic bubbling espresso machine.

'Not in front of the kids,' she cooed.

'Morning, Caleb,' Ralph said. 'What are you doing here so bright and early? Leave something behind yesterday?'

'Ah, no. I'm here to watch Damo and Chelsea unwrap a lot of useless electrical goods they don't want and don't need.'

'Excellent. Excellent,' Ralph said. 'Grab a coffee.'

'Maybe later. Can you point me the way to the groom?'

'Swimming, I do believe,' Rachel said. 'While his bride is outside playing with her wedding present.'

Caleb ambled over to the kitchen window, which looked out on the large garden. It was so green and clean nobody would have guessed they'd had two marquees and nearly four hundred people dining there the night before.

A squeak and a giggle drew his attention to the edge of the terrace. Chelsea's heels dug hard into the paving, her blonde pony-tail wagging madly as she held tight to a length of hot-pink rope in both hands, while a tiny black and white fox terrier puppy had the other caught between its teeth. The puppy growled with as much vigour as a puppy could while Chelsea laughed. And laughed and laughed.

The only word Caleb could use to describe his best friend's bride in that moment was *happy*. He realised with some chagrin that that word was making rather a lot of appearances on his radar of late.

Chelsea glanced up, blew her fringe from her eyes, and gave him a big wave. He saluted back, then pointed to where the puppy was making a run for the back steps. She laughed some more, then took off after it.

Caleb realised that, despite having to be there at such a hideous hour, there was no way he could begrudge his friend a moment of the life he'd have with the woman, insidiously happy as she was.

He turned back to face the kitchen at large. 'Either Damo bought Chelsea a dog or a piece of pink rope. Which is it?'

'A dog, I tell you,' Rachel said. 'We tried to convince him to buy her a new car so she would stop having to drive that odd pink business van of hers around the place. But no. Ralph, how did we raise a son with such whack priorities?'

'How indeed?' Ralph said, leaning in to kiss his ex-wife on the end of the nose. Then he took his newspaper, his fresh coffee and himself outside, while Rachel mooned after him until he was out of sight.

His feet itching to get moving, get gone, or get anywhere but around all this happy, smiley coupledom, Caleb was about to scoot out to the pool when Ava came clumping down the stairs.

His feet stayed put and instead he slowly sank back against the kitchen bench.

She was dressed like uni students everywhere. Faded jeans frayed at the cuffs, red sneakers, a baby-blue zipped-up tracksuit top, hair pulled back into a messy bun atop her head, glasses perched on the end of her nose.

The dog-eared novel tucked under her arm was pure Ava. She never went anywhere without one as a kid. Boy, that brought back a flood of memories. Nice ones. Sweet ones.

Ones that threatened to negate the healthy antagonism he'd built up the evening before.

She still wore the leather strap, which she now knew held the locket he'd once given her. What he didn't know was if the picture inside it had been long since changed. They hadn't quite gone far enough the night before for him to find out.

*Wrong,* he corrected himself. They'd gone too far before her motives had come into the light. She'd been jilted and was looking for comfort. He wasn't comfort guy. The end.

So why did the mere sight of her have him feeling like a tightly coiled spring?

'Morning, Avocado,' he called out when she looked as though she might head right on out of the kitchen without even noticing he was there.

She looked up and upon seeing him faltered on the next to last step, catching herself on the stair rail at the last second.

It took a couple of moments for her to collect her breath before she frowned like a champion and shuffled groggily past him.

'My, my,' he said. 'Don't we look tired? Still on Boston time? Or did your conscience keep you up all night?'

'Bite me.'

'Ava, darling,' Rachel said, 'go upstairs and put something more appropriate on, please. We have company.'

Ava looked pointedly around the room. 'I don't see any company.'

'What am I?' Caleb asked. 'Chopped liver?'

'That would be insulting to chopped liver,' she said beneath her breath. 'Why are you here anyway? Too lazy to find another family to bug?'

Caleb laughed at the third Halliburton to question him with the exact same words in as many minutes. 'You're your parents' daughter, that's for sure.'

Ava crossed her arms and glared daggers at him. 'You take that back!'

Caleb glanced at Rachel, who was swanning around the kitchen with white iPod cords dangling from her ears. Totally oblivious, as she had always been when it came to her daughter.

He scratched the back of his head as he explained, 'You all asked the exact same...oh, never mind. I'm here because Damien asked me to help take the gifts back to his and Chelsea's new house.'

He turned towards the coffee machine, grabbed a mug and said under his breath, 'Brat.'

The slap of book against granite kitchen bench-top reverberated through his arm.

'What did you just call me?'

He took his sweet time to finish pouring, added a gulp of cream, then pushed the mug towards her.

Her half-hearted, 'Thank you,' got him off the hook.

As Caleb poured his own strong black coffee Damien came into the room with wet hair and a damp towel slung over his shoulder. 'Morning, all.'

A chorus of hellos echoed around the room. His mother fixed his hair, his father waved with his newspaper from the terrace, and Ava watched it all with a knotted brow.

She glanced back at Caleb, saw he was watching her, then her frown turned to a glare.

He laughed, she frowned all the more, then huffed over to the fridge. She stuck her head inside, her right knee kicked out sideways and her right foot resting snugly against her calf.

All that pose did was pull her jeans tight across her buttocks. From behind she still looked a nubile nineteen. Lean, curvy, and fit as a fiddle. Caleb couldn't have dragged his eyes away for all the coffee in Brazil.

Then she pulled her hair from its elastic band and shook it out, scratching her fingers through her scalp until her hair fell in long, sexy, messy waves. He would have put money on the fact that she had no idea she was doing it. And he would have bet his life savings on the fact that she was doing it because she subconsciously wanted to look good for him.

It seemed he wasn't the only one left feeling as if the night before was unfinished business.

He settled thoughtfully against the bench and took a sip of coffee. The hot drink scorched a layer off the top of his tongue. He glanced skyward and muttered a soft curse at whoever up there might be listening.

She finally came out of the fridge with a piece of pizza that looked as if it had seen better days.

'Don't tell me you've been living on stale pizza for the past ten years,' he said.

'Fine,' she said through a mouthful of just that as she turned and pinned him with a fierce stare. 'I won't tell you that.'

'Stale pizza ain't cheap. How could a poor student afford to live so well, I do wonder?'

She ambled back over to her coffee and leant against the counter beside him, close enough that the back of his neck bristled. He was sure he'd know if she was in the room even with his eyes closed, he was so well tuned to her.

When she didn't deign to answer Caleb filled in the blanks himself. 'Perhaps you work in the college bookstore? Pull beer at an off-campus bar for tips? Sleep on friends' floors and raid their cupboards when everyone else is asleep? Aah, no. I'd forgotten about Daddy's trust fund.'

Her initial verbal response post-swallowing was less than ladylike. Then, 'Look who's talking. I never knew a guy so eager to get to twenty-five so that he could take the money and run. What was the plan again? Blow it all on black at the casino? No, you were going to buy a boat and cruise the Caribbean making friends with the local girls until the dough ran out. How did that work out for you?'

Caleb had forgotten he'd ever said that. Likely he'd been showing off, making noise, trying to get attention from the bright, pretty girl. However, he gave her a slow smile as he said, 'Who says my life plan has changed any?'

Antagonism radiated from her like a spicy perfume. But rather than make Caleb realise he'd dodged a bullet the night before, the intensity of her reaction to him was infectious.

It made him want to taste more of that soft, sweet skin. To kiss her until her knees melted, until she could scarce draw breath. Until she could no longer remember the name of the fool back in Boston who had jilted her, thus sending her into his arms in the first place.

That was what it might well take to get her well and truly out of his system once and for all.

His smile was forbidding. 'Now that we've established my life is hunky-dory, I think we really should be shining the spotlight onto yours,' he said. 'Last night didn't you mention something about a review?'

Ava's mouth shot open but Damien chimed in before she could tell Caleb exactly what he could do with his spotlight.

'Damn, you two are painful. And since I know you'd both rather push each other's buttons far more than you'd like to actually answer a simple question... Ava, Caleb used his trust-fund money to help me buy the business. Without him, then and now, Keppler, Jones and Morgenstern would be another pesky upstart two-man operation rather than the company every other trading company wants to be.'

Caleb shifted on the spot, not all that comfortable being seen as responsible. It hardly did his mad, bad and danger-ous-to-know image any good.

Ava's mouth snapped shut, and when she looked back at him her expression had changed. She looked at him differently. As if maybe she ought not to have sniped at him after all.

His skin contracted agreeably. The night before hadn't been an anomaly. He wondered if she had any idea that sniping was the only thing staving off the kissing.

'And, Caleb,' Damien said with a warning tone that Caleb could not mistake.

'Yes, Damien,' he said, loading the two words with as much indolence as he could.

Damien simply didn't pay him any heed. 'Apart from the numerous scholarships she's earned, Ava tutors and guest lectures at universities around the States. She's written numerous articles about human behaviour for magazines including a couple of hilarious ones for *The New Yorker*. She has recently become a darling of the business conference circuit. And she lives on campus in order to save money. She does all right.' Damien reached out and ran a hard hand over Ava's hair, mussing it up even further.

She quickly flattened it down and glanced at Caleb from beneath her fringe. While Caleb held tight to his coffee and wondered if she had any idea that he was itching to run his hands through those sexy waves himself.

He said, 'You must be so proud of your little flag bearer for the great unwashed.'

Damien rolled his eyes. 'Why I ever thought that getting the two of you together again would take me back to the fun, fabulous days of our youth I have no idea. Now I remember you were always at each other's throats. I must have blocked that part out.'

He shook his head and took up Ava's place standing at the open fridge.

Having finished her pizza, Ava twisted to pick up her

coffee. Her jacket tipped forward ever so slightly, but just enough Caleb caught a hint of white lace bra. He gritted his teeth and swallowed. Who knew having one more layer between them than they did the night before would prove to be an even bigger turn-on?

He shifted closer. She noticed and frowned. But she didn't move away.

'I had no idea you'd become so conscientious,' she said.

'Sure. And I spend my Saturday nights helping little old ladies across the street too,' Caleb said. 'Now I don't think we actually sorted out the subject of your trust fund…'

'I gave it up.' She took a slow sip of her coffee, those big blue eyes of hers just waiting for his reaction.

Caleb realised he must have looked like a fish out of water, his mouth dropped open so fast. He ran a finger over the edge of his mouth before saying, 'Right, and I've been contemplating the priesthood.'

'Do you want me to take you upstairs and show you? The paperwork is collecting dust in my bedside drawer as we speak.'

She took a step away from him.

Caleb snaked a hand out and grabbed her wrist. 'You want me to come up to your room with you? Right now? Just the two of us?'

Ava's cheeks turned beautifully pink and her gaze shot from her wrist to her brother. Damien was whistling beneath his breath and pretending he hadn't heard a thing. But Caleb was on the right angle to see the guy was smiling.

'No,' Ava said. 'I don't. How about I fax them to you later when you've left? When will that be, exactly?'

He slowly let her go, smiling as she rubbed the spot where he'd held her, as though trying to erase his touch.

'No need,' he said. 'I can tell by the clothes on your back you're obviously skint.'

'And you're insufferable,' Ava said.

'Nah,' Caleb said, 'I'm lovely. My mother told me so every day until I moved out. Heck, that's why I moved out.'

Damien's shoulders began to shake. He was enjoying this. Mostly because he knew way too much for Caleb's comfort. Caleb wanted very much to get his friend in a headlock until he cried mercy. Even then he might think long and hard before letting the pain come to an end.

Caleb was pretty sure Damien wouldn't be smiling if he knew while he'd been feeding cake to his bride, the two of them had been up to all kinds of no good upstairs. In fact if Damien knew the kinds of no good Caleb was yet contemplating perpetrating on his sister he might be the one in danger of gross pain.

He'd even dreamt of ways to teach her lessons, in great detail. Until his stupid alarm had woken him so that he could come here and ooh and aah over all the wedding gifts.

'Remind me never to get married,' he said beneath his breath.

This time Ava heard him loud and clear. 'Never get married. For the sake of the human race, please never get married.'

Before Caleb had the chance to come back with some pithy remark Chelsea came bounding inside with the puppy in her arms.

*Thank God,* Ava thought. The more people in the room to take her focus off Caleb, the better.

She had to admit he looked good today. If at all possible, even better than he had in his tuxedo the night before. Loose jeans clung to his narrow hips, a navy V-necked jumper with a red T-shirt underneath did very little to hide the hard planes beneath, and the lightweight pale grey blazer he wore over the top just dripped money. His hair was slightly more mussed and his stubble more grown in. He really was just about the most naturally gorgeous guy she'd ever known. If only he didn't know it.

He looked up and caught her staring. And he didn't look away. The air between them crackled and she was hit with a sense memory of his taste, his touch, and the ease with which she'd gone from seductress to putty in his hands.

She'd gone to him for validation. What she'd found was trouble.

Chelsea's dramatic sigh turned everyone to the kitchen door to find her shucking off her grass-covered shoes. Her cheeks were pink from exertion and delight. She jogged up to Damien and kissed him full on the mouth. He wrapped an arm about her waist and when she was about to pull away he tucked her in close and continued the kiss for a second or two longer. That was all. But it was enough for all of Chelsea's energy to leech out of her as she quite simply sank against him.

Ava leant her elbows on the kitchen bench and just watched them.

She'd never doubted her mother and father would be contented with one another their whole lives, and their relationship had fallen apart. The fact that it had slowly been rebuilt from the ashes didn't negate the dark years in between. She hoped against hope that her brother would have greater luck.

There was only one species she had ever found in her extensive studies on the subject that was absolutely monogamous. In the deepest sea, the tiny male anglerfish found the scent trail of a female, followed her, bit her and hung on. Their skins literally fused, their bodies grew together and they mated for life. She'd always thought it was in its own way terribly romantic.

Her brother gave his bride a kiss on the end of her nose and she beamed up at him. Ava hoped that it wouldn't take something as painful as the fusing of skins for them to last.

If two such substantial people couldn't make it, what hope would she ever have?

Ava couldn't help it. She casually tipped her head just enough so that she could glance at Caleb.

She needn't have bothered with the finessing. He wasn't hiding the fact that his eyes were all for her.

His left hand covered his mouth, his pointer finger ran slowly, hypnotically, across his bottom lip. He blinked. Slowly. And she knew without a doubt he was thinking about kissing her. And so much more.

She looked away before he could see how much she wanted to kiss him right back.

She felt him sink back against the bench, his elbow rested inches from hers. His warmth infused her as fast as if he'd set her sleeve on fire.

His little finger reached out and ran up and down the side of her hand. Her eyes fluttered closed. She'd never known such simple pleasure in her life. What she did know was that she'd been kidding herself thinking the night before might be some kind of cure-all. If anything she felt even more at sea than she had been before.

'Knock, knock.'

Ava jumped so high at the sudden loud voice from the terrace she pulled a muscle in her side. She moved away from Caleb, glancing at him briefly, but long enough to see he was grinning. Then with a hand pressing against her waist she turned to find a brunette with curls and an oversized handbag covered in flamingos standing in the doorway.

'Morning, sis,' Chelsea said, waving at the woman with her puppy's paw.

Damien turned out of his wife's embrace but still kept an arm about her waist. 'Has everyone eaten?'

Chelsea gave him the puppy, then raced to the fridge, but

she was in and out in half a second. 'Give me three minutes to make a couple of boiled eggs, then I'm all yours.'

'Ah-h-h, too late, Mrs Halliburton, that's what the vows and rings and guests and cake and DJ and stuff was all about last night.'

Chelsea slapped a hand to her head. 'Right. I keep forgetting.'

'Oh, how beloved you make me feel. Now we're all here we should get this show on the road. I for one can't wait to see how many Royal Doulton tea sets our nearest and dearest think two people need.'

He held an arm towards the double swing doors leading to the living room. Ralph and Rachel meandered on through. Chelsea's sister waited for Caleb and slung an arm through his elbow and began chatting to him as if they were long-lost friends.

Ava waited for him to send her a look, of explanation or grief, an inclusive smile or a glance that said he'd rather it were her arm through his elbow. But she got nothing.

Her head hurt. Her cheeks felt hot. Her hands felt cold. Her stomach felt tight. Her feet felt numb. She wondered if anyone would believe her if she begged off with a sudden case of the flu.

# CHAPTER SEVEN

'I'M SO glad you were able to make it,' Chelsea said.

Ava turned to find her sister-in-law at the stove with a saucepan full of enough water to boil eggs to feed the household twice over.

She opened her mouth to say so, then decided being a bossy boots wasn't the best way to start a relationship with her only sister-in-law. 'Oh, well, my pleasure.'

'It's all Damien talked about the last days leading up to the wedding. I don't think he would have had as good a time had you not been able to get away.'

'I don't know about that. From what I've seen he only has eyes for you.'

Chelsea let go an exaggerated sigh. 'Do you have any idea how nice that is?'

'What, me? Well, no. Not so much. Unfortunately.'

'Mmm,' Chelsea said. 'Are you quite sure?'

Without her meaning them to, Ava's eyes shot to the now still swing doors leading to the living room. There was a man behind those doors who she'd caught staring her way more often than not. But the only reason she knew that was because she hadn't been able to stop staring at him.

She glanced back at Chelsea, who was looking that way too, before her gaze swung back to Ava.

'Would you like an egg?' Chelsea asked, an all too knowing half-smile on her face.

'No. No, thanks. All filled up on stale pizza. A student's staple meal,' Ava said. And then after a moment of panic she added, 'Hard-boiled eggs will spin on a flat surface. Uncooked or soft-boiled eggs will not.'

'I did not know that.' She smiled, her soft brown eyes telling Ava what politeness would not. That she was there, a friend. Happy to talk if she needed it. And that Damien had obviously told her about the situation with Taylor.

But Ava had never had a sister. She'd never even had a really close girlfriend. She'd grown up with boys, then concentrated so hard on her studies through high school then had moved from subject to subject, course to course, college to college, boyfriend to boyfriend, country to country, ever since.

Maybe talking would have been a sensible problem-solving alternative to throwing herself at Caleb. But it was a tad late for all that.

She pointed a thumb towards the living room as she backed away. 'I'd better go in there. In case he's wondering where I am. Damien, I mean.'

Chelsea smiled and nodded.

Ava grabbed *Love in the Time of Cholera* off the kitchen bench and backed away.

Once in the lounge, Ava slid her book beside her and sat on the edge of the couch, tucking her feet beneath her meditation-style.

Caleb leant against the mantle laughing with Damien. When her brother realised Chelsea still hadn't joined them he patted Caleb on the arm and went to find her.

Caleb pushed away from the mantle and headed towards the lounge. She fully expected him to take the farthest point in the room so that he could have prime position from which to toss conversational grenades at her without fear of getting hit back, but instead he veered past the mammoth teak coffee table and sat on the long couch beside her.

She turned to glare at him instead, but he was watching some vague point in the distance with a small serene smile on his face. Eventually he turned to her and smiled as though he'd only just realised she was even there.

Was he serious? Barely two minutes earlier he'd been seducing her with little more than his little finger.

She gritted her teeth and motioned to the other end of the long couch with her chin.

His brow furrowed.

She motioned again, this time raising her eyebrows in the general direction of 'as far away as possible'.

He mouthed, Are you okay?

Rather than lose it at him, she looked away. Her mum was pulling up an oversized ottoman so as to be closest to the gifts piled in the corner of the room. Her dad took his place on his usual wing chair.

Caleb poked her in the leg.

She glowered at him.

He grinned and let his hand linger by her thigh. Half of her wanted him to leave it there, tantalising her, the other half wanted to snap it in two.

She wondered how on earth she could tell him to shove over without making a complete scene. But if she moved her chin again she feared she might dislocate something.

By the time that thought was thought it was too late. Chelsea's sister Kensey sat on Caleb's right and they were trapped. He moved closer to her on the pretence he was giving Kensey more room. Ava knew he was merely taking every opportunity possible to punish her.

Meaning she would have to spend the next hour drinking

in the faint scent of Safari aftershave Caleb had always worn. And feeling the shuffle of his jeans against hers every time he leaned forward to take a sip of his coffee.

'Didn't think you had it in you to drag yourself here so early, Caleb,' Kensey said, her voice bright and cheerful.

'Lovely to see you again, Mrs Hurley.'

'So you remembered I'm married this time?'

'How could I not? I have caffeine trickling into my system, the sun is shining and you're no longer wearing hot-pink taffeta. My brain is able to function better under these circumstances.'

Ava scoffed loudly. Then regretted it the second she felt Kensey lean forward. She fought against the urge to screw up her face and instead turned into the conversation.

'Hi there. I don't think we met yesterday…' Kensey began.

Ava reached across Caleb and held out her hand. 'I'm Ava, Damien's sister.'

When she leant back, Caleb's arm was resting along the back of the couch behind her. Even though she knew she'd end up with a terrible neck ache she leant forward just enough they weren't touching.

'I didn't think you could come,' Kensey said. 'Something about your uni professor keeping you strapped to your desk.'

This time it was Caleb's turn to scoff.

Kensey smiled, then frowned. 'I feel like I keep stepping into conversational minefields without knowing it.'

'Not at all,' Ava insisted as she leant back suddenly, trapping Caleb's wandering hand between her shoulder blades and the couch. His sharp intake of breath was most satisfying.

And then he, oh, so slowly, began manipulating his hand until it flipped and tucked along the back of her neck, beneath her hair. And then he began to stroke, soft, leisurely, heavenly strokes.

'This guy ever conveniently forget you were married too?' Kensey asked.

'Ah, no,' Ava said, her voice croaky. She cleared her throat. 'Not married.'

'But he must have hit on you, right? He's so bad, and you're an utter doll. Why didn't Chelsea tell me you were such a doll?'

'Maybe she doesn't think I'm a doll.'

'How could she not?' Caleb interjected, but was promptly ignored by both women. Or ignored by Ava as much as he could be while he had his fingers curled deliciously hard within her hair.

'I wonder if he ever hit on Chelsea?' Kensey said, eyes bright at the thought. 'She never said, but that doesn't mean it didn't happen. Far too discreet, my sister.'

'Wouldn't surprise me,' Ava said, getting into the swing of things, and trying her best to disregard the warmth tingling down her back and making her feel as if she were floating off the couch. 'He always was the brazen type.'

'If I sat back with a napkin over my eyes and had a little nap you guys could just carry on without me, I take it,' Caleb said.

'Gladly,' Kensey and Ava said at the same time.

Kensey grinned. While Ava bit her bottom lip to stop from groaning when Caleb started massaging her neck.

'There's too many women in this family now, Ralph,' Caleb called loudly across to Ava's dad.

He looked up from his newspaper with a slightly bewildered expression.

Caleb poked his spare thumb at each of the brunettes bookending him and said, 'Suddenly the women in this family outnumber us. When did that happen?'

'Complain about it all you like, Caleb, my boy, but I'm afraid I won't be joining the naysayers. The more women the better has long since been my motto.'

Caleb's mouth turned down and he nodded as his gaze flittered briefly to Kensey. Then he turned to look Ava dead in the eye. 'Good point, Ralph. What was I thinking?'

Ava breathed deep through her nose and sniffed in a compelling waft of that drinkable aftershave. Her heart rate sped to a gallop as his hot hazel gaze pinned her to the back of the chair. If he wasn't reliving every moment in her arms the night before then she was more clueless than even she imagined she was.

'Oh, yeah,' he said, staring at her far longer than was in any way civilised. 'I remember what I was thinking. They may smell great and be pretty to look at, but they did have to steal one of our ribs to get here.'

Her father's laughter echoed across the room. That sound was the only thing that could have dragged Ava's eyes from Caleb's gaze. Her dad's dark blue eyes were twinkling. Ava felt a smile building inside her seeing her father content. It had been so long…

The simple lazy hazy days of her childhood, when her dad taught her how to ride a bike along the path by the golf course. When they and the Gilchrists had spent every Melbourne winter water-skiing in Belize and every Melbourne summer snow skiing in Aspen. Her life had been simple then. Safe. Happy. Until the day the fighting had started and everything she'd ever known had begun to crumble at her young feet.

She blinked and realised her father was looking at her, a small crease between his bright blue eyes.

Terrified of doing or saying something that would wipe that smile off his face, Ava did that thing people did when caught staring: she shifted her gaze an inch to the left, then slowly let it trail away.

'Get more than one man in a room and they all revert back to childhood,' Kensey said. 'I'd know, I have four. Kids, not men. So do you have kids, Ava?'

'Ah, no.'

'A fella?'

Caleb snorted loud enough that Ava jumped and his fingers tangled in her hair, tugged, and hurt. Her eyes watered, but she couldn't do anything about it because then everyone would know what he'd been doing to her all along.

Kensey's smile merely grew wider. 'You two are all about the in jokes, I see. Would you prefer I sit somewhere else?'

Ava said, 'I'd prefer he sit somewhere else.'

'Ooh,' Kensey said, eyes darting from one to the other. 'It's like that, is it?'

'It's not like anything. We're not like anything,' Ava shot back, quickly lifting her hair from the back of her neck and sitting forward, the second Caleb dropped his guard.

Nevertheless Kensey tapped the side of her nose as though she knew better.

'So where is your husband this fine morning?' Caleb asked, casually pulling his hand back to rest beside him on the couch.

Ava could have kissed him for getting her off the hook. Well, not kissed him. Punched his shoulder in camaraderie. Shaken his hand…

'Babysitting,' Kensey said. 'His first day alone with our newborn and the other three. If I don't go home to the lot of them hyped up on sugar then I'll eat my foot. So, Caleb, no kids for you either?'

'Not that he knows of,' Ava muttered.

Caleb slapped his hand down on her thigh. It stung and set her blood racing so fast through her veins she only hoped her face didn't turn bright pink.

'How could I,' Caleb asked, 'when the woman of my dreams won't do me the honour of incubating them for me? Don't you think our genes would make one beautiful baby? Ava? Honey bunny?''

She gritted her teeth to stop from groaning, then said, 'Keep your hands off my genes, Caleb Gilchrist.'

'Yeah,' he said, pulling his hand away and wiping it on his own jeans. 'I guess it would be hard for us to raise a family living on a friend's floor and eating stale pizza. I hereby withdraw my offer to father your children. So stop asking me.'

Ava lifted her leg to her chest, crossed her arms over it, getting as far away from the guy as possible, and said, 'Oh, shut up.'

'Ava,' her father chastised from his chair.

'He started it.'

'She made me,' Caleb shot right on back.

'Get a room,' Kensey added with a grin, and that shut the both of them up more than any other three words could have.

'Play nice, you two,' Damien said as he and Chelsea entered the room, arms around one another, bodies tucked tight, faces lit by the brightest smiles two people could have.

Ava somehow managed to rein herself in before she gave in to the desperate desire to poke her tongue out at her big brother. Mostly because she was certain Caleb would use it as a way to make her feel even more warm and fidgety than she already did.

An hour later only a tenth of the presents had been opened and they had all had too much coffee, too much left-over wedding cake and were all feeling a tad silly.

Kensey had been put in charge of folding the wrapping paper. Ava had no idea why as her mother would never deign to reuse any such thing. But it also meant that she and Caleb now had the couch to themselves.

The chair beneath Ava's bottom lifted as Caleb leaned towards her. He came so close she would have leant away if not for the high arm of the chair digging into her ribs. So instead she was left looking deep into a pair of cheeky hazel eyes that were flashing with the thrill of adventure.

Adventure she was certain by that stage had everything to do with her and the couch.

'Caleb…' she warned under her breath.

He reached over her and threw a couple of gift cards he'd been pretending to be interested in into the pile in her lap. 'I'm going stir crazy here.'

'Well, tough. You're the best man—this is your duty.'

'Who are you to talk of duty, Ms Prodigal Daughter?'

She shot him her dirtiest look complete with curled lip. Caleb reached up, put a finger over her mouth to wipe the look away. She grabbed his hand, held it tight in her lap then quickly looked out over the crowd to make sure nobody noticed. Thankfully everyone was watching Chelsea hold up a crystal bowl to the light, much more excited about the fact that her puppy was chasing the rainbow prisms the bowl was creating on the walls than the extravagant label dangling noticeably off the side.

Ava laughed despite herself and felt a little happy thrill shoot down her centre that her brother had found himself such a truly down-to-earth bride. If Chelsea didn't bring the Halliburton household down a peg or two nobody could.

A sudden tickle of hair against her neck had her whipping her attention back to Caleb, who was brushing her hair from her shoulder.

'Are you trying to drive me crazy?'

'Not at all. You had a…thing on your neck. I was just brushing it off.'

He continued staring at the point where her neck met her shoulder and the happy thrill she'd felt for Damien had nothing on the flash of energy that poured through her every vein at the look in Caleb's eyes.

'A thing?' she repeated, her voice giveaway deep.

His gaze slowly meandered up her neck to her face and she felt every centimetre his gaze touched heat from the inside out.

When his eyes met hers they were dark. Shadowed. 'Can we please—?'

'I like the look of this one,' Chelsea called out as she picked up a foot long silver box and shook it.

Caleb breathed out hard through his nose and his frustration seeped into Ava until she had to wiggle her toes to lose some of the excess energy coursing through her.

'Ooh, what if it's those new Versace salad servers?' Rachel said, eyes bright.

'No, I recognise the paper,' Kensey said. 'I think it's something from that fancy candle place at Chadstone.'

By this stage even Ralph had put down his newspaper and was staring at the box as though he could see through it. 'I'm thinking…sterling silver scroll container in which to put your wedding certificate.'

Everyone in the room oohed at Ralph's inspired guess. He pinked a bit about the ears. 'My mother gave Rachel and me one for our wedding,' he explained.

'How much will you pay me to shout out the obvious?' Caleb murmured into her ear. 'The looks on your parents' faces would be a treat.'

She laughed through her nose. It *was* just the right shape for it to have come from an adult supply shop. 'Please, this morning has been the most pleasant time I've spent with my family as long as I can remember. Don't ruin it by throwing a vibrator into the mix.'

'Possible vibrator,' he said, his voice a mite louder.

She turned to glare at him to find he was close enough she could make out every speck of stubble on his fabulous jaw. She swallowed as circumspectly as possible before saying, 'I'll give you five bucks not to say it and ten if you'll keep your mouth shut for the rest of the day.'

He smiled so wide she was privy to every perfect tooth, and

was forced to remember just what he could do with them when given half a chance. She needed to swallow again.

'Ten, eh?' he said. 'Tempting. But I do think the offer needs a little sweetening.'

She looked back into his eyes, hoping for reprieve, but instead found them brimming with so much unsuppressed hunger her throat squeezed shut. She managed to choke out, 'Pretty please with sugar on top?'

'Mmm.' His deep voice rumbled down her spine. 'Not exactly the kind of sweetening I had in mind.'

'What goes on in your mind is a mystery to all mankind.'

She glanced back to the proceedings, lest he see in her eyes how much he was getting to her and how much she was enjoying just being herself. With him. It was so easy.

'Then how about a hint?' he offered.

'Ah, not necessary.' The thought of Caleb spelling out in any kind of detail that which he thought tempting and sweet that she could supply made her knees itch. 'I've decided to rescind the offer altogether.'

'Caleb,' Chelsea called out, her hand ready to tear the paper, 'what do you think it is?'

He opened his mouth, took in a deep breath.

'Don't.' Ava clamped down on his hand, which she realised she still held in her lap.

He closed his fingers over hers before she could let him go, thought for a few seconds, then said, 'I'm going with fridge freezer. No ice-maker included, unfortunately. Cheap-skates.'

Everyone laughed appreciatively.

Ava let go of the breath she'd been holding. And at the same time gave up and let go of her resolution to appear unaffected. Being affected felt too good. Indulging couldn't hurt. She turned her hand until it fitted snug in his, their fingers intertwined.

'You owe me,' he rumbled.

Ava decided it best not to ask how much.

Chelsea tore open the package and inside was a marble statuette of a naked woman writhing around a tree trunk.

Kensey peeled the card from the discarded wrapping. She opened it and read, 'From Aunt Gladys.'

Everyone nodded in understanding. Everyone bar Ava, who was busily biting her lip as the back of Caleb's hand ran up and down her zipper.

'Next!' Damien said from his position on the far couch where he had a good view of his wife having too much fun opening all the presents.

Ava shifted position, lest Caleb go a centimetre further. Their hands fell apart. But at some stage she and Caleb had come to be sitting so close she was all but leaning against him. If this didn't end and soon she was going to end up sitting on his lap and there'd be no hiding their games from her family then.

'Open the little one,' Ava said, pointing to a small black box. 'It's from me.'

Chelsea picked it up, held it to her ear and shook it.

'It's a matchbox collection,' Caleb muttered near her ear.

She waved a hand at him to shoosh him as she watched Chelsea unpick the sticky tape.

'No? Then it's a pack of cards.'

'Will you keep it down, please?'

'Just tell me now if you made it yourself so I don't accidentally say something stupid when all is revealed.'

'There's nothing I could say to stop you.'

'The first step is admitting it,' he whispered, and she had to close her eyes to stop from screaming, 'though, to put you out of your misery, my final guess is…matching harmonicas.'

All shooshing from Ava ceased as she turned to glare at Caleb.

There came a final ripping of paper and a slide of cardboard, then Chelsea's bewildered voice said, 'It's a pair of harmonicas.'

'Get out of here!' Damien said, leaping out of his chair and grabbing them out of her hands to inspect them.

But Ava was staring at Caleb, gob smacked. And his gob seemed smacked right back.

'You cannot be serious,' he said.

At the same time she said, 'How did you possibly know?'

She felt the rumble of his laughter shake against her side. She frowned. 'Don't you dare laugh at me, Caleb Gilchrist. You know how much I hate it.'

'Well, then, lucky for both of us I'm not laughing at you, I'm laughing near you. A harmonica? Twice over. Are they meant to serenade one another on their honeymoon?'

'The harmonica is the world's best-selling instrument. And look!'

She pointed at her brother, who was already playing with it. And he was holding Chelsea's to her mouth and she was laughing at the horrible cacophony of sounds their duet produced.

'And look,' she whispered, placing a soft hand on Caleb's knee and angling her chin towards her father who was now on the edge of his seat.

'Well, I'll be,' Ralph said, watching his son with delight written across his face. 'A mouth harp. I used to have one of those darned things years ago. Was a fine player in my day. I wonder what happened to it.'

Ava knew.

She and Damien had loved it when their dad used to bring it out late at night and played beautiful sad songs by the firelight. But it had been swept away, out of sight, out of mind, during the dark years of The Divorce, just as she had been.

Damien looked her way with a slight gleam to his eyes. He held her gift up in salute. She felt her throat catch.

'What do you know?' Caleb said.

'A heck of a lot more than you've given me credit for, my friend,' Ava said as she crossed her arms and sank back into the couch, vindicated. And with a lightness about her that she hadn't felt in days. Weeks. Months. Years. As if the world around her was finally beginning to make sense again.

'Come on, kids,' Rachel said when the production line had ground to a halt for too long. 'Next gift, please.'

The next box Chelsea chose was a similar shape to the naked lady statue, only bigger and wrapped in flesh-coloured paper.

Ava tipped her face into her open palm. She felt Caleb shaking with laughter beside her.

# CHAPTER EIGHT

SOME time after midday Caleb stood, stretched his arms over his head and twisted his back to loosen up while the others filtered from the room. 'I've been sitting in that damn couch so long I'm afraid my backside shape will never be the same again.'

Kensey tilted her head to have a look. 'Looks fine to me.'

Caleb smiled and looked to Ava, who was staring hard at his backside with a small frown on her face. 'Care to give your opinion?'

She held her book to her chest and blinked. 'I'm not checking out your backside and I'm certainly not grading you on it.'

He let his arms drop. 'You don't need to. I'm onto you.'

With that he walked back into the kitchen, knowing she couldn't help but follow.

'You're onto me how?' she asked as she jogged up behind him.

'You couldn't keep your eyes off me in there.'

'Excuse me! My eyes were all for the lovely shiny presents.'

'Of course they were,' he said as he mingled with her family.

'You're one to talk,' she said, having to get really close so her voice wouldn't carry. 'You couldn't keep your hands off me.'

'You're right,' he said. 'I couldn't. In fact I'm struggling not to touch you right now.'

She snapped her mouth shut and looked like a firecracker ready to pop. Caleb had every intention of being there when she went off.

He grabbed a mini-focaccia from the batch the Halliburtons' cook had whipped up, popped it in his mouth and pretended to pay attention to Damien and Chelsea's rundown on their honeymoon plans.

All the while he was thinking of how he could get Ava alone. And as far as he could tell Ava wasn't taking the hint.

She always had been book smart far more than street smart. Which was a hazard in itself. Caleb found that there was something immeasurably seductive about a clever woman. The quick wit, the utter absorption in whatever held her fancy, a whole world going on behind those sexy glasses.

It was time to get to the point.

'Do you want to get out of here?' he murmured.

The flare in her eyes gave her away before she said, 'I'm not sure I can.'

She glanced over to her parents, who were starting to head off into their separate zones. Her mother was limbering up and her father had found yet another newspaper to read. 'I probably should stay and—'

'Ava, honey,' Rachel called out, unaware as always of anything else going on around her, 'stand up straight or your boobs will hit your navel before you're forty.'

Caleb lost it. He laughed so loud even Rachel stopped jogging on the spot and stared at him.

When he'd collected himself he smiled at Ava and lifted an eyebrow.

'Get me out of here,' she begged.

'Done. Damo,' he said, 'there's nothing more you need us for imminently?'

Damien dragged his eyes away from his bride to stare through Caleb as his words infiltrated. 'Ah, no. Not imminently.'

'Excellent. Rachel, you don't mind me stealing your precious daughter away, do you?'

Rachel flapped a hand at him. 'Not in the least. Go, go.'

'Great.'

Caleb grabbed Ava's hand and headed to the terrace. He caught Damien's eye on the way out and what he saw in his best friend's eye wasn't comforting. It wasn't even all that friendly. But he'd deal with that later.

'Later, Ralph,' Caleb said as they zoomed past.

Ralph lifted his head, stared at their joined hands and frowned. 'Caleb,' Ralph said, nodding slightly. 'Ava. Will we see you tonight?'

Her hand clenched in his and Caleb clenched back. And just like that she relaxed.

'Of course, Dad. Maybe we can get you to play a tune or two on Damien's harmonica.'

Caleb heard the catch in her voice and he pulled her a tad closer. She sank against him as though she needed the support in that moment. And he let her. No matter how good it felt and how much he'd regret allowing her vulnerability to get to him by the time the two of them were away from this place and alone together.

Ralph nodded again and the frown cleared up. 'Perhaps,' he said, then went back to his paper.

Caleb then pulled her down the stairs until he felt her pulling back.

'What's the hurry?' she asked.

'No hurry.'

'Good, because I don't have my purse, or keys to the house or anything.'

'You won't need them where we're going. Besides, you

still have that book clutched tight in your hand—what else have you ever needed?'

She grinned. 'Fair point. So where are we going exactly?'

'You'll see.'

In fact he thought he'd better come up with somewhere fast or else they'd be driving around in circles with that warm body and warm scent sending him further and further around the bend.

They reached the front of the house, complete with its two-storey columns, twin chimneys and wide sprawling white brick and charcoal shingle facing it looked like something the Kennedys would feel right at home in.

'Tell me that's not your car,' Ava said, tugging against his hand as they neared the low-slung, curvaceous, canary-yellow sports number parked at an askew angle on the white gravel drive.

'Ava, meet my favourite blonde. This is Mae West,' he said as he opened the door and swept an arm towards the cream leather passenger seat.

Her expression was mightily unimpressed, with him or the car. He only laughed. There weren't that many women in the world who'd not swoon over such ridiculously expensive an example of motor engineering while they dreamed of diamonds and cruises and fabric samples for the summer house.

But not Ava. She tucked herself into the seat as though she was trying to touch as little of the surrounding luxury as possible.

'You're a snob, you know that?' he said.

'Hey—'

He shut the door on her wounded expression.

He didn't have time to argue. He'd just spent the past four hours indulging in the longest concentrated foreplay of his young life. He needed her away from this place. It messed with her head and he wanted her thinking to be crystal-clear.

He opened the driver's side door, slid into spot and before she'd even got a word out said, 'Put on your seat belt.'

'I was. I am.'

'Good. It's just that with the way you've been all over me today I don't trust you not to get a sudden desire to jump me while we're driving.'

He turned the key, revved the noisy engine and he shot down the driveway and out onto Stonnington Drive. And anything she might have said in response was lost within the sound of the engine.

Hundred-year-old oak trees on either side of the road shaded the wide old street, lending the already elegant large houses a peaceful, austere quality. Though very few of the people living behind the façades were peaceful or austere. Most of them were stark raving mad.

But Caleb wouldn't begrudge a one of them a dime. They'd all made his childhood an interesting one to say the very least.

Ava made a small sigh beside him. He glanced sideways to find her looking out the window. Twelve-foot fences, ostentatious security gates and overly manicured brush-box hedges flickered over her reflection. But they couldn't hide her frown.

He slid into a higher gear and picked up speed. He felt as if he was losing ground. While her mere proximity still had him thrumming from head to toe.

There was no way that would all come to nothing. He had every intention of finishing what they'd started the day before. Especially after the way she had trembled at his every touch, and her skin had pinked every time they'd made eye contact.

His car growled at him as he took the corner a tad too fast.

Once they were off Stonnington Drive she seemed to come to as if from a trance. Her shoulders relaxed against the back of the seat and her head lolled sideways to face him.

That face. Who knew that after all these years that face could still drive him crazy? The speed limit soon became more of a guide than a rule.

'I'm not a snob,' she said.

And he laughed, enjoying feeling crazy a heck of a lot. 'Welcome back.'

Her mouth twisted. 'Sorry. Did I zone out mid-conversation?'

'Something like that.'

'Bad habit.'

Caleb took another sharp left, poor Mae West moaned from his rough handling. But now he knew where he was going he wanted to get there fast.

'Any chance you're going to fill me in on where you're taking me?' Ava asked when they swerved down a long driveway lined by massive pine trees.

'Weren't you the one who told me people don't like being asked too many obnoxious questions?' he said.

She couldn't hide her smile. 'That sure doesn't sound like me. Though if you answer my question there will be no more need for questions.'

He slowed the car to a crawl, the deep rumble of the engine rocking them from beneath. 'I can turn around and take you back home to the Halliburton Horror Mansion, or you can decide that where you really want to be more than anywhere else right now is where I have every intention of taking you.'

She stared at him for several long moments without blinking. The car began to feel hot as he waited for her response.

'Fine,' she said, the word shooting from her lips as though it had to fight its way through every last bit of common sense.

But Caleb wasn't looking for common sense. He was looking for submission. Now he had it. He pushed the accelerator to the floor.

Caleb slid his car into the private garage at the Stonnington Golf Links he spent a yearly fortune on so that his precious Mae was safe from little presents from the sky whenever he played there.

'You have to be kidding me,' Ava said when sensor lights flickered on as they drove in, showing off the wood-panelled walls and carpeted floor.

She spun on her seat, peering through the small back window as the garage door closed slowly behind them.

Caleb cut the engine.

Without the guttural roar the world around them suddenly fell quiet.

Ava turned back to face him, her eyes wide, dark, her breaths coming harder as she realised that they were well and truly alone for the first time since he'd left her the night before.

And that he'd planned it that way.

Her throat worked as she swallowed hard. But she didn't look away.

'Hi,' he said.

Her answering smile was fragile. 'Hi.'

He reached out and tucked a wave behind her ear. He left his hand around her neck, his thumb tracing the side of her throat.

'I was thinking we could go see if that spot by the fifth hole you used to like so much was still there.'

'How do you know about my spot by the fifth hole?'

'Every time I played as a kid you'd be there. Pretending to read.'

She nodded, then realised what he'd intimated. 'Hey!'

He slid his hand around the back of her neck and she melted against his touch. He hadn't imagined her response to him the night before. Thank the Lord.

'It was a very good spot for reading and reading only,' she said.

He'd always thought it a good spot for spying on him, but the last thing he wanted was to break the glorious sexual tension weaving its way around them by suggesting such a thing.

Ridiculous as it would seem at any other time, right then he desperately wished he owned a family sedan. One with nice big front seats that bent back all the way. Mae West's rather cramped interior was not conducive to what was about to happen.

He slid his hand away, only able to as he knew he'd be touching her again soon. He alighted from the car and went around to her side to open her door for her. She held out a hand, he took it and lifted her out.

They stood chest to chest.

He could feel the thunderous beat of her heart. It more than matched his own.

He'd held off long enough. He practically felt like some kind of saint for lasting as long as he had.

'Oh, to hell with it,' he said, wrapping a hand behind her neck and dragging her into his arms and kissing her.

Fireworks exploded behind Ava's eyes as she closed them tight and kissed Caleb right on back. Hard, fast, no holds barred.

Until that moment she had no idea how much she'd been craving this. Craving him. His touch, his taste. How little the night before had done to assuage the tension brimming between them.

That had been about a purely selfish, desperate need to clear her head, by using a man she knew could do just that.

As he pressed her back against the car, the hot metal no match for the heat sluicing between them, she didn't want to analyse what *this* was all about. She just wanted to live it. No motives, no consequences, just feelings and experience and pleasure.

She shut down the voices in her head and wrapped her arms around him, pressing herself along his length and sinking into his kiss as if it were the only way she could hope to ever breathe fully again.

He let her go to rid himself of his jacket, but their lips didn't part. The kiss was too good to forfeit. She unzipped her own tracksuit top and ripped it off her arms, letting it land in a heap at her feet. Hell, the floor in this garage was likely cleaner than the one in her dorm.

Then his hands were beneath her T-shirt, sliding over her skin. So warm. No, so *hot*. Knowing just where and how to touch her to make her melt. She shuddered deliciously.

All too soon, feeling as if she was about to pass out from the intensity of it all, she pulled away. Lay a hand on his chest. Took several deep breaths.

Caleb merely took it as an opportunity to rid her of her T-shirt, sliding it up her torso and over her head.

Memories of their first time came swarming back to her, but were soon crowded out by the current of sensation sweeping over her in the here and now.

Caleb's teeth at her neck, his hands cupping her bottom, his big, masculine body hard against her.

This had none of the innocence, none of the gentle finesse of anything they'd experienced together before. They were both grown-ups now. Both more well versed in desire. And both more desperate to simply have one another to bother with romance.

'You smell better than anyone I've ever known,' she said, sinking her face into his neck.

He brushed her hair aside and smiled against her cheek. 'I bet I do.'

She turned her head to give him better access. 'Though that could be because my sense of smell has been permanently damaged from too many years spent living in student accommodation.'

He moved to her ear lobe, sucking it into his mouth, before blowing soft, hot air across it. She arched against him.

'That'll teach you to sass me, Doc,' he said.

She slowly wrapped her leg around his calf and ran her hands through the back of his hair. God, she'd always loved his hair. The adorable curl, the preppy colour. It was beautifully coarse beneath her fingers.

He looked deep into her eyes.

'Is that all it took to get you to finally up your game? Sass,' she said, her voice as husky as all get out. 'Noted.'

His smile became a grin. A knowing, devilish grin that made her stomach clench in a mix of jitters and intense anticipation.

He slowed, brushed her hair from both shoulders. Slid a bra strap down one arm. Released her left breast to the open air. Cupped it with his hand. All the while watching her eyes cloud with the bliss of it all.

'You done sassing me?' he asked.

She nodded. Yes, yes, yes! Whatever it would take for him to stop the sweet torture.

As though she'd said the words aloud he ran his hand down her chest, circling her nipple, stroking her sensitive waist, pressing into her hip bone, and tugging open the top button of her jeans.

The sound of her zip split the air, his fingers slid beneath her panties and before she even had the chance to prepare herself for his touch he was working his magic.

She clung to him, her fingers curling into his sweater as the world around her slipped away and she felt every single sensation bombarding her.

Caleb's slow steady breaths tickled her hair. The robust curve of him clenched beneath the knee she had curled about his leg. And he stroked her until every feeling inside her, every sensation outside her collided into a small hot ball of pleasure that only built and built and built to such a crescendo she thought she might implode.

Just as she made to cry out Caleb kissed the sound away, taking her breath, her thoughts, her words, her release into him.

As she came down she realised the fingers clinging to his sweater hurt from hanging on so tight. She uncurled them just enough to let the blood back into her hands.

Then gathered her strength and looked up into his eyes. They were dark as night yet brilliant with desire. She could feel how great his strain from holding back.

She felt utterly powerful and terribly weak all at once.

She slowly pulled him towards her, and kissed him long and slow and deep.

And soon she was lost to his longing, his expertise, his burning heat all over again.

He lifted her so that her legs wrapped around him. Her eyes locked with his as he walked her to the front of the car. Then sat her upon the still-hot bonnet.

'Hot, hot!' she cried out.

'Tell me about it,' he murmured, and the car had nothing on the temperature of her skin.

'I meant the car,' she managed to breathe out. 'It's scorching.'

He frowned. Whipped his T-shirt and sweater over his head in that sexy back to front way men had of doing so. Silly the way that small move made Ava's already weak knees begin to quake.

He lay them on the hood, slid his hands beneath her backside, lifted her, then set her back upon his clothes.

'Better?'

She smiled, running hands over the tight hard muscles of his bare arms. 'My hero,' she purred.

His neck pinked. 'Don't go getting any ideas, Ava. I'm no gentleman.'

'Lucky me,' she said, before she dragged him down with her.

Caleb showed no mercy, touching, stroking, kissing, caressing every erogenous zone she had, plus a few she was sure only worked under his ministrations. And just as she began to peak all over again Caleb shucked off his shoes and jeans, tugged hers off with such dexterity and speed she found herself laughing from the craziness of it all.

When he fished a condom from his pocket, and fitted it, her laughter dried up in her throat. He poised his large form over her and looked into her eyes, letting her know that this was truly the point of no return.

As if she hadn't already leapt over that cliff.

He slid inside her, filling her so deeply her eyes closed and she held on for dear life as he took her places she hadn't even imagined she could go.

Never in her life had she felt as free. As liberated. As much all woman. To get there it had taken someone who was truly free, truly liberated, and all man.

And as together they moved and clung they fell apart in one another's arms.

The roar in Ava's head wafted away and slowly everything went quiet again. Her body took longer to come back to earth.

The room felt like a sauna. Her skin was drenched in sweat. Tendrils of her hair clung to her cheeks. She licked her lips to find they tasted of salt.

'Whoa,' Caleb finally said, his voice sounding as if he'd swallowed sandpaper.

'That's the word I've been looking for,' she said back.

He slowly lifted her upright, of which she was glad. Her equilibrium was not what it used to be. He slid his arms from around her, leaving her be, sitting atop the bonnet of the luxury car like some creature at an auto show. Funny, it was so outside her everyday existence it only made her feel even sexier.

'Pleased in the end that I brought you here?' he asked, standing before her butt naked and not in the least embarrassed about it, though why he should be she had no idea. All those tight, hard, youthful, male planes.

'Ecstatic,' she said, crossing her legs, her arms, anything she could to cover up as the cool fluorescent light flickering in the metal ceiling above did its best to illuminate everything in its path.

'Mmm,' he said, taking her hand and leading her off the car to where their clothes were scattered on the plush carpet. 'Next time you'll not argue and simply trust that I know best.'

'Next time?'

All she got for her sass that time was a slow, sexy smile.

And this time, rather than turning their backs and trying to forget what they'd done, they helped one another get dressed.

Caleb held out her jeans for her to step into. She bit her lip to stop from laughing as he nibbled at her hip bone.

Her eyes roved over his athletic chest as she took her time turning his inside-out T-shirt and sweater back the right way around for him.

And every time she slid her bra strap over her shoulder, he casually slid it back down again.

'Caleb,' she warned.

'Ava,' he said with a glint in his eye that made her completely satiated body begin to buzz with expectation again.

When she was again fully dressed he gave her one last tidy, straightening her top, zipping her jeans, wiping her damp hair back off her face with two sure hands. His eyes roved over her, making sure she looked put together, then he gave her a confident nod.

If the sex had been explosive, the aftermath was just about the most tender experience of her life.

At first she couldn't find the words to tell him so. And by the time she could she'd decided those intimacies were things best left unsaid.

It had been sex. Pure and simple. There was no mistake bigger than believing with Caleb it could ever mean more.

'So how about we head down to the fifth tee?' Caleb asked.

She flattened her palms over his sweater, ironing out the creases she'd put there. 'That's why you brought me here, right?'

He tucked her hand in his, pressed a button to open the garage door and said, 'Think that if you must.'

Ava blinked against the sunshine, hoping it would allow her a little time to bask in the aftermath before its bright restorative light brought everything back to real life.

# CHAPTER NINE

FIFTEEN minutes later Caleb and Ava lay beneath a cloud of drooping willow leaves in a small thicket of trees on the edge of the fifth hole of the Stonnington Golf Links.

Caleb used his jacket as a cushion and her head rested on his thighs. Her sneakers and his rested in a haphazard pile at the base of a tree. And she felt as if the afterglow would last for ever.

She glanced sideways to find him leaning back on his forearms. A large round diving watch gleamed expensively at the end of a well-sculpted, tanned arm. His dark jeans wrapped around his thighs as though his muscles were straining to be free. A long piece of grass twirled between his teeth.

Her insides did that awful twisting thing they'd been doing all weekend. Ten years studying at the hardest schools in the world and her constitution had been fine. One weekend back on Stonnington Drive and she was developing an ulcer.

In front of them the perfect green rolled away from them towards a lake filled with waving rushes and brown wood ducks. While behind them and down a deep gully was a meandering creek which cut through her parents' backyard. 'You couldn't have taken me further away, by any chance?' she asked.

After a lazy pause he said, 'Now that's not what you came back to Melbourne for, was it?'

She grimaced. He was right.

He'd been spot on earlier too. She had been able to secretly, or not so secretly as it turned out, watch Caleb and his father during their weekly game from this vantage point. Even as a teenager he'd fitted in as though he'd been genetically engineered for the lifestyle they'd been born into.

With his boyish curls and his neat white teeth. His long, lanky, lackadaisical stride. His utter cool in the face of anything life threw at him. His ace tennis serve, his perfect golf swing, the packs of girls who'd followed him around like bees to pollen.

Yet the spark of brilliance he'd always carried with him had nothing to do with advantage or privilege. It was deeper than that. He had the exceptional kind of innate magnetism that meant a regular girl like her found herself naked atop a sports car.

Caleb breathed long and hard through his nose and the muscles of his chest pressed against the fabric of his T-shirt. The boy was all grown up. And didn't she now know just how?

A fly buzzed by her nose. She swatted it away, angry at it for spoiling the decadent idyll she was thoroughly enjoying. But it only came back.

*Buzz buzz buzz. This can't last.*

The last of her happy haze wore off as life rudely intruded. But it was for the best. She only had a couple of days before she was due back at school and if anything in her life was ever going to be different, if she was ever going to stop repeating the same mistakes over and over again, she had to begin with a clean slate. With her parents. With this place. With this man. And that didn't just mean exorcising lingering feelings she had for him.

She picked up a leaf from the ground and began peeling it apart. 'Do you remember the last time we played golf here?'

Caleb's eyes narrowed, but he kept his gaze on whatever he was staring at in the distance. 'You mean the only time. When you lost every one of the dozen balls you started out with. And the golf pro suggested perhaps you have lessons. Elsewhere.'

'Yeah, that time. I thought I was showing some potential.' She sat up, leant back on her hands so that she looked down into his untroubled face and chose her next words carefully. 'If I hadn't have left I may have become some kind of golfer.'

He rolled onto one elbow, pulled the grass from his mouth, flicked it away and looked into her eyes. 'Well, then, I guess you should never have left.'

She blinked down at him. The guy was just too cluey. She should have remembered that. She might well have duxed every school she'd ever attended, but Caleb had always managed to make her feel as if she was playing catch up.

'I had to leave,' she said, resolutely sticking to her train of thought. 'My life here wasn't healthy.'

'I can't imagine a healthier life to be had.'

'You think? I found out about the birds and the bees from Caroline Vance out the back of the Science lab in third grade. She'd given Jamie Crowson her lunch money to show us what he had down the front of his shorts.'

Caleb's laughter echoed so loudly in their little grove it created waves of pleasure over her skin.

'It's not funny!' she said. 'I close my eyes and I can still see his Spiderman underpants.'

Caleb's laughter only grew.

Ava sank her face into her open palms and tried to think of a happy place. But she realised that sitting beneath this tree, next to this guy, his laughter reverberating dizzily in the back of her head, was about the happiest she'd been in some time.

'I can't believe I felt I might now be able to share a torturous childhood moment with you.'

'What, now that I've had you naked against the bonnet of a Lamborghini suddenly you see me as your Dear Diary? How nice.'

'No,' she said, putting the backs of her hands against her hot cheeks. 'I meant now that you're supposedly all grown up. But you haven't changed.'

'You have.' He glanced her way before finding his naked toes suddenly fascinating. 'As to your predicament, true, your parents can be a pain in the proverbial, but you can't possibly tell me you didn't have everything to stay for.'

*Everything to stay for…*

The only thing she'd wanted to stay for had been him. Choosing between the slight possibility of him and the reality of Harvard had been ridiculously difficult. In the end her own indecisiveness had been the clincher.

'I did not want to become my mother,' she said.

His eyes narrowed. 'What on earth—?'

'Playing tennis three times a week but never finding time to do kinder duty at my kids' schools. Redecorating the kitchen every two years because I have nothing else to do. Drinking martinis at nine in the morning.'

'Bloody Marys.'

'Excuse me?'

'She's moved on to Bloody Marys. On a health kick, don't you know.'

She shook her head. 'I hate tomato juice so that only shows how much I would have regretted that life. You know I love her. I do. She's so stunningly oblivious one can't help but love my mother. But the last thing I ever want to become is her.'

'You couldn't become Rachel Halliburton if you dyed your hair blonde and wore a tennis skirt twenty-four-seven.'

'Who says? I love the house I grew up in. I loved hanging out with the kids on the block. With you.' She glanced his way to find he was staring out into the distance again. 'I loved my private education and having no government debt to worry about. It's a slippery slope.'

He shrugged as much as a man resting back on his elbows could shrug. She kind of wished he'd sit up and face her. She didn't see how anyone could have a serious conversation when they looked so relaxed. So cool. So provocative all stretched out like a lion basking in the sun.

She wondered if he ever really cared about anything the way she couldn't help but care so much about everything.

'Your father misses you terribly,' he said, catching her unawares.

She shook her head, vigorously, enough that she had to fix her hair afterwards. 'I'm pretty sure he has no clue I ever left. Probably looks up from his newspaper once a month and figures I've gone out for ice cream again.'

'He knows,' Caleb said. 'He adores you, Doc. Damien was always self-sufficient. I reckon the guy was born in a suit and tie. But you were always your father's little princess. Anyone seeing the two of you together could see it. Everyone including your stunningly oblivious mother, who no doubt wondered what she had to do to get the same level of attention.'

Ava had never seen it that way. Yet it somehow made all kinds of sense. She pulled her knees to her chest. 'Once upon a time maybe.'

'Uh, no. When he saw us coming down the stairs together last night for a moment I actually feared for my life.'

'Don't be ridiculous.'

'I'm serious. Your father has always been a bear of a man. The only times I've ever seen him smile with teeth is when he's beating someone at golf or if the stock reports in that day's financial section of the paper were in his favour. But when he saw you yesterday, his eyes, they melted. You reduced him to a puppy dog. And then when he saw I was with you, the kid he'd always kept a close eye on lest I lead his respectable son astray, and deduced where we had been...'

Ava held her hands over her eyes. 'No-o-o. My father did not deduce anything.'

'Then why did he look at me as though he was trying to remember where he'd last seen a meat cleaver? He's a large man, your father. Possibly the only man I've ever met who I'd not back myself against in a street brawl.'

Ava rested her chin on her upper arm and stared at him. 'And when have you ever pictured yourself in a street brawl?'

Caleb laughed some more, the deep, heavenly sound lulling her into wanting to stretch out sideways until she was lying beside him. Tucked in against his solid chest.

As though her need had reached out to him, he placed a hand around her bare foot. His simple touch made her feel hot and loose all over again, heaven help her.

'You, my sweet,' he said, 'obviously have no idea how men's minds work.'

'That,' she said, curling her toes into the grass, 'is an understatement.'

As Caleb softly massaged her foot the world beneath her began to tip and tumble. She reached down and let the dirt and twigs at her sides dig into her soft palms.

So much for exorcising him from her system.

They'd locked horns since the day they'd met and still didn't quite know how to disentangle them. Perhaps because neither of them truly wanted to. Oh, boy...

'Did you know that dendrophobia is the fear of trees?' she blurted.

Caleb blinked just the once, then he let go of her foot and let his gaze wander back to the fairway. 'Sure. Everybody knows that.'

Ava frowned. 'Really?'

'No. Nobody knows that. Why would anybody know that?'

'If they'd spent any time studying the basics of psychological phobias they might.'

'Right. Of course. In my spare time between women's studies and advanced keg emptying I must have missed that class at uni.'

Thankful for the chance to keep her own problems out of the limelight for the moment, she said, 'From what Damien has told me, you are some kind of star in the business world. Unmatched at what you do. You shouldn't demean what you've achieved.'

'Me? Why on earth would I do that? I'm a hell of a guy. Just ask me.'

'Yet before I left you seemed to be trying your very best to have as dissolute a university life as you could.'

'As opposed to…'

'As opposed to the extraordinary one I always thought you capable of. I wondered if that was the result of your being an only child. The expectations must have been exhausting.'

She blinked several times, waiting for his response to what she thought a well-reasoned proposition if she did say so herself.

He gradually pressed himself into a sitting position so that they saw eye to eye. So that she could feel his breath against her cheeks. That sexy smile of his tickled at the corners of his mouth before he said, 'You thought me extraordinary?'

'With the opportunities we had we had no right not to be extraordinary.'

His smile deepened. *Oh, boy, oh, boy, oh, boy…*

Then he reached up and ran a hand through her hair. Her breath hitched in her throat. Her every muscle froze. Until his fingers came away with a twig. He held it between them, then crushed it between his strong fingers.

He stared at the broken pieces as he said, 'So it wasn't just that you thought me *extra* special.'

She felt her cheeks pinking. Then as his eyes once again found hers she frantically searched the ground for another leaf to decimate, but it seemed she'd pretty much made a mess of every one within a metre radius of her position.

'Perhaps you're right,' he said.

'About what?' she croaked.

'I was doing my very best to negate the advantages I'd been given. The day I realised it everything changed. The good life and I have been firm friends ever since.'

He made fun. But she knew it was more than that. He was a success in every sense of the word. While she'd lived a life of perpetual adolescence sleeping in smelly dorms, or on friends' foldaway beds, dating father-figures in search of some kind of substitute approval she hadn't had from her own dad.

Yeah, she wasn't as clueless as people seemed to think she was. She'd learnt a thing or two about herself while studying psychology. But a person who knew themselves didn't necessarily make a person who knew how to fix themselves. Except, it seemed, for Caleb.

'I guess I can't have expected ten years to have gone by and nothing have changed,' she said.

'Though some things will never change no matter how many years you give them in the hopes they might.' The shadow of a sensitive smile darted across his face before it was quickly swallowed up by his usual intentionally indolent expression. And it made her heart thump in several wrong directions before it found its rhythm again.

She searched for some random snippet of trivia she could throw into the mix to snap the loaded tension. But his proximity muddled her brain. Made her ache for him. Made her lick her lips and imagine going for round two right here, right now under the noses of goodness knew how many Sunday golfers.

She had no excuse, no beer, no music, no romance of a wedding, or rumble of a fast car to use as an excuse for the feelings devastating her.

Just the scent of fresh grass clippings, the soft song of birds in the trees above, and Caleb filling her vision. Big, bad, beautiful Caleb.

As though he knew exactly what she was thinking he leaned across her, resting his hand on the other side of her leg so that she was trapped. 'So tell me,' he drawled, 'did you ever meet any guys like me over across the sea and far away?'

'Thankfully there is no one else in the world quite like you. You?'

'Hmm?'

'Ever find yourself with anyone quite like me?'

'What—opinionated, in need of a hairbrush, two left feet?'

Time swirled about her, sliding back into the past for a brief moment before it settled right back to the present. She hadn't seen the man in nigh on ten years and he'd summed her up in a sentence. No one anywhere in the world knew her quite so well.

And then just before she quite came back to earth he kissed her. Yielding, slow, timeless kisses that made her bones dissolve.

His stubble tickled her cheeks. His teeth nipped at her bottom lip. The thumb of his right hand trailed up and down her bare ankle.

Feelings and sensations tumbled inside her. She grabbed a handful of his T-shirt in an attempt to stay steady. But it was no use.

Everything in her life was already so far out of control and this was the only kind of out of control she could take more of.

The kiss ended. Her hand uncurled from the front of his shirt. And her heart felt as if it were sitting outside her chest. Bare. Naked. Exposed.

'That night, in the boat shed, before I left,' she said, the words bubbling up from goodness knew where, 'you were my first.'

He reached up and ran a hand through her hair, and this time he twirled a wave around his finger before letting it fall back to her shoulder. 'I know,' he said.

She cringed. 'Was it that obvious?'

He nodded just the once. 'In the best way.'

'Now you're just being nice. I'm not sure I can handle you nice.'

'Why? What do you think you might do?'

'Heavens. Nothing worse than what we've already done.'

'We haven't done anything wrong. Or bad. In fact I think it's all been pretty good.'

She licked her bottom lip and his eyes grew darker.

'Maybe that's why it feels so good,' she said. 'Because we both really know it's bad.'

'I like bad.'

'No surprise there. I had no idea that *I* liked bad. But now I'm kind of getting the hang of it.'

His face eased into the kind of smile that would have crumpled the knees from beneath her had she not already been sitting. 'I can attest to that.'

'Why, thank you.'

'No,' he said. 'Thank you.'

Ava let her gaze rove over every inch of his face. She'd need something good to take back with her to school where she was about to face more than just the review committee, but possibly the ridicule and collapse of her academic future.

It was a beautiful face. Charming, sinfully arresting, full of character. Those hot hazel eyes of his made her heart race.

And he knew it. She could see it in those same eyes. She tipped her head forward, hiding behind a curtain of hair. 'I didn't come to you that day in the boat shed looking for what I found.'

'I never for a moment thought you had.'

She shook her hair from her face and looked him dead in the eye.

She waited for him to say more. To say it had been special, important, or even the slightest bit meaningful. In the end, his silence spoke volumes. They might well have been naked in one another's arms an hour earlier, but she was the only one with her heart on her sleeve.

As such, confession time was over.

She managed to get herself to her feet without touching him. With that kind of dexterity she could have been a gymnast in another life.

She grabbed her shoes and brushed herself off. 'Come on, Caleb. Even though I'm sure nobody even remembers we're gone, we'd better get back. This weekend is all about the bride and groom, after all.'

He lifted a hand to her and she had no choice but to grab on with both of hers and pull. He pushed his heavy self to his feet and looked down at her, dark eyes further shadowed by the waterfall of willow leaves concealing them from the world at large.

'So do you feel better now?' he asked.

'Excuse me?'

'Now that you've ticked me off your list?'

'What list?'

'The I'm-going-to-make-up-for-past-mistakes list.'

She looked down. 'That's not what I'm doing.'

He held a finger beneath her chin and lifted it until she had no choice but to look in his eyes. 'You don't need everybody in the world to like you, you know. Hell, even some of my closest acquaintances can't stand me half the time.'

'I don't need everybody to like me,' she said. *Just the ones who should love me.*

His finger left her chin and ran down the side of her cheek, tucking her hair behind her ear. 'Maybe you haven't changed that much after all.'

He leaned in, kissed her softly on the mouth, then turned her and gave her a little shove out of their secluded glade and into the overbright sunshine.

*Easy for him to say,* she thought as she stamped down the path back to the car. *Everything has always come so easily to him.*

She'd been too studious to be popular at school. Able to chug back beers with too much ease to fit in with Taylor's wine and cheese friends. And after the divorce she'd always been too needy of garnering her father's attention to get it.

She'd never been able to find a place where she really fitted. No matter how far and wide she'd searched.

Then again sitting beside him on the couch sharing private jokes had been something she could have spent the whole day doing. And lying in her favourite glade with her head on Caleb's lap had felt like a little piece of heaven. But could any of that compare with how right it had felt to have her body intertwined with his?

It seemed the only place in the world she really fitted was with him. Rather than depressing her, for all its inconvenience it set off a light bulb inside her head.

Perhaps this weekend she ought to give the guy everything until she had nothing left to give. Then with a perfectly clean slate maybe she'd finally be able to form a healthy relationship with someone more suitable. More available. More local. And less likely to turn her head so far she'd end up facing the wrong way.

She'd just have to make sure that this time, unlike last time, she'd be okay. She was older. Stronger. This time she was forewarned.

For the last time she'd loved him and left him she'd spent the whole plane ride to London in tears. So much so the stewardess had taken her into a spare seat in first class to calm her down and let the others in economy get some sleep.

# CHAPTER TEN

LATER that evening, after everyone had played their part in the procession of luxury cars ferrying the trillion-odd wedding gifts to Damien and Chelsea's new nearby house, the Halliburton family circus returned home for a family-only barbecue.

Ava sat on a white cane chair on the terrace, her finger unconsciously running back and forth beneath the leather strap at her neck. She wished she'd thought to bring a book downstairs. A book had always given her a wall of privacy even when the Halliburton world raged around her.

Instead she was forced to watch on, from the outside looking in, as Damien manned the barbecue, Chelsea chased the naughty puppy off into the garden, her mother was in the kitchen likely giving the cook what for and Ralph stood by the barbecue, one hand in the pocket of his chinos, the other holding a beer, laughing.

Caleb was right. A lot had changed in the years since she'd been gone. She didn't remember her father ever drinking anything as pedestrian as a beer. Though it was imported…

He'd also said that some things never changed no matter how many years you gave them in the hopes they might. The guy was too laid-back to ever waste a breath, much less a dozen words. So just what had he meant by that?

Ava flinched at the sudden squeak of sneaker on tessellated tile.

Her mother appeared from outside the blur of her tunnel vision. 'Where's Caleb?'

She sank down deeper into the chair. 'How should I know?'

Her mother gave her one raised eyebrow. Ava felt her neck warming. Had she been the last one to figure that she and Caleb had unfinished business?

Ava said, 'He's not family, so I assume that's why he didn't show up to this family-only do.'

Her mother, long since immune to sarcasm, gave a small shrug, then bounced over to the barbecue.

Ava watched on as her mother touched her father on the shoulder as she leaned in to ask him something. He leant his cheek against the back of her hand a moment. Then he turned and kissed her knuckles, then walked back into the house.

It was a simple move. Yet achingly intimate. Ava might not have even noticed if she hadn't been paying such close attention.

It wasn't just about reciprocal needs met. Or the comfort and ease that came from knowing someone half your life. But care. Tenderness. Love.

'You see that?'

She blinked as Damien's voice cut into her reverie. He was standing over her shoulder, a plate of juicy cooked steaks on a platter in his arms.

She nodded slowly. 'They really are back together, aren't they?'

'I told you you'd need to see it to believe it.'

'You can't blame me after having a front-row seat as it all fell apart the first time.'

Damien squeezed her shoulder. 'Since he retired he and

Mum began catching up for coffee every now and then. Then they joined forces on the local seniors' tennis circuit. Mum still officially has her apartment but she's always here. I think they really don't know that the world knows they're back together. It's like a romantic little secret. And I'm happy for them to keep it that way if it makes them happy.'

Ava's eye twitched. And she bit at her bottom lip. For them to remain happy she couldn't say a word about it. But for her to find any kind of closure on that part of her life she knew she had to talk about it.

Her legs began to jiggle with all of the energy she was having to hold back.

She turned to her brother and tucked her feet beneath her on the chair. 'And you? You're deliriously happy, I take it.'

'Thanks to Chelsea, you bet I am,' her brother said, but his smile was all the answer she needed. 'Hey, where were you this arvo? Chelsea and I were hoping to have some time together, just the three of us. I feel like I've barely had any time with you this weekend.'

'Understandable, brother,' she said, chucking him on the arm. 'You have other things on your mind.'

His eyes narrowed. 'Where were you?' he repeated.

Ava swore beneath her breath that her little smoke-and-mirrors act hadn't worked. 'I was…umm—'

'With Caleb,' he finished for her.

She clicked her fingers. 'Right. With Caleb. Haven't seen him in years, you know. We just, you know, chatted about stuff we've done in the last ten years. Had a giggle about old times. My golf game. Stuff like that.'

Several taut seconds passed before Damien said, 'Well, so long as he's behaving himself. I made him promise to play nice.'

That had her sitting upright. 'You did what?'

He instantly backed out of hitting distance. 'The two of

you were always at one another as kids, and I wanted to make sure your trip home was as uneventful as possible without him making things more complicated.'

Complicated? The poor guy had no idea how complicated things had become and how much his words had just complicated things all the more.

'Caleb is not that complicated,' she said with as uncomplicated a smile as she could manage while she framed all sorts of words she'd have with Caleb when she next saw him.

Damien smiled back, but she wasn't sure she truly had him fooled. 'No. I guess he's not.'

And when his bride came bounding up the back steps with their new puppy in tow he gave Ava a kiss atop her head, then strode towards Chelsea as fast as his two feet could carry him.

Damien brushed stray waves from Chelsea's face and kissed her, and all Ava's energy simmered to a low boil.

She belonged in this scene less now than she ever had. Only now it was because everyone there was perfectly happy without her.

It was suddenly too much for Ava to bear. She felt as if she should never have come home at all.

She hopped off the lounger and went inside looking for space. And what she found was her father paused in the doorway, newspaper folded under one arm, a fresh beer in the other hand, a startled look in his eyes as though he was hoping he hadn't been seen.

'Dad,' she said on an expulsion of breath.

'Ava,' he said with a sharp nod.

That was all she was going to get? Again? She was quite simply too ruffled to let it slide this time. She stared at him as if to say, *And whatcha gonna do about it?*

He looked up and down the long terrace as though hoping to

find a private little area in which he could hole himself up. Alone.

She threw her arms out in defeat. 'Don't panic. I was just leaving.'

'No. There's no reason—'

'Like hell there isn't. If I had a mainsail and a keel I'd get more of a look in than I ever did in this family. I should never have come back here. Hoping it might be different. I might be different. You…'

He *was* different. The way he'd taken her mother back proved that. She was the one who still felt as if she were bobbing in unfamiliar seas.

'Oh, forget it.'

She knew it wasn't really him she was angry with any more. It was her. Or Caleb for not opening up to her as she had to him. But her dad was unfortunate enough to be in the line of fire, and she'd been angry at him at one time and never let him know about it. It seemed she was making up for a lot this weekend.

'I'll see you later,' she said as she angled past.

But before she even made it two steps he said, 'I'm no fool, child.'

She slowed up and her gaze shot to his. She looked from one dark blue eye to the other, hoping to find a flicker of consideration, or compassion. But all she saw was the man she'd grown up thinking hung the moon and the stars, the one who'd given her her first book, who'd never told her how to spell a word of her homework if she didn't first look it up in the dictionary, but who'd turned out to have feet of clay after all.

She took a deep breath to stop from turning into the heart-broken fourteen-year-old she always felt like around him. 'Dad, I never said you were a fool.'

'But you thought it,' her father said. 'I see it in your eyes, even now. You thought I was wrong to ask your mother to leave and you think I'm wrong now to have taken her back. And you've never forgiven me for either decision.'

Ava stared at him. Speechless.

He blinked twice before saying, 'I still remember the day you were born like it was yesterday.'

She gulped down a mouthful of dry air, which did nothing to soothe her suddenly aching throat.

'Your eyes always followed the sound of my voice. Your first smile was mine. The first time you reached out and gripped anything it was my little finger. When Damien was born I could have exploded with pride. But you were precious. My little girl. And now I look at you standing there, the same age I was when your mother and I had you, and I can't imagine where the years since have gone.'

His eyes were so sad it hurt her heart.

She squared her shoulders to open her chest so that she could breathe. 'I don't remember you picking up the phone to call me either, you know.'

He slapped the newspaper down onto the table, and when he looked back at her she might as well have slapped him fair across the cheek for the shock and anger she saw in him. And any kind of headway they might have made by her simply turning up came to a screeching halt.

'Dad—'

He held up his now free hand. 'You should never have gone to that blasted school. I should have made you stay. I shouldn't have counted on Caleb to do the asking. It should have been me.'

If she'd needed anything to help find her voice again that was it.

'Oh, you've got to be kidding me!' she cried. 'Did the guy

pay a town crier to go up and down Stonnington Drive that day?'

A muscle twitched in her father's jaw. 'At least he talks to this family about such things.'

It was too late by then. She was good and riled and nothing was going to stop her. 'And do you wonder why I don't?'

Her father dropped his chin and shook his head. It was several moments before he looked up again and if he'd been any other man she might have thought that glint in his eye was a tear. 'I don't wonder. I understand. And I lament the fact every day.'

A small breathless 'Oh,' escaped her lips. But before she had the chance to even come to terms with what that might mean, her father said:

'I lament that I was too caught up in the grand failure of my marriage to see that you were floundering on the sideline. And I lament that by the time I realised it, that the influence that boy had always had over you wasn't enough to get you through. He may have been as corrupting as all get out, but he has a good heart, a good head, good sense, and he always preferred you.'

Her galloping heart took a little stumble.

Caleb… Preferred her? Always?

She swallowed hard and lifted her chin. 'I shouldn't be surprised you wanted Caleb to do your dirty work. Nobody in this family bar Damien ever managed to string two words together in my direction from the moment Mum first walked out of here.'

Her father shook his head. 'I never thought I'd see the day when that little girl who once looked upon me with such adoration could become so flinty. And so unforgiving.'

She felt as if a hot knife had sliced through her heart.

Why she'd thought coming home would help her find her

path again, goodness only knew. At least from a distance she felt a little sad about the relationship she had with her parents.

And now... Now her father was looking at her with pure and unadulterated disappointment. She'd never in her life felt worse.

She turned her back on him and walked. Just walked. Through the kitchen, across the terrace, down the wide marble steps, across the back lawn and towards the bank of pristine conifers lining the edge of the property.

Pushing through the scratchy lower branches, she came upon the small cliff face that led to the river. The old mouldy steps Damien and Caleb had carved into the cliff face so that they could sneak out of the house as teenage boys were still there. Surely. Geography was one thing that couldn't change that much in ten years.

Unable to see them, she began to panic. She slid to her knees and scrambled about in the brush for the white stone marker, not caring that the knees of her jeans were soon covered in grass stains or her hands in mud.

She heaved a huge sigh of relief when she found the top step, then, placing one fast foot after the other, she half walked, half slid down the bank, hit the dank mossy edge of the stream cutting the house off from the golf course, stepped across the flat stones, her feet squelching in mud and low trickling water, until she was near the other side.

And that was where her life really hit its straps.

Not only was she not as practised or as nimble as she'd been at nineteen, her feet were a half-size bigger. She hit the last stone, her toes curled over the edge and her heel dangled off the back. There she teetered for a good five seconds, swaying back and forth, her arms held out like a tightrope walker.

And then with as much grace as a hippo trying ballet for the first time she landed butt first in the inch-high water.

Everything changed. Yet nothing ever changed.

*Hang social anthropology and family politics,* she thought. *Philosophy might be my calling after all.*

# CHAPTER ELEVEN

CALEB wiped the shower fog from his bathroom mirror, and slapped cologne on his neck. He was preparing himself for what he hoped would be a big night out, a night of wine, women and song. Whatever it took to lose the constant slideshow of images of Ava Halliburton from the front of his mind.

Sure, they were nice images, but for some reason they were beginning to make him feel edgy. Wobbly around the edges. It wasn't a feeling he cared to name, or encourage.

There was a knock on his apartment door.

He poked his head out of the bathroom and glanced at the wagon-wheel clock over the bar. It was a little after seven in the evening.

He rubbed his towel over his still-wet hair, then wrapped it loosely around his hips and padded through the sunken lounge and up the three wide steps to the front door, leaving faint footprints on the hardwood floor.

He opened the door expecting it to be Pedro, his neighbour across the hall who was always in need of rubber bands, or self-raising flour, or a vase, or some such oddment.

But it wasn't Pedro. It wasn't even close to being Pedro.

It was Ava. The bottoms of her jeans were caked in mud. There were grass stains on her knees. And a small scratch on her chin, which looked as if it had been bleeding. But it was her bright eyes, shiny and wide as though she'd been crying, that made his heart twist in his chest.

'Barbecue over so soon?' he asked.

She burst past him, not even registering his state of undress. Something must have been really wrong.

'Something I can help you with?' he asked, rehitching his towel.

'It's my dad.'

'What a shocker,' Caleb said beneath his breath as he leant his backside against a hall table on the far side of the room.

'We just had an altercation at home. I knew I should never have stayed there. I should have stayed at the hotel as planned. Made this a civilised visit. In and out. But no-o-o. The minute my dad asks me to stay and I'm putty. Weak-willed little girl just wanting to please him. And you!' she said as she turned on him.

'And this has what to do with me—?'

'You told my father I was leaving.'

'I assumed you had a return ticket.'

'Not now. Then. When I went to Harvard. After that night…' She waved a fast hand over her face as though wiping out what she'd been about to say.

'I never said I hadn't told him.'

Her big blue eyes snapped to focus on his face then, her chin as stubborn as he'd ever seen it. 'What gave you the right?'

'Oh, I don't know. The fact that I knew that your parents would be beside themselves if they woke up one morning and you were gone.'

'That was my choice. Waiting until I got there to tell them had been my decision. I was terrified to call them when I arrived in London and they already knew!'

She took up her pacing with such frenzy she was leaving track marks in the plush cream rug by his fireplace. 'I'm twenty-nine, for goodness' sake. These things shouldn't affect me the way they do.'

'When you're fifty-nine you'll still be your father's daughter whether you like it or not.'

She glanced at him as though seeing him for the first time. And even though he was doing his very best to remain unaffected by her, his skin was of a different mind—heating, itching—as he imagined her in nothing but a towel, and then less as she wrapped herself around him.

'This is some place you've got here,' she said, turning from him and jogging up the steps to the wall-to-wall windows overlooking the Melbourne city skyline. 'Wow, that view is gorgeous.'

It was just the kind of view that put a woman in a romantic mood. All multicoloured city lights sparkling off the Yarra. And the great Flinders Street train station reposing like a great sphinx on the far bank.

Yet for some reason Caleb was careful to keep a piece of furniture between him and Ava at all times.

His phone rang. Ava spun and stared at it as though it might be about to explode. Caleb let it go to his machine.

From the phone her eyes moved to rove over his loft-style apartment. Over the plush leather sofas in the sunken lounge. Over the polished wood floors, the state-of-the-art raised kitchen and up the winding staircase to his second-floor bedroom.

It changed her focus. Calmed her. The manic whirlwind settled. Her movements became more relaxed. The great accommodating whoosh of air that had clouded his head the moment she'd exploded into his home subsided.

And he couldn't take his eyes off her.

At some stage she'd changed into dark denim jeans and a pink T-shirt with a picture of Little Miss Sunshine on it. It was fitted, and short enough that every time she moved it revealed a sliver of creamy skin above the beltline of her jeans.

Her hair was up in a shaggy mess atop her head. Her foul mood had only served to put apples in her cheeks. And her lips were hot pink from her biting at them continuously since she'd come in.

He clenched his teeth and dug his fingers hard into the knot of his towel to stop himself from moving an inch in her direction.

Once her tirade was over she'd go. He'd make her. He'd turn her around and send her on her way and he could go back to getting ready to go out. Away from here. Away from her.

Her gaze slunk down the stairs and back to him. It seemed to linger on his towel for a few moments. Her chest expanded as she took in a deep long breath. Then she looked him dead in the eye.

Her eyes narrowed. 'Do your parents own this place?'

If he'd needed something to quench his urge to push aside every piece of furniture to get to her that did it.

'No, Ava, I am a grown man with a big-boy job for which I earn dollars to pay for such nice things.'

'That's right, you work for Damien.'

'We're partners at Keppler, Jones and Morgenstern. Fifty-fifty profit share split down the middle.' *Thank you very much.*

She frowned some more.

'I'm not sorry that I come from privilege, Ava. I feel privileged to have come from privilege. I like that I don't have to worry about where my next Lamborghini will come from. Sorry if that messes with your socialist outlook. I only hope it's kept you warm at night as much as my five-hundred-dollar sheets and goose-down comforter have me.'

'You have a point. Who needs autonomy when one has central heating?' She turned away from the window and ambled back down the stairs towards him and that was when he saw the glint in her eye.

She hadn't come here because she was in a snip at all. She knew just what she was doing and right now that entailed teasing him.

A primal growl rumbled to life in his throat. Oh, he ached to make her pay. For leaving all too easily all those years ago. For making him so crazy now. He did not need this. Didn't need her. But damn it if he didn't want her still.

It was then that he realised there was now no longer anything between them but wide-open space and a black Egyptian cotton towel.

'How did you get here, Ava?' he asked, his voice tight.

'Taxi.'

'Not the proletariat train for you?'

She pointed a finger at his chest. 'I thought Damien told you to be nice to me.' Her mouth twisted for a second before she smiled. 'His wallet was on the kitchen bench. So I nicked twenty bucks.'

Caleb laughed.

Ava snuck closer. 'I was upset. With Dad for putting me in my place. And Mum for always getting what she wants. And Damien and Chelsea for being so happy. It seems being bad is for me after all.'

She was beside him now. She picked up a piece of unopened mail, turned it over in her hand to read the sender's address, then put it back on the glass bowl on the hall table.

'So your dad put you in your place, did he?'

She nodded. 'He called me flinty and unforgiving.'

Caleb winced.

She shrugged. 'I know. Harsh. But no less than I deserved. The cab ride over here was long enough for me to admit that you were right about one thing.'

'Just the one?' He looked at her mouth. He couldn't help himself. It was just so pink, and soft, and he could still feel its imprint on his.

'I think he's sorry. I think he wishes we'd had a better relationship. I think, I think, I think, but I won't know unless I do forgive him and stop being such a sorry excuse for a daughter and blah blah blah.' She shook out her hands. 'Okay. Enough for today.'

She glanced at his towel again and this time licked her lips. 'Did I interrupt you doing something?'

'Me?' Caleb put a hand to his naked chest.

Ava's eyes followed. Darkened.

He cleared his throat. 'I was getting ready to go out.'

She looked up. Frowned. 'Oh. I was kidding. I'm sorry, I just, I needed to clear my head and somehow every time I spend time with you I seem to think more clearly for some reason, so I thought… I guess I should leave you to get ready.'

'Fine.'

She didn't move an inch.

'Do you need money for a cab?' he asked.

She shook her head, and her shoulders and her hips. Swinging left to right and back again until he felt as if he were fast becoming hypnotised.

'Right, then.'

He moved to the front door. Opened it. She slunk past and out into the hall. The scent of orange blossoms filled his nose. He gripped the door handle until his knuckles turned white.

'You're a good guy, Caleb Gilchrist.'

'Don't you go thinking that now, Ava Halliburton. I've known smarter women than you get into a whole load of trouble thinking such rubbish.'

Her brow furrowed. 'You've known smarter women than me?'

He laughed. A belly laugh that rumbled all the way to the ends of his naked limbs and back again.

He reached out and ran his thumb down her chin. 'Never have. Never will.'

She glanced down the hallway, biting at her lip. Her brow furrowed as though she hadn't thought past this part. 'Well,' she said, 'I guess I'd better head back.'

'Perhaps you should.'

He could have closed the door in her face. Hell, he could have taken a solo chair that morning for the present-opening ceremony. He could have said hello the night before then spent the rest of the evening chatting up a wedding guest.

But Ava Halliburton was his Achilles' heel. Always had been and by the looks of things she always would be. From the second he'd seen her sitting in the church he'd been toast.

The only answer was to reduce her the same way. To teach her that playing with fire would only get her burnt.

He reached out, slid a hand sensuously down her arm. For the first time since she'd landed in his apartment she seemed unsure.

'How about a proper goodbye?' he said, his voice gruff.

Slowly. Achingly slowly he drew her back inside. And when she was close enough he could see her eyes were dark pools of anticipation.

'Goodbye, Ava,' he said, smiling as he leaned in to kiss her.

The kiss was slow, sensual and searching. As ever before she melted into him with such effortlessness, such trust. She made it so easy for her pleasure to become his pleasure and that was enough.

Her cool hands slunk around his waist. The texture of cotton and flesh sliding against his naked torso and his warm skin contracted delectably beneath her touch. He reached up and pulled the comb from her hair. Her waves tumbled heavily into his hands until they became blissfully knotted.

And they kissed and kissed and kissed.

Their lips parted as they came up for breath. His gaze tangled with hers. Those wild, brilliant blue eyes filled with longing and desire and history and amity. He knew in that second that this time with her had nothing to do with her need to feel liked, or his need to teach her a lesson.

It was about saying goodbye.

He slowly slid her T-shirt over her head, threw it to the couch, then tucked a hand into the hair at her neck as he kissed her long and deep. She held on tight and let him show the way.

The only one with an intimate knowledge of his apartment, Caleb lifted her in his arms and carried her to the stairs.

She leant back and looked into his eyes. Hers were feverish. He told himself it was because she was deep in the throes of passion for him, but even as he thought it he knew it wasn't totally true.

She was a mess. A beautiful mess but a mess all the same. Even if his head felt like cotton wool he doubted hers ever felt that way. There were way too many facts, too many figures, too many memories and worries and ideas rattling around in there for her to ever fully switch them off.

This was not just about sexual gratification for her. It never would be. No matter how much she might hate the fact she was more thoughtful than that. More sensitive.

'Last chance, Doc,' he said, his voice hoarse.

'Caleb,' she said, her voice hoarse and hopeless as she pressed one gentle hand to his cheek. 'Please.'

He didn't need to be asked twice even as he now understood what this was costing her.

He was a cad. He was wicked. He was a selfish bastard.

He was taking advantage of the situation in every possible way. But that was his nature. And it was for the best if she knew it.

He carried her carefully up the skinny winding staircase to his loft bedroom. Once there he let her down, her lean body sliding against his so slowly it was almost unbearable.

She sat back on the bed, bounced a couple of times, then crawled backwards until she was lying on it. Willing, waiting. Her long dark hair splayed across her perfect shoulders. Her chest lifting and falling with each heavy breath. A sexy smile upon her lips. The brightest of internal lights in her eyes.

He got down on his knees at the foot of the bed and grabbed her feet. Her brow furrowed. Not what she was expecting? Good.

He ran his thumbs up her insteps and her head lolled back, eyes closed, mouth open. 'Oh, God, yes, more of exactly that, please,' she said.

He grinned and did as he was told. Just long enough for her to fall into a state of complete relaxation. Then he wrapped his hands around her feet and tugged. Her elbows slid out from beneath her and she landed flat on her back with a bounce.

Her breath whooshed out of her lungs in a great squeal of surprise. Followed by a peal of laughter. 'That was just cruel,' she said.

'Ava, my sweet, you haven't yet seen how cruel I can be.'

He took one foot, covered it in his warm hands and blew hot air along her sole. He half expected her to feign indifference, to hold back, it was what he would have done, but her hands gripped mounds of blanket and she arched away from him. When she came down it seemed she couldn't get enough air.

Her susceptibility to his every touch shouldn't have surprised him. Not after the times he'd been with her. But here, now, this time everything felt strangely heightened. He actually wondered if she might come before he'd even moved higher than her foot.

He clasped a hand around her ankle and tugged. She slid further down the bed, her hair splaying out beneath her head like a fan of dark silk. He ran a hand beneath her jeans, and up her calf. Only then did he remember her jeans were knee-deep in dry mud.

'What on earth were you doing before you came here?' he growled.

She opened her eyes, lifted her head and glanced at her jeans, then grinned. 'Wouldn't you like to know?'

'What I'd like is to not get mud all over my clean bed sheets.'

She moved up onto her elbows again and looked him right in the eye as she said, 'If you want me to take my jeans off, Caleb, you only have to ask.'

'Where have you been all my life?' he asked.

She laughed. Her laughter sang through him. Soft, pretty, familiar, and much missed. He vowed to collect as much of it as he could before she left.

His stomach clenched.

He ignored it and instead paid close attention as Ava climbed to her knees and slowly, ever so achingly slowly, began to pop the buttons of her fly.

Pop. Pop. Pop.

The top of her panties peeked out from the V of her jeans. He looked again at her bra. It was white cotton and covered in yellow daisies. He looked down. Her panties were pink hipsters with pictures of fairies on them. It took him a moment to realise they didn't match. He wasn't sure he knew that women had it in them to wear mismatched underwear. But Ava, being Ava, wasn't like other women.

It was so ingenuous, so darling, so lacking in ego his hands actually shook. He clenched them into fists at his side so that she wouldn't notice. So that he could pretend it had never happened.

'Ready?' she said, head down, eyes stormy, hair out of control.

God, but she was beautiful. And not just that. She was unique. Never in his life had he known another woman quite like her. And never would he again.

'Ready as I'll ever be,' he said.

She fell onto her back, lifted her legs in the air, yanked her jeans off and hung them from a single finger off the edge of his bed. 'Where do you want 'em? Wouldn't want to dirty your precious floor,' she said.

'Say the word dirty one more time and only you're to blame for what I might do.'

'Dir-r-rty,' she purred.

'Right.' He leapt onto the bed, grabbed the jeans and threw them so far they sailed over the balcony and onto the living-room floor below.

She laughed so hard her knees tucked up to her chest. Her pale knees covered in a smattering of tiny freckles. The muscles beneath his eyes twinged. How could he have forgotten that about her? He kissed one, then the other in reparation.

Then he slowly lowered her legs until she was lying flat. Naked bar her underwear. Looking up at him. Trusting. As though she knew he'd never really hurt her. Where she got that idea he had no idea.

'Hi,' she whispered.

'Hi,' he said.

He leaned down and kissed her. A deep lusty kiss that he'd be perfectly willing to see go on for ever. But he didn't have for ever. He only had tonight. And thus he planned to make every minute count.

He gently caressed her flat tummy with his open palms. She writhed beneath his touch.

He kissed his way up one arm and down the other starting and finishing with the tips of each finger. Her deep sensual breaths punctuated the weighty silence.

He tugged at the peak of her bra until her breast was exposed. She bit her lip, anticipation seeping from every pore. Then he took her nipple in his mouth, suckling until he thought he might be the one to fall apart with the best still yet to come.

She tucked a leg around his back, found he was still wearing the towel and whipped it off with her toes.

'So that's what they teach you at those fancy schools.' He kissed his way back up to the edge of her lips and wondered then how he'd been able to stay away from that heavenly mouth for so long.

He felt her smile against his mouth. 'And that's just in orientation.'

He slowly circled her belly button with the tip of a finger. 'Did they teach you this?' he whispered between kisses.

'First year,' she said on a release of breath as her eyes fluttered closed.

He let his fingers trail slowly down her belly, until they tickled her soft dark hair. 'How about this?'

'Wait,' she said, her voice ragged, 'hang on. Yep. Uh-huh. That was for extra credit.'

'Then how about this?' His fingers didn't move. Yet her whole body tensed in expectation of what was to come. He slowed his kisses until their lips barely touched. It was sweet agony. And for a guy who never denied himself anything it was a revelation.

Then he cupped her, stroked her, and she was rendered speechless. Her right knee fell sideways as she opened herself up to him and he let himself marvel at the woman she had become.

He found himself wanting to prolong everything. To take as long as she'd let him to please her. And only after she fell apart and long after her trembling ceased did he find a condom in his bedside drawer, slide it into place and lever himself above her.

He waited for her to open her eyes so that she could see who it was who could break her down as he had. She looked deep into his eyes and she smiled. Her lovely, sweet, sexy, debilitating smile.

*Ava…*

This time her name came to him in his own voice. Deep, croaky and wretched.

He sank inside her, a perfect fit. She wrapped her legs about him, ran her fingers through his hair and moved with him as though they were listening to the exact same beat in their heads.

She clung to him, her fingers biting into his shoulders, her sweat intermingling with his.

Eons later she released his name on a long forlorn sigh. And just as he felt the sweet tension peaking inside him she tumbled into bliss in his arms. And he in hers.

They fell back to earth together, holding one another close, their breaths easing slowly, slowly.

She continued to press herself against him as closely as she possibly could. It felt as though she was trying to get under his skin.

If only she knew she had been there all along.

# CHAPTER TWELVE

AVA stood out on Caleb's balcony, wearing an oversized T-shirt of his she'd found hanging over a chair in his room. And nothing else bar the leather strap and locket he'd bought her for her sixteenth birthday.

The locket which to this day still had his picture inside.

As she blinked up into the dusty night sky her limbs were warm, her mind racing. But for the first time in as long as she could remember her heart felt settled.

She loved Caleb. Had done as long as she'd known him. There was no other man for her out there in the big wide world. She'd looked. She'd sampled and she'd only been disappointed again and again.

Because the only place she needed to have looked was in her own backyard. It was so obvious to her now she couldn't even imagine the mental roadblocks she must have steadfastly kept in place all these years so as not to see it.

The light spring breeze tickled the bare skin at the edges of the T-shirt.

Could it ever be possible that the reason he'd been such hard work this weekend was because he might in fact love her, too? And had all this time?

She shivered and wrapped her arms about herself, wanting to feel the lingering heat of his touch as long as she could.

The swoosh of the sliding door told her she was no longer alone. A satisfied smile stretched across her face as Caleb slid behind her, tucking his length along hers, and nibbling the soft spot below one ear.

'Have you ever seen such stars?' she asked.

'You asked me that last night. You need some new material.'

'Well, they're worth a second mention.'

Caleb's nuzzling stopped for as long as it took for him to look up, then he was back at it again, creating wave upon wave of goose bumps over every inch of exposed skin. 'Don't get the appeal myself,' he said. 'Then again I'm not in the least bit romantic. As far as I'm concerned stars are stars.'

She shrugged into Caleb's T-shirt, the scent of him corrupting her every which way. 'You forget I haven't seen these exact stars in a very long time. See there, low in the east Pisces, the fish, and Cetus, the whale. Mira, a star within Cetus periodically changes its brightness.'

This time when Caleb stopped nuzzling, he wrapped his arms about her waist and looked up, tucking her head beneath his chin. Her lungs squeezed tight with pure happiness.

'Don't tell me you studied astronomy too.'

'Only enough basic concepts of astronomy and astrophysics to pass the Harvard post-grad written placement examination. But by then I realised how much applied maths and how little star-gazing would be involved in the post-grad studies, so I let it go.'

'Mmm, all work and no play. Doesn't sound like my cup of tea, either.'

'Big shock.'

'So,' he said, 'tell me what's so special about these stars that has kept you away from my bed for far too long.'

She slid her arms along the top of his, the rasp of masculine hair creating a whole new level of shivers within her. 'These stars are special because they only look like this in this part of the world. Looking up at the Milky Way, arching across the sky from north-east to south-west, I know I'm home. See?'

'Nothing I didn't learn at the school trip to the Brisbane Planetarium so far, Ms Ivy League. I'd ask for my money back if I was you.'

'Fine. Then look directly overhead and you'll see Capricornus, the sea-goat, and Aquarius, the water carrier.'

She held up her arm and pointed, leaning back into him so that he could have the best view. His hand found her elbow and slunk along her arm until it was wrapped around her hand. She leaned back even further, his warmth became her warmth and the stars almost became irrelevant. Almost.

Knowledge had been the one thing that had helped her make sense of the crazy, chaotic, confusing world around her, and now she just loved imparting everything she'd learned to others. Having a doctorate under her belt would bring her place in academia to an end, releasing her out into the big wide world to share what she knew with kids just like her.

The thought of her doctorate, of Harvard, of the review committee, and of leaving this place, lassoed her freed spirit and brought it back down to earth.

She leant deeper into Caleb's sinew and strength, allowing his indomitable strength to cushion her.

'And over there,' she said, 'towards the south-west there's the Southern Cross. It can't be seen from the northern hemisphere yet its visible here throughout the entire year. It never disappears below the horizon. Isn't that something?'

'It's gorgeous.'

'It's constant is what it is. Standing anywhere in this city, on any given night, looking skyward, and seeing those five stars is about the only thing I've ever been able to truly count on.'

Caleb's grip abated, just a tad. But just enough.

She let her arm drop. Suddenly the cool of the night enveloped her, winding itself around her even though to all intents and purposes she was still in Caleb's arms.

But she no longer felt as though she was in his embrace.

'We can do this, right?' she whispered.

'Do what?' he asked, sliding a hand beneath her T-shirt to trace his fingers along her naked ribs.

It felt decadent, it felt delicious, and she knew he was trying to distract her. It was working.

But out there on his balcony, staring at the wide Australian sky, her train of thought had been important. Imperative. The next five minutes might well decide the course of her life.

'Stop, Caleb, I can't think when you do that.'

'So stop thinking.' He replaced his fingers with the palm of his hand, making gentle yet insistent tracks across her belly. It flinched agonisingly under every small caress.

She turned in his arms to find he was shirtless. All hard, tanned muscle gleaming in the moonlight. Blue and white striped pyjama pants hanging low off his hips. And by the feel of him he wore nothing underneath.

He was gorgeous. Just far too gorgeous and charismatic and provocative for it to be in any way fair. 'Caleb…'

His answering smile was flirtatious. Deliberately so. 'Yes, Ava?'

'I'm going back to Harvard.'

His eyes grew dark, and not from desire. 'Of course you are.'

She bit her lip. That wasn't the response she'd been hoping for. Neither had she expected him to get down on his knees and beg her to stay. Something in between would have been helpful. So she explained herself further to make sure he really heard her.

'Going back won't be pretty. In fact, it's going to get pretty ugly. But a lot of people have put a lot of faith in me over the years. The scholarships alone have saved me hundreds of thousands in student debt. I owe the companies and organisations who've sponsored me to finish what I started. To be all they thought I could be.'

'Ava, honey,' he said. 'You're going to have to let go this desperate need of yours to be liked or you'll for ever be turning in circles trying to please everybody but yourself.'

'You're right,' she said. 'I know you're right. This weekend has shown me the time has come to do what I have to do to please myself as nobody else is going to do it for me. Of all the schools I've been to Harvard really fits. It's one of the finest schools in the world and I'd be a fool to give up everything I've worked so hard for.'

The fact was, when all was said and done, she was her parents' child. She was a Halliburton. It was in her blood not to accept less than everything she'd ever wanted.

She wanted to finish out her schooling at Harvard.

She wanted to ace her doctorate.

And she wanted Caleb.

'I guess what I'm asking,' she said, 'is if you'll wait for me.'

He didn't move. Didn't flinch. He didn't even blink. He just looked at her with those dark shadowed eyes. And suddenly she felt very cold.

'I have a year left on my dissertation. And then I could teach, or speak, or consult anywhere in the world. I could come home for good. But with the right incentive I'd do everything in my power to finish sooner.'

Eventually the muscles in his jaw worked as he squinted

off into the distance. 'It must help having such sway on the panel,' he said. 'Well done there.'

'Such sway?' *No. He did not just say that.* Her voice was reed-thin as she said, 'Caleb, that's over. I see now that it was over before it even began. You have to believe me.'

She reached a hand up to his cheek and he jerked away. Her hand closed in on itself as though burned.

He wasn't really being as mean as he was trying to be. He was protecting himself. She knew him well enough to know that his bravado was a shell. Beneath his slick surface was the most genuine, deep, tender man she'd ever known. That man was the man she loved.

Her next words clogged in her throat. But if this blistering affair was ever to become anything more they had to be said.

Trying not to feel as if this was her last chance to get this right, she took a deep breath and said, 'But you've already waited all this time.'

After several long seconds, he stepped away from her, distancing himself physically and emotionally. It left her shaking, and wishing she'd thought to put on a robe.

'You said it yourself,' he said. 'The opportunities over there are unmatched. Why come back at all?'

She rubbed a hand across her forehead, which suddenly felt abnormally tight. 'Well, for you. For us. For this. Caleb—'

'I don't do stale pizza,' he said. 'I don't do sleepovers. I don't do commitment. I do five-star luxury all the way. Blithe self-indulgence. Absolute independence. Are you saying you're sophisticated enough to handle that?'

His words made no sense. Not after the way he looked at her, and treated her, and the way she felt when she was with him. The way the first place she'd wanted to run when she'd felt backed into a corner was not as far away as possible but into his arms. And not after the way he'd taken her in.

Had she been the one to read everything the wrong way? Heck, she'd done it enough times in every other relationship she'd ever forged—why should her relationship with Caleb be any different? Could she truly be the world's greatest fool?

She grabbed a tight hold of the freezing cold metal railing and glared at the stars that twinkled back at her: pretty and completely unhelpful.

'Why?' she asked them, the hot sting of humiliation burning the backs of her eyes. 'Why is it that I always get the same response?'

At the hitch in her voice, she felt Caleb finally stir.

She turned on him with a vengeance. 'Don't you dare look at me like that.'

'Like what?'

'Like I'm some poor washed-up kitten in need of coddling. I'm not a kid, Caleb. I'm a grown woman. I'm smart, I'm not cross-eyed, I can hold a conversation, I can cook a mean pot roast, mothers always seem to like me.'

Ava felt her breaths coming more shallow and more frequently. But now she'd started she couldn't stop. After she'd given herself to Caleb the way she had, and received so much more of him than she'd ever thought possible, her emotions had become a runaway train.

She looked deep into his eyes and asked the one thing, despite all her schooling, that she'd never been able to figure out:

'What makes me so hard to love?'

*A-w-w-w, hell,* Caleb thought, his throat constricting to the point of physical pain.

What had begun as a night of sexual fireworks, of passion reignited, of fantasies lived out, of the most sublime, free, spontaneous release of his young life, had suddenly spun on a dime and become very very real.

He was a proud man, a strong man, a man who was used to having things fall his way. But the time had come to admit the memory of the day he'd asked her to stay for him and she'd walked away had scarred him deep. And he never wanted to feel that diminished, that fallible, that way ever again.

'Honey,' he said, the words feeling like acid on his tongue, 'I'm not the one to ask.'

'Why not you?' she asked, her big blue eyes shimmering, wounded.

He dug his toes hard into the tiles until they hurt. 'Because I'm not the till-death-do-us-part, happy-family-guy type. I can't do long distance. Hell, I'm not even all that good at short-distance relationships. I'm not the one you want.'

'So you're telling me that you don't want me. After what just happened in there, and everything else that went on between us this weekend, you are standing there and telling me that it was all just sex.'

'Maybe I am.'

'Maybe?' Her eyes were so full of hope. But it wasn't the hope of someone looking forward to a bright rosy future. It was the hope of someone clinging to a life raft.

'Honey, there's no maybe about it. I told you I'm no good at being nice. I'm rotten to the core.'

To prove it he dragged her to him and kissed her. It was intense, stupefying, consuming.

She melted in his arms, clinging to him, kissing him with such unchecked ardour that for the first time in his entire privileged life he wished he were a different kind of guy. And it was all her fault.

The kiss suddenly tasted of salt. He pulled away. Wiped his thumb across his lips and came away with her tears.

All he could do was stare as her bright blue eyes became great wells of sadness. The fact that it was his fault, his Ava, made him feel as if he'd just entered the seventh level of hell.

'Ava…'

She held up a hand while she collected herself. Her voice was ragged, and so tired when she said, 'Damien and Chelsea are going on their honeymoon tomorrow. Perhaps I should take that as a sign I ought to go back then too.'

She glanced at him, for a few long seconds, giving him one more chance to be a man and take up her tender-hearted request that he be the one to love her as no one had ever loved her.

He might well have been stubborn and selfish, but keeping her dangling for his own ends was beneath even him. 'That sounds like a plan,' he said.

Her face crumpled before she looked down at her bare feet. She nodded once, then said, 'Can you do me the favour of staying out here while I collect my things and go? I feel ridiculous enough without having you watch me crawl around on my hands and knees looking for my bra.'

He opened his mouth to ask how she was getting home, but she held up a hand, her eyes dark and smudged and so, so sad he actually found breathing a struggle.

'If you ask me if I need cab money I will push you off the balcony.'

He shut his mouth. And smiled as he was meant to do.

She smiled back, or at least tried her very best.

Then she leaned in and kissed him on the cheek. Orange blossoms mixed with his cologne to form the sweetest scent he'd ever known.

'Goodbye, Caleb,' she said. Then her hand slid from his chest and she was gone.

He stayed out on that balcony for a long time after she closed his front door. Staring at the stars. Wondering what a sky without the Southern Cross would look like. He'd never paid attention when he'd had the chance to before.

He decided the thought of looking skyward and not recognising a thing was the reason he suddenly felt as if something were missing inside him.

# CHAPTER THIRTEEN

MONDAY morning Caleb sat in his spacious corner office at Keppler, Jones and Morgenstern, the crack day-trading sensation he had run alongside Damien for the past six years.

His right knee jiggled in rhythm with the pen he tapped against the leather pad atop his desk and he stared blankly at the tropical fish populating the screensaver on his computer screen.

The markets had been open for over an hour. He had a dozen leads on new mid-level clients looking for representation. And he had yet to pick up the phone.

It was all Ava Halliburton's fault.

When she'd left the first time he'd cut her from his life cold turkey. This time, while he should have been ambivalent at best, he found he didn't like the idea one little bit.

For the time he'd spent with her over the past thirty-six hours made him feel like a super-fast train hitting a coin on the tracks. Everything he was once so content with in his life was becoming steadily and rapidly unstuck.

A sound had him glancing up to find Damien lounging in the doorway, relaxed and cool in jeans and a black cashmere jumper.

'Jeez, you startled me, mate.' Caleb let his bouncy office

chair tilt forward and took to shuffling random papers on his desk. 'Aren't you on your honeymoon yet? What the hell's wrong with you?'

Damien grinned. 'This afternoon we head off. Two weeks on the beach in Antigua. Just me, the wife, a kilometre of pure white sand, a hammock, margaritas on tap, the wife—'

'You can't imagine how happy I am for you.'

Damien's grin only widened. 'So are you really happy to run the place on your own while I'm away?'

Caleb leaned back in his chair and feigned ambivalence. 'Mmm. Happy? Happy's a strong word. And I did just download Space Invaders and I was hoping to spend the next fortnight beating my top score from when I was sixteen…'

'Shouldn't be hard. You always sucked at Space Invaders.'

'Says the man who looks at anything silver with buttons and lights and calls for help. But worry not, my friend, when you return I will hand the puppet-master strings back to you. Too much admin and not enough schmoozing for me. If that's why you're here.'

Damien pushed away from the door and sauntered over to the window, hands clasped behind his back, shoulders straight. 'It's not.'

'No, I didn't think so.'

'I tried to call you last night and couldn't get a hold of you.'

Caleb let the silence swell, knowing Damien's temperament meant he'd be more likely to bend to fill it. While he himself was stubborn enough to keep his lips buttoned for a lifetime if need be. He'd proven that well enough.

He ran a hand hard across the back of his neck, a move he'd perfected since Ava had come back to town. He let his hand drop.

'So is that where you were?' Damien asked. 'Schmoozing new clients?'

'Nope.'

'Trawling the seedier parts of Melbourne for a new place in which to schmooze clients?'

'Nuh-uh.'

*Just ask me, buddy,* he thought. *At least give me that much credit.*

This conversation had been six months in the coming, ever since he'd stupidly opened his big mouth and told Damien how he'd once felt about his sister. Hell, it had been coming from the day they'd first met.

Caleb and his family had just moved into Stonnington Drive during his last year of high school and he'd been dragged along to play golf with his father, Damien's father and Damien. The neither of them had much taken to the other: two teenage bulls locking horns.

Until Ava with her long dark hair in plaits, glasses perched atop her small nose, mouth in a tight line, had stormed out from the cluster of willow trees to the side of the fifth hole, jeans knee-deep in mud, bright blue eyes fierce enough to cow a grown man.

She'd ramped up to Damien, kicked him in the shin, called him something that in the eyes of a fourteen-year-old had no doubt seemed the worst she could come up with, glared at Caleb for being in her brother's general vicinity, then stormed off.

Ralph Halliburton had laughed uproariously, Damien had blushed, and Caleb, empathetic soul he had been at that age, had felt sorry for the guy and patted him on the back. The two of them had forged the tightest of friendships then and there.

Funny, he'd never asked what had made Ava so angry that day. He looked to Damien, the words tickling the tip of his tongue, then he realised this was not the time.

Damien was no longer looking out the window, he was staring at Caleb.

If Caleb was in any way honest with himself, which he tried his very best not to be much of the time, he'd been a little smitten with his best friend's sister from that very moment.

He'd never met such a tough, feisty or fantastic woman. To this very day…

Caleb pushed his chair back and stood. Eye to eye with his business partner. 'Come on, Damo,' he said, 'spit it out. I haven't got all day.'

'Fine. Were you with Ava last night?'

Caleb's bristling neck hairs felt so on end they were likely horizontal. 'Some of the time, yes.'

Damien's cheek twitched. Caleb looked from one eye to the other trying to decipher if his friend was preparing himself to throttle him or to welcome him to the family.

Caleb had no intention of laying down to the first. And as to the second… A Halliburton. With Ava. Til death do they part. The indecipherable empty space that had appeared in his chest the night before squeezed a size smaller.

'Are you really prepared to ask what we were up to?' he asked.

'Not likely. Though I am prepared to ask what your intentions are regarding my sister.'

Caleb laughed, though the sound hurt the back of his throat. 'You're kidding, right?'

Damien's usually friendly face gave nothing away. 'I'm not kidding,' he said. 'You are you, after all.'

Caleb stood taller, hoping this wouldn't turn any more difficult than it was. Damien was his partner in a multimillion-dollar business, but he was also his best mate.

Would it all come down to this?

And why was telling Damien that he had no intentions so hard?

'Meaning?' he asked.

'Come on, buddy. This is me you're talking to. I know your history with women. It might be enviable but it ain't pretty.'

Caleb had no words. Because Damien was spot on. He was never hard up for a date. Yet, of all the desirable segments of his life, on that front alone he was a restless man.

'She's been through a lot,' Damien said.

'So I gather.'

'I'm not mucking about here. I've seen enough tears from that girl to never want to see her cry again. And if that means I have to stick my nose where it's not wanted in order to ensure her happiness, or at the very least to ensure she's not unduly unhappy, I will.'

Caleb knew Damien was doing what he had to do: protect his sister from the big bad wolf. But what he hadn't realised until that moment was how completely he wanted to protect her, too.

He didn't want to see her hurt. Especially by him.

He didn't want to see her run. Especially from him.

He loved the woman far too much to let anything stand in the way of her getting *everything* she ever wanted.

He loved her?

By Jove, he loved her. He, Caleb Gilchrist, the shark of Collins Street, the last of the confirmed bachelors, was in love.

Well, what do you know? That explained a hell of a lot. The fact that he'd never allowed another woman to get too close. The fact that sleeping with Ava had been more intense, more spectacular, more…everything than with anyone else. It explained the sense of a great gaping hole in his chest the moment she'd left. The ensuing fuzz in his head where his brain had once been. It was the only explanation why he'd been silly enough to be with her again despite the fact that she'd left him once before.

He let his head sink into his hands. If only he'd figured that out twelve hours beforehand. Then maybe she wouldn't be out there in the world feeling as bewildered as he was.

'I don't want to see her hurt any more than you do,' he muttered through his fingers as he ran them over his face.

When he peeked at Damien the guy seemed royally unconvinced.

He could have told him what he now knew, but some latent sense of honour made it impossible to tell anyone how he felt about her before he was able to tell her.

Caleb swallowed down the lump in his throat, looked his best friend in the eye and said, 'My relationship with Ava is between the two of us. Always has been, always will be.'

Damien watched him closely for several long seconds before his shoulders relaxed, then he reached over and took Caleb in his arms, giving him two manly slaps on the back. 'You know what: I think that's the best answer you could have given me. Best of luck there, buddy. She's a livewire. I don't envy you your future one little bit.'

'Right,' Caleb said, not quite sure what to do bar slap his friend back. 'Thanks.'

After one last extra-hard slap that Caleb thought was a bit past the edge of friendly, Damien let go.

'Will you be here when I get back?' Damien asked.

And while three days earlier that might have been the most ridiculous question he'd ever been asked, Caleb found himself floundering for an answer.

When Caleb said nothing, Damien nodded as though that was the right thing to have said, or not said, as well.

'Well, I'm off,' Damien said. 'Ava's flight leaves only a couple of hours after ours. But you knew that, right?'

Caleb, feeling completely and utterly out of his depth,

another new experience to add to the many he was enduring that day, still said nothing.

Damien laughed, gave him one last pat on the arm, then was gone.

Ava stood on the back terrace of her family home, staring out across the pristine garden, past the conifers to the golf course beyond the creek.

Beyond that was the city of Melbourne and somewhere in the middle of the hustle and bustle, wheeling and dealing and making more money than any one human could ever possibly require, was Caleb.

She felt as if she were coming down with the flu, but she knew better. Her body still ached for him. Ached because of him. She had come down with love for a man who didn't love her back. Or at least didn't love her enough.

It was the story of her life.

She glanced at her watch. Fifteen minutes before Damien and Chelsea would have to leave if they didn't want to miss their plane.

Her bags were packed and she had her passport and her airline ticket in the back pocket of her jeans. And while the last time she'd gone she'd felt almost giddy with the pleasure of cutting every string capable of holding her back, this time she felt herself wanting to cling to the strings so tight she was desperately afraid they might snap for good.

Because the last time she had been a little kid running away from home. From a place where she'd felt she didn't belong. And finally from the very adult knowledge that she already cared for Caleb deeply enough that she would change for him, then one day, when it all crumbled and fell apart, as her parents' supposedly solid marriage had done, she would crumble and fall apart with it.

This time she was twenty-nine. Her range of experience was far greater. Now she knew more about risk and reward, about joy and regret, and even about the many different kinds of love. She now understood that most people found it so difficult to show love for fear they might not get it in return.

At one time the whole Halliburton family could have been poster children for keeping their hearts dark and private places. Herself included. But now…

Damien was married.

Her parents had reconciled.

And the night before, in Caleb's arms, she had realised that the reason she had kept the splendour of her heart a tightly closed secret was that there was only one man on earth who already held the key.

She wouldn't take back a second of the journey that had led her to that revelation; in the end it would be her salvation, but, boy, did the growing pains hurt.

'Ava?'

She took in a shaky breath as she turned. 'Hey, Dad.'

He moved to stand beside her, no coffee, and no newspaper to hide behind. 'You're heading off today, I hear.'

'Any minute now.'

He nodded. 'When you didn't come home last night I…' He stopped. Swallowed. 'I was hoping that this time you wouldn't see the need to leave without saying goodbye. No matter how much I had it coming. Then and now.'

'Dad, it's okay—'

'No,' he said, holding a hand in front of him. 'It's not. You didn't deserve my censure. Not you. Not ever. You've always been a good girl. My sweet girl.'

Ava ducked her head so that he wouldn't see that her cheeks were beginning to tremble. 'Dad—'

He kept his gaze dead ahead. 'I always loved this house.

I thought it was the kind of place a man couldn't help but raise a happy family.'

'Are *you* happy?' she asked.

He finally glanced her way, surprise etched across his handsome face.

'I know there was a long time there that you weren't,' she said. 'But now? Are you and Mum both happy?'

His face softened. Melted. And Ava saw in him what Caleb had seen the other night. Love.

Clever Caleb. Sensitive Caleb. Tender Caleb. If only he had a clue that he wasn't the granite-hearted hedonist he did his very best to be. If only…

Her father said, 'You know your mother—so long as she has access to a tennis court and a blender she does not know how not to be happy. But as for me, I can only truly be happy if I know that you and your brother are both happy.'

She smiled. There was no way she was going to burden him with all the ways she knew she could be happier. This was more than the two of them had said to one another in years and it felt so precious she didn't want to do a thing to ruin it.

'Ava!' Damien called out from deep within the house. 'Move it or lose it!'

She took a deep breath of Melbourne air. 'Time to hit the road. Thanks for letting me stay, Dad. I'm really glad I came home.'

His chest puffed out, chin up, warmth hidden behind his usual strong façade. 'Just don't be gone so long next time, you hear?'

She leant her head on his shoulder for just a moment and he let her. 'I love you too, Dad.'

'Ava!'

She lifted her head and screamed, 'Coming, Damien! Jeez.'

Her father followed her into the house and carried her suitcase to the front door. 'Come back soon.'

'I'll try.'

'I mean it. I'll need saving from your mother's intervention once you're gone. And from Damien's holiday snaps. And Caleb's sulking. Oh, Lord, I'd forgotten about Caleb's sulking. Last time you left it must have been a good year before he cracked a ribald joke again. You really have always been his favourite.'

She gave her dad a quick kiss on the cheek, knowing too much too soon and the poor man would likely expire from the indelicacy of it. And knowing there was no way she could make a ribald joke herself under the circumstances.

Then she grabbed her suitcase and headed out into the bright spring day, letting the overbright midday sun do its dandiest to burn away the image she couldn't seem to shake from her mind.

Caleb, standing half naked on his balcony. Moonlight silhouetting his beautiful body against the stunning city skyline. His shadowed eyes giving nothing away as she offered him her heart.

The only man for her.

But not her man.

Caleb glanced at the clock on the wall.

It was just after midday. Ava would be heading to the airport right that minute. Likely in the back of some smelly cab in which the driver would have decided to take her the long route the second he saw that sweet mug coming out of that big house.

'Sir?'

He looked around the oval conference table at his team, who all had mugs of steaming hot coffee in their hands, and looks of faint concern in their eyes that their intrepid make-shift leader obviously wasn't firing on all cylinders.

But he was deep in thought. Important thought. Out-rageous, putting-an-end-to-the-easy-life-as-he-knew-it type thoughts.

He was a big fish in a small pond. He was infamous for getting the ungettable gets. He was feared by other firms and adored by their clients. He had a swanky apartment with a knockout city view, he was known by name at all of the top clubs in town, and his little black book was peopled with the kinds of women men of his ilk would kill for.

Yet Caleb was sitting there at his one-of-a-kind conference table looking out over his million-dollar view contemplating throwing it all away. And for what?

For her, that was what.

She had run once before and, being that he'd been a novice in the ways of love, he'd simply let her go. Now he was all grown up he knew that kind of connection, and history, and friendship, and *égalité* in any relationship was rare. It was more than rare; it was once-in-a-lifetime stuff. But at least the years had taught him another thing that might be of conse-quence in his current state of upheaval: the only way to get what you wanted was to go out there and get it.

And he wanted Ava. If she was about to run again, then by Jove this time he wasn't going to let her get away.

He scraped his chair back so loud the whole room went quiet.

'Mindy,' Caleb said, waggling a finger at Damien's execu-tive assistant, a tall, strong-featured, diligent sort of woman Caleb had always thought very able, when he'd thought of her at all, 'you can take over from here, right? Run the joint for a bit?'

'How long's a bit?'

'Your guess is as good as mine.'

Her mouth hung open for a brief second before her shoulders squared, her eyes narrowed and she nodded. 'Of course I can.'

'Good for you, Mindy.'

Caleb rounded the table, kissed her atop her curly head, gave a big wave to the Keppler, Jones and Morgenstern crew who must have thought he'd caught the bug that had turned Damien from a cool, sharp, focused boss into a man who took half-days three times a week.

And they were right.

He jogged down the hallway, stopping only to grab his car keys.

Only once he and Mae West were stopped in traffic did he hope against hope that her cab driver was taking Ava on a really, really long route to the airport.

Because he had a couple of quick stops to make before he got there.

# CHAPTER FOURTEEN

AND that was how Caleb found himself at the airport on a mission to stop Ava from leaving. Again. He refused to let the overwhelming sense of déjà vu temper his mood.

To his left ceiling-to-floor windows showed the coming and going of countless multicoloured planes. To his right a stream of interchangeable fast-food outlets was a blur on the edge of his vision. And all around him people were either meeting or leaving loved ones.

He felt the heightened emotions running through the place like a terrier nipping at his heels. But for all that he didn't have time to empathise, or the inclination to wonder if it was all that manly to do so. All he could do was use every instinct in his arsenal to reach out and find Ava.

Because this time was different. Because the three things burning holes in the pockets of his suit jacket *made* this time different. As did the years lived, the things realised and admitted, at least to himself. And the way he felt in his heart.

Ava…

The only woman who'd ever really seen him as more than a good time or a road to the good life. The only woman he'd ever let close enough to see beneath the playboy façade he'd spent a lifetime protecting. The only woman for him.

He ducked sideways so as not to run smack bang into a wall of boys in matching team tracksuits. Once through, he headed towards the international food court at a jog.

He, Caleb Gilchrist, the shark of Collins Street, the man least likely to let fancies run away with his cool heart, was running through the Melbourne Airport terminal with his heart well and truly on his sleeve.

'Caleb?'

His name called in that voice brought him to a screeching halt so fast he skidded into a pile of luggage balanced precariously high on a trolley. He banged his shin, hopped on one foot and watched in slow motion as the luggage toppled to the floor.

He glanced over his shoulder, looking for Ava. It had been her voice. It had been his name. Unless he was so far gone he'd been imagining it.

'Oh, dear.'

He looked back to find the owner of the luggage was an older woman not much taller than half his height. What could he do but smile through his teeth and repack her ridiculous amount of baggage? Seriously, where could the woman be going to need that much luggage in this day and age—?

'Caleb?'

He turned to find Ava weaving her way through a row of seats, sliding a dog-eared novel into her leather backpack, glasses on the tip of her nose that was suspiciously pink.

His poor, newly unfettered heart clunked mercilessly against his ribs. He and his damn pride had made her cry. If his shin wasn't already pooling with blood where it had met with what must have been a bowling ball inside one of the lady's bags he would have kicked himself until it hurt just as much.

'What are you doing here?' Ava asked.

'Dear, do you mind…?' the old lady said, looking as helpless as an old lady with skis, and a guitar case, and a tent bag on her pile of luggage could.

He held a hand out to Ava. 'Give me a second.'

She nodded. Caleb tossed the luggage back up onto the trolley. When he bent down to pick up one of the more awkward ones, shaped something like a harp, Ava grabbed the other end.

'Thanks,' he said over the top of the bag as his eyes roved over every glorious underdressed inch of her that he'd half feared he'd never see again.

'Any time,' she said, seemingly unable to take her eyes off him either.

Once the lady was packed and trundling towards the exit Caleb brushed his suddenly damp palms down his suit trousers and drank his fill of Ava.

Hair pinned up into a messy pony tail, denim jacket with a red hoodie underneath, beige cords slouching off her fine frame, flat red leather shoes that looked as if they'd been pre-owned a dozen times over.

And that face. That pale skin, those apple cheeks, those dazzling blue eyes, that wide mouth. That beautiful, familiar, lovable face…

The urge to just take her in his arms and kiss her sense-less, and touch her all over, and make love to her until they fell asleep in one another's arms, was almost overwhelming. How he'd thought he could ever let her go again he had no idea.

'Hi,' he said.

'Hi,' she said, her voice breathy. Unsure. And no wonder after the way he'd behaved. 'What are you doing here?'

This was it. His moment to convince her he'd been a fool, but now he was ready to admit that at least he was her fool. Never in his entire life had he felt so nervous.

He took a deep breath and reached into his pocket, wrapped his hand around the enabler within. 'Thought you might need this.'

He held her white daisy bra from one finger.

Ava stared at it for a few seconds before she realised what it was. She snatched it out of his hand. 'I looked everywhere last night. Where did you find it?'

'It was sticking out from under my couch downstairs. If my memory serves, you were in some kind of hurry to get rid of it last night.'

Ava held up her hand, realised it was the one holding the bra, then slapped it back down beside her. 'I was there. I don't require a play by play. It didn't occur to you that you could post it to me?'

'I don't have your address.'

'Ah, Damien might. Or my parents.'

'Well, silly me, I wasn't thinking of them when I found your bra.'

She hitched her bag higher on her shoulder and gave him nothing. Which was exactly what he deserved. Lucky for him he was an ace at always getting far more than any one man could possibly deserve.

'So,' he said, 'you're really heading back.'

'Yes, I am. I am going back to Harvard, and I'm going to blow the review committee out of the water with my doctoral dissertation. I called Taylor this morning to tell him just that.'

A muscle in Caleb's jaw twitched. If he'd come all this way only to lose her at the last post… He would have no one to blame but himself.

And then she said, 'I asked him to excuse himself from the committee for my doctoral review.'

The words, 'You did not,' shot out of his mouth before he could stop them.

It only made her smile, bringing out the glimmer in those sultry eyes, the adorable apples in those beautiful cheeks. She was so his scruffy beautiful girl it physically hurt to look and not touch.

'I did too,' she said.

'How did he take it?'

'Not well. He seemed to think his partiality would be questioned. And I said that I certainly hoped so. I'm not sure he likes me all that much right now.'

'Fine with me,' Caleb said.

'You know what?' she said. 'It's fine with me, too.'

He got a glimpse of teeth as the smile became a grin. The glimmer of hope that had sent him rushing to be with her was beginning to grow wings.

She blinked up into his eyes, glancing from one to the other as she tried to figure him out as if he were a theory she hadn't quite yet mastered.

Obviously unsuccessful, she bit her lips and looked over her shoulder to the inundation of planes out the window. 'If you came to see Damien and Chelsea off you've missed them.'

'Well, that would have been a great pity if that's why I was here.'

'Oh,' she said. 'It's not?'

'It is, in fact, not.'

They could so small talk like nobody's business. Between them it was practically foreplay, but he'd delayed long enough. Precious seconds were slipping away. Seconds he could be spending with her, not just near her.

He took a deep breath, reached into his left jacket pocket and…

'Young man?'

Caleb frowned and turned to find the old lady with the insane luggage had returned.

'Since you were so kind before I was hoping—'

He held a hand up in front of her face. So kind? Since when did he start to give off good-guy vibes? Just because he was in love, and happy about it—yes, happy, go figure—didn't mean he wasn't still mad, bad and dangerous to know.

'Oh, no, you don't,' he said when she opened her mouth to ask again. 'I'm kind of in the middle of something important here. So, just give me a second.'

Her lips turned down and he actually felt it.

Jeez! He'd brought the triple-threat dream team of the Revolution Wireless owners over to Keppler, Jones and Morgenstern with little more than sweet talk. He could do this.

The lady's pursed lips were soon swept from his mind as he turned back to Ava, his Ava, his sexy, smart, sweet, hopeless, beautiful Ava, took her by the hand and sank to one knee.

The hand still holding her white daisy bra fluttered to her throat. 'Caleb…?'

'Yes, Ava.'

'What are you doing?'

He grinned. 'Sometimes I do wonder what it is they teach you at those fancy schools.'

Ava glanced around at the gathering crowd. 'Caleb, all these people…'

He smiled and waited until her focus was purely on him. Her eyes softened, her shoulders relaxed, and her mouth spread into the beginnings of that glorious wide smile that had chipped away at his heart each and every time he'd seen it in all the years he'd known her.

'No more running,' he said.

'I wasn't, I—' She took a deep breath and let it go.

He nodded. 'Ava. Sweetheart. It's me you're talking to. Me.

Caleb. The boy who riled you, and ribbed you and thought you the cutest, funniest, smartest girl he'd ever known. The young man who knew no better moment than that one beautiful night spent in your arms, but who was too young, too spoilt and too scared to do more than ask you to give up your dreams and stay. The man who thought fast cars and business success and easy living were enough. The man who now realises he would give it all up if you asked him to. The man who won't wait for you because he wants you now. From this day on. For ever.'

As though her legs could no longer hold her upright, she slowly sank down on her knees in front of him. He took her in his arms and hugged her. Just hugged her until she stopped shaking. Then he held her away from him just far enough so he could look into her eyes.

'I know we've been here before,' he said, 'almost in this exact spot, in fact. And I know I screwed everything up last time by not being completely honest about what I wanted, what I needed, and how I felt about you.'

She shook her head as she leaned in and placed a feather-light kiss upon his lips. Sparks exploded behind his eyes before every part of him settled into the most exquisite slow burn.

She said, 'I've never been in this exact place before.'

Tears welled in her big blue eyes. Caleb took in a deep breath lest he join her. Then he pulled a ring box from another inner pocket of his suit jacket.

She took it, opened it, her eyes growing exceedingly wide as she took in the large solitaire. 'Oh, my.'

'Oh, my hurting bank account,' he said.

She laughed her gorgeous laugh and the crowd around them began to cheer, led by the lady with the luggage who was telling them all how the nice man in the suit and tie had helped her earlier.

Caleb stood, helped Ava to her feet, cut through the crowd, looked around for the signs leading to the nearest private lounge and didn't stop until they got there. He tipped the guy at the desk everything in his wallet until he'd secured a couch in a secluded corner.

Ava was still staring at the ring, and he wouldn't have been surprised if she had no idea they'd even moved.

To get her attention back he said, 'Did you know pure gold is so soft it can be moulded by hand?'

She glanced up at him, a slow, steady, sultry smile growing across her face. 'Actually I did.'

'Of course you did. You likely have a degree in molecular chemistry you'd simply forgotten to mention.'

'Only a class or two while I was still at high school.'

She grinned, all bright happy eyes and hope. No wonder he loved her. She got him. And he got her. There was no better feeling.

'Caleb,' she said, then gulped down a lump in her throat. 'Before you say anything else, I want you to know that I have a ticket to return home, booked for three months from now. I planned to achieve the fastest doctorate in the history of the Ivy League so that I could come home and see you and try to convince you that you missed me.'

If Caleb had thought himself skating around the edge of happiness earlier when she'd simply smiled at him, now he knew that was nothing compared with the bloom of feeling invading his every pore at the knowledge she had no intention of letting him go either.

He took the ring box from one hand, the bra from the other, and placed them behind him. For this he wanted her full attention. He reached into the final inner pocket of his suit jacket and pulled out his passport and the printout of confirmation of his plane ticket to Boston that afternoon.

She stared at it. 'But the business...'

'I called Damien from my mobile just before he boarded the plane. He has agreed to buy me out.'

If she'd been surprised to see the ring it was nothing compared with the shock in her eyes. 'But your clients, all the time and money and work you've put into the place—'

'I have the funny feeling rich Americans aren't that different from rich Australians.'

'But—'

'Seriously? Are you trying to talk me out of moving to Boston, opening up a boutique trading firm of my own, and buying an obscenely expensive apartment halfway between the university and the central business district for us to live in? Don't you dare try to talk me out of buying a Cadillac with white-walled tyres and one of those musical horns.'

'You're giving up your whole life. For me?'

He reached out and cupped her cheek. 'I'm taking control of my life. For us. For the longest time I've felt like a big fish in a small pond. And there's nothing I like better than a challenge. And you, my capricious young friend, are the greatest challenge I've ever met. How could I resist?'

He took the ring from the box, held it between his fingers and raised an eyebrow. 'Marry me, Doc.'

Ava nodded, a determined, sure little nod. 'You just try and stop me.'

She leapt into his arms and kissed him. They clung to one another with such intensity he could barely breathe. But breath was overrated compared with what he was getting in return.

When they pulled apart he ran a finger over her cheek, her

chin, her lips. 'Do you have any idea how much I love you Ms Halliburton?'

'If it's even a tenth of the amount I love you, Mr Gilchrist, then I have a pretty good idea.'

He let the ring hover over her hand. 'Even so, I'm not eating stale pizza. Ever.'

She laughed. The sound trickled warmly down his spine.

'Fine,' she said. 'And I'm not ever joining a tennis club.'

Caleb ran a hand over his chin. 'Is that a clincher?'

She slapped him on the arm.

'Whoa. Deal. Anything else I should know about now?' he asked, keeping the ring just out of reach.

Her mischievous face turned serious. 'Even when we drive each other crazy I never want us to end up sleeping in separate bedrooms. Promise me.'

'Honey, if we manage to end up on the same continent then I'm not letting you out of my bed for a week. Separate bedrooms? You'll be lucky to take a separate shower.'

Ava slid her arms around his waist and tucked herself neatly against him, curling her legs over the top of his. 'Is it bad how much I like the sound of that?'

Caleb kissed her on the end of her nose. 'So-o-o bad.'

'Can I have my ring now, please?'

'Are you sure it's not too ostentatious for your liking?'

Her mouth twisted, her cheeks pinked, her eyes devoured the Tiffany setting as if it were the biggest piece of chocolate cake she'd ever seen and she'd just come home after ten years in the desert. 'Nah,' she said. 'It's just ostentatious enough.'

He slipped the ring onto her left ring finger.

It was a perfect fit. It had only taken them fifteen years to realise it.

Caleb shifted Ava until he had access to all the bits of her he planned to get far more up close and personal with the second they found a preposterously sumptuous hotel in Boston.

And he smiled as he leant in to kiss the woman he loved. For he was a happy, happy man.

* * * * *

# PLAYBOY BOSS, PREGNANCY OF PASSION

BY
KATE HARDY

**Kate Hardy** lives on the outskirts of Norwich, England, with her husband, two small children, a dog—and too many books to count! She wrote her first book at age six, when her parents gave her a typewriter for her birthday.

She had the first of a series of sexy romances published at twenty-five, and swapped a job in marketing communications for freelance health journalism when her son was born, so she could spend more time with him. She's wanted to write for Mills & Boon since she was twelve, and when she was pregnant with her daughter, her husband pointed out that writing medical romances would be the perfect way to combine her interest in health issues with her love of good stories.

Kate is always delighted to hear from readers. Do drop by her website at www.katehardy.com.

For Michelle Styles—good friend and fellow
history aficionado—with love.

# PROLOGUE

'SO WHAT'S her name, Luke?' Karim asked as he and Luke left the squash court.

'Whose?'

'The woman who's distracting you.' Karim gave his best friend an appraising look. 'Why else would I beat you by this much of a margin?'

Luke smiled despite himself, recognising his own question thrown back at him. The difference was, when *he'd* asked, there had been a woman distracting Karim—the woman who was now his wife. It wasn't the same for Luke, who had no intention of letting anyone that close to him. 'Not my social life. Work,' he said economically.

'Sounds as if you need some TLC, Lily-style. Come back with me and have dinner with us.'

'What, tonight? It's hardly fair, dumping a guest on Lily at the last minute.'

'You're not a guest.' Before Luke had the chance to protest further, Karim had already speed-dialled home. Two minutes later, he hung up and, in his best attempt at Luke's East London drawl instead of his own cut-glass accent, said, 'Sorted.'

Luke, knowing that Karim was laughing with him rather than at him, gave in gracefully. It wasn't as if he was going to find a replacement for Di tonight. The temp agency was sending someone first thing in the morning, and hopefully the temp would stay long enough for him to find proper maternity cover for his personal assistant.

Even though that was going to take time he'd prefer to use more profitably, he was just going to have to be patient.

Ha. Patient. A word that barely existed in his vocabulary. When Luke wanted something, he went for it. He didn't waste time. And having to wait around on other people's schedules was the quickest way to drive him crazy.

To his relief, Karim didn't press him to talk on the way back to his home. Karim simply let them in, headed straight for the kitchen and kissed his wife lingeringly.

'Put the girl down. For pity's sake, you've been married for three months. You should be over this stage by now,' Luke said from the doorway.

Lily just laughed. 'You really *are* out of sorts, Luke. Here. These will keep you going until dinner.' She gestured to a plate of canapés on the island unit.

Luke suddenly realised that he'd forgotten to eat lunch—he'd been too busy fixing things to think about food, and now he was ravenous. He needed no second invitation to grab a bar stool and work his way through the canapés. 'Thanks, Lily.'

As always, her food was wonderful. Restorative. 'Fabulous,' he said after the first mouthful.

She inclined her head in thanks. 'So are you going to tell us what's bugging you?' she asked.

He sighed. 'I just wish I understood why on earth women want babies in the first place. Di hasn't stopped throwing up since the day she did the pregnancy test, and—' He stopped abruptly as he caught the glance that Karim and Lily were sharing. The kind of glance that could mean only one thing.

He grimaced. 'Sorry. I don't have a shred of manners. I apologise—and of course what I just said doesn't apply to you. I'm really pleased for you both.'

'You'd better be,' Karim said, 'as you're going to be an honorary uncle.'

For all Luke knew, he might already be an uncle.

He blocked the thought. The decision he'd made was harsh, but it was also the only one he could have made. If he'd stayed, he would've gone under and ended up like the rest of the men in his family.

Doing time.

'Thank you,' he said politely. 'I'm very honoured. When's the baby due?'

'Six months.' Lily laughed. 'You're really trying hard to say the right thing, aren't you, honey?' She ruffled his hair on her way to the fridge.

She was treating Luke as if he were her big brother and it made him feel odd. As if there were an empty space deep inside him. A space where he really wanted to be part of a big family.

Which was ridiculous. He was perfectly fine on his own. Much, much better than he had been as part of a family. Been there, done that, no intention of taking a backward step. 'I'm only being nice because you're cooking and I want to be fed,' he retorted.

She laughed even more. 'Don't give me that. I know you're just a pussycat.'

Karim was laughing, too; he'd scooped his wife onto his lap and he had both hands resting protectively round her abdomen.

Luke joined in the fun. 'For you, Lily, I could be.' Then he grinned. 'But unfortunately you have a husband who might not be too happy about that, so I'll settle for being fed.'

'Your wish is my command,' Lily teased back. 'So what's wrong? Your secretary's got morning sickness?'

'And lunchtime sickness. And afternoon sickness. My office is a mess, she hasn't been there to do a proper handover to the temps—when they turn up, that is—and neither have I, and…' He broke off and shook his head in exasperation. 'I've had enough of the chaos. I've sent Di home for the rest of her pregnancy.'

Lily looked worried. 'Luke, I don't mean to interfere, but…is that legal?'

Luke knew exactly what she wasn't asking. 'Don't worry, Lily,' he said dryly. 'She's on full pay and her job's open until she decides what she wants to do. But right now she's not capable of doing her job properly and it's unfair to expect her to keep up with me when she's feeling so rough. And I need someone who can sort this mess out before I lose any more opportunities.'

'Someone who's a good organiser.' Lily looked thoughtful. 'I might just be able to help you out there. My favourite supplier, Louisa—her sister's a freelance office troubleshooter.'

'A what?' Luke asked.

'Organised, efficient, and good at sorting things out. You know those reality TV programmes about people who come to your house and make you sort out your clutter? Well, that's apparently what Sara does in real life. Except in an office. And she does the sorting out for you.'

If the woman was no good, Lily wouldn't have mentioned her. Luke knew that Lily realised the importance of business networking—that your recommendations reflected on you. And this sounded like the solution he needed. 'Do you have her number?'

'No, but I've got her sister's, which is the next best thing.' Lily disappeared for a couple of minutes, then returned with a card. 'Here.'

Luke read the card. 'Fleet Organics.'

'They do apple juice, apple balsamic vinegar and—well, everything else you'd expect from an organic orchard,' Lily explained. 'Ask for Louisa, tell her I gave you the number and say that you need to talk to Sara.'

'Thanks.' He slid the card into his wallet. 'And if this troubleshooting woman's that good…'

'She might be busy,' Lily warned.

'Hmm, that's what someone told Karim about you. But he still charmed you into cooking for him,' Luke reminded her with a grin. 'I'll call her. See what she can do for me. Thanks for the tip.'

Lily checked something in the oven. 'OK, it's done. Go through to the dining room, you two.'

Karim and Luke did her bidding.

Luke took a first mouthful of the food. 'Lily, this is wonderful. If you ever decide you're bored with being a princess, you can come and be my housekeeper.'

'She won't be bored,' Karim informed him. 'Find your own princess.'

'I'm not a prince,' Luke countered. 'And I don't need a princess.' What he wanted was a good assistant at work, a part-time housekeeper who would sort things while he was out and wouldn't nag him about being a slob, and a string of girlfriends who wanted to have fun and accepted the fact that he wasn't looking for anything permanent.

Apart from the assistant problem—which, hopefully, this office troubleshooter would help him fix—that was exactly how his life was, at that moment.

And it suited him just fine.

# CHAPTER ONE

SARA checked the address in her diary. Yes, this was the place. A former warehouse converted to a mixed-use residential, office and retail block, all sparkling clean brick and lots of glass. The ground floor was full of bijou shops and coffee bars—she made a mental note to check them out later, and drop in some of the family business cards—and she guessed that the top two floors were offices. It looked as if the architect had taken advantage of a partially collapsed roof at one end and had put up a tower with one wall of sheer glass—though it had been sympathetically done and looked in keeping with the building. That, she guessed, was the residential part of the building; the rooms on the side with the glass wall would have stunning views of the Thames.

You'd need a small fortune to be able to afford that sort of flat. But, hey, she was fine with the room she'd begged in her oldest brother's flat. Just because she didn't have a place of her own, it didn't mean she was a failure. She had a family who loved her as much as she loved them, a great social life and a job she enjoyed. She didn't need anything else.

She took the stairs to the first floor, where a receptionist sat behind a light wood desk.

'Can I help you?'

'I have an appointment to see Luke Holloway. Sara Fleet,' she said.

'Through the corridor, last door on the right,' the reception-ist said with a smile.

Luke Holloway. He'd sounded crisp on the phone, the kind of man who knew what he wanted and didn't waste time. Which made it all the more surprising that he needed an office trouble-shooter. She usually dealt with people who stuffed things into drawers and scribbled things on sticky notes which they promptly lost and didn't have a clue what a filing system or diary was—and Luke hadn't given her that impression when he'd asked her to meet him at his office. So what kind of man was he?

Well, she was about to find out for herself.

The last door on the right was closed. She knocked and waited. 'Come in.' The voice sounded slightly harassed.

She'd been expecting someone in a sharp suit and handmade shoes; the man leaning back in a chair, talking on the phone with his feet on the desk, looked more like a rock star. He was wearing a black round-necked sweater that she guessed was cashmere, teamed with black trousers, and his short dark hair was expensively tousled—the kind of haircut that made him look as if he'd just got out of bed. Teamed with eyes the colour of cornflowers and the most sensual mouth she'd ever seen, it was enough to make Sara's libido sit up and beg.

Though she knew better than to mix business and pleasure. This man was her client. Well, *potential* client. They'd agreed to meet today and discuss the situation; she'd learned in the past that someone might sound reasonable enough on the phone, but in person they were a nightmare to work with, so it was easier to discuss things face to face. Particularly as she prided herself on her ability to judge people quickly yet fairly: in business, she'd never once been wrong.

Personally... Well, now wasn't the time to start brooding over that.

He put his hand over the receiver. 'Are you Sara?' he asked quietly.

She nodded.

'Good. I'm Luke. Sorry about this. I'll be with you in two minutes—take a seat or a look round the office, whichever you prefer.'

And he was as good as his word; he'd wrapped up the call before she'd had time to absorb more than the fact there were two desks in the room, both with state-of-the-art computers and completely clear work surfaces, and a bank of filing cabinets. The view from the office window over the river was stunning; she could see ships sailing down the Thames, and on a sunny day like this the water sparkled.

'Right—I'm all yours,' he said.

The thoughts that put in her head... Very, very unprofessional thoughts. Thoughts of him lying naked on crisp cotton sheets that were just about to get seriously rumpled.

Sara pushed the idea away and really hoped that her face hadn't turned as red and hot as it felt. What the hell was wrong with her? She never, but never, started fantasising about her clients. Even the good-looking ones.

Though Luke Holloway was a little more than good-looking. He was the most gorgeous man she'd ever seen. The sort whose smile would make any woman's heart feel as if it had just done a somersault.

'Can I get you a coffee?' he asked.

'Thanks. That'd be nice.' Though what she really needed was a cold shower.

'Bathroom's over there, if you need it.' Luke indicated the door in the far corner.

Oh, no. Please don't let her have said that thing about cold showers out loud. Then her common sense kicked in. Obviously he meant if she needed the loo. 'Thanks, I'm fine.'

He opened another door to a small galley kitchen. 'Milk, sugar?'

'Just milk, please.'

He added milk to one cup and sugar to another, then took a tin from the cupboard and removed the lid. 'Help yourself.'

Extremely posh chocolate biscuits.

Clearly her amusement must have shown on her face because he laughed. 'My only vice. Well, almost.'

She caught the gleam in his eyes and could guess the other one. It dovetailed with the thoughts she'd had when he'd told her he was all hers. And it made her mouth go suddenly dry. She had to make a real effort to force her mind back to business. He wanted a troubleshooter, not a lover.

She wasn't in the market for a lover in any case. She liked her life as it was. Happy and *single*. Uncomplicated.

'So what makes you think I can help you?' she asked.

'You come highly recommended,' he said simply.

'So,' she countered, 'do you.'

He inclined his head, acknowledging the compliment. 'Lily warned me that you might be busy.'

'Usually, I am.' She shrugged. 'I'd planned to take the summer off to do a bit of travelling. Spend a month in Italy or Greece.'

'Good food, decent weather and plenty of sandy beaches?'

'Plenty of ruins,' she corrected. A beach holiday, sitting still and doing nothing, was her idea of boredom. She liked exploring. 'It's one of the perks of being self-employed—I can choose when I want to take a holiday.'

He handed her a mug of coffee, then picked up his own mug and the tin of biscuits and ushered her back into the office. 'Most self-employed people have to be forced to take time off.'

Was he talking about himself? She looked straight at him. 'It's important to take time off. If you don't refill the well, you end up with burnout and you're no good to anyone. Good time management helps a lot.'

He didn't look convinced, but at least he didn't try to argue with her. Which was good. After Hugh, Sara had had enough of workaholic men. Ha. After Hugh, Sara had had enough of men, full stop. She kept her relationships light, flirty—and absolutely not committed.

'My office isn't usually this disorganised,' he said, shepherding her back into the main room and indicating a chair.

'Disorganised?' The place was spotless. Unless she was missing something huge.

'As I said on the phone, my personal assistant's pregnant and she's been off sick a lot. I've had temps in, but Di—that's my assistant—hasn't been able to brief them properly, and I haven't been here enough to do it myself.' He rolled his eyes. 'Today's temp didn't even bother turning up. I was talking to the agency when you came in, asking them what had happened.'

Sara couldn't resist the impulse to tease him. 'Are you telling me you're so scary that the temps have got your name on a blacklist and refuse to come and work for you?'

'I'm not scary in the slightest. I just expect a fair day's work for a fair day's pay. And if you can't do basic things like answering the phone politely and taking a proper message, then you shouldn't take a job as a PA.' He raked a hand through his hair. 'Actually, one of the temps was excellent, but when I asked if I could have her back for a long-term assignment, the agency said she'd already been given a placing somewhere else and wasn't available.' He propped his elbows on the desk and rested his chin on his hands. 'Which leaves me in a mess. I need someone to go through all the filing and put my office back into the order I'm used to, and to keep this office ticking over until Di decides whether she wants to come back after she's had the baby.'

'I can do the first bit,' Sara said, 'but I do short-term assignments only. Maternity cover—that's way too long a time for me.'

'Understood.'

'So how much filing are we talking about? Because, unless I'm going mad, I can't see any filing at all.'

Luke walked over to the other desk and removed a large cardboard box from underneath it. It was full of papers, stuffed in haphazardly. 'This,' he said. 'I know, I know. Do the filing daily and it's a small job. Leave it, and the next thing you know it's overwhelming. But Di felt too rough to do it. She knows I hate clutter, so she put it all into this box out of the way, meaning to do it later.'

'Except now she's not here, and your temps have consistently ignored it.'

'Exactly. And Di usually weeds the files. My guess is she hasn't done that for a while, either.'

'So would I get carte blanche to reorganise your filing system?'

'If it's a genuine time-saver, yes; if you're trying to justify your bill, no.'

She liked the fact that Luke Holloway was this blunt. It meant she'd know exactly where she stood with him. No pussyfooting around, no hiding behind a façade of being a polite, bumbling upper-class Englishman, the way that Hugh had.

Not that Luke could pretend to be upper-class. Not with that accent.

'So what exactly is it you do?' she asked.

'Are you telling me you didn't look me up on the Internet?'

She flushed. Of course she had. 'It didn't tell me very much. You're twenty-eight and a self-made millionaire.' And his girlfriends were all the model type—tall, long legs, exotic looks and impossibly shiny dark hair. He dated a lot, was on the guest list at the best parties and changed his girlfriend frequently. Extremely frequently. 'But newspaper stories and online gossip columns aren't always accurate.'

'It didn't tell me much about you, either. Apart from the fact that you don't have your own website.'

So he'd looked her up, too?

Well, of course he had. Even if she'd come recommended. Luke was the kind of man who'd pay attention to detail. 'I don't need a website. My clients come from word of mouth.'

'Which is the best form of advertising. It's accurate and it can't be bought.'

How come they were discussing her business? She was meant to be finding out about his. 'You still haven't answered my question,' she pointed out.

'I buy and sell businesses.'

She blinked. 'You're an asset stripper?' No way was she going to work for someone like that. Even if he did come highly recommended, and had the sexiest mouth she'd ever seen. She had standards. Standards that, post-Hugh, she wasn't going to compromise.

'No. I get bored easily and I like a challenge.' He shrugged. 'So I buy failing businesses and turn them into going concerns. And, once they're back on their feet, I normally manage to arrange a management buyout.'

So the people who put the work in with him to sort out the company reaped the rewards. A man with a conscience, then.

The complete opposite of Hugh.

Not that she was going to think about Hugh the Betrayer.

'I'm good at solving problems.' He rolled his eyes. 'Usually. This is the exception that proves the rule.'

'What sort of businesses?'

'Sport and leisure. Gyms, health clubs, spas…and I'm thinking about expanding a bit.'

'And you do all this on your own?'

'With a good PA. And decent managers in each business who are savvy enough to talk to me well before something becomes a major problem—and who come to me with solutions rather than expecting me to sort it all out.'

Luke liked the way Sara Fleet questioned him. The way she cut right to the nub of the problem. He could work with her.

'So why are you freelance?' he asked.

'I guess it's the same thing as you—I'm good at solving problems and I get bored easily.'

Better and better. He could *definitely* work with her.

'And I like decluttering and sorting out mess.'

'Are you mad?' He slapped a hand against his head. 'Sorry. That wasn't meant to be an insult. I loathe filing, so I'm grateful to find someone who actually likes it. I don't understand you at all but, believe me, I'm grateful.'

'I like putting things into order. I suppose I'm a bit of a neat freak.' She glanced round his minimalist office. 'Looks as if you are, too.'

'Look, I'm being rude here, but your sister tells me you had a first-class degree. How come you're working as an office troubleshooter?'

'A glorified filing clerk, you mean?'

He blinked. Had he been that obvious, or had she just heard the question too many times? 'I wasn't going to be quite that blunt, but yes.'

'It's information retrieval. I suppose I could've been a librarian or archivist,' she mused, 'but I like the challenge of sorting out new places. My family nag me about my degree, but frankly I'd had enough of academia and all the backbiting and I couldn't face staying on to do my doctorate. So I temped for a bit, while I decided what I really wanted to do with my life.' She shrugged. 'Then Lou worked out that what I love doing most is a business asset, and I'd be better off working for myself than working for an agency.'

He ignored the mention of her family. It was irrelevant to his business. He didn't care if she could trace her family back ten generations and was best friends with all her fourth cousins three times removed. If she could do the job, that was all that mattered. And so far she seemed pretty clued-up. 'It sounds sensible to me.' He paused. 'So do you do other things, besides decluttering?'

'Such as?'

The first thing that came into Luke's head shocked him. He'd only just met the girl, for pity's sake. Sara was the complete opposite of his normal type—well, apart from the fact that she had long legs. Her straight blonde hair was pinned into a neat chignon, whereas his girlfriends always had dark hair with that just-got-out-of-bed look, and her eyes were sharp and blue instead of a wide, soulful brown. She was dressed totally for business, in a little black suit teamed with a demure cream-coloured top; a choker of black pearls added a classy note.

But then there were the shoes.

Killer heels. Shiny. And bright pink.

A touch of the exotic.

He took a deep breath, willing his libido to go back to sleep. This wasn't appropriate. Even if Sara Fleet did have a gorgeous mouth and legs he'd like to see more of. This was *business*. And he wasn't going to act on the impulse to ask her out to dinner. Or the even stronger impulse to yank her into his arms, unpin her hair and kiss her stupid.

*Focus*, he warned himself.

'I don't know how long it's going to take you to sort this lot out. Or how long it's going to take me to find maternity cover.' He gave her a speculative look. 'I think your mind works the same way that mine does. You're going to get bored sorting out my filing.'

'Your information retrieval system.'

He laughed. 'Don't try to dress it up in fancy words. It's a box of filing, and you know it.'

'Plus a potential overhaul of your systems, if you show me what you already have in place. What else did you have in mind?'

Again, he thought of her body wrapped round his. Which was crazy. Apart from the fact that Sara Fleet wasn't his type, he knew better than to mix business with pleasure. It always ended in tears.

Except for Karim and Lily. But again they were the exception that proved the rule.

And he knew he was going out on a limb here, but his hunches were usually right. 'The kind of business I'm looking at—I could do with a female viewpoint. An honest one.'

She frowned. 'What sort of business?'

'A new venture, for me.'

'Which tells me *so* much.'

He loved her sarcastic tone. It meant she'd speak her mind,

rather than telling him what she thought he wanted to hear. And he valued honesty and straightforwardness. 'I'm looking at buying a hotel. I have three or four options, and I want to check them out, so it means there'll be some travelling involved. Would that be a problem?'

'No. Justin won't mind.'

Justin? Obviously her partner, he thought. Good. That made her very firmly off-limits. Because he only dated women who were single and who didn't have wedding bells in their eyes. Sara was already spoken for, so he could lock away that instant attraction and simply work with her. 'Fine. Right—systems.' He took a swig of coffee, then talked her through the bank of filing cabinets, answering her questions as they went along. 'That's the paper side of things. Computer…' He drew a chair round to his side of the desk, then tapped into the computer and flicked through the various programs. 'Accounts, payroll, correspondence, past projects, current projects. All bog-standard stuff. I assume you can deal with spreadsheets and graphs.'

'Yes.' She asked a few more questions—sensible ones, and not just for the sake of it, he noticed—and then it was decision time.

He knew what he wanted. So he did what he always did and played it straight. 'So that's the set-up here.' He paused. 'Would you be prepared to sort out my office and act as my PA until I find maternity cover?'

'Yes.' She told him her hourly rate.

'That's less than the agency charges,' he remarked.

'Because agencies,' she said dryly, 'pay temps about half the rate that they bill the clients. To cover overheads and profit.'

'True.' And he liked the fact she was sharp enough to realise that. 'Though you could get away with charging more than you do.'

'I thought clients were supposed to haggle for a reduction in fees, not an increase?'

He spread his hands. 'A fair day's work deserves a fair day's pay. If you're as good as I hear you are, you'll be worth it.'

She inclined her head in acknowledgement of the compliment. 'When do you want me to start?'

He glanced at his watch. 'How about…now?'

# CHAPTER TWO

LUKE was surprised at how quickly Sara settled in. By the beginning of the following week, it felt as if she'd always worked with him. He'd persuaded her to man the office and take phone messages while he was out, and Sara turned out to be brilliantly organised. If he was out of the office she emailed the messages to him so he could act on them if they were urgent. Or she dealt with queries herself and sent him an email to tell him what she'd done.

He loved the fact that she used her initiative instead of running to him with questions.

And whenever Luke reached a point in his work when he was about to stop and make himself a mug of coffee, Sara was there before him. Just as he was about to look over to her desk and ask if she wanted a coffee, too, she'd place a mug on the coaster on his desk. Rich, smooth coffee, the exact strength he liked, with no milk and one spoonful of sugar. Perfect.

'Have you been talking to Di or something?' he asked when he'd finished his coffee.

'How do you mean?'

'Because you second-guess me, the way she did. It's almost like having her back—and she had four years to get used to the way I work.'

Sara laughed. 'No, I haven't talked to her. Not about *you*, at any rate. She called the other day to see how everything was and I told her to put her feet up with a mug of ginger tea and stop feeling guilty.'

'Good. That's what I told her, last time she rang.' He paused. 'So how did you…?'

'Know how you work? Observation,' she said. 'Most people have routines.'

'So you're saying I'm set in my ways?'

She spread her hands. 'Work it out for yourself, boss,' she teased.

'You're just as set in your ways,' he retorted, slightly nettled.

'Meaning?'

If she was going to be straight with him, then he'd be straight with her. 'You're here on the dot of nine, you always take exactly an hour's lunch break and you leave at the dot of five. And you never, ever work late.'

'Because I'm good at time management.' She returned to her own desk. 'Besides, the longer the hours you work, the more your productivity drops. By the third day of working late, you're actually running behind.'

'How do you work that out?'

'Easy.' She scribbled something on a piece of scrap paper, then walked over to his desk and put it in front of him. 'One curve. The $x$ axis is time, the $y$ axis is your productivity rate. Now, would you agree that it's higher in the morning, when you're fresh, and lower at the end of the day, when you're tired?'

'Yes.' Though he could see exactly where this was heading, and he had a nasty feeling that she'd boxed him neatly into a corner.

'So if you're not fresh, because you're tired from the previous day, you'll start further along the $x$ axis, from a lower productivity point, as if you've already worked a couple of hours. And the more days you work late, the further along the $x$ axis you start each morning.' She folded her arms. 'My point, I think.'

'Hmm. And what about personal variables? Some people are best first thing in the morning, others are better later in the day.'

'True.'

'And some people thrive on working long hours. Point to me.'

'Some people *think* they thrive on it,' she countered. 'I hate that culture where you have to be seen to be in early and work late. Presenteeism isn't good for you. The way I see it, if you want to get more done, you need to work smarter, not harder.' She frowned. 'Do you ever take time to smell the roses, Luke?'

'I don't need to smell any roses.'

She looked at him over the edge of her rimless glasses— glasses, he'd noticed, she only used for computer work. 'Yes, you do. Everyone needs to refresh themselves, or they'd burn out. So what do you do?'

He shrugged. 'I go to the gym.'

'You own several gyms. So that doesn't count. It's work.'

'No, it's not.'

'Can you tell me, hand on heart, that whenever you go for a workout or what have you, you don't start appraising the place and thinking about how to maximise the use of the gym?'

'When I play squash or have a workout, I focus on what I'm doing. Otherwise,' he said with a grin, 'I'd be at the bottom of the squash ladder.'

'Whereas you're at the top?'

He spread his hands. 'Top or second. Whatever.'

'And the moment your workout or your match ends, you switch over to business, don't you?'

'It's who I am.'

'No,' she said. 'It's what you do. Who you are is…' Her voice faded and for a second he caught an odd look in her eyes. Something that made his pulse skip a beat. But then it was gone, and he had to remind himself she was off-limits.

'So aren't these parties you go to any fun?'

'They're overrated,' he admitted. 'Or maybe I'm getting old. But, yeah, I'm starting to find them boring.'

'Is that why you change your girlfriend so frequently, too?'

'Probably.'

'Maybe,' she said thoughtfully, 'you're seeing the wrong kind of woman.'

He nearly asked what kind of woman she thought fitted the bill. But maybe it was better not to know. Better not to wonder if a certain bossy blonde would fill the empty spaces he almost never admitted were in his life.

Before he realised what he was doing, he asked, 'How about you?'

'I go to the theatre and the cinema with my friends. We might go out for a meal—anything from a pizza to tapas to Thai, as long as it's good food. Or I'll go home to be spoiled by my parents and play with my toddler niece and take the dogs for a long run in the orchard.'

Hmm. She hadn't mentioned her partner. Or maybe the guy was so much part of the furniture that she didn't bother mentioning him by name.

But there was a bigger danger area here. Even if she had been free, she was clearly very close to her family—a world away from his own life. So it was definitely better to keep things strictly business with her.

'So I take it you don't work weekends?' he asked.

'Absolutely not.'

'That's a pity,' he said. 'Because I could do with you this weekend.'

'How do you mean?'

'I'm going to see a hotel,' he explained. 'And, as I think you have a gut feel for what needs fixing, I'd be interested to see what you thought of it.' He spread his hands. 'Of course I'd pay you for your time, because it'd mean an overnight stay, but if you came with me I'd respect your right to clock-watch—and I promise you can stop answering my phone and let it go to voice mail at five o'clock on the dot. And you can take a couple of days off next week—paid—to make up for the time.'

She gave him a speaking look at the phrase 'clock-watch', but when she spoke her tone was mild. 'This weekend.'

'Unless your partner will have a problem with it?'

'Partner?' She looked mystified.

'Justin,' he enunciated. Saying the man's name helped him remember that she was spoken for. That she was off-limits.

Her face cleared. 'Oh, *Justin*. He isn't my partner. He's my oldest brother. I share a flat with him.'

Luke's heart missed a beat. He'd managed to keep his hands off Sara so far by telling himself that she was attached and therefore off-limits.

Now it turned out that might not be the case.

Given how blank she'd looked when he'd asked her about her partner…it made him pretty sure that she wasn't attached at all.

All of a sudden the room seemed to shrink. Right now, Sara was close enough to touch.

And, oh, he wanted to touch.

Taking her to Scarborough would be a spectacularly bad idea. Way too full of temptation—temptation he wasn't sure he'd be able to resist.

Then he realised that she was speaking. 'Sorry?'

She rolled her eyes. 'Pay attention.'

'Yes, ma'am. Would you mind repeating that?'

'Please,' she prompted.

He'd like to hear her saying that word in other circumstances. In a different tone. All husky and sensual and on the edge of losing her control.

All the blood in his body went south, and he had to swallow hard and close his eyes for a moment to regain control. He just hoped she didn't look down at his lap, because the evidence of his thoughts was pretty clear. 'Please.'

'I said, did you mean telling you honestly what I think?'

'Given that half my clients will be female, I need a female point of view. Which, obviously, I don't have. And you tell it like it is—which is what I want to hear. You don't have a hidden agenda.'

'You said the weekend,' she said. 'Would you want to leave on Friday?'

'Yes. We'll stay Friday evening and Saturday, and come back Sunday. And I'll let you have Monday and Tuesday off to make up for the time, as well as paying you while we're away.'

'It's not about the money.'

He raised an eyebrow. 'It should be. You're running a business, not a charity.'

'Staying in a hotel with you.' Her eyes narrowed. 'That means separate rooms, yes?'

'Of course it means separate rooms. I'm asking you to join me as my consultant. My colleague.' Even though he would've liked to ask her for a different reason, he knew that mixing business and pleasure was a stupid idea. Besides, although it had turned out that Justin was her brother, not her partner, she hadn't actually *said* she was unattached. 'So your partner won't mind?'

'I already told you, Justin's my brother.'

'Which is why,' he pointed out, 'I didn't ask you again if Justin would mind. I asked you if your *partner* would mind.'

'I'm single, if that's what you mean.' She lifted her chin. 'I could ask you the same. Will your partner mind me accompanying you?'

'I'm not seeing anyone right now,' he said, 'so it's not a relevant question. That's why I asked you to come with me: to give me a female viewpoint.'

'What about your mother? Your sister?'

'I don't have either.'

She flushed. 'I'm sorry, Luke. I didn't mean to stamp on a sore spot.'

'You weren't to know,' he said lightly. He knew Sara would assume that his mother was dead; he had no idea whether his mother was still alive or not, but he'd lost her a long time ago. Even before he'd walked out on his family, nearly half a lifetime before. 'Let's change the subject, hmm?'

'Good idea.' She looked relieved. 'Um…what sort of dress code are we talking about?'

He shrugged. 'Whatever you want. I should warn you now,

it's not a posh hotel. It might've been, once. But now it's...'
He stopped, trying to think of a nice way to put it.

'Shabby genteel?' she suggested.

'Pretty much.'

'And you're going to turn it around. Restore it to its
former glory.'

'If all the figures stack up and my gut feeling tells me to go
for it—yes, that's the idea.' And he needed to get out of here.
Before he did something utterly stupid. Like swivelling his
chair round, taking Sara's hands and pulling her off balance so
she landed in his lap and he could kiss her until they were both
dizzy. He glanced at his watch. 'Right. I have a meeting. I'd
better go.'

'There isn't a meeting in your diary.'

Well, of course she'd know his schedule. She was acting as
his PA. 'I forgot to put it in,' he fibbed. 'I'm going to see the
temp agency. Interview a few potentials.' And that was exactly
what he was going to do. Even though they weren't expecting
him. Because right now he needed to put space between himself
and Sara. For both their sakes.

Sara forced herself to concentrate on the task in hand when
Luke had gone. Strange how the office felt empty without him.

And she still felt guilty. Not about the banter—she was
pretty sure he enjoyed it just as much as she did, and she knew
that he'd come up with a dozen valid reasons why working
overtime was good for you, to counter her arguments—but
about the fact she'd inadvertently hurt him. There had definitely
been a flash of pain in his eyes when she'd mentioned his
mother and he'd told her he didn't have one. It was a fair bet
that the rest of the men in his family were the sort who'd bury
themselves in work rather than discuss their feelings, and Luke
himself had admitted that he dated a different girl every couple
of weeks. So he probably didn't allow himself to get close to
anyone in case he lost her, the way he'd lost his mother.

A man alone.

It made her want to put her arms round him, give him a hug and tell him that everything would be fine.

Not that she had any intention of doing that. Because she knew it wouldn't stop at a hug. Several times in the last week she'd looked up and met Luke's gaze; he'd quickly masked his expression, but not before she'd been aware of the flare of heat. Desire. Interest.

Exactly the same way she felt. And, the more time she spent with him, the stronger those feelings became.

Perhaps she should've refused to go to Scarborough. They'd be stuck in a car together for a long journey. They'd spend the whole weekend in each other's company. And, even though it was business, it would be all too easy for it to slide into something else.

Uh. *Slide.* Bad analogy. Because now she had other pictures in her head. X-rated ones.

She dragged in a breath. 'Don't be so stupid. You've already been there, done that and got your heart broken,' she told herself loudly. 'Remember Hugh? He was just as much of a workaholic as Luke is. It didn't work then and it won't work now.'

Though Hugh's mouth hadn't had such a sensual curve as Luke's.

And whereas she'd eventually been able to wipe Hugh's kisses from her memory, she had a feeling that she wouldn't be able to do the same with Luke's. She'd get hurt. Badly.

She'd just better hope that he managed to find a PA to cover for Di, and she could finish this job before the temptation got too much for her.

# CHAPTER THREE

SARA had managed to compose herself by the time Luke returned—literally five minutes before she was about to leave. 'Any luck?' she asked.

'No. Clearly it's not my week for finding new staff. So if I can ask you to stay just a little longer?'

'Yes,' she said, before her common sense had a chance to stop her.

'Good.' He sat on the edge of his desk. 'Sara, I bulldozed you a bit about Scarborough.'

'A bit?' She arched an eyebrow.

'OK, a lot,' he admitted. 'And I know it isn't fair, giving you such short notice to rearrange your weekend. So don't feel you have to do it.'

'It's all right. I wasn't doing anything in particular,' she said. 'I had vague plans to go to the cinema with friends, but nothing definite.' Nothing that couldn't be changed. 'Besides, it'd be nice to get out of London and go to the seaside.'

'We're going to Scarborough to *work*,' he reminded her.

She smiled. 'Maximum eight hours a day. Which means we'll have time to smell the roses—well, the sea air, anyway.'

He didn't take the bait. 'As long as you're sure it's not a problem.'

'It's not. But I do insist on having a paddle in the sea. And one of those whippy ice creams with a chocolate flake stuck in it.'

He shrugged. 'Do what you like in your lunch break.'

'So you're too chicken to paddle?' she teased.

'Too *busy*,' he retorted.

'A five-minute paddle isn't going to take much out of your day. And the break will do you good.'

'Refilling the well?' There was a slight edge to his voice.

'Good. The man's learning,' she said, resisting the urge to walk over to him and ruffle his hair. Touching would be a bad idea. She might not be able to stop at ruffling his hair. And she needed to be professional with him. She wasn't looking for a relationship right now; even if she had been, Luke wasn't the man for her. He kept too many barriers round himself. She wanted someone less complicated. 'Right. I emailed your messages to you as they came in, there's a report on your desk next to a pile of letters that need signing—and I'll see you tomorrow.'

'OK. And, Sara?'

She paused by the door.

'Thanks. I do appreciate you. Even if I don't say it.'

'You know, that's why you're on the temps' blacklist,' she said with a grin. 'You're too grumpy, too uptight, and you grunt instead of talking.'

'There isn't a temps' blacklist—and I don't grunt.'

'No?' she teased.

'No. Go *home*,' he said, flapping a hand at her and going back to the proper side of his desk.

No doubt he was going to work late again tonight, Sara thought. From what she'd seen of Luke, she was beginning to wonder where on earth the press got those photographs of him at parties and why his name was linked with a string of women. As far as she could see, he didn't have a social life. He just worked.

Maybe on the way to Scarborough she could start to draw him out a bit. Make him talk to her. Find out what made him tick.

\* \* \*

On the Tuesday, to Sara's surprise, Luke was actually in the office at lunchtime. 'I'm going to call down to the sandwich bar and order something. Do you want anything?'

This was where she knew she ought to smile politely and say thanks for the offer, but she'd get something while she went out for her usual lunchtime walk.

Though she couldn't resist the mad impulse to try to reform him. To teach Luke Holloway to smell the roses. To make the smile on his mouth reach his eyes. 'Thanks, that'd be lovely. But I've got a better idea. Instead of having sandwiches delivered here, why don't we pick up some lunch on the way?'

'The way where?' he asked.

'Call it an experiment in boosting productivity. If you go for a walk at lunchtime, you get more done in the afternoon. It's something to do with getting extra oxygen to your brain.'

'This,' he said, 'sounds to me like one of your flaky ideas.'

'I'm not flaky. I'm *enlightened*,' she said loftily. 'And you're a workaholic.'

He held both hands up in the classic surrender pose. 'Guilty as charged, m'lud.' Except his grin was completely unrepentant.

'Seriously, Luke, taking a complete break and doing a bit of exercise is good for you.'

'Exercise.'

How did he *do* that? How did he manage to make her think of sex, whatever he said? She wasn't sure if it was the glint in his eyes, or the fact that when he spoke she couldn't take her eyes off his mouth. 'Walking,' she said, then immediately took a swig of water from the glass on her desk, hoping he'd think her voice was husky simply because she needed a drink. And she really, really hoped her thoughts hadn't shown on her face.

He glanced out of the window. 'You have a point. It's a nice day. A walk would be good.'

She checked her watch. 'Let's leave in half an hour.'

He raised an eyebrow. 'What happened to working smarter?'

'Just trust me,' she said. If they went now, the place she had in mind would be crammed with office workers. If they took a late lunch, it would be just how she liked it. How she wanted to share it with him.

'You're the boss. We'll order the sandwiches anyway, to make sure they don't run out. I recommend the crayfish wrap. Unless you're allergic?'

'No, that'll be fine. I'd love to try the crayfish.'

Half an hour later, after they'd picked up their lunch, she ushered him towards the tube station.

'I thought you said we were going for a walk?'

'We are. Not here.'

'We're going to the Tower of London?' he asked when they left the train at Tower Gateway and headed towards Tower Hill.

'Not quite. Trust me,' she said, leading him down a narrow path and surreptitiously glancing at his face to see his reaction when they arrived at their destination.

'A church?' Covered in ivy.

'Not quite.' And then she led him inside, gratified by the utter surprise on his face, followed quickly by an expression of disbelief and…was that delight?

'Wow. I had no idea this place was here.'

'St Dunstan in the East. It was bombed in the Blitz, but instead of knocking it down the authorities turned it into a garden.'

Instead of pews there were park benches, instead of a font there was a fountain, and instead of glass fronds climbing shrubs filled the arched window frames.

'Refilling the well,' she said softly, sitting on one of the empty benches and patting the seat next to her. 'If I'm working in the city, this is where I come for lunch. Outside the lunch rush hour, that is.'

'It's beautiful,' he said. 'And so quiet. You'd never believe you were in the middle of the city.'

'Exactly. It reminds me a bit of home,' she said.

'You miss the country?'

She nodded. 'But I love the buzz of the city, too. So I suppose I have the best of both worlds—I live here in London, but I can go home to Kent whenever I want.'

'The garden of England.'

'Absolutely. We're spoiled with castles and stately homes and gardens on our doorstep.'

'I've always lived in London,' he said reflectively.

'So you've never spent any time in the country?'

'The occasional weekend. Nothing much.'

She smiled at him. 'You'll have to come back with me some time. I'll show you some of my favourite places.'

'Are you asking me on a date, Sara?'

For a second, she couldn't breathe. The air felt as if it were crackling with electricity—even though the sky was a clear blue and there wasn't so much as a single wispy white cloud, let alone purple-grey storm clouds.

A date.

She'd meant it as a throwaway but genuine offer. To share some of her favourite places and spread a little sunshine into his life.

But it could be construed a different way. That she'd just asked him out.

Her heart skipped a beat.

Would he accept?

Another missed beat.

Did she *want* him to accept?

The world suddenly felt precarious, and she backtracked. Fast. 'Not a *date* date. An offer to a friend—because I like you, and I think we could be friends.'

'What, even though you boss me about?'

She was relieved that he'd slipped back into teasing banter. That, she could cope with. 'Hey, I'll have to be bossy if I'm navigating.'

'What about sat nav?' he countered.

'You can't beat local knowledge.'

'True. Point to you.' He regarded her seriously. 'The way you see life…everyone's a potential friend until proven otherwise, aren't they?'

She thought about it. 'I suppose so,' she admitted. It was the way she'd been brought up—around people who loved her and always showed their affection.

'Don't you get disappointed?' he asked.

'Not often.' She had with Hugh, but he was the exception that proved the rule. 'Are you saying that you see everyone as a potential enemy, then?'

'Hardly. I'm not the paranoid type.'

'But you don't let people close.'

He shrugged. 'It makes life much less complicated.'

It also made life lonely, she thought. Not that there was any point in saying so. She had a feeling that Luke would claim he didn't need anyone and that his life was just fine as it was. 'You see the glass as half empty, then?'

He smiled, but it didn't reach his eyes. 'It's obvious you see it as half full. I'd say it's simply half a glass. Telling it as it is, no flowery description.'

His words were light, but she could hear the warning signal: she might want to be friends, but he'd keep her at a distance. She kept the conversation completely impersonal for the rest of their lunch break, telling him what she knew about the history of the church, and he seemed to relax again with her. And, although Luke spent most of the afternoon either on the phone or in meetings, he was back at his desk just before she left the office for the evening.

'Sara?'

'Uh-huh?' She glanced up from her computer and was rewarded with a smile that did actually reach his eyes. A smile that did seriously odd things to her insides.

'I just wanted to say thanks. For sharing that garden with me today.'

'Pleasure.' And it warmed her that he'd enjoyed it. 'See you tomorrow.'

'Yeah. Have a nice evening.'

'You, too.' On the surface, it was polite office chit-chat. Though Luke wasn't the sort to do chit-chat. He was always charming, but she knew he hated wasting a single second. So the fact he'd bothered to thank her and wish her a nice evening… Maybe he was learning to trust her. Opening up to her just that little bit.

Though Sara was completely thrown the next morning, when she walked in to find a beautiful bouquet of roses on her desk, all pink and cream. 'What's this?'

'You made me stop and smell the roses yesterday. I thought I'd do the same for you today,' he said. His smile was just the wrong side of wicked. 'A thanks for helping me out.'

She shrugged. 'Strictly speaking, you're my client. You're paying me to help you out.'

'If you had the builders in, you'd make them tea and bring them cake and make a fuss of them so they did a good job for you, yes?'

'Ye-es.' Where was he going with this?

'Same thing,' he said. 'Except you're not a builder. You're a girl.'

'You noticed?' she deadpanned.

'I noticed.'

There was a flare of heat in his expression that triggered a corresponding flare in her body. To the point where she really needed a cold shower. She took refuge in being sassy. 'Basically, this is a business expense.'

'No. It's from me to you, to say I appreciate you.'

'And so you should.' No way was she going to let him know that his comment, even more than the flowers, had just turned her into mush. She buried her nose among the blooms. Their scent was sweet, yet heady. 'Thank you. They're beautiful. How did you know I'd like pink roses?'

He coughed and gestured to her shoes.

She smiled. 'Busted. OK, so it's my favourite colour.' She breathed in their scent again. 'Thank you, Luke. These really are lovely.'

And when she made them both a coffee and put a mug on his desk, she gave in to the impulse and kissed his cheek.

'What was that for?' he asked.

'Just to say I appreciate the roses.'

'Pleasure.' But he was staring at her mouth.

Just as she was staring at his.

*Wondering.*

She was used to giving hugs and kissing cheeks and ruffling hair. It was how she'd grown up, in the middle of a close and noisy and affectionate family. But kissing Luke's cheek just now, being close enough to smell his clean scent and feel the softness of his skin against her lips…that hadn't been her best idea. Because it had made her all too aware of him: an awareness that could be dangerous.

An awareness that grew and grew over the morning. Luke had a lunchtime meeting—one that had been in his diary since before she'd started working with him, so she knew it wasn't an excuse to avoid her. She had lunch on her own, sitting on a bench overlooking the river. Giving her time to think.

Things were definitely starting to change between her and Luke; although Sara still didn't really know what made him tick, she liked the glimpses he'd allowed her to see so far. Liked them enough to want to know more. To get to know him properly. And…

She took a sip of her ice-cold water. If she let her thoughts go much further in that direction, she'd need to up-end the bottle over her head to cool her down.

* * *

'I'm pulling rank,' Luke said the next day. 'We're having a working lunch.'

She coughed. 'Lunch is meant to be a *break*.'

'Refilling the well. Yeah, yeah, you told me.' He flapped a dismissive hand. 'But I need to brief you a little bit about this weekend.'

'The operative word being "little". I thought you wanted me to do it completely as a mystery shopping kind of thing?'

'Even mystery shoppers need a brief. Look, it's time for lunch. If you don't have anything better planned, there's a very good pizza place round the corner.'

He'd dressed it up as a business thing—but he knew full well that wasn't what he was offering. This was the same as her offer to him the previous day of a weekend in the country: a date that wasn't a date.

He'd enjoyed spending time with her in that tiny, perfect garden. And even though the alarm bells were ringing in his head, warning him that this was a dangerous game, he wanted more. Something about this woman made him want to break the rules. Get to know her better.

'Sounds good to me. As long as we split the bill.'

'You,' he said, 'are the boss.'

She laughed. 'Yeah, right.'

He loved the way she laughed. It made him feel as if the sun had just come out after a dull, grey morning.

And why a beautiful, clever, warm woman with a sense of fun was still single was beyond him. He wouldn't have been surprised to learn that Sara Fleet had been snapped up the second she'd turned sixteen.

Or maybe that was it. Maybe she was a widow. True, she was very young to be a widow—but life wasn't always fair, and if she'd loved her husband that much… Then again, she was using her maiden name.

And why was he speculating about something that was

none of his business? He shook himself. 'Let's go so we can beat the rush.'

They arrived in time to grab a seat under one of the umbrellas on the terrace overlooking the river.

'Do you recommend anything?' Sara asked.

'It's all good. The pizzas are wood-fired, so they're fabulous. Wine?'

'Thanks, but I'll stick to sparkling water. If I drink at lunchtime, it makes me want to curl up and go to sleep.'

Luke suppressed the thought that he'd like to watch her curled up and sleeping, satiated after making love. He was meant to be keeping this strictly business. But there was something about her that drew him.

They settled on pizza, and sharing focaccia bread and a simple salad. But when the waiter arrived, he was clearly struggling to write down their order.

'Luke, would you mind if I ordered?' Sara cut in gently.

He spread his hands. 'Be my guest.'

She said a few words in what Luke guessed was Italian, and the waiter beamed at her before bursting into an absolute torrent of language. Sara was smiling back, speaking just as rapidly. Luke didn't have a clue what they were talking about, but he liked the lilting sound of the words from her mouth.

The waiter was clearly also charmed, because he disappeared into the kitchen and returned almost immediately with a rose in a vase.

A pink rose.

She thanked him, and he gave her a deep bow before disappearing to see to another customer.

Luke grinned. 'Trust you to make sure we take time to smell the roses.'

She flushed. 'Sorry. I wasn't showing off, just then— Gianfranco was struggling and it's hard enough dealing with customers without the language barrier. He's only been in

England for a week; he's come over to work in his uncle's business in his gap year.'

Luke was impressed that she'd found out so much information in such a short space of time. Then again, there was something about Sara that made you want to trust her.

Which made her dangerous.

He pushed the thought away. 'It was kind of you to help out. So you speak Italian fluently.' Then he remembered. 'And I've stolen your week in Italy.'

She shrugged. 'I hadn't booked my ticket, so it wasn't a problem. I can go to Sorrento some other time.'

'Well, I feel guilty.'

'Good.' She grinned at him. 'You can buy me pudding to make up for it.'

That zest for life, that love of food…and it was so refreshing, after the time he'd spent with women who nibbled on a lettuce leaf and made a fuss about counting carbs. 'Deal. So do you speak any other languages?'

'French. A bit of German. And I can scrape by in Greek, provided I have a dictionary.'

'Impressive.' He smiled ruefully. 'I never really learned languages at school. I haven't needed to, for work.'

'You can speak the universal language, though. Money.'

'Well enough.' He shrugged. 'Have you been to Scarborough before?'

'No—we always tended to go south, down to the coast at Sussex. You?'

'A long time ago,' he said. It was one of the few memories from his childhood that was happy.

'You're right. The pizza's excellent,' she said after her first mouthful. 'And so's the bread—I love it that they do it with rosemary here. It reminds me of Florence.'

'So you like ruins?' He remembered her degree was in history, so it was pretty obvious she'd be interested in that kind of thing.

'It's the way the past still echoes down through to the present, and the beauty never fades.'

When she talked about something she enjoyed, she was really animated, he noticed. And her enthusiasm was infectious. 'You could've been a teacher. You would've really inspired your classes,' he said.

She wrinkled her nose. 'I did think about it. But there's so much red tape in education—it would just suck the joy out of it, for me. Besides, I like what I do now.'

And if she'd been a teacher, she wouldn't have walked into his life.

Although Luke didn't join her in having a pudding, he indulged in a rich, dark coffee, and when they returned to the office he was shocked to discover they'd been out for an hour and a half. Considering that lunch for him was usually just long enough to eat a sandwich… He made a mental note to put in the extra time that evening, and forced himself to concentrate on figures and phone calls for the rest of the afternoon.

He'd just replaced the receiver when she put a mug of coffee on his desk. 'Problem?'

'Nothing major. The guy I was playing in a league match tonight—he needs to reschedule because something important cropped up at work. Which means I have a court booked but no partner.' He looked speculatively at her. 'I don't suppose you…?'

'Absolutely not.'

'I thought you said exercise was good for you?'

She shook her head, laughing. 'I'm hopeless at racquet sports. Justin tried to teach me, and I was so embarrassingly bad that he had to admit defeat.'

'I could teach you.'

Her eyes met his and awareness zinged through him. Both knew he hadn't been talking about just squash.

'Thanks for the offer, but it's not really me.' This time, she was the one to give the speculative look. 'Though if you're at a loose end…'

'What?'

'You didn't look that convinced at lunchtime when I told you why I loved ruins. Come and see something with me. And you don't have an excuse—you just told me your squash match was cancelled.'

'Has anyone told you that you're a bulldozer in disguise?'

She laughed. 'Yup. So are you game?'

He should say no. Use the time to work. But his mouth didn't seem to be working in synch with his brain. 'Sure.'

'Something' turned out to be the British Museum. 'I love the courtyard here,' she said. 'It's the light and shade—just lovely.'

A big, wide open space with a glass ceiling, triangles radiating out from a central column. He could see exactly what she meant.

He'd never really spent any time in museums. But when she took him to see the Egyptian mummies and the Roman mosaics, he could see it through her eyes and was enchanted.

'Haven't you ever done this before?' she asked, clearly surprised.

'I guess when you live in a place, you take it for granted and don't get round to doing the touristy things.'

'True, and doing them on your own's not such fun because you don't get to share them and talk about them with someone.' She reached out and took his hand for a moment, squeezing it. 'Maybe we can come back together some time.'

'That'd be nice.'

What really shocked him was that he meant it. He wanted to spend time with her. He liked the sound of her voice and could've listened to her all day when she told him about the things that clearly grabbed her attention. And he *really* liked the touch of her skin against his.

Ah, hell. This wasn't supposed to happen. He didn't *do* relationships. He always had brief and mutually satisfying affairs with women who knew the score. Women who moved in the same glittering social circles. Women who didn't have wedding bells in their eyes or want him to meet their families.

Sara Fleet was a mass of contradictions. Efficient and businesslike, and yet warm and touchy-feely at the same time. He still hadn't quite recovered from that kiss on the cheek earlier that afternoon. God only knew how he'd stopped himself turning his face to hers and capturing her mouth.

And right now her hand was curled round his.

It was oh, so tempting. All he had to do was raise her hand to his lips. Kiss the backs of her fingers. Turn her wrist over and press his mouth to the pulse point, see if it jumped as hard and fast as his own heart was beating right then.

It didn't matter that they were standing in the middle of a public place. The rest of the world just faded away. He could pull her into his arms. Cup her face. Lower his mouth to hers. Taste the sweetness on offer...

'Luke?'

Uh. He really was losing the plot. He never, but never, allowed himself to be distracted like this. 'Yeah, fine,' he said, not really sure what he was agreeing to, but the warmth of her smile promised him it was something good. 'Listen, I'd better let you go. You'll need to pack for tomorrow.'

'And you, no doubt, are planning to squeeze in some work.'

'A teensy bit.' Which might just stop him thinking about kissing her.

'You,' she said, 'are impossible.'

'So I've been told.' He disentangled his fingers from hers and was dismayed to find that he actually missed their warmth and pressure.

Not good at all.

He was twenty-eight, not thirteen. Time he remembered that and acted like it. 'Come on. I'll put you in a taxi.'

'I'm perfectly capable of getting the Tube.'

'I know. But humour me.'

'Depends.'

'On what?'

'I'll take a taxi,' she said, 'if you agree to paddle in the sea with me on Saturday.'

'And you say *I'm* impossible?' He rolled his eyes. 'Come on.' He hailed a taxi, paid the driver and waved her goodbye.

And the worst thing was, he couldn't wait to see her tomorrow.

'You,' he told himself loudly, 'need your head examined. She's a complication you don't need.'

Though he had a nasty feeling that he was protesting just a little too much.

# CHAPTER FOUR

'IT'LL take us five hours to get there,' Luke said when Sara walked into the office the next morning. 'So we'll leave at two, when you're back from lunch. That way we'll get there at seven, we'll have time to unpack and have a quick shower and then we'll have dinner.'

Sara looked surprised. 'We're not stopping on the way?'

'Not unless you need a comfort break.'

'What about you?'

He wrinkled his nose dismissively. 'I'd rather just get there.'

'You're the boss.'

There was definite sass in her tone, but Luke didn't rise to the bait. He spent the morning in meetings and his lunchtime reading reports. Sara was back at two o'clock precisely, as he'd expected.

'Only one suitcase—and a small one at that?' he queried.

'We're only away for two days. Why would I need more?' She rolled her eyes. 'Clearly you mix with the wrong sort of woman.'

'Meaning?'

'High maintenance—the sort who can't open a door without checking for damage to their nails. And whose top drawer is full of make-up and emergency hair spray, and who travel with six changes of clothes per day.'

He laughed. 'Point taken. But it's refreshing.' Like her shoes, though he refrained from commenting. Today's were suede, in a deep teal colour to match her camisole top.

Then he wished he hadn't thought about matching shoes. Because it made him wonder if her underwear matched, too. And what she'd look like in just teal-coloured lacy underwear and those shoes and the black pearl choker, with her hair loose instead of worn up, and…

'I'll carry that. You can lock up behind us,' he said gruffly.

'I can carry my own case.'

'As you say, I mix with the wrong sort of woman. I'll carry the cases. And my laptop.' He lobbed the bunch of keys at her; as he'd expected, she caught them automatically. She gave him a speaking look, but locked up and followed him down the stairs to his car.

'Nice,' she said, clearly appreciating the sleek lines of his car, then frowned as he opened the back door. 'Aren't you going to put the cases in the boot?'

'There's no room.'

'What, you're taking half a filing cabinet with you or something?'

'It's a hybrid car,' he said. 'The one downside is that the battery takes up most of the space in the boot.'

'You've got an eco car?' She raised an eyebrow. 'I'd have expected you to go for a really flash sports car. A limited-edition thing.'

He laughed. 'Absolutely. I have my name on the list for an eco sports car that's going to be on sale in about…oh, seven years' time. But this'll do for the time being.'

'It doesn't look like the one my sister drives. Hers is eco too, but it's…well…' She wrinkled her nose.

'Ugly?' he finished. 'I'm with you all the way. Just because a car's environmentally friendly, it doesn't have to *look* worthy. You can be green and still have fun.'

'But you don't have fun,' she pointed out.

'Oh, but I do,' he purred. He moistened his lower lip, aware that she was watching every move, and enjoyed the way her colour heightened. Good. So she wasn't quite as cool and collected as she made out.

He stowed their cases on the back seat, then opened the passenger door for her. 'And don't give me a hard time about being perfectly capable of opening a door yourself.'

'Would I?' She gave him a wicked grin, then sat on the seat and swung her legs gracefully into the car in a move that could've come straight from finishing school. And her knee-length skirt rose up just enough to make his own temperature rise accordingly.

Well, it served him right for playing games.

And he was going to need the air con on full to cool him down.

'This car was really expensive, wasn't it?' she asked when he slid into the driver's seat.

'That depends on your definition of expensive.' He gave a half shrug. 'I like to drive in comfort.'

'I can see that. A real wood and leather interior. Justin would just drool over this.' She laughed. 'Well, he'd drool more if it was an E-type Jag.'

'If it was a red one, so would I. But classic cars need a lot of maintenance and a lot of time.'

'Which you're not prepared to spend.'

He smiled ruefully. 'You said it.'

'Hmm. I really didn't have you pegged as an eco warrior.'

He indicated the building behind them. 'This place is carbon neutral. It's one of the reasons I chose the office space.' She didn't need to know that he owned a sizeable chunk of the building. 'And my hotel chain is going to be carbon neutral, too. Using as many local materials as possible.'

'That's why Dad turned the orchard organic when my grandad let him take over the reins,' Sara said. 'It means our costs are higher, but it's worth it.'

Something else they agreed on.

It was beginning to scare him, just how well she matched him.

He wasn't in the market for a relationship. Didn't want the commitment. Didn't need the hassle and misery he knew that a family could bring.

He really needed to get his head straight and concentrate on this new venture instead of thinking about how sexy the curve of Sara Fleet's mouth was.

'So why Scarborough?' Sara asked.

'I'm looking for a hotel in a spa town. Scarborough was famous for its waters in its heyday. I'm looking at another in Cromer, and one in Buxton.'

'Why not somewhere closer to London, so you don't have so much travelling time?'

Because Scarborough was the only place he could ever remember having a family holiday. Not in a hotel—they'd stayed in a little guest house—but they'd had a week of sun and sea when he was tiny. Before his mother had turned into a shadow of herself and his father had let them both down. Not that he was going to explain that to Sara. It was irrelevant. 'I'm just exploring my options at this stage,' he said.

'So this place in Scarborough…'

He shook his head. 'If I tell you the facts and figures it'll colour your view. I want to know what you think of the place as a customer. What's good, what's bad, what's missing.'

'Do they know you're thinking about buying it?'

'No. As far as they're concerned we're just customers, and that's the way I want it. I'm not trying to catch anyone out. I just want to see things as they are on a normal day—not when they've made a special effort.'

For the first three hours of the journey, they worked. Sara answered his phone, made appointments, sorted out his schedule for the next three weeks and talked business.

And then she stopped.

'Five on the dot?' he teased.

'Five on the dot,' she agreed—and, to his horror, switched his phone off.

'What are you doing?' he asked.

'I've put your phone on to voice mail. Turning it off means it'll be much less stressful for you than hearing the three rings before your voice mail cuts in—because, knowing you, you'll start nagging me to bend the rules and answer it. And no, you're not putting it onto hands-free and answering it yourself.'

Bossy didn't even begin to cover it. And Luke was too surprised to argue.

'Righty. Now this is a fabulous sound system.'

'It has nineteen speakers,' Luke said.

'Nineteen? That's excessive.' She groaned. 'Boys and their toys. Rupert—he's my baby brother—he would just *love* this. Let's see. What have we here?' She fiddled with the playlist. 'Oh, I should've guessed. Dinosaur rock.'

'It's not dinosaur, it's indie. And it's great to drive to,' he protested.

'Yeah, yeah.' Though at least she switched it on.

'I suppose you're into ballet music,' he retorted.

'What makes you say that?'

'You're all posh and pearls,' he said with a grin. 'See, I can do stereotypes, too.'

She paused. 'Actually, I do like ballet music. And, before you ask, yes, I did have ballet lessons when I was young.'

'And piano and horse-riding?'

'Don't be chippy.'

'I'm not. It's just…how the other half live.' He gave her a sidelong glance. 'I can just see you in a tutu.'

'You don't wear tutus for practice,' she said loftily. 'You wear leotards and footless tights.'

He could imagine her in a leotard, the material clinging to her body. And then wished he hadn't, when his body reacted predictably.

'Anyway, I stopped doing ballet when I was twelve.'

'Why?'

'To be any good, I would've had to spend hours a day practising,' she said. 'And I didn't want to be a dancer when I grew up, so it wasn't fair for me to take a place in the class if it meant that someone who really wanted to dance missed out. But I enjoyed it while I did it.'

Ballet. That certainly explained the grace with which she walked.

'What about you?' she asked.

'No, I never fancied being a Billy Elliot.' He pushed away the thought that, if he had, his family would've put a stop to it. Ballet didn't exactly go with their lifestyle.

To his relief, she let it go and seemed contented enough to look out of the window and listen to music—the same music she'd just decried, he noted with wry amusement. And it was fine until the traffic information report on the radio cut through the music, at about the same time as he noticed the queue of traffic on the motorway.

'Oh, great,' he said, switching off the engine as they came to a halt at the end of the queue. 'And we're miles away from the next junction, so I can't even take us cross-country to avoid the tailback.'

'Hey, it's not your fault. Accidents happen. We'll just have to wait for the road to clear.'

Though waiting wasn't one of his strong points. When he asked her for the third time to check the Internet on his phone to see if there was an update on the traffic situation, she sighed. 'You can't stand being still, can you?'

'No. I hate wasting time.'

'I doubt very much if anything's changed in the last five minutes. We're stuck,' she said dryly, 'so live with it.'

'Mmm.' He drummed his fingers on the steering wheel.

'You could always talk to me, to take your mind off it.'

Talk? In his experience, when women wanted to talk, it meant trouble. That they'd changed their minds about not wanting a commitment—and they expected him to change, too.

Then again, he wasn't in a relationship with Sara. Officially, they were working—even if she had clocked off. So that made things easy. 'Oh, you want a proper rundown on the hotel.'

She tapped her watch. 'Remember, it's gone five. I'm off duty. So no work talk.'

'What do you want to talk about, then?' He knew it was a mistake even as he uttered the words.

'You,' she said simply. 'I want to get to know you better.'

He wanted to get to know her better, too. Much more intimately. But he knew it was a bad idea. That it would turn his life upside down. And he'd fought too long and too hard to get where he was to throw it all away.

When he didn't reply, she sighed. 'OK. So you're the strong, silent type. Give me your hand.'

'Why?' But he did so.

She inspected his knuckles. 'Wow. No grazes. I'm impressed. What did you do, wear gloves?'

To stop his knuckles dragging on the floor, she meant. He couldn't help laughing. 'I'm not a Neanderthal, Sara.'

'You're not a new man either, I'd bet.'

'You want a *personal* conversation?'

She must've seen the warning glitter in his eyes because she flushed. 'Not that kind of personal. I just wondered what made you tick.'

'Same as most people. Oxygen and food.'

She rolled her eyes. 'You made your first million before you were twenty. Given that you're not a computer geek…at least, I don't think you are?'

She was fishing. Not good. He needed to head her off. 'No. I'm just good at economics.'

'So how did you find that out? You worked in a family business?'

His family had definitely had a business. Generation after generation had gone into it. But he'd chosen not to. 'No.'

'Then how?'

She clearly wasn't going to let this rest. And, given that all three lanes of the motorway were jammed solid, he couldn't go anywhere. So he'd tell her some of it. 'I was good at maths, and my teacher had a hunch.'

She didn't need to know it was the teacher who'd bailed him

out of the police station when his family had proved impossible to contact.

Ha. Everyone knew the rules: get caught, and you're on your own. It had been a waste of time even trying to get hold of his family, and the police had known it. They'd had to follow procedure—but they'd wasted little time before contacting his school.

And they'd struck gold.

So had he.

Literally.

'Hunch?' Sara queried.

'That I'd be good at economics as well as maths.' He smiled wryly. 'It didn't do much for my street cred, having extra lessons at lunchtime.' Not that anyone would've dared say anything to him about it. They knew who his family was. The school bullies chose targets without any implied muscle behind them.

'But it paid off.'

'Yep. I got a job on Saturdays and school holidays, working on a market stall.' Again, thanks to his teacher, who'd happened to live next door to the trader—and who'd guaranteed that Luke wasn't like his family and there wouldn't be any trouble. 'The original barrow boy, that's me.'

And he needed to get his patter back. Fast. Get her away from the subject of families. 'I talked the stallholder into giving me a share of the stall instead of an hourly wage, and put most of my profits back into the business. Worked out some new lines. And within a year we'd expanded. By the time I was fifteen, I had my own stall and I paid someone to work on it while I was at school.'

And he'd refused to launder any of the family's money. It had caused rows, but he'd stood his ground. And when his cousin had tried to teach him about family loyalty...that was where his other extra-curricular lessons had come in handy.

Boxing.

He'd broken his cousin's nose.

And it had sickened him, how easy it had been to fall into

the spiral of violence and crime. He didn't want to be like his family—and yet the only way to prove it to them had been to act the way they did. Wrong, wrong, *wrong*.

Luke had also been the one to clean up his cousin's face and take him to hospital. And when they'd returned to the house, he'd quietly explained to his family that he wanted to stay straight. That he didn't want to have any part of what they did. And he'd given them an ultimatum: they had to accept that or let him go.

They'd turned their backs on him.

Every single one of them.

Even his mother.

He'd learned then what family really meant. Toe the line or you were out. Try to follow a different dream, and they wouldn't be there to encourage you.

He was on his own.

So he'd packed and left that evening. Slept on the street because it was too late to find somewhere to stay. And the following day—after he'd returned to hospital and discovered that the reason why his hand still hurt was because he'd broken it— he'd found himself a bedsit where the landlord accepted cash and asked no questions.

'So you ended up owning half the market, did you?' Sara asked.

'No. It was the start of the Internet revolution. I found someone who could do me a website, someone else who could handle the postage and delivery side of things and a wholesaler who'd give me a bulk discount. It was a bit of a gamble, but it paid off. The business went just the way I hoped it would.'

'You decided not to go to university, then?'

He shook his head. 'I wanted to be out in the real world. Making money instead of listening to other people talk about it.' That, and the fact that he hadn't sat his exams. With his writing hand broken, there hadn't been any point in even turning up for the papers. So he'd left school at fifteen without any formal qualifications. Which meant no A levels. Which meant no university.

Though Luke had always known that he wouldn't make it in the money markets. Not with his family background. Who would trust the son of a thief, the grandson of a fraudster? And quite how he'd managed to talk his way onto the MBA course where he'd met Karim, he'd never know.

'So you were a dot-com millionaire.'

'Yes.' He shrugged. 'And then I got bored.'

'And that's when you started buying failing businesses, to see if you could make them work again?'

He knew he should give her a one-word answer and change the subject. And yet...there was something about Sara. Something that encouraged him to talk. So, against his better judgement he told her. 'It was by accident, really. The gym I went to...I used to have a beer with the owner, from time to time.' A friend of his old boxing teacher—who'd lectured him like mad on the idiocy of bare-knuckle fighting and who'd said he needed to learn the discipline of martial arts instead. 'Anyway, Lin told me that the landlords were hiking the rent yet again and he wasn't going to be able to cover his costs, so he was having to sell up. I didn't want the hassle of finding another gym that suited me, so I talked him into letting me have a quick look at his books to see if I could do anything.' He smiled. 'I could see the problems, and I managed to fix them. In return, Lin gave me a free pass to the gym and taught me kick-boxing.'

'Kick-boxing? Isn't that...well, violent?'

'Not if it's done properly. It's controlled and disciplined.'

'Like you.'

'Like me,' he agreed. 'Best thing ever if you've had a bad day and you want to get rid of the stress.'

'By kicking hell out of someone, you mean?'

'No.' That was what certain members of his family had done. Maybe even still did. Another reason why he didn't want anything to do with their life, ever. 'Kick-boxing's fast-paced but it's *controlled*. And the discipline you learn from it helps with other sports.'

'So you're a sports freak.'

'What do you expect from a guy who owns several health clubs?' he asked mildly. 'I play squash a couple of times a week, I do kick-boxing a couple of times a week and I do some training in the machine room the rest of the time.'

She groaned. 'Don't tell me—and you never miss a sporting event on television.'

'Actually, I don't have a television.'

She stared at him, looking surprised for a moment. 'Let me guess. You don't bother watching because you'd rather spend the time working.'

'Got it in one.'

'But don't you…? Well, you must do something to relax.'

'I do.' It often involved a party with some fairly tedious conversation, followed by hot sex. He even considered telling her so, just to see if it would shock her. 'Sometimes I go and see a band. Dinosaur rock, as you'd have it. You can't beat it when it's really loud.'

'What about the cinema? The theatre?'

'Not really my cup of tea.'

Then, to his relief, the traffic started moving. 'About time, too,' he commented. He glanced at the clock on the dashboard. 'We're going to be about an hour late. But it'll still be early enough to eat.' And from now on he'd keep the conversation to safe topics. Such as work.

# CHAPTER FIVE

AT FIVE past eight, Luke pulled up in the hotel car park. Sara schooled her face into neutral as she looked at the building. The paint was peeling off the stucco and the woodwork; she had to remind herself that seaside buildings always looked scruffy because of the salt content in the air. And maybe the place would be better inside, less run-down.

But her hopes faded as they walked into reception.

'I'm sorry, there's been a problem.' The receptionist looked ready to burst into tears when Luke started to check in. 'We had a burst pipe this afternoon and we can't put you in the rooms you booked.'

'Not to worry. We don't mind taking two different rooms,' Luke said.

The receptionist bit her lip. 'That's the thing. The water damage…it means we only have one room left. A double.'

Sara stared at her in horror. Surely the girl wasn't suggesting that they should *share* a room?

But that seemed to be precisely what she was saying.

'Luke. We need to talk,' she said in an urgent whisper, nudging his arm.

He let her lead him away from the desk. 'What?'

'We can't share a room. We'll have to go somewhere else.'

'At this time on a Friday night in the middle of summer, we'll be lucky to find anywhere else.'

'There must be *somewhere*.'

Luke rolled his eyes. 'For pity's sake, Sara. We've been stuck in the car for the last six hours. Right now all I want to do is eat, have a shower, check my emails and sleep. OK, so we didn't plan on sharing a room. But it's only for one night. We're adults and we're colleagues and we're perfectly capable of sharing a room without having sex.'

She wasn't so sure. 'Uh-huh.'

He sighed. 'Look, I'm not going to leap on you.'

There was no answer to that. And she couldn't exactly tell him she thought it was more likely that she'd leap on *him*. So she said nothing.

He clearly misread her silence, because he closed his eyes briefly. 'Before you say it, it's not because I think you're unattractive either, because you are. And telling you you're attractive doesn't mean I'm going to try making a move on you.' He shook his head. 'Why do women have to be so bloody *complicated*?'

He meant *needy*, she knew. She lifted her chin. 'I'm not complicated.'

'I'm not in the mood for an argument. I'm tired and I want a shower and something to eat. We'll cope. Look, I'll ask for an extra duvet or something and I'll sleep on the floor.'

'Uh-huh.'

He walked back over to the reception desk. 'Thanks. We'll take the room,' he said.

Sara simply followed him when he pocketed the room key and picked up both their cases.

The room was even worse than she'd feared. Small, with only just enough room for the bed, one narrow bedside table, a built-in wardrobe and a chest of drawers. No way was there enough space for him to sleep on the floor. They'd have to share the bed.

'Don't say a thing,' he warned, dumping their cases on the bed. 'Right now, my first priority is food.'

The meal turned out to be as awful as the room. Apart from

the fact it took ages to arrive, her grilled chicken was so dry it tasted like ashes, the sauce was decidedly gloopy and the vegetables were soggy. His food clearly wasn't much better, because he picked at it and finally pushed his plate away.

'Maybe everything seems so bad because we've had a rotten journey,' she said. 'Maybe everything will seem better tomorrow.'

'Maybe.' He didn't look convinced. 'Right now, the only thing this place has going for it is the staff.'

A receptionist who'd gone into panic mode, a cook who—well, couldn't—and a waitress who'd whispered at them.

But that wasn't fair. For all she knew, the burst pipe had affected the kitchen as well. Perhaps the cook had had a lousy day and this wasn't the normal standard of the food here.

Even so, surely Luke wasn't really intending to buy this place?

On the other hand, he'd said how much he liked turning round businesses that were in a mess. This one definitely seemed a mess, and it was just the sort of challenge she had a feeling he'd love.

'Right. I need a shower and I want to check my emails.'

And then…they'd be going to bed.

Together.

Her mouth went dry.

As he'd said, they were adults. They were perfectly capable of sleeping in the same room—the same bed—without having sex. But even so she felt the adrenalin flooding through to her fingertips as she followed Luke to their room.

He opened the door and stood aside, letting her through first. And then her stomach rumbled. Really loudly.

She grimaced. 'Sorry.'

'Not your fault.' He shrugged. 'We could go and find the nearest fast-food place.'

True, but she also knew he was tired. Just as she would be, had she spent six solid hours driving. 'I've got a better idea. Hang on a sec.' She rummaged in her suitcase and produced a large bar of chocolate. 'My emergency stash.'

'You carry emergency chocolate?' He looked amused.

'Don't knock it.'

'I wouldn't dream of it.' He sat on the bed and gratefully took the large piece she broke off for him. 'This is good stuff,' he said after the first taste. 'Thanks.' He smiled ruefully. 'I'm sorry I've dragged you into this. The hotel wasn't meant to be this bad. A bit run-down—shabby genteel, that's what the agent told me.'

'Sexing it up.' Oh, hell. She really shouldn't have said that word. Sara avoided Luke's gaze. 'I mean, it might look better in the morning.'

'I don't think so, somehow.' He paused. 'Do you want the first shower while I check my emails?'

'Thanks.'

At least the water was hot. But there weren't any complimentary toiletries; Sara was glad she'd thought to bring shower gel with her.

Though there was nothing she could do about her pyjamas: a little strappy top and cropped trousers which emphasised her curves. Still, she'd worked out very quickly that Luke was a man of honour; she could trust his word.

Whether she could trust herself was another matter.

He was sitting on the edge of the bed, rapidly typing on his laptop, when she emerged from the bathroom. He glanced up at her. 'That's the first time I've seen your hair down.'

She usually wore it up for work.

'I like it,' he added. 'Given that I know your low opinion of high-maintenance women, dare I ask if you use straighteners on it?'

'It's naturally like this.' She smiled wryly. 'Dead straight. And I used to hate it when I was younger. I used to go to bed in plaits, even though they were uncomfortable.'

'All for the sake of curls? You needn't have bothered.'

'I know. They usually fell out by the time I'd had breakfast.'

'That isn't what I meant—I was trying to pay you a compliment. It suits you like that.' Then he scanned her from top to toe. 'I'm glad one of us has something to sleep in.'

Sara felt her eyes widen. 'What do you mean?'

'I don't normally bother. And, as I wasn't expecting to share a room with you, I don't have any pyjamas with me.' He smiled wryly. 'Actually, I don't think I even possess a pair.'

She could well believe it. And the idea of sleeping next to him while he was completely naked... Her face felt hot, so she guessed that she'd blushed deeply. Really obviously.

He lifted a shoulder. 'Don't worry, Sara. I'll make myself decent so I won't embarrass you. I'm going to have a shower.' He climbed off the bed. 'Choose which side you want. I'm not fussy.'

When Luke came out of the bathroom a few minutes later, wearing just a pair of jersey boxer shorts, Sara had arranged herself in bed, on the side with the light and the bedside table, and was busily studying a puzzle magazine. She just hoped that Luke didn't look over her shoulder at the page, or he'd see that she was filling in the answers randomly—and she knew he was sharp enough to work out that it was because her concentration was shot to pieces.

His skin was still damp from his shower, his hair was tousled and he looked utterly edible. Her pulse rate went up several notches.

'The shower was freezing,' he remarked.

Guilt flooded through her. 'Sorry. I didn't realise I'd used all the hot water.'

'In a hotel, you're not supposed to be able to use all the hot water,' he reminded her.

'Maybe it's to do with the burst pipe. I never thought about it.'

He spread his hands. 'No matter. It's probably just as well. I needed a cold shower anyway.'

Her nipples tightened. Was he saying he was just as attracted to her and needed to cool his desire? And he'd said earlier that he thought she was attractive...

She didn't dare meet his gaze, just made a noncommittal murmur and continued pretending to do her puzzle.

As he climbed into bed beside her, the mattress dipped under his weight. He shifted, then shifted again, turned his pillow over and shifted yet again.

'I've changed my mind about shabby genteel,' he said crossly. 'This place is just *shabby*. The mattress is lumpy, too.'

Sara couldn't help laughing.

'What?' he demanded.

'Complaining about the mattress. Isn't it meant to be the princess and the pea, not the prince and the pea?' she teased.

'Very funny.' But then, as she lowered her puzzle book to glance at him, he smiled wryly at her. 'Ah, ignore me, Sara. I'm tired and grumpy. I'm going to get some sleep. Goodnight.'

'Goodnight.'

He turned so that his back was to her. She pretended to do a couple more clues, then closed the book and switched off the bedside light. But she couldn't sleep; she lay awake in the darkness, aware that Luke's body was very close to hers and that he was wearing very, very little.

And it was oh, so tempting to turn on her side and curl into him. Slide her arm round his waist and press her cheek against his back, absorbing the warmth of his body—despite the fact that it was the middle of summer, the night had a distinct chill to it.

And if she cuddled in to him, what then? Would he lace his fingers through hers? Or would he turn so that he was facing her, holding her close to his heart? Would he dip his head, steal a kiss?

She knew there was an attraction between them. One neither of them had acted on, because they were being sensible and businesslike and adult about things. But she also knew that there was no reason why they couldn't act on that attraction. They were both free, both single.

Except…

After Hugh, Sara had promised herself she would only get

involved with a man who'd commit to her. A man who'd put her before his job.

Luke Holloway wasn't that kind of man. He was a self-confessed workaholic who got bored easily. Who thrived on change. Who hadn't committed to any of his previous girl-friends—his relationships lasted a matter of weeks. Given the little he'd told her about his past, she was pretty sure he had huge barriers in place to make sure nobody came too close.

No, Luke wasn't Mr Right.

And she'd do well to remember that.

She heard his breathing deepen and become regular; he was clearly asleep. And then Sara, too, turned on her side with her back to him, relaxed and allowed herself to drift off.

The following morning, Sara was aware of light filtering through the curtains. Drowsily, she started to open her eyes—and then she realised where she was.

In bed with Luke Holloway.

But not as she'd gone to sleep last night, with her back facing his.

No, somehow, in the night, they'd moved into each other's arms. Her head was on his shoulder, her leg was draped over both of his, her hand was curled intimately round his inner thigh and her fingers were resting under the hem of his boxer shorts. Against his bare skin.

Which meant there were just a couple of millimetres between her fingers and his erect penis.

Oh, no.

She was practically *groping* him.

How on earth could she possibly face him?

The one good thing was that his breathing was even and regular and deep; clearly Luke was still asleep. If she could just move her leg without waking him, remove her hand from its intimate position and wriggle out of his arms, she could rescue the situation.

She'd just started to move, very carefully and very gently, when she became aware of a rumble of laughter in his chest. And his voice was full of amusement when he said, 'So Sleeping Beauty wakes at last…'

# CHAPTER SIX

MORTIFYING.

This was utterly, utterly *mortifying*.

Luke had been awake all the time—and he'd been well aware of exactly where her hands were.

'Have you been awake long?' she asked, silently praying that the answer would be no.

It wasn't.

'Long enough,' he said.

Worse and worse. So he must have been lying there for ages. And the situation must be just as awkward for him: after all, he was the one being draped over. Being groped. Hastily, she shifted so she was no longer sprawled over him and removed her hand. 'I'm sorry. Um…Luke, I didn't mean to…' Her voice faded and she could feel her face heating.

'I know you didn't. And I don't mind.'

But she did. She was practically squirming with embarrassment.

'It's a little more than not minding,' he said softly. 'Actually, I liked having your hands on me.' He drew his free hand down her side, moulding his palm to her curves. 'And I like having my hands on you, too.'

She dragged in a breath. 'I thought you said…' That they could be adult about it. That they could share a room—a bed—without having sex.

'That was last night. This is now. Different day, different viewpoint.' He gave her a wicked grin. 'And I could point out that I wasn't the person with one leg sprawled over you and my hand up your pyjamas.'

This time, she did squirm. 'That's a bit below the belt.'

His grin widened. 'So was your hand.'

Oh, help. This was getting worse and worse.

He shifted so that he was facing her. He still had one arm wrapped round her, holding her close to him; his cornflower blue eyes were lazy and sexy and irresistible.

'Good morning,' he said softly.

'Good morning.' She just about managed to get the words out; right now, with that hot, sexy expression in his eyes, she could barely breathe. Even though she knew it wasn't physically possible, desire seemed to have taken the place of oxygen in her lungs.

He dipped his head slightly and kissed the tip of her nose. 'Sara.'

This was tempting. Incredibly tempting. She could see in his face what he wanted.

The same thing that *she* wanted.

Though if they gave in to their mutual urge and made love, it would make their working relationship seriously awkward.

'We shouldn't do this,' she warned, her voice shaky.

He stroked her face. 'I know. This is a seriously bad idea. I should have more self-control.'

'We've only known each other for a couple of weeks,' she pointed out.

'That's long enough. I already know you. You're bossy.'

'Bossy?'

'Yeah, but I forgive you because you're good at what you do and you're good to work with.' He stole a brief kiss. 'You love the colour pink. You're a history nut, you like girly films and the theatre, you believe everyone's nice, you're mad enough to enjoy filing, you play the piano and you have a thing about ice cream and paddling in the sea. What else do I need to know?'

'Nothing, I suppose.' She bit her lip. 'I know hardly anything about you. Just that you're a hotshot businessman who hates clutter. You like posh chocolate biscuits, you take your coffee black with one sugar, you do kick-boxing and squash and you never watch television. You listen to dinosaur rock, and you have a seriously expensive taste in cars. That's not a lot, Luke.'

'There isn't much more to me than that.'

'I'm sure there is.'

'Shallow as a puddle, that's me.'

'Like hell. You're more like still waters running deep.'

'Still.' He tested the word. 'Hmm. Interesting. I don't think anyone's ever said that about me before. And I'm not sure whether it goes with the other description you use for me—workaholic.'

'All right, so you live your life at a hundred miles an hour and I'm mixing my metaphors,' she said crossly.

'I've just thought of something else about you. You talk too much and there's only one way I can think of to shut you up.'

She lifted her chin. 'That's so corny.'

'True, though. The only thing I can think about right now. Kissing you. Touching you.'

'That's two things.'

He groaned. 'I mean it. I really want to kiss you.' He moistened his lower lip. 'I've wanted you for *days*, Sara—probably since the moment you walked into my office and started bossing me about.'

It was the same for her. The moment she'd seen him with his feet up on the desk, talking on the phone, his hair sexily rumpled. Which was why she'd let him talk her into staying longer, being his temporary PA, instead of just finishing the trouble-shooting job and moving on to the next client. 'Me, too,' she admitted.

'So there's a pretty logical conclusion here.' He traced her lower lip with his thumb and Sara's lips automatically parted.

'I'm so glad you agree with me,' he said softly and bent his head to kiss her. His mouth brushed against hers, the contact light and teasing and tempting her to respond. When she tipped her head back slightly, he deepened the kiss, offering and demanding at the same time.

Sara had kissed men before. Been to bed with men before. But this… This was something else. The feel of Luke's mouth against hers made every nerve-end tingle, made her blood feel as if it were fizzing through her veins.

His fingers slid under the hem of her pyjama top. He stroked her waist, the pads of his fingertips brushing against her skin, and she shivered, wanting more. Taking the invitation, he let his hand slide slowly up her body until he cupped one breast. His thumb rubbed across her hardened nipple, which suddenly felt supersensitive to his touch. A touch that wasn't enough for her. She needed more.

He broke the kiss. 'Do you like that?' he asked softly.

'Mmm.' She couldn't quite manage a proper word.

'Then how about this?' He shimmied down the bed and, to her shock, he opened his mouth over her nipple, sucking her through her pyjama top. A pulse started to beat rapidly between her thighs and she couldn't help sliding her fingers through his hair, urging him on.

'I'll take that as a yes,' he whispered, and bunched her top upwards. He nuzzled his way over her stomach, pausing to tease her with the tip of his tongue circling her navel, and then at last, at last, closed his mouth over one nipple. Without the thin jersey of her top in the way, it was even better: the teasing flick of his tongue, the pressure of his lips and the light graze of his teeth against her nipple made her arch against him in pleasure.

And then he slid his hands between her thighs, cupping her through her pyjama bottoms. He rocked his hand, so the base of his thumb rubbed against her clitoris, and she couldn't hold back a whimper of longing. 'Luke.'

He kissed her mouth, hard, then hooked his fingers into the

waistband of her pyjama bottoms and started to pull them down. She raised her hips, letting him pull the material clear, and shivered as he kissed his way down her thighs, caressing every millimetre of skin as he uncovered it.

And then her breath hitched as he worked his way back up again. He paused at the hollows of her ankles, and again at the backs of her knees. By the time he reached her inner thighs, Sara was shaking; gently, he eased her thighs further apart and knelt between them. She couldn't open her eyes; all she could do was whisper, 'Luke, you're driving me crazy.'

'That's the idea.' His voice sounded husky, sensual and sexy as hell.

She wriggled in anticipation, and heard him laugh softly. And then, at last, he drew a finger along her sex—and then all the way back again.

'Please,' she whispered.

He did it again. And again. And then he shifted slightly and she felt his breath against her skin. She held her breath, waiting, willing him to do it. And when she felt the slow stroke of his tongue, she shuddered and fisted her hands in his hair again.

'You taste so sweet,' he whispered against her skin.

In response, she tilted her pelvis.

She felt him shift back slightly. Surely he wasn't going to stop now? She screwed her eyes shut and tipped her head back against the pillows. 'I can't believe you're going to stop now.'

'I'm not intending to stop.'

'Then what?' She opened her eyes and stared at him.

'I'm just checking that you're sure you know what you're doing.'

'Of course I do.'

'Because, if you look at this logically, as you said, this is a seriously bad idea.'

True. Though, right now, stopping felt like an even worse idea. Maybe she'd spoken the words aloud, or maybe he'd just read it in her expression, because he simply said, 'Yeah, it's the same for me.' Then he took her hand and curled it round his erection.

She tightened her grip and rocked her hand slightly, wanting to tease him the way he'd teased her, and he groaned. 'Sara. I can't think straight now. All I want to do is bury myself in you. Deep.'

'Then do it,' she said, 'because I'm going to…to *implode* if you don't carry on.' And, just to make sure he got the message, she tightened her thumb and forefinger round his shaft again and drew the circle slowly up and down.

Just once.

He swallowed hard. 'I need a condom. Now.' He vaulted out of bed, and Sara realised that he must have taken his boxer shorts off at the same time as he'd removed her pyjama bottoms. Naked, Luke was glorious—completely unselfconscious and gorgeous. His body was sculpted and perfectly toned.

And the way he moved, graceful and sure as a dancer, turned her on even more.

He retrieved a condom from his wallet and returned to the bed.

Then it hit her that he carried condoms in his wallet. And how many names she'd seen his linked with.

'Do you do this a lot?' she asked.

'What?'

'Sleep with your staff.'

'Never.' He looked serious. 'It's an unbreakable rule.'

One he was about to break?

As if he'd read her mind, he said softly, 'Strictly speaking, you're not my staff. You're my consultant. You're your own boss.'

'I think you're splitting hairs.'

He reached over and wound the end of her hair round his fingers. 'Mmm. You have lovely hair. I wanted to do this last night. Except I was tired and grumpy and I wouldn't have made it good for you.'

She shivered. 'And you're intending to make it good for me now?'

'Sara, I've barely started.'

She knew she should leave it there, but this nagging voice in her head wouldn't let up. 'So you're good at this. You get a lot of practice.'

He sighed. 'Without being arrogant, yes, I tend to be good at things I like doing.'

*Like making love.*

'And yes to the practice—in the past. I haven't had a lot of time lately, so I haven't seen anyone for a while.'

Which didn't answer her real question.

Her thoughts must have shown on her face, because he stroked her cheek with the backs of his fingers. 'But I know what you're really asking, so I'll tell you. I date a lot, but I'm fussy. Whatever you might read in the gossip columns, I don't sleep with just anything in a skirt.'

He leaned down and brushed his mouth against hers. 'Stop thinking. Just *feel*.' He looked at her and hooked one finger under the strap of her pyjama top, easing it down over her shoulder. The top he'd pushed up earlier to bare her breasts. 'I like this. A lot. But it has to go: I want you skin to skin.'

She couldn't quite get past the implications of what he'd said. 'You have a lot of sex.'

He sighed. 'Sara, I like sex. I like good sex. And, yes, I like lots of it. But, as I told you, I'm fussy.' He paused. 'One thing I should be clear about, though. I'm not in the market for marriage and happy-ever-afters. So this is just you and me, here and now. It's not a declaration of intent, and it's not going to get in the way of work. It's just getting this craziness out of our systems so we can go back to normal and work together. Sara. I like you. I think you like me, or you wouldn't be working with me. Neither of us is seeing anyone else. So where's the problem?'

'Just so you know, I'm not looking for a relationship.'

'Fine.'

'And I'm not in the habit of sleeping around.'

He smiled. 'If it makes you feel better, I don't think you're a tart. That isn't why you're naked—well, almost naked—and in bed with me. That's…'

'…because the hotel's a mess and we had no alternative but to share a room?' she finished.

'I guess. Though I'd also say that it's serendipity. As I said, I've been having trouble keeping my hands off you. When I'm in the office, I keep looking over at you at the computer, and thinking about walking over to you and lifting you out of your chair and laying you on your desk and…' He slid one hand between her thighs again, his fingertips brushing her skin but staying milli-metres away from her sex. 'Touching you. Tasting you. Easing my body into yours and making you come so hard that you forget where you are. Making you come until you scream with pleasure.'

The image flickered in her mind and her mouth went dry. 'Luke,' she whispered.

'I want to be inside you, Sara. Right now. And I think that's where you want me, too.' He moved his hand to cup her sex again. 'You feel hot.'

So hot that she was burning up. 'Yes.' She barely got the word out.

His fingertip skated over her clitoris, with just the right pressure and at just the right speed to push her pulse rate up another notch. She dragged in a breath, and it turned to a gasp of sheer pleasure as he pushed one finger inside her. 'And wet,' he said, his voice dropping an octave.

'Yes.'

'And ready for me.' He paused. 'Say it.'

'I'm ready for you.' Each word was punctuated with a dragged-in breath.

He withdrew his hand. 'Now, lose the top.'

She sat up; her fingers were shaking as she pulled the top over her head. And she felt suddenly shy; even though her hair was long, it wasn't long enough to cover her breasts. And she was sitting there in front of Luke, completely naked. Practically displaying herself to him.

He twirled the ends of her hair round his fingers again. 'You're gorgeous, Sara Fleet. You turn me on—in a big way.'

'All words and no action, Mr Holloway?' Her voice was raspy, but she was determined to give as good as she got—not to be all shy and embarrassed, even though she felt it.

He gave her a wolfish smile. 'I'm going to make you take that back, Ms Fleet. I'm going to make you beg.' He ripped the foil packet open and rolled the condom onto his penis.

'Is that a threat?'

'A promise,' he corrected, his blue eyes glittering with desire.

This time, his kiss was hotter. More demanding. It made her head spin, and then he eased his hand between her legs again, stroking and teasing until her whole body felt hot, almost molten.

'Luke,' she whispered.

In answer, he pushed his finger into her. Very, very slowly. So slowly that it drove her crazy. She tightened her internal muscles round him, and he smiled.

'Anything you want to say to me?' he teased.

She narrowed her eyes at him. 'You *know* what.'

'I'm not a mind-reader,' he added, his eyes glittering. 'Say it.'

'I want you,' she said. 'Inside me.'

He'd said he was going to make her beg. If he made her wait any longer, she'd go crazy. 'Please, Luke.'

He smiled and fitted the tip of his sheathed penis against her sex, and slowly, slowly eased in. He stayed there for a moment, letting her get used to the feel of him, and then she wrapped her legs round his waist, urging him deeper.

Taking his weight on his arms, he dipped down to brush his mouth against hers; she opened her mouth under his and he responded with a kiss that demanded and gave in equal measure.

This man, she thought, could be addictive. Because he paid attention to detail—he noted the change in her breathing when a particular touch or caress excited her, and repeated it until she was quivering and spiralling out of control.

The lumpy mattress was forgotten. All she could focus on

was the way Luke made her feel, the sensation of his body moving inside her and the touch of his skin against hers.

And just as her orgasm hit, he held her closer, murmuring her name over and over like a litany; she could tell from the way his body tensed that he, too, had reached his climax.

When the aftershocks of pleasure died away, he withdrew carefully, moved onto his back and shifted so that he was holding her close. Neither of them spoke; she was happy just to feel the beat of his heart against her cheek.

'I need to deal with something,' he said eventually, stroking her hair. 'Excuse me a moment.'

But as he moved from the bed and she heard water running, the spell broke and she thought about what they'd done. How stupid she'd been.

Her doubts must have shown on her face because he raised an eyebrow on his return from the bathroom. 'What's up?'

'You're right—this was a bad idea. We work together.'

'We've been through this already. It's OK. Relax. We're both professionals, so this isn't going to interfere with work.' He kissed her lightly. 'I'll let you have the first shower. Though it had probably better not be with me, or we won't be out of here until well after lunchtime.'

Oh, the thought that put in her head. If she'd been standing up, her knees would've buckled.

'Go and have a shower,' he repeated. 'Then we're going to have breakfast, look round the hotel and discuss things over lunch.'

'OK.' She paused. 'Um, would you mind handing me my pyjamas? Or closing your eyes?'

'It's a bit late for that. We've seen each other up close and very personal.' He kissed the tip of her nose. 'But if it makes you happy…' He retrieved her pyjamas and handed them to her. 'I'll sit with my back to you and my eyes closed, OK?'

He obviously thought she was being ridiculous—and she probably was, given how intimately they'd explored each other's bodies—but at least he'd humoured her. 'Thank you.' She put her pyjamas back on again, retrieved her clothes from the wardrobe and dresser and locked the bathroom door behind her.

She'd have a shower. Wash her hair. And maybe she could dredge up some common sense in the middle of it all.

# CHAPTER SEVEN

When Sara emerged from the bathroom, fully dressed, Luke was sitting up in bed, covered by a sheet up to his waist, working on his laptop. There was a pile of clothes on the bed next to him; clearly he intended to follow her lead and put his clothes on with a closed door between them.

'The bathroom's all yours,' she said.

'Thanks.' He saved his file, switched off the laptop, then headed for the bathroom while Sara averted her gaze.

While he showered and dressed, she busied herself tidying the room. Putting the bed back into a semblance of decency and trying not to think about just how she and Luke had rumpled the sheets only a few minutes before.

'Shall we go down to breakfast?' he asked as he came out of the bathroom.

His hair was damp and tousled and he looked thoroughly gorgeous, but his tone was casual and neutral. As if they were colleagues who'd had separate rooms and he'd merely knocked on her door at the agreed time. As if they hadn't just blown each other's minds.

She suppressed the throb of disappointment. This was how she'd wanted it, wasn't it? 'Sure. Is that your idea of casual?' She indicated his formal trousers and crisp white shirt.

'I'm not wearing a tie.' He shrugged. 'How else am I going to dress?'

'We're at the seaside. You can't paddle in trousers; you need shorts.'

'No, I don't. Besides, shorts don't exactly go with shoes.'

Especially as his were highly polished and looked handmade. Though he'd look great in shorts. The sort that came down to the knees—cut-off black chinos, with that white shirt unbuttoned a little more and his sleeves rolled up a bit. Add a pair of dark glasses and bare feet, and he'd be stunning. Like a pirate.

'Unlike some people around here,' he added, clearly oblivious to the thoughts running through her head, 'I don't have the contents of half a shoe shop in my wardrobe.'

'I don't have that many pairs.' Not with her, at any rate.

'You've worn seven different pairs to the office already. And the ones you're wearing right now are different again.'

He'd noticed her shoes?

She wasn't quite sure what to think. In her experience, men didn't notice shoes. Then again, Luke was the kind of man who could make you think he was wool-gathering, but would get ten out of ten if you told him to close his eyes and then asked him detailed questions about his surroundings.

'You don't wear shoes when you paddle,' she said.

'I'm not buying a pair of shorts just to please you.'

She shrugged. 'Your choice. You'll just have to roll your trousers up to your knees.'

'I'm not going…' His voice faded and he held both hands up in surrender. 'OK. I submit. Otherwise you'll argue with me until breakfast is over—and I'm starving.'

They went down to the hotel restaurant together. Clearly they were here towards the end of the hotel's allotted time for the meal, because only one other table was occupied—and the elderly couple looked as if they'd almost finished their meal. There was a help-yourself cold buffet set out on tables at one end of the room, or the menu stated that they could order a full English breakfast. Remembering their meal from the previous evening, Sara decided to go for the safe option, sticking to fruit and yoghurt. Luke was clearly thinking along the same lines, as he opted for toast.

The coffee, when it arrived, was stewed. Maybe it was their fault for arriving so late, she thought, but did it really take that much effort to make half a pot of fresh coffee? And when she glanced at Luke's plate, she noticed that the butter hadn't melted into his toast. Which meant it was probably cold and chewy, like the stuff she remembered from her student days. She wasn't surprised when he left most of it.

'So what's the plan for this morning?' she asked.

'Look around. Mental notes. Actually, there's a spa here, so you could go for a treatment.'

'What sort of treatment?'

He spread his hands. 'Anything you like. My bill. And, before you protest,' he added with a grin, 'I can't exactly try it out myself, can I?'

'There's no reason why men can't have a facial.'

He groaned. '*Please*. Do you talk to your brother like this?'

She thought about it. 'Yes. Both of them.'

'Just book something,' he said. 'And I'm going to use the hotel pool.'

Ten minutes later, she texted him. *Beautician fully booked. Going for a walk on the beach. Call me when you're ready.*

Almost immediately, her phone rang.

'I'm ready now,' Luke said, 'so I might as well take that walk with you.'

'I thought you were going for a swim?'

'The pool's out of action because of the burst pipe,' he said. 'So I think we need a discussion over coffee.'

'Provided it's somewhere else,' she said in a low voice. 'This morning's was undrinkable. I could really, really do with a latte.'

'Does this mean you don't want lunch here, either?'

'I've got a better idea. We skip lunch and have an ice cream on the beach.'

He sighed. 'You're going to nag until you get it, aren't you?'

'Absolutely. And my paddle in the sea—*our* paddle,' she corrected herself.

'Where are you?'

'Reception.'

'Stay put. I'll meet you there.'

He joined her in a couple of minutes and they headed towards the seafront. They found a small café overlooking the sea where the coffee smelled good and the scent of bacon was mouth-watering.

True to form, her stomach rumbled.

Luke stifled a grin, but not before she noticed. 'Emergency chocolate required?' he asked.

'An emergency bacon sandwich would be better.'

'That,' Luke said, 'is the second-best idea you've had this morning.'

Was the first making love with him? Though she wasn't sure she dared ask.

'Find us a table—I'll go and order. Latte, wasn't it?'

'Thanks.'

He joined her, carrying the coffee. When the bacon sandwich arrived, the bread was thickly cut from a bloomer loaf, incredibly soft and fresh; the bacon was home-cured and grilled to the perfect crispness, and the tomato ketchup definitely tasted home-made.

'This,' she said after finishing her first mouthful, 'is fantastic. And this is what that hotel should've been offering this morning. I bet you anything you like, their bacon would've been microwaved and their bread would've been soggy.'

'You're really not impressed with the hotel, are you?' Luke asked wryly.

'Let's face it, they don't have a clue. And if you really need me to list what's wrong…'

'Go for it,' he invited.

It took her eight minutes.

'You're absolutely right,' he said when she'd finished.

'But?' She could see the word in his face.

'But doesn't that feel like a challenge for you?' he asked. 'Doesn't it make you want to go and sort it all out?'

She sighed. 'I know you like a challenge, Luke, but I think the place needs too much work. And it's probably listed—so you'll end up going through tons of red tape if you want to do so much as painting a window frame, let alone anything structural.'

He raised an eyebrow. 'So you're an expert on listed buildings?'

'My family home's listed,' she explained, 'so I know from work my parents have had done in the past that it can be a nightmare. Luckily we know this brilliant architect, Max Taylor, who specialises in restoring listed buildings. And he's got fantastic contacts—that saves a huge amount of time. He tells us exactly what needs to be done and who can do it, and the local planning department know he knows what he's doing so they trust him and don't drag things out.'

'He sounds like a very useful contact. Perhaps you can introduce me to him.'

'Sure. But I can tell you now he won't come all the way up here,' she warned. 'Unless it's a really special building—which that hotel most definitely isn't—he only works within the area of the M25.'

Luke frowned. 'I thought your family lived in Kent.'

'We do. Anyway, that doesn't include us.' She flapped a dismissive hand. 'We were clients before.'

'Before what?'

'Before he got married and had kids. He's a really hands-on father.'

'I see.'

Although his expression hardly changed, she was aware that there was a barrier between them. His eyes might just as well have had steel shutters pulled down; she had absolutely no idea what he was thinking. What had she said to produce that effect so quickly?

Then she remembered what Luke had said about not having a mother and her own supposition about the men in his family.

It looked as if she was right; Luke clearly had issues about families. And, if she didn't want him to clam up on her completely, she needed to get their conversation back on track—onto something he found safe. Work. 'Anyway. I don't think it's viable because it would take up all your time. It'd be closed for months while you made the repairs and alterations, so you'd be losing money hand over fist.'

Luke smiled. 'I think my cash flow would be able to withstand it.'

She rolled her eyes. 'Of course. I forgot. You're a millionaire. That's why you're looking at buying a truly awful run-down place.'

'It's calling speculating to accumulate. And I did warn you it wasn't going to be luxurious,' he reminded her.

'A place can still be comfortable without costing an arm and a leg,' she pointed out. 'I don't doubt that you could do it.' Luke Holloway was the kind of man who could do anything he set his mind to. 'But is it going to be worth the cost? And I don't mean just financially.'

'My time, you mean?'

'And your social life. Either you'll have to fly from here to London—that is, if there's an airport nearby—and that'll scupper your plans about being green, or you'll have to give up the parties.'

He shrugged. 'As I said before, I'm getting bored with the parties.'

And bored with his gorgeous, exotic-looking model-type girlfriends?

She pushed the thought away. It was irrelevant. He'd already made it clear that he wasn't looking for a relationship. What had happened between them this morning was clearly a one-off.

And she wasn't even going to let herself think about tonight.

'Have you thought about your clients?' she asked. 'Are they going to be local, or would you expect people to travel five hours from London?'

'That's something to think about,' he said. 'But, as I said,

I'm looking to build a chain. All in spa towns and seaside resorts, like this. All with good, simple food cooked with local ingredients. Old-fashioned good service and spa treatments—I could even offer genuine local spa waters, just as people took them a hundred years ago.'

She stared at him, horrified. 'Luke, have you ever actually tasted spa water?'

'Have you?' he countered.

'Yes. And it's vile. Anyway, I thought spa therapy meant bathing in the stuff, not just drinking it?'

'Depends if the water's warm or cold,' Luke said. 'Or hot.'

Suddenly the heat was back in his eyes. And she had a feeling that the idea inside her head matched the one inside his: just the two of them and a hot tub. Her hand was shaking slightly as she lifted her mug of latte; she really hoped he couldn't see it. Didn't guess what kind of effect he had on her.

She really had to get a grip. Even if Luke was changing his mind about a relationship, she wasn't. 'Right. Enough work for now. I want my walk on the beach,' she said, forcing herself to sound all bright and chirpy, and not in the slightest as if she wanted to drag him back to their awful hotel room and rip all his clothes off.

'And the whippy ice cream with a chocolate flake in it. Yeah, yeah. I get the message.'

As they walked across the beach, Luke saw a man teaching his small son how to fly a kite.

More than twenty years ago, Luke had stood on this self-same beach, doing exactly what the little boy was doing now: giving every scrap of attention to the man who was holding the reel of string and explaining how to hold it. His father.

Sara clearly noticed what he was looking at, because she asked softly, 'Did you ever do that as a kid?'

He nodded. 'I remember having a blue kite, the traditional shape with a really long red and yellow tail. Actually, it was on this beach my dad taught me to fly it. I must have been about four or five at the time. I couldn't keep the tension and the kite kept dropping out of the sky, but he didn't give up. He rescued it and brushed the wet sand off, and we kept going until finally it flew and I could feel the wind tugging at it. And it was so good to see my kite flying up there and knowing I was doing it all myself…' He shook his head. 'Ah, it was a long time ago. Not important.'

She curled her fingers round his. 'Memories help to make you who you are.'

'Even the bad ones?' The words were out before he could stop them. Horrified, he shook his hand free. 'Forget I said that.'

'Even the bad ones,' she said, recapturing his hand, 'because they teach you what you don't want out of life.'

Something in her voice alerted him. He looked at her, shaken out of his own nightmare. 'That,' he said, 'sounds personal.'

'I've made some pretty bad decisions in the past. You know what you said about me believing everyone's nice until proven otherwise?' At his nod she explained, 'I discovered someone who wasn't so nice.'

He had a pretty good idea that the person in question was male, and had hurt her badly. So he tightened his fingers briefly round hers, to show her he understood and he sympathised without pitying.

'But there's always a positive. Making that mistake hurt— a lot—but it helped me to realise what I don't want. And I won't repeat my mistakes.'

Was that a warning? He needed to know. 'Was this morning a mistake?' he asked softly.

'I don't know.'

At least she'd been honest with him. Even though it stung.

'Was it a mistake for you?' she asked.

He could see the vulnerability in her eyes. No way could he say yes and hurt her. On the other hand, he had a feeling that, despite their agreement that morning, Sara believed in happy-ever-afters. Something he wasn't sure he could offer her. The only thing he could do was to be honest. 'I don't know, either. I didn't plan it to be like this.'

'Maybe,' she said, 'we both plan too much. Maybe we should just…see how things go.'

It shocked him that he was still holding her hand. It shocked him even more to realise that he didn't want to let it go. 'Yeah. Though it might be a bit late for taking things slowly.'

Colour bloomed in her cheeks. And he wanted to kiss her all over again, lose himself in her. 'We'll see how things go,' he said, and he kept his hand in hers.

As they reached the harbour, Sara nudged him and gestured towards the chalked signs for boat trips.

He read them swiftly. 'You want to go out in the bay and see the seals?'

'And the puffins,' she added with a smile. 'It's only for an hour and a half. I'll swap it for the paddle in the sea.'

'Feel free to go, if you want to. Though it's not my kind of thing.'

'Hey, if you're going into seaside hotels and leisure, you need to know what's on offer locally—so you can advise your guests.'

'If I'm not going to invest here, there isn't much point in scoping out the local facilities,' he pointed out.

'Ah, but you need a benchmark. Something by which you can judge other operators. Besides, a bit of sea air will blow the cobwebs away.'

He sighed. 'All right. If you insist, we'll go and see the seals.'

'Are you sure you can take sitting still and not using your mobile phone or sneaking in some work on a report—for all of an hour and a half?' she teased.

'No. But we'll do it, if it shuts you up about shorts and paddling.'

She wasn't the slightest bit abashed. 'Good. Oh, and as this is my idea, I'm paying.'

'Bu—'

'No arguments,' she cut in.

Well, OK. He was picking up the bill for everything else that weekend; if she wanted to do this, he wasn't going to refuse and make her feel bad. Even though it was far from his idea of being a treat. 'Thank you,' he said politely.

She bought the tickets, and their timing was perfect because the next trip was about to depart. There was just room enough for them in the boat, so he had to sit very close to her. And nearly everyone on the boat seemed to be in a family.

Well, he'd just have to live with it.

He pretended to be absorbed in the commentary. On the rocks, seals were basking in the sun. One rolled over and flapped a flipper, causing one of the children to yell that the seal was waving at him.

And even the seals were in family groups. The bull, large and protective, the cow, secure next to her mate, and the pup, settled happily and cuddled up to its parents.

Even though he usually avoided family situations as much as possible, part of him was charmed by the seals' huge dark eyes and almost spaniel-like faces. Some of the seals, more inquisitive than the others, made their cumbersome way into the water—and then suddenly they were gliding along, their heads bobbing up and disappearing and bobbing up again an impossible distance away.

He glanced at Sara. She was smiling; although her sunglasses hid the expression in her eyes, he'd bet they were all warm and soft. Right at that moment, she looked like a real English rose. And he really had to make an effort to stop himself pulling her close and kissing her.

'They're gorgeous, aren't they?' she asked.

'Yes,' he admitted.

Though he was glad she hadn't asked him if he was glad she'd pushed him into this. Because he really wasn't sure. Although the waters around them were so calm it was practically like a millpond, suddenly it felt as if he were sailing a tiny dinghy in high seas. Nothing was quite the same as it had been yesterday, and he couldn't put his finger on why he felt so thrown. Though he suspected it had something to do with her.

He listened to the crew's tales about the Old Horse Rocks and the seals, watched the puffins bobbing on the water, far tinier than he'd expected them to be, and then, as they sailed in close to the smugglers' coves, listened to tales of the rum-runners and pirates.

'You know, you'd look great as a pirate,' Sara said with a grin.

'I am *not* wearing shorts. Or an eye patch.'

'Arrr,' she mocked, in her best pirate impersonation, 'you're a chicken, you arrr.'

He just loved the way she teased him. And what was sauce for the goose… He bent his head so he could whisper into her ear. 'If you're asking me to play pirate tonight, honey, and rip your clothes off and ravish you, then it can be arranged.'

And he grinned when she blushed like a beacon.

Good. He was back in control of things again. And that was just how he liked it.

# CHAPTER EIGHT

WHEN they reached dry land again, Sara said, 'So are you going to admit you enjoyed that?'

'The seals were cute. And the puffins.'

'But?'

Well, she'd asked him straight. He had to be honest. 'It's not really my kind of thing.' When she didn't say anything but the *why?* was clear in her expression, he sighed. 'Too many kids.'

'You don't like children?'

'My idea of hell,' he said, 'would be having to work in a nursery or a classroom. And be on playground duty.'

'You'd hate what my mum does, then—going out to local schools and telling them all about apples and old-fashioned Kentish recipes.'

'Mmm.' Not his scene at all.

'So you don't ever want children of your own?'

Absolutely not. He'd had a miserable childhood with a dad who hadn't been there half the time and a mum who had been physically present but too full of tranquillisers to notice anything. OK, so Luke wasn't his dad, but he wouldn't know how to begin to be a good father. And he had no intention of trying. 'Marriage and babies,' he said, 'are seriously overrated.'

'There's more to life than work.'

'True.' He shrugged. 'And there's more to life than babies.'

'Actually,' she said, 'babies are the point. Without them, the human race would die out.'

Trust her to zero in on that. 'I guess you're right. Someone has to produce children. But it's not going to be me.' A nasty realisation struck him. 'So you're looking for marriage and babies?'

'Not at the moment. But eventually, yes. When I meet the right person.'

'Mr Right? Do you really believe in all that hype?'

She spread her hands. 'My parents have been together for thirty-five years. My sister Louisa's happily married with a toddler. My brother Rupert's engaged. And I think Justin is seeing someone—though he's probably keeping it quiet because he knows that, the minute Lou finds out, she'll start planning his wedding.' She smiled. 'She has this terrible habit of matchmaking. She claims credit for three weddings and two engagements, excluding her own.'

Luke made a mental note to stay well away from Sara's sister.

He was being paranoid. His relationship with Sara was strictly business, or had been until this morning. Well. Physically, it had been strictly business. He'd been fantasising about Sara Fleet from the second he'd met her.

'Whatever floats your boat,' he said, aiming for cool. And he really wanted to stop talking about weddings and families. It was way, way outside his comfort zone. He glanced at his watch. 'I need to make a couple of calls, and I left the relevant paperwork back in the hotel. Do you mind?'

'No. Though I think I'll just go for a walk on the seafront. I might have that ice cream I've been promising myself.'

'Sure. I'll see you back at the room whenever you're ready.'

Though she didn't look too enthralled at the idea of going back to their hotel.

As he approached the place, he could see exactly what she meant. It wasn't genteel shabby at all. It was forlorn. The sunshine was unforgiving because it made the place look even worse.

Yet it had so much potential…

He shook himself. Forget the calls. They could wait. There was something else he needed to do first.

A couple of minutes on the Internet found him exactly the right place. A larger version of the sort of place he'd thought about turning his hotel into. Old-fashioned and yet with all mod cons. A place with a history and stunning views over the bay, and, better still, their best suite was free due to a last-minute cancellation.

He settled their bill at reception. 'Sorry, something cropped up and we have to leave,' he said. It was a fib, but the receptionist looked miserable so why make her day worse than it clearly already was? 'But of course I'll pay for tonight's room.'

He'd just finished packing their cases when Sara walked back in.

'What are you doing?' she asked, looking shocked.

'We're leaving.'

'What, now?' She glanced at her watch. 'At this rate we won't be back in London until ten o'clock—and that's if we don't stop on the way.'

'We're not going to London,' he explained. 'We're moving.'

'What?'

'I think we both deserve a non-lumpy mattress tonight.'

'And you just packed for us both.'

Was she going to have a hissy fit about the fact he'd packed her stuff? 'Yes, because it was quicker than waiting for you to get back, and I folded your stuff carefully. Let's go.'

Once Luke had made his mind up to do something, Sara thought, he didn't hang about. There was no point in discussing it further, so she simply followed him out to the car.

The hotel he'd booked was only a few minutes away and it was spotless from the outside. Perfect paintwork, without even the hint of a chip or a crack, the windows sparkled, and the car park at the back had tubs of summer flowers to brighten it up.

Inside, it was even better. Again, Luke refused to let her carry her case; when he'd picked up the key from the friendly, smiling receptionist, they took the lift to the top floor. Every surface was clean and, even in the lift, the carpet was so thick that you sank into it.

'Our suite,' Luke said, unlocking the door and ushering her in. 'Take a look around and see what you think.'

It was huge. A living room with comfortable sofas, a low coffee table and another table with a kettle and a selection of coffee, different kinds of tea and hot chocolate, plus fantastic biscuits. Another table held a beautiful display of fresh flowers. The French windows led onto a balcony with stunning views of Scarborough Bay—and she realised with pleasure that they'd actually be able to watch the sun set from there. There was a wrought-iron bistro table and two chairs on the balcony and another tub of the beautiful summer flowers like the ones in the car park.

There were two bathrooms, to her surprise, one with a power shower and one with a whirlpool bath. Complimentary toiletries, thick fluffy bath robes hanging on the door and plenty of room for spreading out.

Though there was only one bedroom. With an enormous bed, admittedly—but it was just *one* bed.

'This doesn't mean I'm expecting you to sleep with me,' Luke said softly from the doorway. 'I'll do the gentlemanly thing and sleep on the sofa, if you like.'

He was giving her the choice.

'It's a big bed,' she said.

'Super-king size, according to the girl on reception,' he told her.

'And we're perfectly capable of sharing it without…' Then she saw the smile on his face. 'What?'

'I was just remembering waking up this morning.' There was a distinct glitter in his eye. Amusement mixed with desire.

She felt her face heat. 'Um.'

His smile broadened. 'I don't mind sharing, if you don't.'

She was hardly in a position to protest. Especially as the suite was enormous, and he'd changed their hotel for her sake. 'I'm sorry. This must've cost a small fortune.'

He shrugged. 'It's not a problem.'

'Look, I ought to pay my share of it.'

'No. I'm the one who dragooned you into coming to Scarborough. So it's my bill. No arguments.'

'Then thank you.' She grimaced. 'I'm sorry I made such a fuss—I could've coped with another night in that other hotel, you know.'

'No, you couldn't. And neither could I.' He smiled wryly. 'You saw the "before". This is what I saw the place being "after".'

'And it's fabulous—but it'd take so much time and effort to make it like this. You'd really have to do a proper cost benefit analysis.'

'And a building survey and get quotes for the work that needs doing. True. But there's also my gut instinct.'

'Which is?'

'Usually right,' he said.

She groaned. 'That's infuriating. You know what I meant.'

'Be nice to me, or you'll be eating fish and chips on the harbour instead of a posh dinner,' he teased.

'There's nothing wrong with fish and chips. Anyway, I don't have the right clothes with me to have dinner in the restaurant here.' Her beige linen trousers and cream top and black loafers could pass muster as smart casual, but this was more a little black dress and strappy shoes sort of place.

'Actually,' he said, 'there's more than one restaurant—there's the formal dining room, and a café bar for something less formal. Pasta, pizza and burgers. But I was thinking room service. Dinner on the balcony, overlooking the sea and watching the sun set.' He proffered a menu. 'I checked this out online before I booked. It's pretty good.'

She scanned it quickly. 'I think I'll have to close my eyes and pick at random. This is just… Wow. I like *everything* on it. And it's all local produce. Organic, too.' She looked up at him. 'So this is the sort of thing you're planning to do?'

He nodded. 'Probably not on as big a scale as this. I like the idea of having a boutique hotel, maybe fifteen or twenty rooms. Small and exclusive.'

'Expanding to a chain.'

'Yup.'

And he'd do it, she knew. He'd find the right sort of place to change—somewhere a little less run-down than the hotel where they'd stayed the previous night, but a place that could still be transformed from something run-of-the-mill into something spectacular.

In the end, she chose the oven-baked breaded Brie with cranberry relish, followed by local cod served with a basil and parmesan risotto.

He raised an eyebrow at her choice. 'So you're a foodie, then.'

'Definitely. I'd rather enjoy my food than sit nibbling on a lettuce leaf, knowing that I'm fashionably stick-thin but being utterly miserable because I also know just how much I'm missing out on.'

Then she remembered some of the names she'd seen him linked with. Stick-thin model types, the lot of them. 'Sorry. I wasn't commenting on your…um…taste in female company.'

He laughed. 'I know. But I also know what you mean. It's easier to enjoy a meal with someone who's interested in what they're eating rather than someone who orders a starter for their main course and refuses pudding and you know they're counting calories and carbs the whole time.' He'd chosen grilled tiger prawns with lemon, followed by a plain steak, salad and new potatoes.

'Going for the manly option?' she teased.

'No. I just like my food simple and good quality.'

'How about pudding?' Although he'd skipped pudding at the pizza place, Sara knew he had a weakness for posh chocolate biscuits. The chances were, he'd also enjoy chocolate pudding.

'I'm not that bothered, but choose what you like.'

'The one I'd like is a sharing pudding—the fruit platter with white chocolate dip. But it's a bit too much for one.'

'Fine. I'll share it with you. Now, wine—you're having fish, so we'll go for white. Chablis OK with you?'

'Lovely—but you're having steak.'

'Which can cope perfectly well with good white wine. It doesn't have to be red,' he said. 'I suppose we could have champagne, but personally I think it's overrated. I'd rather have a decent Chablis—a Margaux or a Nuit St Georges.'

She smiled at him. 'And there's you teasing me about being posh.'

'You're saying a barrow boy can't enjoy wine?' he fenced.

She laughed. 'I'm not a wine snob—Justin is, but I guess that goes with the territory of being a barrister. I just know what I like.'

'Which is?'

'Pretty much the same as you, actually.' Though her budget didn't usually run to drinking it in restaurants.

'If we eat at seven,' Luke said, 'we can watch the sun set. So I'll order from room service; then we can unpack and maybe have a cup of coffee on the balcony.'

It didn't take long to unpack. And sitting on the balcony, watching the sea swishing in and out, was incredibly relaxing. The perfect weekend break. And even Luke had lost that slightly watchful look she was used to. He'd rolled the sleeves of his shirt up slightly, exposing a sprinkling of dark hair on his arms, and he looked utterly edible.

Down, girl, she told her libido silently. Luke, despite his teasing in the boat, might not appreciate being pounced on. And he certainly hadn't made a move towards her; when her fingers had brushed against his earlier as she'd handed him a cup of coffee, there hadn't been even the tiniest flicker of awareness on his face. No spark, like the one that had coursed through her.

Or maybe he was just better than she was at masking his feelings.

She had no idea what was going on between them right now. Whether they were colleagues or lovers. Not friends, certainly: on the boat, she'd noticed his barriers going up. When she'd touched his hand, he hadn't relaxed and laced his fingers through hers. In fact, he'd looked distinctly uncomfortable.

Probably because, as he'd admitted, he didn't like children—and their trip had definitely been family-oriented. Someone, she thought, must have hurt him very badly. There hadn't been a mention of a wife and children in his past, but she knew better than to ask straight out. Though a messy divorce would explain why he was so against relationships, why he didn't believe in love.

Right at that moment, he was calm. Reposed. And she wasn't going to risk ruining the moment by asking him where she stood or pushing him to talk about his past.

A knock at the door heralded room service—a waitress who swiftly laid the table on the balcony with a damask tablecloth, shiny cutlery and sparkling glasses, followed by a waiter who brought the wine and their starters.

The food turned out to be as good as the service. 'This,' she said after the first mouthful of her Brie, 'is perfect. Try it.'

He gave her an amused look, but allowed her to feed him with a forkful. 'Agreed, it's good,' he said. 'Try this.'

There was something decidedly sensual about opening her lips and allowing him to slide a tiger prawn into her mouth, and her heart skipped a beat at the look in his eyes. 'It's good,' she said. And she didn't just mean the food.

The idea of sharing a platter of fruit and melted chocolate with him made pleasure slide all the way down her spine. Would he keep things strictly professional with her—or would he feed her morsels of fruit? Would it start out as pudding and end up as something else?

Their main courses were just as spectacular, and then the waitress brought the fruit platter. There was a pot of melted chocolate over a tea-light candle to keep it warm, and as well as the pineapple and strawberries and papaya there were bite-size squares of home-made Yorkshire parkin and tiny short-bread rounds.

Sara speared a square of the ginger cake and dipped it in the chocolate. She was just about to draw it up to her mouth when Luke leaned forward and nibbled it off her skewer.

'Hey! That was mine,' she protested.

He raised an eyebrow. 'It's a sharing platter. I think,' he said, 'this is how it's meant to work.' And then he dipped a square of parkin into the chocolate and lifted it to her mouth. 'Open wide,' he said, his voice slightly husky.

This was a game she liked. And she could tell by the way his pupils were expanding that he enjoyed it, too. The setting sun was forgotten; all she could concentrate on was Luke.

'There's chocolate on the corner of your mouth,' he said when they'd finished, then leaned over and licked it off.

She wasn't sure which of them moved first, but the next thing she knew she was sitting on his lap, his mouth was jammed against hers and her hands were in his hair.

'I think,' he murmured when he broke the kiss, 'we'd better go back inside. Or anyone looking up is going to get an eyeful of something they shouldn't.'

Oh, help. She'd been so involved in his kisses that she'd actually forgotten where they were.

'Just as well I said we'd leave the stuff outside our door when we've finished.' He stole another kiss. 'Because I really do *not* want to be disturbed for the rest of this evening.' He lifted her as he stood up, then strode with her into the bedroom and laid her back against the pillows. 'Wait for me. Two minutes,' he said, brushing his mouth against hers.

She heard the clatter of china and cutlery—clearly he was dealing with the remains of their meal—and a door closing, and then he was back in the bedroom. Closing the heavy curtains. Switching on the bedside light.

'Sara,' he said.

She stood up and walked into his arms. Matched him kiss for kiss, touch for touch.

'I need this, too,' she whispered.

'I'm all yours,' he said.

So she'd tamed the pirate king, had she? Somehow, she thought not. But she took pleasure in unbuttoning his shirt and pushing it off his shoulders, exploring his muscular chest and broad shoulders. Unwrapping a parcel was half the fun, and she was going to enjoy every single moment of taking Luke's clothes off. Looking and touching and tasting.

'A proper six-pack,' she said, letting her fingers drift down over his abdomen. 'So this is what kick-boxing does for you, is it?'

'And the training for it.'

'Good,' she said, and unbuttoned his trousers. Slid the zip down incredibly slowly, keeping her gaze fixed on his—and she revelled in the fact that his breath hissed as her fingers moved lower. His earlier coolness had been a sham. Luke Holloway was definitely interested.

'Lose the shoes,' she said.

'Bossing me about again, are you?' But he kicked them off.

She smiled. 'And now…'

But as she was about to push the material of his trousers over his hips, his hands grasped her wrists. Firmly enough to stop her, yet gently enough not to hurt.

'My turn,' he said. 'Arms up.'

She let him tug the hem of her strappy top and pull it over her head.

Then he undid the button and zip of her trousers. She'd already kicked her shoes off much earlier, so when the linen fell to the floor she simply stepped out of them.

'Now there's a picture,' he said. 'I knew you'd be the type to wear matching underwear.'

'Did you, now?'

'Those teal suede stilettos you were wearing yesterday…I could imagine you wearing just them and your underwear— matching teal silk and lace—and that string of black pearls.'

'You've been fantasising about me in my underwear?' The idea sent a kick of desire through her.

'Yes. And a bit worse than that,' he admitted with a mischievous grin. 'Like taking it off.'

'Show me,' she invited, and colour slashed across his cheekbones.

Firstly, he loosened her hair so it fell about her shoulders. Then he slid the narrow straps of her bra down her arms. 'You have beautiful shoulders,' he whispered, nuzzling kisses along them. 'And your skin's so soft. It makes me want to taste you.' He nibbled gently at the curve of her neck, making her shiver and tip her head back.

'And it makes me want to do this.' He dipped a finger under the lacy hem and traced the edge of her bra; every nerve-end seemed to come to life under his touch. Then he unclipped her bra slowly, with one hand; as it dropped to the floor, he let her breasts spill into his hands. 'You're stunning, Sara.'

Given the kind of women he dated—women who were a little taller and a lot thinner—she wasn't convinced—but then he bent his head and kissed her shoulders again, tracing kisses along her collarbone and then nuzzling down between her breasts. When he dropped to his knees in front of her and took one nipple into his mouth, her knees buckled and she had to hold on to his shoulders for support.

'Hold that thought,' he said, and hooked his thumbs into the sides of her knickers. Slowly, teasingly slowly, he drew them down to her ankles, then lifted her foot to help her step out of them. Then he rocked back on his haunches and looked up at her. 'Sara Fleet, you blow my mind.'

It was pretty much mutual. Not that she wanted to tell him yet. She held her hands out; when he took them, she tugged him to his feet. 'My turn.'

And then she copied his actions, dropping to her knees in front of him. She finished unzipping his chinos and stroked the material down over his hips; when they slid to the floor, she helped him step out of them and removed his socks at the same time.

She could see his erection outlined by the soft material of

his jersey boxer shorts; giving him a wicked grin, she breathed teasingly along it, so he'd feel the heat of her mouth, and she was rewarded with a husky groan of pleasure.

She stroked his thighs, firm and muscular. 'You're beautiful, Luke Holloway. If I was any good at art I'd love to paint you. Sculpt you.'

'Sounds like an excuse to look at me naked.' His words were teasing but his voice was slightly shaky. Her touch obviously affected him more than he was prepared to admit.

'Now there's an idea,' she teased back. 'And, considering that you took my clothes off…' She removed his soft jersey boxer shorts.

'Enough,' he said, reaching down to take her hands and pulling her to her feet. 'Much more teasing and I'm going to lose control.'

'Which would be a bad thing?'

'Considering that I want to make sure it's good for you— yes,' he told her baldly.

He lowered his mouth to hers, then picked her up and, still kissing her, carried her to the bed and set her back against the soft, soft pillows. He opened a drawer in the cabinet next to the bed to retrieve his wallet and remove a condom from it. She closed her hand over his. 'Mine,' she said softly.

He gave her a smouldering glance and the sexiest grin she'd ever seen.

He lay back against the pillows and she opened the foil packet; she rolled the condom onto his erect penis, teasingly slowly, looking him straight in the eye as she did so.

'Hear that shredding sound?' he asked.

'No.'

'I can. It's my patience and my self-control. If you're going to do it, Sara… Just do it.'

'What happened to finesse?' she teased. But she loved the idea that she could turn this quick, clever man into a pile of mush. So she finished rolling on the condom, straddled him and slowly lowered herself onto him.

'Yes.' The word was a hiss of pleasure. He shifted slightly so he could push more deeply into her, and she began to move over him, varying the pace and the pressure. He'd reached back over his head to grip a rail on the wrought-iron bedstead, and his knuckles stood out white; his breathing was growing shallower and faster as his climax built.

This was power.

And she loved every second of it.

Loved the fact that she was taking him to the edge of pleasure.

Then he released his grip on the bedstead and twined his fingers through hers. 'Look at me, Sara,' he whispered. 'See what you do to me.'

She did. Exactly the same as he did to her. She could feel the ripples of pleasure starting to spread and overlap. And she could see in his face, the moment that his climax hit, dovetailing with hers. The moment when they both fell over the edge.

He wrapped his arms round her, drawing her down to him; Sara rested her cheek next to his, enjoying the way he held her close. She knew that Luke wasn't a man who let people close but, after this, no way could he possibly put the barriers back between them. They'd shared too much.

And after he'd dealt with the condom, he curled his body protectively round hers, wrapping an arm round her waist and holding her close to him. She laced her fingers through his and he brushed a kiss against her shoulder. 'Sleep well,' he said softly.

'You, too.' And tomorrow… They'd deal with that when it arrived.

## CHAPTER NINE

THE next morning, Luke woke Sara with kisses. Soft, sweet kisses that made her feel warm inside—a warmth that turned to heat when he began exploring her body with his mouth and his hands, finding places that made her want to purr with pleasure.

'I have an idea,' he said.

'Mmm.' As long as he carried on doing exactly what he was doing, she'd say yes to almost anything.

'You need to put your hair up first.'

'Why?'

'Health and safety.'

How come his brain was still functioning, when hers was out to breakfast? she wondered. She sat up—and then she remembered he'd loosened her hair the previous day. So she had no idea where her hairpins were. 'Sorry, no can do. Unless you tell me what you did with my hairpins.'

He looked blank for a moment, then grinned. 'Ah, yes. Give me a second.' A quick hunt on the floor, and he'd retrieved most of them from among their discarded clothes.

She put her hair up and let him lead her to the bathroom.

So that was what he had in mind. Sharing a bath.

He switched on the taps. 'What you said yesterday about the spa bath—it made me think this might be nice.' He picked up the three little bottles on the side of the bath, sniffed each in turn, then added a couple of drops from one to the water.

Foam began to form on the surface, and Sara frowned. 'Hang on. If we're having a whirlpool bath—I thought you weren't supposed to use bubbles in one?'

'A couple of drops is fine, as long as it's low-foam and not oil-based. Too much, and we'll have to mop the floor.'

Well, of course he'd know. He owned spas and health clubs.

He helped her into the bath, then slipped into the water next to her. He turned off the taps and switched on the whirlpool, and immediately the tiny layer of froth was whipped into deep bubbles.

She'd once accused him of not having fun.

Ha. She hadn't had a clue. This man definitely knew about fun.

She pushed aside the thought that he'd probably done this quite a few times before. With quite a few different women. This was here and now. That was what they'd agreed, wasn't it?

He dabbed foam on the end of her nose, then laughed at her.

She retaliated, and a vigorous foam fight ensued. And then Luke pulled her onto his lap. 'It's a shame your hair has to stay up—because in this bath, with your hair down, you'd look like a mermaid. All alluring and sensual.'

She laughed. 'Hardly. Apart from the fact I have legs instead of a tail, my singing voice isn't great.'

'You'll have to dazzle my senses with a kiss instead, then.'

She did.

And he responded, to the point that they were almost too late for breakfast. Sara still felt guilty about the fact that their sheets were damp—Luke hadn't waited for either of them to dry themselves properly before he'd carried her back to bed—but he was completely unrepentant.

Despite the fact that they were the last ones in the restaurant, the waitress greeted them cheerily and brought them freshly squeezed orange juice along with really good coffee.

'It's Sunday, so I'm having a proper breakfast,' Luke said, and ordered soft creamy scrambled eggs, granary bread toast and crisp bacon.

The sea air—or maybe making love with Luke—had given Sara an appetite, so she joined him.

When they'd finished, she leaned back against her chair with a sigh of pleasure. 'That was an excellent choice on your part. Right now, I feel as if I could conquer the world.'

'I think your parents misnamed you. They should've called you Scary,' he teased.

She pulled a face at him and laughed. Right at that moment she felt eighteen again. And Luke, too, looked younger. More carefree.

It didn't take them long to pack and check out. 'I cheated you out of your paddle yesterday,' he said. 'So we'll do it today.'

'You really don't have to.' She'd pushed him into the seal trip and he'd hated that.

'No. You're right. It'd be fun. The sun's shining, it's summer and we're at the seaside.'

'Am I hearing things?' She blinked. 'Are you going to tell me next that you're not going to work today?'

He laughed. 'I'm not going *quite* that far.'

After he'd put their things in the car, they headed for the beach. To Sara's surprise and delight, at the edge of the beach Luke removed his shoes and socks, then rolled his black trousers up to his knees. With his white shirt partly undone and his sleeves rolled up, he looked just as she'd imagined him, all barefoot and sexy and gorgeous. And only the fact that they were in a public place stopped her grabbing him and kissing him stupid.

'Remember that film with Burt Lancaster in it?' she asked as they walked along the edge of the sea, the waves swirling round their ankles.

'Film?' He looked blankly at her.

'I forgot, you don't do TV or films. Anyway, there's this film from the 1950s called *From Here To Eternity*—a real classic. Deborah Kerr and Burt Lancaster kiss on this Hawaiian beach among the crashing waves. And…' Her mouth went dry.

She couldn't see his eyes behind his dark glasses, but she

was pretty sure she could guess at their expression because his voice had grown deeper, sexier. 'We could,' he said. 'But, apart from the fact that this is North Yorkshire, not Hawaii, and the sea's pretty calm today, I think we could end up getting arrested.' He drew the tip of his forefinger down her bare arm. 'Because we don't seem to be able to stop at kissing.'

Very true. They'd already proved it several times, to their mutual satisfaction. She moistened her lower lip, and he groaned.

'Don't. Because it makes me want to taste you.'

It was the same for her.

'I need a cold shower,' he said.

'I could push you into the sea.' Except then his chinos and his shirt would be plastered against his skin, reminding her of the lake scene in *Pride and Prejudice*—a moment she'd savoured on several occasions with friends and wine and chocolate. 'Uh. Scratch that. We need ice cream.'

'After the breakfast we've just eaten?'

'To cool down,' she said.

He didn't take her hand as they walked to the little kiosk. Which was just as well. She had a feeling that as soon as they touched they'd combust. She bought them both a whippy cornet with a chocolate flake, then wished she hadn't when she watched him eating his; the way his tongue curled round the ice cream reminded her of the feel of his mouth against her skin.

In retaliation, she sucked on the end of her chocolate flake, and was rewarded with a groan. 'I'm going to have to turn my back,' he said, 'because you've put all sorts of ideas in my head, and they're definitely not suitable for the middle of a public beach.'

'You started it.'

'How?'

'Licking that ice cream.'

There was an impish quirk to his mouth. 'It's how you're supposed to eat ice cream.'

'Even so. It was positively indecent.'

He laughed. 'And what you just did was demure, was it?'

In answer, she just licked her lips, and he groaned. 'You're a bad, bad girl. And I'm very glad you are.'

When they'd both dried off and put their shoes back on, Luke drove them back to London. Though it wasn't quite the same as their journey north—apart from the fact that there were no traffic jams, Luke didn't ask her to make calls or check his diary, and they stopped halfway for a late lunch in a little pub in a village off the motorway.

Back in London, Luke parked the car outside Sara's block of flats in Camden.

'I'll carry your suitcase up for you,' Luke said.

'Thanks. Do you want to come in for a coffee?' Sara asked.

At six in the evening, there was a fair chance that her brother Justin was home. Luke really wasn't in the mood for meeting any of Sara's family—but, then again, how bad could it be? Justin knew they'd gone away on business, so it wasn't as if he'd start playing the tough big brother, grilling his baby sister's new boyfriend about his intentions. Besides, Luke could see in Sara's eyes that she'd be disappointed if he said no. So he could do this. Treat it like a business meeting. 'Sure. Coffee would be lovely.'

She tapped in the code on the keypad by the front door, then led him up the stairs to the first floor and unlocked the door to the flat.

'Oh. Justin isn't home.'

'Pity,' he lied. 'Where do you want me to put your case?'

'Leave it here in the hallway. Come through,' she said, ushering him into the living room. 'I'll bring the coffee in.'

Sitting and waiting patiently wasn't Luke's thing, so instead he wandered round the living room. The mantelpiece was full of photographs, including graduation photographs; one was Sara, and the family likeness told him that the others were her two brothers and Louisa. There was another photograph with

Louisa wearing a wedding dress, Sara in a bridesmaid's dress and their brothers in top hats and tails, another that was obviously of their parents, and less formal ones of a toddler he assumed was Louisa's. There was a photograph of their father walking through an orchard with four assorted dogs, and one of their mother up to her arms in flour in a farmhouse kitchen, clearly spontaneous rather than posed—her smile, he thought, was very like Sara's.

A close-knit family.

A world away from his own—well, his was close, but only if you toed the family line. Which he hadn't wanted to do. Whereas Sara's family... He had a feeling they'd all encourage each other to follow their dreams, even if they weren't in line with the rest of the family. After all, Justin was a barrister and Sara was an office troubleshooter—neither of which had anything to do with their parents' orchard.

Unsettled, he joined Sara in the kitchen. 'Want a hand with anything?'

'No, you're fine.' She was reading a note and smiling; she looked up at him over the edge. 'Justin left me this in the middle of the table, so I couldn't miss it. He went home for lunch today. Mum says she missed me and she's sent me some apple cake.'

'Apple cake?'

'Kentish speciality. And obviously Mum's big on apple recipes because of the business.' She grinned. 'Justin's a star. He stopped off at a supermarket on the way home and re-stocked the freezer with my favourite ice cream.'

'You and your ice cream,' he teased.

'Absolutely. And I love this bit. "Hope you had a chance for your paddle and you didn't work all weekend."' She laughed.

It was all affectionate and warm—and it scared the hell out of Luke because it was so far from what he was used to. In the days when he had a family, they never used to do little things to please each other; everything had been focused around the family business and the strange code of honour among thieves. Looking back, he remembered that his mother had diamond earrings, but he could never remember his father bringing her flowers or a box of chocolates or some little thoughtful token. And any paintings he'd done at school had always been left on the side, never pinned up on the wall.

Sara finished making the coffee; she added sugar to his mug and milk to hers. 'So can I tempt you?'

'Tempt me?'

She rolled her eyes. 'Wake up. *Apples.* Would you like some Kentish apple cake?'

'No, thanks. I'm fine.'

'Your loss,' she said. 'My mum's cooking is the best. OK, so this is reheated, but even the smell of it reminds me of home. She cooks this in the Aga and the whole house smells of apple and cinnamon. It's gorgeous.' She took a covered box from the fridge and spooned some of the apple cake into a bowl. 'Do you mind if we sit out here?' she asked.

'No, it's fine.' And there were fewer photographs to unsettle him than there were in the living room. Just postcards attached to the fridge with little magnets.

He sat at the table, his hands wrapped round his mug of coffee, while she warmed up the apple cake. The scent of cinnamon made his mouth water.

'Sure you don't want a taste?' she asked as she retrieved the bowl and added ice cream.

He thought of the way they'd shared a pudding the previous night. And how easy it would be to do it all over again. And how embarrassed Sara would be if her brother came home while Luke was still naked in her bed. So it was best not to start anything. 'Sure.'

'Good. All the more for me.' She looked slightly put out. 'I didn't know Justin was going home today.'

'So I've kept you from your family.'

She shrugged. 'It doesn't matter. I'll go next weekend.'

'Go tomorrow,' he said. 'Remember, you have the next two days off in lieu for this weekend.'

She looked straight at him, her blue eyes just a little too bright for his liking. 'So now what? We go back to a formal office relationship?'

'Yes. No.' Oh, hell. Whatever he said, whatever he did, he was going to hurt her. He really shouldn't have been so self-indulgent. Why hadn't he kept her at a proper distance, the way he'd meant to? He dragged a hand through his hair. 'Sara, I don't do happy-ever-after. And I don't want to do the wrong thing by you.'

'But?'

'But right now I don't want it to end,' he admitted. 'And I'm never indecisive like this. I always know what I'm doing.' He sighed. 'This has thrown me. I didn't expect to…' His voice faded. Of course he hadn't fallen in love with Sara Fleet. Even if he believed in love—which he didn't—he knew it didn't happen that fast. It couldn't possibly happen that fast.

'So what do you suggest?' she asked softly.

'As we said yesterday. Take it day by day. See how it goes. No pressure. No promises.' He spread his hands. 'I'm sorry, Sara. I can't offer you more. I just…'

'You've been focused on your business. And you don't want any distractions.'

He was relieved that she understood. 'I know it sounds selfish.'

'Sounds?' She arched an eyebrow.

'*Is*, then. But it's all I can offer you right now.'

'I wasn't looking for a rel…' Her voice faded.

He took her hand. Kissed her palm. Folded her fingers round it. 'He hurt you that much?'

'Who?'

'The guy who's made you wary of relationships.'

'What makes you think there's a guy?'

He noticed that she didn't actually deny it—just answered a question with a question. 'Because you,' he said simply, 'aren't the closed-off sort.' Those photographs, all smiles and hugs, had told him exactly what sort of woman Sara was. Warm and sweet—and way too good for him. 'So someone must have hurt you to make you back away. And I'd guess that it was the person you told me "wasn't so nice".'

'I don't repeat my mistakes.'

'And you think I'll be a repeat mistake?' he asked.

She swallowed. 'You're a workaholic. Like Hugh was.'

'No. I'm a workaholic, I admit, but I'm not Hugh,' he corrected. 'I'm *me*. I don't claim to be perfect, but I won't hurt you intentionally.'

'Hmm.'

He sighed. 'Just remember that I'm a man, not a mind-reader. If you're not happy about something, I need you to tell me. Be straight with me. Remember, I'm used to being on my own.'

She coughed. 'More like, you're used to being with a string of women.'

'I've never dated more than one woman at a time,' he said. 'That's dishonourable. Not my style.'

She said nothing. So was that what had happened? Her ex had two-timed her? But even if he asked her straight, he had a feeling she wouldn't tell him. The guy must have hurt her really badly—and he was surprised to feel himself tensing up. Wanting to flatten him. Ridiculous. Especially when he knew that violence solved nothing.

He stroked her face with the backs of his fingers. 'If it's easier for you, we could play it safe and go back to being business associates.'

'But?'

Clearly she'd picked up his line of thought. 'But I'd always wonder if I should've been a bit braver and taken the risk. And I think you would, too.'

She looked serious. 'So you think it's worth a try?'

'Only one way to find out. Live a little,' he said softly.

He was about to kiss her goodbye—chastely—and leave,

when he heard the sound of a key in the door. A couple of seconds later, the kitchen door opened and a man strode in—clearly Justin, because Luke recognised him from one of the photographs.

'Hello, Shrimp! Sorry I was out when you got back.' Justin greeted his sister warmly with a hug, a kiss and a ruffle of her hair.

'I'll forgive you. You restocked on ice cream for me.' She beamed at him.

'Well, I have to keep my little sister happy.'

'Absolutely, if you want me to cook for you. Justin, this is Luke. Luke, this is my ancient, elderly brother.'

'Nice to meet you, Luke.' Justin's handshake was firm, dry and professional, and Luke found himself relaxing slightly. 'I hope Shrimp here remembered her manners and offered you some apple cake rather than scoffing the lot herself.'

'She did.'

'Good. So, how was Scarborough?'

'Crossed off my list. I would've seen it as a challenge but—' Luke looked over at Sara '—luckily I had someone with me with some common sense.'

'No doubt you paid for it in whippy ice creams,' Justin said with a grin. 'I'm surprised she hasn't managed to persuade Dad to open a dairy.'

'It's a brilliant idea. It'd complement the apples. Ice cream and apple cake are the perfect partners. And we could do apple sorbet,' Sara said. 'Expand that to elderflower, from the trees at the edge of the orchard. And maybe—'

'Enough, enough!' Justin held up his hands in surrender, laughing.

Luke found himself liking the man: he had the same warmth and sense of fun as Sara. And he ended up staying much longer than he'd expected to. When he left and Justin shook his hand and said, 'Good to meet you', Luke was able to echo the sentiment and mean it.

Though he also shook hands with Sara, rather than kissing

her. He wasn't quite ready to go public on a relationship where neither of them was completely sure where they were going. 'See you Wednesday,' he said.

She smiled back. 'See you Wednesday,' she echoed.

# CHAPTER TEN

THE next morning, Sara woke at her usual time. And although she tried turning over and going back to sleep—knowing that she was officially on a day off—she couldn't settle.

Eventually, she gave up and looked at the clock. Seven o'clock. It was pointless just lying there. She might as well get up, have breakfast…and go into the Docklands office.

When she walked in at nine o'clock sharp, Luke glanced up from his desk and stared at her, looking surprised. 'Hello. I thought you were on a day off?'

'I changed my mind,' she said simply.

'What about your theory about the twenty per cent productivity drop?' he asked.

She shrugged. 'You'll have to live with it.'

He smiled. 'Then sit down. I'll make us some coffee.'

'I've been thinking,' she said when he returned with the coffee. 'We need to set some ground rules.'

'Sounds like you've already worked some out.'

'I have.'

'And?'

'One—and this is *not* negotiable—you don't sleep with anyone else while you're with me.'

'Fine. And it goes both ways,' he added.

'Agreed. Two, we're taking this day by day.'

'Agreed.'

'Three…' She'd been thinking about this one. A lot. It was where things had started to go wrong with Hugh. 'You spend time with me. You don't work ridiculous hours.'

'I don't work ridic—' He stopped, mid-protest. 'OK. I'll compromise—I won't work quite as late as I have in the past.' He could always catch up early in the morning. 'But I should warn you I have some standing dates. Including Monday nights.'

'Dates?'

'Yup. You know. Things that involve me getting hot and sweaty. With lots and lots of physical action.'

Her eyes narrowed. 'Indeed.'

He leaned back against his chair. 'But if you want to be responsible for Karim not having his weekly game of squash with me on Monday nights and getting really unfit and flabby, sure, I'll cancel.'

The rat. He'd strung her along. Teased her. And she'd been gullible enough to fall for it. 'Squash.'

He spread his hands. 'I told you I play squash a couple of times a week. Monday's with Karim and Thursday's a league match. And kick-boxing's on Tuesday and sometimes Wednesday.' He paused. 'You can come and watch, if you want.'

He didn't sound too enthused about the idea, though. She could guess why. 'It'll cramp your style.'

'No. It'll just be incredibly boring for you.'

That wasn't the real issue, she was sure. 'You don't want anyone to know about me, do you?'

'Sara, any man would be happy to boast that he was dating you.'

The word hung in the air—she said it for him. 'But…?'

He sighed. 'If you come to the squash court, Karim will take one look at you, leap to conclusions and get Lily to nag me stupid. I'll never get another minute's peace. And, right now, this is very new—for both of us. So I want to keep things just between us until we're sure of where it's going.'

She couldn't argue with that.

'But I could meet you afterwards. I know an excellent

Chinese restaurant not far from the squash courts, if you don't mind eating a bit late. They make the best dim sum ever.'

He was trying to compromise, she could tell. And it wasn't as if she wanted to spend every single evening with him. 'I still want to see my friends, too.'

'Good. Because cutting yourself off from your social network to spend all your time with one person is incredibly unhealthy.'

Did that mean he still intended to go to all those flash parties? And, most probably, on his own?

It must have been obvious what she was thinking, because he smiled. 'Hey, I'm bored with the party circuit. I'd offer to take you, but I can assure you that you'd be bored to tears within minutes. And, anyway, men aren't like women. They don't need bonding sessions.'

'No? What about football and beer?'

'I'm not into spectator sport,' he reminded her. 'Sure, I have the occasional beer with Karim after squash, but men don't sit around dissecting emotional stuff the way women do.'

'That's a bit sweeping.'

'Largely true, though.' He wrinkled his nose. 'Anyway, there's another reason why you have to keep up with your female friends—because there's no way you're dragging me off to see some tedious chick-flick.'

'You never know, you might enjoy it.'

He shook his head. 'I might enjoy sitting in the back row with you and kissing you stupid…but then again, I'd rather kiss you in private, so I can take things to their proper conclusion.'

'Proper?' she teased.

He laughed. 'OK, so what I have in mind is improper. But possibly not at this time of the morning, when I have meetings to go to and work to do.'

'How long have you been here?' she asked.

'Not long.'

'Crack of dawn?'

'No. I had a workout first,' he admitted.

'In one of your gyms?' At his nod, she sighed. 'And I bet you managed to get a meeting in there, too.'

'A teensy, teensy one.' He held his thumb and forefinger a couple of millimetres apart.

'There's no hope for you, is there?' she asked ruefully.

He grinned. 'No. But if you want to try any persuasion techniques, I'm open to suggestions.' He glanced at his watch. 'Gotta go. See you later.'

For a second, she wondered if he was going to kiss her goodbye. Then again, this was the office. And of course Luke would be professional with her here. She damped down the disappointment, waited for her computer to boot up, and started working through the emails.

Two seconds later, the office door opened and Luke strode back in. 'Forgot something,' he said.

'Uh-huh.' She could be just as professional as he was. She carried on working, assuming that he was going over to his desk.

And then he spun her chair round. Leaned over her. And kissed her. Thoroughly.

'Later,' he said softly, and left the office.

And it took a good ten minutes before Sara was calm enough to concentrate on her work.

Luke was out of the office for most of the day, and Sara was in the middle of emailing him to say she was leaving for the day when he walked in.

'Hi there. Sorry, got held up,' he explained. 'Is everything OK?'

'Fine.' She smiled at him.

'Is there anything I need to know about?'

'Apart from what I've already sent you? No. I was just about to go home.'

'Five o'clock on the dot?' he teased. 'You weren't supposed to be here anyway. You could've left earlier, if you'd wanted. Gone shopping or something.'

'Shoe shopping?' she teased.

He took a look under the desk. 'Yet another different pair. Are you sure your name isn't really Imelda?'

'No, but Lou changed our spaniel's name to Imelda, because he steals shoes and piles them up in his bed. He never chews them—just cuddles them. And it's always one from everyone in the house.' She laughed. 'Lou says it's because he thinks it'll mean we can't go out without him.'

She noticed that Luke looked faintly awkward. Because he wasn't a dog person? Or was it the fact that she was talking about her family? Despite telling her about his dad teaching him to fly the kite, Luke never said a word about his family, so it was a fair bet they weren't close.

'Are you still OK to eat with me tonight?' he asked.

'Sure.'

'Good.' He took the notepad from her desk and scribbled down an address. 'This is the restaurant. Meet you there at eight?'

'Fine.' So he planned to meet her there rather than outside the squash courts. He really did like to keep his life compartmentalised, she thought.

He opened his wallet and took out a couple of notes, proffering them to her. 'Take a taxi.'

She folded her arms. 'I'm perfectly capable of getting the Tube.'

He sighed. 'You're female, you're on your own and it's the evening.'

'It's still light at eight o'clock,' she pointed out.

'I don't care.' He put the notes on the desk in front of her. 'Take a taxi there, and I'll see you home.'

'Has feminism completely passed you by?' she asked.

'No,' he said. 'I believe in equal opportunities. But I also believe in not taking stupid risks to make a point. It's not a particularly rough area, and I know you're streetwise—but you also don't know the area, which makes you vulnerable. So stop being stubborn about it and take a taxi. And wait inside the restaurant for me. I'll book a table in my name.' He folded his arms and stared at her.

Sara knew when she was beaten. 'All right. Thank you. Even though I think it's completely unnecessary and over the top.' She tucked the notes into her purse, then switched off her computer. 'See you at eight. Have a good match.'

'Thanks.' He smiled at her and headed for his own desk as she left the office.

He was going through his emails when she returned.

'What?' he asked.

'As the saying goes…"I forgot something."' She spun his chair round, the way he had to her that morning, bent her head and kissed him, deepening the kiss and exploring his mouth.

By the time she broke the kiss, his pupils were enormous, there was a slash of colour across his cheeks and his mouth was slightly swollen and reddened.

'How the hell am I supposed to concentrate after that?' he demanded.

'You're the genius. I'm sure you'll work something out.' She gave him a cheeky grin and sashayed out of the office, knowing that he was watching every move she made.

At five to eight that evening, she was waiting in the restaurant; true to his word, Luke had booked them a table. She sat facing the door so he'd see her as soon as he walked in, ordered a mineral water and was browsing through the menu when something made her look up.

Luke.

Funny that her senses were so attuned to him, she knew the second he'd walked in the door. It had never been like that for her before. Not even with Hugh—and she'd been so sure that she and Hugh would marry and settle down and have children.

With Luke, she wasn't sure of anything. They were taking this day by day, and he'd been up front about the fact he disliked children. Quite what the future held for them, she didn't know.

But, for the life of her, she couldn't just walk away without seeing where this took them.

'I'm so glad you don't believe in making a man wait for you to make a dramatic entrance,' Luke said, brushing his mouth against hers and sliding into the seat opposite hers.

His hair was still damp from the shower, and he looked utterly gorgeous in plain black trousers and a black cashmere sweater. He'd drawn admiring glances from several tables on his way over to her; it wasn't just the way he looked, but the way he moved. All loose-limbed and sexy.

And all *hers*.

'How was your squash match?' she asked.

'Someone completely destroyed my concentration earlier,' he said. 'So what do you think?'

She batted her eyelashes. 'Are you saying you lost because of little ol' me?'

'Yup. So the very least you can do is kiss me better.'

'In the middle of a restaurant?' She wagged her finger at him. 'Tut, tut, Mr Holloway. You need to learn some patience.'

'You're trying mine right now.'

She just laughed. 'I'm hungry.'

'So,' he said, 'am I.'

'Then let's order.'

He sighed. 'You really don't take a hint, do you?'

'You promised me food. And I thought you hotshot business-men made a point of under-promising and over-delivering?'

'Yeah.' He laughed. 'You know, that dress looks fabulous.'

It was a red linen shift dress, teamed with a black lacy shrug and her black pearls. One of her favourites.

'Thank you. This all looks fabulous. What do you recom-mend?'

'Dim sum to start, then crispy duck. Then maybe share a mixture of dishes.'

It was the perfect evening. Good food, good company, good conversation.

And he held her hand all the way home on the Tube. He even came in for a coffee and chatted to Justin about cars and sound systems. To the point where Sara let herself begin to hope that this was going to work out. True, he didn't sit anywhere near her and he gave Justin the impression that dinner had been business rather than personal, but at least he stayed and talked.

'I'll see you tomorrow,' she said when she finally saw him to the door.

'No. You were supposed to take today off, and tomorrow you're definitely not in the office. Go and buy some shoes or something.'

'You're a bad influence,' she said with a smile. 'I never need encouraging to buy shoes.'

'Show them to me on Wednesday,' he said with a grin.

So he wasn't planning to see her tomorrow at all. OK. Well, this was new for both of them, and taking it slowly would be sensible. 'Mmm. And it'd be nice to have new shoes for tomorrow night—my regular pizza night with the girls.' Just so he'd know she wasn't pining over him. 'They, at least, will appreciate them.'

'And you're saying I won't?'

'You're a man,' she said loftily. 'Of course you won't. I'll see you Wednesday, then.' She reached up to kiss his cheek.

In response, he drew her closer. Kissed her mouth. Not with the hunger he'd kissed her that morning: this was a sweet, soft kiss of promise. The kind of kiss that made her feel as if her bones had just melted. The kind of kiss that stole her heart. 'Sweet dreams, Sara,' he said, and waited until she'd closed the front door behind her before walking away.

When Luke got home, he really intended to work. There were some reports on potential properties that he wanted to compare and contrast. But he couldn't concentrate the way he usually did. Every report he looked through, he found himself staring at the pictures of the hotel rooms and thinking of Sara and wondering how soft the bed was.

And it drove him crazy.

He never, but never, had a problem compartmentalising his work and his love life.

Or maybe it was because she worked with him. It couldn't be anything else, he was sure.

But he missed her the next day. Missed the sassy comments mingled with sound common sense and good ideas. Missed bouncing ideas off her. Missed her ready smile.

And the kick-boxing turned out to be even more of a disaster area than his squash match.

'Either you're working too hard or she's utterly gorgeous,' Mike, his sparring partner, said afterwards.

'Working too hard,' Luke fibbed. He knew exactly what the problem was. Sara. He couldn't stop thinking about her. And, against his better judgement, he ended up texting her later that evening.

*Hope you're having a good evening. L.*

It was completely innocuous, in case one of her friends picked up her phone by mistake. But enough to let her know he was thinking of her.

The reply came an hour later. *I am. Very girly. You'd HATE it.*

He almost—almost—suggested that she came over to his place for coffee afterwards. But that would be too needy, and he wasn't needy. Ever.

He left it half an hour before enquiring casually, *You busy tomorrow night?*

*Why?*

*Have dinner with me?*

The gap before she replied felt incredibly long, and Luke was cross with himself. Ridiculous. Sara wasn't a game player; she was probably on the Tube and didn't have a signal.

And then his phone beeped. *Thought you had kick-boxing on Weds?*

*Skipping it.* His concentration was so shot this week, he knew it was pointless. *So, dinner?*

*What time?*

*After work.* He suppressed the thought that tomorrow night he might get to find out whether her underwear co-ordinated with her shoes and her tops. *Any food you don't like?*

This time, instead of beeping to signal the arrival of a text message, his phone rang.

'Rather than playing text ping-pong, isn't it easier to have a conversation on the phone?' Sara asked crisply.

'You were out for the evening. I thought it was easier to send a text so you could answer at your leisure.'

'Well, I'm home now, so you can talk to me.'

He laughed. 'Now that's a dangerous invitation.'

'Why?'

He couldn't resist teasing her. 'What would you do if I gave you a dirty phone call?'

She laughed back. 'Probably enjoy it.'

He was speechless. She'd really called his bluff; right at that moment, he felt as if his tongue had been glued to the roof of his mouth.

'What did you have in mind for tomorrow night?'

*You, me and nothing in between.* He just about stopped himself saying it. 'Just dinner. Is there any food you don't like?'

'I'm easy to please. What's the dress code?'

'Whatever you like. Oh, and your new shoes.'

'I didn't buy any.'

'Oh.'

'But I did buy something else.' Her voice was full of amusement. And there was a sensual note that made him feel as if she were stroking his skin. Kissing her way down his body.

Uh.

He really, really had to get himself back under control. Before he said something really stupid. Like begging her to come over and show him this very second. And he really, really didn't want her to know just how needy he was feeling right now.

He didn't do needy. He'd spent half his life standing on his own two feet, and it was going to stay that way.

'Aren't you going to ask me what?' she teased.

'No. I'll see you tomorrow,' he said, more abruptly than he'd intended. 'Goodnight.' But when he cut the connection he felt awful.

What was wrong with him?

He *liked* Sara, for pity's sake. He enjoyed her company. So why was he blowing hot and cold like this, behaving like a moody teenager whose hormones were running riot?

There was an explanation—but it wasn't one he was prepared to countenance. How could you fall in love with someone when you didn't believe in love?

Utterly ridiculous.

So instead he went down to the office and worked through various sets of figures until he was too tired to see straight.

# CHAPTER ELEVEN

'WHY didn't you tell me?' Sara asked as Luke unlocked his front door the following evening.

'What?'

'That you live above your office.'

He shrugged. 'It wasn't relevant.'

'Wasn't relevant?' She stared at him. 'Luke Holloway, I can't believe you sometimes.'

'What's the problem?'

'You work crazy hours *and* you live right above your office.'

He sighed. 'All it means is that I have a short commute to work. And I do leave my work in my office. I never bring work home with me.'

'You don't need to, do you? All you have to do is walk downstairs.' She shook her head. 'There's no hope for you.'

'Sara, I don't see what the fuss is about.'

'No. You wouldn't.' And it wasn't Luke's fault that her ex was out of the same mould. She shouldn't take out her insecurities on him. 'Sorry,' she muttered.

'Women. They're another species,' he said lightly. 'Come and see the views.' He ushered her into the living room. 'What do you think?'

It was as stunning as she'd guessed it would be, the very first day she'd seen the building. Luke lived in the duplex penthouse apartment, and his living room was right at the top of the tower. The side overlooking the Thames and the city was floor-to-ceiling glass, so the view was incredible. And, with the sun still out, the river sparkled—it was like looking down onto a magical world.

'It's fabulous,' she breathed.

'And that wall means the room gets lots of natural light. It's one of the things I love most about living here.'

In most other male preserves, she thought, there would be a state-of-the-art TV and several games consoles as the focal point of the room. But Luke's living room was furnished extremely simply. No clutter anywhere. Just three enormous leather sofas, which looked as if they'd be butter-soft to the touch, grouped round an extremely modern fireplace; a coffee table near one of the sofas; a stereo system which looked sleek and stylish and she'd just bet was the very top of the range; and a bookcase which seemed to contain mainly business-oriented textbooks. There was also a glass-topped dining table with eight chairs on the other side of the room. At one end of the table, two places had been set opposite each other with what looked like granite place mats, cutlery that shone with the lustre of real silver and the finest, thinnest crystal glasses. A fat white candle stood in a scooped silver bowl, nestled on top of flowing curved legs: a Celtic knot design, she thought, stripped down to its simplest form.

There wasn't a single photograph: nothing at all personal to give away what kind of man Luke was. They could've been standing in an extremely posh hotel suite. Admittedly, with that incredible glass wall, Luke didn't really need any pictures: the views were enough. Over the mantelpiece—bare of anything except a small unadorned clock—there was a large mirror, reflecting the views. And it made it very clear to her that Luke was completely self-contained. He didn't need anything or anyone.

This really didn't bode well for the beginning of their relationship, she thought.

Yet there had been moments in Scarborough where he'd

seemed to let her in. When he'd told her about his father teaching him to fly a kite, when he'd walked with her at the edge of the sea, when he'd shared the chocolate dipping platter with her. Or was she deluding herself?

'It's gorgeous—though it's pretty minimalist,' she remarked.

He shrugged. 'I hate clutter.'

She knew that already, from his office. He really wouldn't be able to cope with Louisa's toddler, Maisie, she thought—the little girl was going through the stage of trailing clutter everywhere.

'Would you like a glass of wine before dinner?' he asked.

'Thank you.' She followed him through to the next room; the kitchen had granite worktops, what looked like handmade pale wood cabinets and a state-of-the-art range cooker. There was practically nothing on any of the work surfaces, apart from a wooden fruit bowl and a kettle. No cork pin-board on the wall above the breakfast bar, crowded with memos and recipes and business cards, as there was in her parents' kitchen; no postcards or photographs held onto the stainless steel American fridge with little magnets.

And, more to the point, she couldn't smell anything. Nothing cooking, nothing marinating.

Odd.

He took a bottle of Chablis from the fridge and poured them both a glass. 'Cheers,' he said, raising his glass in a toast.

'Cheers.' She paused. 'So if we're having dinner here tonight—does this mean you're cooking for me?'

'Not exactly.'

'I'm not with you…' Then the penny dropped and she grinned. 'Ah. You cheated and bought stuff you're going to heat up in the microwave.'

'Slightly worse,' he said.

'How much worse?'

'I sweet-talked the café manager at one of the gyms to make something for me that I could heat through,' he admitted. 'It's in the fridge.'

Unbelievable. 'You have a kitchen like this and you don't cook?' she asked, flabbergasted.

'I don't need to cook, apart from breakfast—and even then I might nip down to the coffee bar and grab a bagel because it's quicker. If I'm in the office, I'll have a sandwich for lunch.'

And eat it at his desk, with his other hand annotating reports, she thought. Apart from the occasion when she'd taken him to St Dunstan's and the time they'd gone to the pizza place. Lunch dates they hadn't repeated.

'Though if I'm at one of the businesses, I'll eat in the café there.'

'And you do the same for dinner.'

'Pretty much. I eat sensibly.' He shrugged. 'It's better than living on burgers and doughnuts. And it also means I get to do some quality checking on the health club cafés; I can make sure the food and the service are what I'd want them to be. Double whammy, you might say.'

She shook her head. 'You're missing out on a lot, you know. Cooking's one of the best ways I know to relax.'

His eyes lit with amusement. 'I know other ways. Though, if I give you a demonstration, dinner will be very, very late.'

She could guess exactly what he was talking about. And the remembered feel of his hands and his mouth against her skin sent a shaft of pure desire through her. To cover her confusion, she took a sip of wine and pretended he hadn't said a thing. 'I used to love cooking with my mum—mind you, I drove her insane because I was always rearranging her cupboards.' She smiled. 'Mum used to rearrange them right back and leave me sarcastic little notes for the next time I sneaked into the kitchen to do it.'

'Then you've always been the orderly type?' At her nod, he raised an eyebrow. 'So why were you giving me a hard time just now for having a tidy flat?'

'There's tidy, like me, and there's extreme minimalist,' she said.

'I get it. You like having all the clutter—but you also like having it all lined up and put away.'

'Yup.'

'I would really like to know,' he said, 'just how many pairs of shoes you have. And whether you arrange them by colour, style or fabric.'

'That,' she retorted, 'would be telling.'

'Come and sit down and I'll feed you,' he said. He held the chair out for her that faced the view.

'But that means you can't see the view,' she protested.

'I see it all the time.'

He was being polite, and she was the guest. She'd better remember that.

He lit the candle and the scent of vanilla filled the air.

'This is lovely—and I like that holder. The legs look a bit like a Celtic knot, only simpler.'

He smiled. 'What do you expect from—I quote—"an extreme minimalist"?' He walked over to the stereo system and pressed a couple of switches.

Sara raised an eyebrow as the first notes slid into the air. 'What, no dinosaur rock?' she teased.

'Hey, you're the one who had piano lessons as a kid. I assumed you'd like this.'

'You can never go wrong with Mozart,' she said. Good food accompanied by candlelight and the most beautiful piano music. Utter bliss. 'This sonata's one of my favourites.'

'Don't tell me—you can play it?'

'I used to be able to,' she admitted. 'But I haven't played for ages. I'd make a real mess of it now.'

'Would you rather I changed the music?' he asked.

'No, this is fine. Do you want a hand in the kitchen with anything?'

'No, that's OK. It's practically all done.'

He brought through two plates of prawns mixed with avocado and baby spinach leaves, drizzled with lime juice and olive oil.

'Wow, this is fantastic,' Sara said after the first taste.

'Exactly. So when I have food like this available, why would I bother cooking?'

'Point taken.'

The main course was cold chicken with baby new potatoes and salad. 'Are you telling me you actually sullied a saucepan with this?' she teased.

'You must be joking. Too much washing up,' he retorted.

'I love the dressing.'

'Pomegranate and orange. Apparently Cathy got the recipe for this one from Lily after we did a tasting thing for her.'

And pudding was utterly perfect. Fresh raspberries and best-quality vanilla ice cream. Had he remembered her favourite? she wondered.

'This,' she said, 'is bliss. My brothers and sister tease me about it, but you just can't get better than really good vanilla ice cream. Especially with lovely tart English raspberries.' She smiled. 'It always makes me think of the summer holidays when I was a kid, raiding the garden. There's nothing like fruit that's freshly picked and still warm from the sun when you eat it.'

'Glad you like it.'

'Well, that was fabulous. Even if it was utterly cheating on your part.'

'Hey, I washed the raspberries myself,' he protested, laughing.

'That,' she said, 'isn't cooking.'

'Yeah, yeah.' He cleared the table. 'Go and sit down in comfort. I'll bring the coffee through.'

Sara curled up on one of the huge leather sofas and just looked at the lights. Now it was dusk, the lights had come on outside, brilliant whites and deep blues reflected on the Thames. 'This is beautiful,' she said as Luke returned bearing coffee and a box of chocolates.

'Wait a second.' He went over to the table and blew out the candle. 'How about now?'

That little extra bit of darkness inside made the outside seem even brighter. 'Just stunning,' she said. She could understand exactly why he'd chosen to live here.

'It's even better late at night,' he said. 'The Thames is like polished ebony reflecting it all back.'

'Like a Whistler painting.'

He smiled. 'Trust you to know the art.'

'Don't be chippy.'

'I'm not. I don't know a huge amount about art, though I'm not that keen on abstract stuff. I like a painting to look like what it is.' He settled next to her, sharing the chocolates.

For a second, Sara could imagine every evening being like this. Living with Luke, sharing his space—cooking with him, laughing with him, making love with him.

Then she shook herself. She wasn't supposed to be letting herself fall for him. This was supposed to be getting the attraction out of their mutual systems.

Luke took her hand. 'So you like my living room. Want to come and see what I go to sleep to?'

Which didn't necessarily mean he was planning to make love with her, Sara reminded herself; he might be just offering her a guided tour of the rest of the flat. 'Sure,' she said, hoping that her voice didn't sound quite as breathless as it felt.

He led her downstairs. Although he didn't switch on the light in his bedroom, the glow from outside was enough to show her the contents: a huge, huge platform bed with plenty of pillows, a bedside table with a lamp and lots of space. As with the living room, one wall of the room was floor-to-ceiling glass; the bed was positioned to face the glass and, instead of curtains, he had narrow black Venetian blinds. Again, there were no pictures on the rest of the walls, and all the furnishings seemed to be in shades of grey and white.

Then she realised that the Mozart was still playing—and she could still hear it. 'How do you do that?'

'It's probably what you'd term boys and their toys.' He

gave her a wry smile. 'It's a sound system that follows you round the flat.'

'If you'd told me about it before I heard it for myself, I would've said you'd been reading too many sci-fi novels.' She shook her head in wonder. 'I had no idea that kind of technology even existed.'

'It's based on wireless networks,' he explained.

'It's impressive.' And she'd just bet it was hideously expensive. Especially given how good the quality of the sound was.

He inclined his head. 'Thank you.'

She wandered over to the window and looked out. 'This is astonishing.'

'I like it. And with all the glass…it makes me feel free.'

'You're claustrophobic?' she guessed.

'I couldn't have worked in the market if I was, with all the stalls right up together and everything piled high—no, I just like my space.'

Was that a warning, a reminder that he wasn't going to let her any closer? But, then again, he'd invited her here, shown her round the place.

She stood with her hands on the rail of the window, looking out and drinking in the view. Luke stood behind her and slid his arms round her waist. He brushed his mouth against the nape of her neck. 'I really can't work out whether I like your hair up or down best. Up means I get access like this…' He drew a trail of nibbling kisses along the sensitive curve at the side of her neck. 'And down makes you look much more touchable, less remote.'

'You think I'm remote?'

'When you're all elegant and sophisticated… Yes. And I'm glad today you wore a dress rather than a suit.'

'Why?'

'Because—' his fingers found the tab of her zip and lowered it '—it makes things easy for me.'

He was planning to undress her in front of a window? 'Luke, we can't—people might see!'

'Stop worrying,' he said. 'Apart from the fact we're on next to the top floor, there's no light on inside—the light's coming in from outside, so we can see out but people can't see in.'

'But, Luke…'

'It's fine,' he reassured her. 'Live a little.'

He kissed all the way down her spine until she was shivering, then he eased the material of her dress over her shoulders, drawing it slowly down to her waist and letting it fall to the floor.

She turned to face him. 'Luke.'

'I want to touch you, Sara.'

'And I want to touch you.' She unbuttoned his shirt. She could see his face clearly in the light spilling in through the window; his eyes were really dark, there was a slight hint of stubble on his jaw and, with that white shirt undone, he looked as sexy as hell.

He sucked in a breath. 'Do you have any idea how sexy you look right now? In lacy knickers, high heels and pearls, with your hair up?'

'This was what I bought yesterday. Well, except the shoes and necklace.' The pearls were palest lavender, matched to her underwear. 'You like them?'

'More than like.' He picked her up, carried her to his bed and settled her against the pillows while he ripped the rest of his clothes off.

The mattress was firm and the pillows were the kind you could sink into but which also gave support. His sheets were purest cotton with a really high thread count, so soft against her skin, and they were perfectly smooth, not even creased from being folded.

'What are you thinking?' he asked softly.

'Scarborough. The sheets weren't creased there, either.' Not until they'd spent the night in them.

'You can crease my sheets any time you like,' he teased. Then his face went serious and he kissed her, demanding a response from her mouth while he finished removing her clothes.

He paused to protect her with a condom, then eased into her body. And it felt to Sara as if she was really connecting with him—more than just bodily. He lost himself in her, just as she lost herself in him.

Afterwards, he took off her pearls and placed them on his bedside table before taking her through to his en-suite bathroom. His shower was definitely big enough for two, and he paid attention to every centimetre of her skin, lathering it and then rinsing off the suds. The towels were thick and fluffy, and he dried her very tenderly, really cosseting her.

And then amusement lit his eyes.

'What?' she asked.

'You're the only woman I've ever met who matches her toenail polish to her underwear.'

'Details are important,' she said. 'Actually, if my shoes aren't black, I normally match it to my shoes.'

'So you have dozens of bottles of nail polish as well as dozens of pairs of shoes?'

'Could be worse. I only have three handbags,' she teased back.

'We'd better get dressed,' he said. 'I'll drive you home.'

So he wasn't going to ask her to stay. Well, she hadn't expected it. Besides, she didn't have clean clothes and a toothbrush with her, so it was just as well. The fact that Luke had shared as much of himself with her as he had tonight was a huge step forward.

Luke came up to the flat with her. Justin was out for the evening and had left her a note but, to her disappointment, Luke didn't stay.

It must've shown on her face because he said softly, 'If I come in for coffee, you know as well as I do that it won't stop there. And I don't want to embarrass you in front of your brother.'

'Uh-huh.' She tried her best to sound cool and casual and perfectly OK with it all.

And then he kissed her goodnight; it was so sweet and tender and full of promise that it made her want to cry.

'See you tomorrow,' he said.

'Tomorrow.'

One day at a time, they'd agreed. If she pushed him too far, too fast, it would all blow up in her face. She just needed to be patient.

And then it hit her.

She'd fallen in love with Luke Holloway. A workaholic who didn't believe in marriage, who didn't want children and who, despite the fact that he'd been fine with her brother, would no doubt take the long way round to avoid anything resembling a family gathering. A man who didn't believe in happy-ever-afters.

The worst possible man she could fall for.

What made it even worse was that she knew he was definitely the one. Her feelings for Hugh paled into insignificance against what she felt for this man. This went bone deep.

She knew that Luke was going to need patience and time to trust her, to talk to her about whatever was in his head; he was a man who was totally self-contained. But would he ever really open up to her?

All the way back to Docklands, Luke thought about it. New territory. He'd always been careful to avoid his previous girlfriends' families. The fact that he'd met Sara's brother—and liked him—meant that he was getting in too deep for comfort.

He couldn't pull back. Not now. Yet the idea of going forward made him nervous. Crazy. He'd done deals for enormous amounts of money. Taken plenty of risks—calculated, but still risks. Yet he'd never felt upside down and in a whirl, the way he did whenever he thought about Sara.

If this was love, he wasn't sure he could cope with it. He wanted his nice, orderly, *busy* life back.

Though, at the same time, he couldn't imagine life without Sara around. He no longer wanted the shallow, glittering parties that had been his social life. No longer wanted a string of gorgeous women who expected no commitments, just lavish gifts and lots of fun.

What he wanted was something much simpler.

And much more complex.

He wanted Sara.

But if he took the risk—what then? Would he end up hurting them both? Would he end up losing her?

Because if he let her into his heart, took the risk and let her draw him into her family, he wasn't sure that he'd survive losing all that a second time.

There had to be a way forward. But, right at that moment, he couldn't see it.

# CHAPTER TWELVE

OVER the next couple of weeks, Sara and Luke saw more of each other outside work, and she found herself beginning to hope that things might just work out for them. Luke delighted her one Saturday with a trip to a couple of ruined abbeys in Kent, saying, 'Seeing as I've taken up the time you were going to spend wandering round temples in Greece and Italy, this is the least I can do.' A day spent walking hand in hand, with lunch at a little country pub, quiet and intimate and close. Just perfect.

She, in turn, surprised him with tickets for a rock concert; although it wasn't really her thing, she could see how much he enjoyed it and that made it all worthwhile.

And, although Luke still hadn't found a temp, Sara didn't mind that much; she was enjoying working with him and liked the way he asked her opinions of things and stretched her skills by teaching her to read balance sheets and underlying trends. Even better was when he asked her to go with him to scope out potential hotels.

'Can you come with me to look at a place?' he asked.

'Oh, you mean that place you found in Cromer?' She remembered him talking about it: a seaside resort in Norfolk with a Victorian heyday. It was too late in the year to see the poppies the area had once been famed for, but it still held the potential of a paddle in the sea and a walk on the beach in the early evening, just before the light faded. 'Sure.'

'It's another weekend, I'm afraid—is that OK?'

She nodded. 'When?'

'Friday morning. I'll need you to meet me here at eight.'

Norfolk was only a couple of hours' drive away. Maybe, she thought, this wasn't the hotel he'd been talking about; maybe this was a new opportunity and he wanted to get the earliest look possible. 'I'll check my diary,' she said, wanting to make the point that she did have a life outside work and wasn't going to drop everything for him. 'Yes, you're OK. Though, had it been next weekend, I would've had to say no.' Not that it was worth asking Luke to come with her to her niece's birthday party. If he was reluctant to meet her oldest brother, no way would he agree to come to Kent for a Sunday afternoon and meet her entire family.

'Good. You'll need casual clothes. Flat shoes with a decent grip are a good idea.'

She frowned. 'I thought Norfolk was flat?'

'Obviously it's not mountainous like the Lake District but, apart from the fens and bits around Yarmouth, it's not that flat.'

'Flat shoes.' She surveyed the lipstick-red stilettos she was wearing. Definitely not suitable.

He laughed. 'Sounds like it's a chance for you to go shoe shopping. Oh, and your passport.'

'Passport? Why do I need that?'

'Because I need a photocopy of it—and your driving licence—for the insurance company. You know, to insure my car for you to drive.'

'Since when do they ask for a passport?'

He shrugged. 'Maybe they want extra proof of identity.'

Maybe companies were tightening up security.

'Oh, and don't bother with breakfast. We'll stop on the way.'

But on Friday morning he didn't drive her to Norfolk. Instead, they took the Docklands Light Railway to London City Airport.

'Luke? Where are we…?'

'You'll see when we get there' was the irritating reply.

'I thought we were checking out one of your potential hotels?'

'Nope. We're playing hooky for the weekend.'

She stared at him in surprise. 'But you don't play hooky.'

He smiled. 'Maybe you've inspired me.'

Maybe, she thought; she'd certainly noticed that he'd worked fewer hours recently.

Once they'd checked in, he bought them coffee and muffins.

She laughed. 'So Mr Healthy does eat cake sometimes, then.'

He laughed back. 'Sometimes. And you know my weaknesses. Posh chocolate biscuits.' His eyes added the rest of it for him, and desire rippled down her spine.

The airport operated a silent terminal system; rather than a tannoy announcing the flights, there were information screens throughout the airport giving updates on arrivals and departures. There were several flights due, but Sara knew there was no point in asking him which one.

And then she saw it on the screen.

*Private charter. Holloway.*

'Private charter?' she asked. 'You chartered a plane just for us?'

'Don't get too excited. It's not a jumbo jet,' he said dryly. 'I know air travel isn't eco-friendly, but the rest of the trip is.'

'But…can you do that sort of thing? Charter a plane, just like that?'

'You can if you have a friend who owns an airline.'

She blinked. 'You have a friend who owns an airline?'

'A small one. We were on the same MBA course.'

She wasn't surprised that Luke had done an MBA. And she'd just bet that he'd graduated at the top of his class.

The plane was tiny—only six seats plus the pilot—but it meant she could see everything.

Four hours later, they landed at a tiny airport. 'Where are we?' she asked.

'Samos. Greece,' he added, for good measure.

Once they'd disembarked and gone through Customs, they

took a taxi to the harbour. 'Stay there a minute,' he said, and disappeared. When he returned, he picked up their cases and led her further down the marina to where a yacht was moored, its white sails unfurled.

She blinked. 'We're going on that?'

'Yup. You and me.'

'But I've never done any proper sailing.'

He looked amused. 'You don't need to.'

'You've hired a skipper?'

He smiled. 'This isn't a complicated boat, Sara. It only takes one to sail it—and, anyway, I can teach you rigging and steering, if you like.'

'You're kidding.' And he was going to sail the boat himself?

His grin broadened. 'What, you're chickening out on me? If I remember rightly, you were the one who was so keen on boats at Scarborough.'

'A boat trip,' she corrected, 'where I was a passenger and all I had to do was look at the seals.'

'You're still a passenger,' he said. 'You don't have to do anything but sit there with a book.'

'I didn't bring any books with me.'

'Then just enjoy the scenery. We're going to the next island west of here—Ikaria. Its name comes from Icarus.'

'The boy whose father made them wings to escape from prison, but he flew too high and the sun melted the wax on his wings and he drowned?'

'That's the one. Apparently he flew too high because he was so thrilled by the view—the mountains to the south, and fabulous beaches to the north.'

'How come you know about boats and the natural history around here?'

'I do occasionally take holidays.'

'And you've sailed before.'

'I learned in the same place as Admiral Nelson—the Norfolk Broads. If it was good enough for him…'

She smiled. 'That sounds like patter.'

'It is. But it's also true.' He smiled. 'Anyway, I knew you'd like this as you like things in shipshape order.'

She groaned. 'Your jokes are terrible.'

'I know.' He didn't look the slightest bit repentant. He carried their cases onto the yacht, then helped her on board. 'I just need to change, and then we'll go sailing and find a nice place to moor tonight. We can eat at a little taverna somewhere.'

She guessed he'd already researched the island and discovered the best places to eat.

'Just sit there and look at the boats for a minute. Oh, and change your shoes.' At her raised eyebrow, he spread his hands. 'Health and safety regulations.'

Now she knew why he'd told her to wear flat shoes. Not because they'd be walking, but because they'd be on a boat—and flat shoes with a decent grip were safer. 'My shoes are in my case,' she reminded him.

'Take those ones off—gorgeous though they are, I don't want you falling off the deck.' He blew her a kiss. 'I'll bring your sensible shoes up with me.'

When he reappeared, he was wearing a white shirt with the sleeves rolled halfway up his forearms, black chinos rolled up to his knees and deck shoes with no socks. He was also sporting dark glasses and a red bandana over his hair. 'Now, you have to imagine the earring, the parrot and the hook,' he said.

Her pirate fantasy. She loved the fact that he'd tried to indulge her; though she also knew he'd hate it if she went all gooey on him, so she resorted to sass. 'Captain Hook wore a pirate hat, not a bandana, and he had a red velvet coat,' she countered. 'Besides, pirate captains don't wear bandanas.'

'No?' He sat down beside her, placed her flat shoes on the deck and leaned over to kiss her thoroughly.

'You lied to me,' she said when she could catch her breath.

'How?'

'You told me we were going to Norfolk.'

'No. You assumed it. I just didn't correct you.'

'You lied about the reason why I needed a passport.'

'True, but it was a teensy fib to put you off the scent, purely because I wanted to surprise you. I'd never lie about anything important.'

She believed him. Luke was an honourable man. 'You'd never make a real pirate,' she said softly, stroking his face.

'Probably not. But, hey, I'm not the one with the Captain Hook fantasy.' He grinned. 'Oh, and for your information, pirate captains might wear bandanas if they're travelling incognito to do a bit of QC work in their fleet.'

She groaned. 'Please tell me this isn't work. You're not planning to buy a yacht? Or a spa hotel in Greece?'

'It's a thought…' Then he laughed. 'No, we're playing hooky for the weekend. Though there are various hot springs on the island. We can try them out, if you like. Or just moor at one of the harbours and paddle in the sea. Which reminds me.' He'd brought a bottle of sun cream up with the shoes. 'On a yacht, the sun's rays are reflected from the sea so they'll burn you more quickly. You need high protection factor.'

'Going to rub it on for me?' she teased.

'Now there's an offer. Be careful what you say to a pirate captain on a very secluded island,' he teased back. But he rubbed the cream into her skin, making sure it was thoroughly covered, before removing his bandana. 'I should've told you to bring a hat—I'll get you one when we moor, but in the meantime use this.'

'What about you?'

'Pirates don't need hats,' he said.

Sara felt slightly guilty, sitting there watching him do all the hard work of sailing the yacht, but as she knew practically nothing about boats she knew she'd just be in the way. Though she did enjoy the view: the blueness of the sea was stunning. And her view of the ship's pirate captain was even better.

He took her to Nas. 'Apparently, these are some of the best

ruins in Greece,' he informed her. 'There aren't that many of them—just the pier of the ancient port and the floor of the sanctuary dedicated to Artemis survive—but you get to see them in peace and quiet because they're off the beaten track. The villagers reused most of the stone in the church tower and in a stepping-stone bridge.'

'Have you been here before?' she asked, curious.

'No, I just read up about it. It's what made me decide to bring you here. I thought this would be the kind of place you'd like.'

She loved everything about Nas, from the beautiful cove with its soft, pale sand and clear blue water lapping at the shore, to the huge gorge with a river cutting through it, to the ruins themselves. And, when they followed the stream, they found a deep lake with a waterfall.

'This is too good to miss,' Luke said. He removed her shoes, kicked off his own, picked her up and walked straight into the lake.

'Luke!' she protested.

'We don't have any swimming things, and we'll be arrested if we skinny-dip. And I really, *really* want to kiss you under a waterfall,' he said. 'So this is the best option.'

'You're…you're…' she floundered.

'What?'

Gorgeous. Kind. Thoughtful. The man she'd lost her heart to. Not that she'd panic him by telling him so. 'Lovely,' she said.

'So are you.' He drew her over to the waterfall. 'Now kiss me.'

She did, and what started out as a warm, sweet kiss, silently telling him that she loved him, soon turned hot. To the point where they ended up running back to the yacht, and Luke made love to her thoroughly, jamming his mouth over hers to silence her cries of pleasure.

Afterwards, they found a sleepy taverna for a lunch of excellent grilled fish with herbs and salad, and tiny pastries dripping with honey.

Luke refused wine. 'Apart from the fact I'm crewing the boat

so I need a clear head, I'm not a fan of retsina. But feel free to
have what you like.'

She bit her lip. 'Luke, I feel bad about this. I don't have any
local currency on me, and I want to pay for something.'

'Hey, I'm the one who stole your holiday in the first place.
This is my way of making it up to you a little bit. Humour me.'
He smiled at her. 'And to see you enjoying this is payment
enough for me. Money isn't important.'

She coughed. 'Of course you can say that. It isn't an issue
for you.'

'I came from nothing,' he said. 'And on the way I learned
that money really *isn't* important. It's who you are inside that
counts most.'

And Luke Holloway was a good man—one with a huge
heart that he kept barricaded away. Though Sara was beginning
to hope that he was slowly learning to trust her and would start
dismantling the fences.

The weekend was magical, spent sailing round the island.
They visited ruined castles and monasteries with beautiful
frescoes and stunning views, bathed in the hot springs at
Thermae, and late on Saturday they were awed to see a school
of dolphins frolicking in the sea.

'That's just…' Words failed Sara and she simply slid her arm
round Luke's waist, cuddling into him. He rested his arm on
her shoulders and kissed the top of her head.

She had no idea how long they stayed there, just watching
the dolphins arcing out of the water, but she was so glad she'd
shared it with Luke. They moored overnight at another village,
eating a simple yet beautifully cooked meal, and watched the
sun set from the deck of the boat. The stars in Greece seemed
bright and clear, like they never were in London, and, best of
all, she fell asleep in Luke's arms that night.

Late on the Sunday afternoon, they flew back to London.

'It's late. Why don't you stay here tonight?' Luke suggested
when they were back at his flat.

He'd never asked her to stay with him in London. Another barrier down? she wondered hopefully. 'I'll need to call Justin,' she said, 'just so he doesn't worry about whether we've had an accident on the way back.'

'Sure. I'll order us a takeaway.'

It felt oddly domesticated, eating pizza with Luke in his kitchen. Even more so, putting both their clothes in his washing machine. Though she knew better than to hope for too much, too soon. Right now, it was enough to lie in his arms in his enormous bed, watching the rain fall onto the windows and drifting off to sleep with her cheek pillowed against his heart.

# CHAPTER THIRTEEN

ON THE Monday lunchtime, Sara headed over to Greenwich to buy Luke a gift to say thank you for the weekend. Knowing how much he hated clutter, she wanted to get him something useful, which meant something for his desk, but she also wanted it to be something that would remind him of a time when he'd actually relaxed.

In the third shop she tried, she found the perfect thing. And when Luke came back from a meeting, there was a box on his desk tied with blue ribbon.

'What's this?' he asked.

'For you,' she said, leaning back in her chair. 'Just to say thanks for the weekend.'

'You didn't have to buy me anything.'

'I wanted to.'

He untied the ribbon and removed the protective crumpled tissue paper, and simply stared.

'It's Swedish art glass,' she told him. 'A paperweight.' Two dolphins, sculpted from glass, encased in a wave of lead crystal.

'It's beautiful. You really didn't have to, but I appreciate it.'

He walked over to her desk, leaned over and kissed her. His kiss was warm and sweet; this was definitely more than just sexual attraction, Sara thought. And, although she didn't say it out loud, it felt a lot like love.

'I thought the dolphins might remind you of Ikaria. Though the island isn't just linked to Icarus, you know,' she said.

'Sounds as if someone's been doing some research,' he teased.

'I did. It's supposed to be the birthplace of Dionysus—and that's why it's linked to dolphins. When Dionysus was young, some pirates kidnapped him on his way to Naxos, so he stopped the ship and made vines grow over the sails. Then some beasts appeared as if by magic on the deck; the pirates jumped overboard in terror and they were changed into dolphins.'

'I'll think of you and your pirate fantasy whenever I look at it,' he said.

Luke asked her to stay over for two more nights that week; it convinced Sara that he was definitely letting down his barriers. So maybe, just maybe, if she asked him, he'd say yes…

'It's my niece's birthday on Sunday. I was wondering if you'd like to come with me?' she asked on the Friday morning. 'It's nothing elaborate because she's going to be two—just the usual family high tea and a birthday cake.'

'Family high tea.'

There was reservation in his tone, though when she looked at him his face was unreadable.

Clearly she'd pushed him too far, too fast. And hadn't he told her straight that he didn't like children? 'Look, you don't have to. It was just a thought. If you're not doing anything already.'

'It's nice of you to ask.'

She could hear the *but*. And she knew exactly what he was going to say because he always took refuge in work. Which meant she'd gone ten steps back instead of what she'd thought of as one tiny step forward.

'I…' He blew out a breath. 'OK. Sunday's fine.'

It was the last thing she'd expected him to say. So she just stared at him, stunned.

'But I don't exactly come across a lot of children in my line of work,' he added. 'You'll have to help me choose a present for her.'

'Present?'

'Even I know that you don't go to a party without a present for the birthday girl.' His tone was light, but his expression was still unreadable. She didn't have a clue what he was thinking, and it unsettled her.

He logged on to the Internet and typed in the name of the biggest toy shop in London—a name that was familiar even to people who didn't have children. 'What kind of things does she like?'

Then she realised. He was treating this as business; she knew this was his way of coping with things. She almost—*almost*—wrapped her arms round him and told him that everything was going to be fine, that all he had to do was tell her why families made him nervous, and she'd help her...but she didn't want to push him even further away. 'Look, I was going to hit the toy shop this evening. Why don't you come with me?'

'To the toy shop.' It was a statement rather than a question.

'Look, I know you've got something in your diary for late afternoon. Why don't I lock up here and we can meet at the corner of Regent Street and Oxford Circus at…say…six?'

He nodded and turned back to his desk. 'I'll call you if I'm running late.'

She couldn't leave it like this. 'Luke.'

'Mmm?' He looked up from the computer screen.

She laid her hand against his cheek. 'Thank you. I know this isn't really your kind of thing. I appreciate it.'

'No worries.' He made light of it, but his colour deepened. And her heart ached for him. What would it take to show him that he could trust her with himself? With his heart?

At precisely six o'clock, Luke met Sara in Regent Street and walked with her to the toy shop. It was full of families, parents choosing gifts for their children with love. How long had it been since he'd last set foot in a shop like this?

He pushed the thought away. Treat it like business, he told himself. Your goal is to choose a birthday gift for a small child. It's not difficult.

Though it *felt* difficult.

'Look at this.' Sara stood beside a carved wooden rocking horse with a mane and tail made of real hair. 'I always wanted something like this when I was little.'

Of course Sara would know exactly what a little girl would like. She'd been one herself. But he checked anyway. 'Do you think Maisie would like it?'

Her eyes widened. 'Luke, this costs a small fortune!'

He shrugged. 'It's only money.'

She looked away. 'It's nice of you, but…'

He read the answer in her face. 'Not appropriate for a two-year-old? OK. I'm in your hands. You know what kind of things she'd like.' He just hoped that Sara wouldn't drag it out too long. This wasn't his idea of fun.

Eventually, they chose a bright pink easel, several non-spill pots of paint, chunky brushes that would be easy for small hands to hold and lots of paper.

'We're not taking this on the Tube,' he said as they left the shop. 'It's too bulky.' He hailed a taxi and gave the cab driver Justin's address.

'You're coming with me?' she asked, looking surprised, when he slid into the back beside her.

'I'm hardly going to make you carry that lot up the stairs on your own,' he said mildly. 'Give me some credit.'

'I didn't mean that.' She bit her lip and took his hand. 'Just that I've already taken up a chunk of your evening.'

And she felt guilty about it? Ah, hell. Time to make a concession. 'I wasn't doing anything special. And if Justin's home, maybe we can get a takeaway.'

Her smile was reward enough in itself. And sharing a curry and a beer with Sara, Justin and his new girlfriend, Zoe—a simple evening of good food, good music and a lot of affectionate teasing and laughter—Luke was shocked to find that he actually enjoyed it. Much, much more than he'd enjoyed the celebrity parties he used to attend.

Though his gut tightened on Sunday morning as they drew nearer to her family home. Nearer to being involved with a family again. Even though he was pretty sure that Sara's family was nothing like his own—he'd already met and liked Justin, and the rest of the Fleets were likely to be the same—the whole thing made him uneasy. It brought back memories he'd rather keep buried.

The driveway to the house was long and lined with trees. And the house at the end of it was stunning, a mix of honey- and rose-coloured bricks with well-proportioned sash windows. Two dormer windows nestled in the steeply pitched roof and there was a huge chimney at either end with a bowl-shaped top. No wonder Sara loved it here.

'How old is the house?' he asked.

'It's Queen Anne—so about three hundred years,' Sara said.

She directed him round the side of the house; there was a large gravelled area with several cars parked there, plus what looked like a stable block, an oast house and a huge barn. And, although the house hadn't looked that big from the front— three windows on the first floor and one either side of the front door—it went back a long way.

'Nobody ever uses the front door,' Sara said. 'Everyone always goes straight into the kitchen—it's the heart of the house.'

Remembering how much she enjoyed pottering around in his kitchen, he could well believe it. But, all the same, he was glad he was carrying the bulky presents for Maisie—presents that Sara had wrapped in sparkly paper and dressed up with a huge pink bow. Right at that moment, he felt that he could do with a little armour-plating.

Sara opened the door and four dogs—the ones in the pho- tographs in her flat—erupted. Two black Labradors, a Springer spaniel carrying a shoe and a Westie. Sara crouched down and they were all bouncing round her and licking her; she was laughing and not trying in the slightest to calm them down.

Then the spaniel spotted him and barked.

'Hey, it's OK. Luke's a friend,' she soothed.

Luke propped the presents against the wall, crouched down and put his hand out. The dog sniffed him and then licked his hand, before hunting round for the shoe he'd dropped earlier and dumping it at Luke's feet.

'Imelda, I presume?' he asked, laughing and retrieving the shoe before handing it to Sara.

'Yes. The Labradors are Russet and Pippin, and the Westie's Lamborne—Imelda was originally Bramley, until we discovered his shoe habit.'

'They're all named after varieties of apple?'

'What else would you expect, round here?' she teased back.

As she straightened up, an older woman joined them. Her resemblance to Sara was marked; seeing her was like seeing what Sara would be like in thirty years' time, Luke thought. Sara gave her mother a huge hug, then stepped back, grabbed Luke's hand and tugged him towards them. 'Luke, this is my mother, Nina Fleet—Mum, this is Luke Holloway.'

'Pleased to meet you, Luke,' Nina said politely.

'And you,' Luke said, holding out his hand.

To his shock, she didn't shake his hand; instead, she tutted, said, 'Oh, come here' and gave him a hug, too.

How many years had it been since he'd had a motherly hug? Something inside him felt as if it had just cracked.

Part of him wanted to run. But the more sensible part of him knew that if he backed away it would hurt Sara. Nina Fleet was obviously the warm earth-mother type who greeted everyone with a hug. She was warm and plump and smelled of baking.

And, despite his reservations, Luke found himself returning her hug.

'Come in and have some coffee. Lamborne, get *down*. Pippin and Russet, stop pushing—there isn't room enough for both of you to get through the door at the same time as everyone else. And, Imelda, don't you even *think* about it,' Nina warned. 'Sara did tell you about not leaving your shoes anywhere, Luke?'

'Because Imelda will steal one and add it to his pile. Yes.' He laughed, picked up the presents again and followed Nina and Sara into the kitchen.

It was a proper farmhouse kitchen, with handmade cupboards painted cream, a scrubbed pine table and dresser, equally scrubbed red tiles on the floor, two large wicker dog beds near the Aga and a large butler's sink by the window with a view of the orchard.

Luke fell in love with it instantly.

'There's a stack of presents in the living room—leave those there, if you like, then come back and have a seat,' Nina said, gesturing to the table. 'I'm afraid it's a scratch lunch—jacket potatoes and a casserole—because I've been baking all morning and there just wasn't time to sort out a proper Sunday roast. But welcome, anyway. Can I get you a mug of tea or would you prefer coffee?'

'Coffee would be lovely, thanks.'

Sara led him through to the living room—a large, airy room with a huge open fireplace, comfortable sofas that were clearly well used and just the right side of shabby and overfull bookcases. There was a piano in the corner—the piano Sara had learned to play as a child? he wondered—and there were framed photographs everywhere. Weddings, babies, graduations, family get-togethers: they were all celebrated here.

A world away from what he was used to.

But at least Sara didn't push him to talk. She merely helped him put the presents with the rest, then ushered him back to the kitchen.

He noticed how Sara and her mother worked automatically as a team; Sara fetched the cream-and-white-striped mugs and matching sugar bowl while Nina shook grounds into a cafétière. The next thing he knew, there was a steaming mug of coffee in front of him, along with a plate containing a thick slice of warm apple cake. 'Just to keep you going until lunch,' Nina added.

What a welcome. The Fleets were warm and trusting and accepting, right from the start; from what he remembered of his own childhood, everyone was suspect until proven and kept very firmly on the outside.

Probably one of the reasons why he was so suspicious of people in his personal life. It was inbred.

The dogs, who had been lying in their baskets, suddenly erupted again as a middle-aged man walked in, wearing faded jeans, muddy green wellington boots and a T-shirt with a faded slogan about apples.

This, Luke thought, must be Sara's father.

He removed the wellies and left them on the mat by the door. 'Imelda, leave,' he said firmly. The spaniel wagged his tail, as if to ask how anyone could possibly think he'd be naughty enough to run off with a single green wellie. Then the man enveloped his daughter in a huge hug, kissing her soundly. 'And how many pairs of shoes have you bought this week, darling?'

'None. I'm not *that* bad.'

'No?' he teased.

'No.' Sara laughed and hugged him back. 'Dad, this is Luke.'

He strode over to the table and held out his hand. 'Nice to meet you. I'm James.'

'Luke.'

The older man's handshake was firm and dry, and Luke's gut feeling told him that James Fleet was one of the good guys.

This was going to be all right.

The house filled up before lunch—which was a fabulous meal, and very far from being the 'scratch lunch' Nina had described it as—and then, just as Nina was shooing them from the kitchen, Louisa arrived with her husband, Bryan, and his parents.

'And here's the birthday girl,' Nina cooed.

The little girl toddled in and hugged everyone in turn; clearly she was as tactile as the rest of the Fleets, Luke thought.

But she stopped dead in front of Luke and looked up at him, eyes wide.

Of course. He was a stranger.

Dangerous.

Sara scooped the little girl up and lifted her so she was nearer Luke's height. 'Maisie, sweetheart, this is my friend Luke,' she said.

*Friend*, Luke thought. Well. *Lover* wasn't an appropriate word to use to a child. But *friend*... The idea warmed him and scared him in equal measure.

'Lulu,' Maisie pronounced, testing the word. Then she beamed, and a pair of chubby hands seized Luke's arm. 'Lulu.'

Help. He had no idea what to say. And he was well aware that everyone was watching him. Well, he'd pretend this was business. Be nice. Be charming. 'Hello, Maisie. Happy birthday.'

The little girl beamed again. ''Lo, Lulu.'

Sara chuckled. 'You're going to have a hard time living that name down. And what's it worth not to mention it to any of your business associates back in London?'

'How about not smuggling Imelda back to London in the back of my car, and letting him loose among your shoes?' Luke retorted.

Everyone laughed, and it felt as if he'd passed some kind of test. Yet he still found himself on edge. The bond between Sara and her family was close and deep—a world in which he didn't really belong. So much for thinking he could handle this. Even treating it like a business deal didn't make it feel any better.

Luke did his best to smile and be charming, joining in with the birthday tea and singing *Happy birthday to you* along with everyone else when Rupert sat down at the piano and Sara and Justin stood either side of him, adding in extra harmonies. But he was relieved when the presents were unwrapped and the birthday cake candles were blown out and Louisa and Bryan took their sleepy daughter home for bath and bedtime—especially when Sara suggested they needed to start heading back to London.

She'd clearly noticed that he'd gone quiet because, on the way back, she said, 'Luke? I didn't mean to offend you, you know. When Maisie called you Lulu—you know what kids are like.'

Actually, he didn't.

'Maisie has a brilliant vocabulary for her age, but your name was a new word to her. If it makes you feel any better, she calls Justin "Jussie".'

'It's fine,' Luke said.

'Then what's wrong?'

'Nothing,' he lied, not wanting to hurt her. He had to find the right words to tell her—if he really got involved with her, he'd have to open his life up to a family, do what he'd spent all his life avoiding. And he wasn't sure he could do it. 'I'm just a bit tired, that's all.'

Sara wasn't convinced. Clearly there was something in Luke's past that he wasn't telling her. He'd closed up again, and the only thing she could think of that had changed since the previous day was that he'd met her family.

So didn't he like them?

She couldn't imagine why anyone wouldn't like the Fleets. Even Hugh had liked them—before he'd betrayed them.

But why else would Luke be so quiet?

She hoped he wouldn't expect her to choose between them. It would be like being ripped apart; she phoned her mother and Louisa a couple of times a week, emailed Rupert, texted her Dad, had breakfast with Justin…not a day went past when she wasn't in contact with at least two members of her family. No way would she give them up.

On the other hand…she didn't want to give Luke up, either.

She just wanted him to love her family, the way she did. The way they'd love him, if he let them.

Finally, Luke pulled up outside the flat.

'Do you want to come in for a coffee?' she asked.

'Thanks, but I'll take a rain check. I'm a bit tired, and there are a couple of things I need to sort out before the morning.'

'OK. See you tomorrow.'

She kissed him on the cheek, and noted miserably that he didn't kiss her back.

Maybe he'd talk to her tomorrow. Maybe.

But she slept badly that night. And, when she walked into the office, Luke was talking on the phone, only having time to wave an acknowledgement to her. Fair enough—he was running a business—but when he replaced the receiver she noticed that he didn't kiss her hello.

He didn't kiss her goodbye when he left for a meeting, either. So what did this mean? They were back to being just business associates?

It looked as if she was going to have to play this by ear. Take it step by step. And hope that he'd let her get close enough to tell her what was going on in his head.

'Are you all right?' Luke asked when he came back into the office.

'Sure. Why?'

'You're a bit quiet.'

Sara shrugged. 'You haven't been here most of the day.'

'Because there's been a problem at one of the gyms. Suspected subsidence. I needed to talk to a surveyor, and discuss with the manager how we can minimise disruption to the clients.' He shrugged. 'Things happen.'

'Mmm.'

He felt his eyes narrow. 'Sara? I'm not a mind-reader. Spit it out.'

'What's wrong with my family?' she asked.

He blinked. Talk about out of left field. 'Nothing.'

'But you didn't like them, did you?'

'Of course I did. I get on all right with Justin, don't I?'

She folded her arms. 'So why did you go all distant on me yesterday?'

How on earth could he explain that? Not without dragging up a lot of stuff from his past that was best left where it belonged. In the past. 'You're overreacting, Sara.'

'Am I?'

He sighed. 'Look. I admit, I find families difficult.'

'If mine were all selfish monsters, like some of my friends' families are, I could understand it. Of course you'd want to avoid them. But my family are *nice*, Luke. They're decent, kind people who put themselves in other people's shoes.'

Decent and kind. 'Not everyone has a family like that.' His certainly wasn't.

She picked up on it immediately. 'So yours are monsters? That's rough, and you have my sympathy—and I do mean sympathy, Luke, not pity. But it still doesn't mean you have to cut yourself off from everyone else.'

'You're making me sound unreasonable.'

'Because you *are* being unreasonable, Luke.'

'I'm a bit wary, that's all.'

She scoffed. 'That's the understatement of the century.'

'I'm sorry. I'll try, OK? But…look, it's not easy for me. Don't expect too much.' He glanced at his watch. 'I have to be elsewhere, and I probably won't be back before you leave tonight. But we'll talk later, yes?'

'Yes.'

Except he didn't finish until it was way too late to call her. He sent her an apologetic text as a stopgap, and in the morning he called in to a florist's he knew opened early. She'd liked the last flowers he'd bought her, and in his experience this was the best way to defuse a fight.

And, although he was sitting at his desk when Sara walked in, pretending to be absorbed in a spreadsheet, inside he was as jumpy as hell.

She took one look at the hand-tied arrangement of pale pink roses, lilac alstroemeria and silvery-green eucalyptus foliage sitting on her desk and her eyes narrowed. 'What are these for?'

'To say sorry.'

Her mouth thinned. 'I don't need gestures, Luke. I just wanted you to talk to me, so I could understand what's going on in your head.'

'I told you, I have issues.'

She came to sit on the edge of his desk. 'Then tell me. Why do you have such a problem with families?'

'I don't want to talk about it.'

She folded her arms. 'So we're back to square one.'

She really wasn't going to let him off the hook, was she? 'Not everyone gets on with their family,' he said carefully.

'Agreed.'

'I haven't seen mine for a lot of years. We don't have anything in common.'

'No. I guess we're not all millionaires,' she said dryly.

That stung. He lifted his chin. 'It's got nothing to do with money. I didn't have a lot when I left. Just a suitcase of clothes and my share in the market stall.' He stared at her. 'I thought you knew me better than that. I don't judge people on how much they earn or how much they have in the bank.'

'So what do you judge them on?'

'I told you before. Who they are. How they treat other people. And my family…' He sucked in a breath. 'I really don't want to talk about this. Let's just leave it that they don't see things the way I do.'

She looked thoughtful. 'That happens in a lot of families, and it's sad, but sometimes it's the best thing for everyone concerned.'

Relief flooded through him. Thank God. She understood.

And then she looked straight at him. 'But you're using it as an excuse to cut yourself off from the human race, Luke, and that's not good at all.'

'I'm not cutting myself off from the human race.'

'But you don't get involved.'

'Correct.'

'Well, at least I know where I stand.' She slid off his desk and went back over to hers. And although she placed the flowers very carefully on top of the filing cabinets, where they couldn't accidentally be knocked over, he knew that he'd done the wrong thing. Instead of fixing it, he'd made things worse because he'd tried to fob her off with a gesture. One that would've worked on any of his previous girlfriends—but Sara wasn't like them. Money and possessions—except, possibly, shoes—weren't important to her.

She was quiet for the rest of the day, and Luke felt more and more of a heel—and more and more at a loss how to fix this.

At precisely five o'clock she switched off her computer.

'Sara. Have dinner with me tonight?'

'Thanks for the offer, but I'm a bit tired.'

'Look, I can skip my squash. We could eat earlier. Whatever time you like.' He was offering her time, for pity's sake. Wasn't that what she wanted from him?

'Thanks, but I really need an early night.'

In other words, she was still angry with him and wanted some space.

On Tuesday, Luke was out of the office for most of the day and Sara had left before he returned. There was a note on his desk saying that she'd worked through lunch and left three-quarters of an hour early and she hoped he didn't mind.

He did mind.

A lot.

They couldn't carry on like this. Apart from anything else, he missed her.

She was probably on the Tube now, he thought, so there was no point in calling. He left enough time to allow her to get to Camden tube station, then called her mobile.

For a nasty moment, he thought she was going to let it go through to voice mail. Then she answered. 'Hello?'

'Hi. It's Luke.' Stupid—she would already know that from the caller display. 'Um…are you busy this evening?' And then he remembered. Of course she was. Tuesday night was her regular night out with the girls.

Her next words confirmed it. 'I'm going to the cinema with Liz and Sophie. And then we're going to an ice cream parlour.'

'Uh-huh.' He chose his words carefully. 'Maybe afterwards you could come here. I could make you a hot chocolate or something.'

'A hot chocolate.'

'The offer's there. I'll leave it up to you. Enjoy your film.'

'Thanks.'

She didn't make any promises to call in later, and Luke couldn't settle to anything for the rest of the evening. Just when he thought that she'd decided to go back to her own flat, his entryphone buzzed.

'This hot chocolate had better be good,' a voice informed him.

'It will be.' He buzzed her in.

She looked slightly wary when she walked in the door. He said nothing, just walked over to meet her, wrapped his arms round her and buried his face in her shoulder.

Just breathing in her scent calmed him; finally, he lifted his head. 'I'm sorry. I'll try harder. I did like your family.'

'You just have…issues.'

'Yeah. Like you said, there are people, and there are not-so-nice people. People I don't want to be part of. It's in the past now. And that's where I want it to stay—where I need it to stay.'

In answer, she stroked his face. Brushed her mouth against his. 'Just don't shut me out again, Luke.'

'I'll try. Believe me, I'll try,' he promised. And he meant it.

# CHAPTER FOURTEEN

FOR the next couple of weeks, all was fine in Sara's world. More nights than not, she stayed overnight at Luke's flat, and he didn't seem to mind when she filled his fridge and pottered around in his kitchen. He even made the effort to go with her to see her family again.

Although neither of them said anything, she knew how she felt about him.

And she thought she knew how he felt about her.

It was more than just sex. Much more.

But then she had a phone call that worried her sick. To the point where she was so quiet at work that at half past nine on the Friday morning Luke turned off her computer screen and sat on the edge of her desk.

'Hey! I was in the middle of a report,' she protested.

'I don't care. Talk to me,' he said.

'What about?'

'Whatever's bothering you. And don't say it's nothing. You haven't been yourself all week.'

She shook her head. 'It's family stuff.'

'You've fallen out with them?'

'No, of course not.'

'Then what?' He reached over to take her hand and squeezed it briefly. 'Sara, things can't be that bad.'

'They are.' She sighed. 'When things go wrong with old houses it takes loads of time and tons of cash.'

'And there's something wrong with your parents' house?' he guessed.

'The roof. That summer storm the other week blew a few tiles off.' She bit her lip. 'Dad thought it was fixable, but when the builder came round to look at it, he found they've got dry rot in the timbers. It's not covered by the insurance and it's going to cost a fortune to fix.'

'Ah.'

'The problem is, all Mum and Dad's money is tied up in the business and, with the cost of everything going up, there just isn't the cashflow to deal with it. Not with something this big.' She bit her lip. 'I've got some savings, but Rupert's halfway through buying a house himself and Lou's expecting again so she and Bryan are too stretched to help. Justin tried to remortgage his flat to release some equity, but all the lenders wanted to know why he wants the extra money. And when they found out, all of them said no.' She dragged in a breath. 'Which means Mum and Dad will have to sell the business—because no way is anyone going to give them a decent price for a house with dry rot. And the orchard's been in our family for years and years. Since my great-great-grandfather's day. It'll kill Dad to lose it. Especially after—' She stopped abruptly. Luke didn't need to know about the business with Hugh.

'After what?'

'Doesn't matter.'

'Hey. You told me not to shut you out. It goes both ways.'

She was silent for a long, long time. Luke sighed, scooped her out of her chair, sat down in her place and settled her on his lap. 'Right. Talk.'

'Hugh,' she said finally.

'The workaholic?'

She nodded. 'I thought he loved me. Thought he liked my

family. And Mum and Dad were going to expand, float the business on the stock market.'

He stroked her hair. 'What happened?'

'It turned out that Hugh had been advising a consortium—people who cared about profit, not about what my parents were trying to do. They made a hostile takeover bid. Dad just about managed to stave it off, but he and Mum lost a lot of money through it. So it's my fault they don't have the funds to cover the roof repairs.'

'No, it's not.'

'If it wasn't for me introducing him to them, Hugh wouldn't have known.'

'Actually, if he was in the speculative money markets, it would've been his job to know who was floating. The fact he knew you is completely irrelevant. So it *wasn't* your fault.' He gritted his teeth. 'Only a first-class bastard would use you like that—and then make you take the blame.' Luke's fists tightened; he had to make a real effort to relax them. 'Violence doesn't solve anything, but right now I'd like to wipe the floor with him.'

'He isn't worth it.'

'No, but you are.' He leaned forward to brush his mouth against hers. 'Right. There's no point sitting here worrying. I need the facts.'

'What do you mean?'

'It's what I do. Turn businesses round. If your parents will trust me to look at their books and talk me through what they do and how, I might be able to come up with a solution.'

'You'd help them? For me?'

'It's business. What I do,' he said coolly.

She damped down the flare of hurt.

'And I'm not Hugh, if that's what you're worrying about.'

'I know you're not.'

'Good. So I suggest you ring your parents and see if we can go down now.'

'Now?' She stared at him in surprise. 'But you've got meetings.'

'Nothing in my diary is set in stone. You can rearrange my schedules while I'm driving. Say something important's cropped up.'

'You'd really do that?' For her? And he'd been the one to make the suggestion, not her. A warm glow of hope filled her.

'I owe you,' he said. 'You've made me reassess my priorities and learn to fill the well.'

She frowned. 'You don't owe me anything.' Relationships didn't work that way.

'OK. You've also helped me out of a hole and you've let me dragoon you into staying on as my PA.'

'Until you find a temp. And the fact you haven't done so yet, I might add, means you're either too fussy or you're slacking.'

He smiled. 'When you're sassy with me, I know all's right with the world. Ring your parents.'

So now he knew exactly what had happened to make Sara wary of relationships, Luke thought grimly as he drove down the motorway. Someone who'd taken advantage of her good nature, through her most vulnerable spot: her family.

Though wasn't he just as bad as Hugh, in his own way? He was taking advantage of her, too. True, he was planning to help her family out of a hole rather than put them in one—it was the best way he knew to pay Sara back for what she'd given him. But he also knew what she wanted in life. Someone who'd love her. Who'd love her family. Without reserve.

Could he do that?

He wasn't sure.

So it was unfair to keep her hanging on. He really ought to do the right thing: say goodbye, give her the chance of finding someone who deserved her. Someone who'd be able to give her what she needed. Someone…who wasn't him.

And that was the problem.

He didn't want it to be someone else.

But, at the same time, he couldn't get past his wariness of family. Sara wanted children—she'd told him that. The idea of being a father scared the hell out of him. She'd grown up in such different circumstances from his. How would he ever be able to give her the things she needed, the things she was used to? Things that couldn't be fixed by a business deal?

'So how much has Sara filled you in on the situation?' James asked when Luke was sitting at the kitchen table, nursing a mug of Nina's excellent coffee and with Imelda lying on his feet.

'Expensive roof repairs plus the credit crunch,' Luke said, 'and you don't want to sell the business to people who don't have the same ethics that you do and are in it because they're jumping on a bandwagon, not because they care.'

'Got it in one.' James looked grim. 'My family's had this orchard for four generations—five, if you count Rupert coming in on sales and Lou doing the office. And I don't want to lose it.'

And it wasn't just financial, Luke knew. The business was something he cared about. Was part of the family history. Held their roots.

He'd walked away from his family's business. He wasn't going to walk away from Sara's. 'Take me through the business and show me what you do, then we'll look at figures.'

James nodded. 'Look, it's not especially boggy in the orchard, but the grass is long enough and wet enough to mess up your shoes. I don't suppose you brought wellies with you?'

'I didn't even think about it,' Luke admitted.

'Not a problem. We have spares for visitors to use. Come with me and we'll sort you out. Do you mind some of the dogs coming with us?'

'No, it's fine.' Luke couldn't ever remember having a pet, not even a goldfish. And noisy, muddy dogs who insisted on sitting as close to you as they could, or trotting along beside you and nudging your knees every so often, were way out of his ken. But, to his surprise, he rather liked it.

James pulled on his boots again. 'Then let's be going. See you lot later.' He kissed his wife and ruffled both daughters' hair. When they'd left the kitchen, he said softly to Luke, 'I hope you can do something because it'll break Nina's heart if we have to give this up. I would consider selling the house, but in this economic climate it'd be hard to get a buyer, and selling wouldn't change the fact that the roof has dry rot and it's going to cost a small fortune to sort it.'

'I've worked with businesses on the edge of bankruptcy,' Luke said, 'and we've managed to turn it around.'

'By getting rid of half the staff and making the others take up the slack?'

'No. I admit I've had to trim hours back in some places, but if your team's all on the same side and they know you're going to be honest with them, people will be flexible. And once you're out of the rough patch, you make sure everyone shares in the smooth again.'

James gave him a considering look. 'So you're suggesting maybe employee shares?'

'I'll need to look at figures before I say anything. But talk me through the orchard and the factory, and we'll take it from there,' Luke said.

Apart from a brief lunch of home-made soup, home-made bread rolls, tangy Cheddar and apple chutney, eaten round the table with Sara, Louisa and Nina, Luke spent most of the day with James, looking at figures. And, at the end of the day, Nina insisted that they stay for dinner.

'If I'd known we were staying, I would've brought some wine and chocolates as my contribution,' Luke said.

'Don't be silly.' Nina shook her head. 'You've already done enough—you've given up today to work with us. Now, go and sit in the dining room, you lot.'

The house had filled up since lunchtime, Luke thought.

Rupert, the baby of the family, was there with his fiancée, Emmy. Louisa's husband, Bryan, had joined them, along with little Maisie, who insisted on sitting on his lap and kept patting his arm and saying, 'Lulu.'

A big, noisy family who talked a lot and laughed even more. A family who did things *together*. A family who listened to what he had to say about the business and then leapt straight into a full-blown discussion, with ideas bounced off each other and suggestions and offers of help.

The one thing that came out loud and clear was how much they loved each other. Sara offered to take a sabbatical from her business to help her family set up an online shop and to put her savings into converting some of the disused barns into holiday cottages, Rupert offered to put his house-buying on hold and put his deposit into kitting out the holiday cottages, and Louisa knew several other local businesses that would give them reciprocal links to an online shop, through her contacts at Maisie's nursery. Justin intended to call in favours to get all the legal work done for nothing.

And that was when it really hit Luke.

This was a family who really supported each other. And he was absolutely certain that Sara's parents had shown that same support to their children when it had been needed; neither Sara nor Justin worked in the family business, but he'd guess they'd never been pressured to change their career choices to fit in.

This was something, he was beginning to realise, that was worth more than any of the huge business deals he'd done in the past. A family that cared.

He was very quiet for the rest of the evening, letting them do the talking.

'It's getting late,' Nina said. 'Stay the night. It won't take me a second to make up the guest room.'

'That's really kind of you, Nina, but I'm sorry, I can't. I have some early meetings tomorrow.'

'If you're sure? You're not putting us out.'

'I'm sure. But thank you. The offer's appreciated.'

Sara saw him outside.

'Are you staying?' he asked. 'Because if you want to stay that's fine.'

She looked torn. 'I want to be with you,' she said, 'but right now I think my family needs me most. We have a lot to discuss.'

'Sure, I understand.' And he wasn't going to make her choose between them. But the drive back to London that evening was lonely and the car felt empty, even though he filled it with loud music. When he walked into his flat, its clean uncluttered spaciousness somehow felt sterile.

And Luke dearly wished he'd accepted the invitation to stay and be part of them, even if it was only for a little while.

# CHAPTER FIFTEEN

OVER the next three weeks, with Luke's full agreement, Sara cut down her hours working with him and spent half her time in Kent and half her time in London.

At the end of the first week, he gave her a key to his flat. 'This isn't a statement of intent,' he warned, 'and we're not living together exactly, but I was thinking… If you stay here while you're in London, then at least we'll get to see something of each other.'

Sara thought it was as near as a man like Luke was ever going to get to a declaration of intent, and she was happy with that. Even better, Luke unbent enough to spend Sundays with her family, and he really did muck in with everyone else, insisting on doing the washing up and carrying things through to the dining table. He always brought her mother flowers, spent time talking business with her father—and then walked hand in hand with her in the orchard after lunch, kissing her next to every tree.

'You really need to be here at apple blossom time,' Sara said. 'It's lovely; you lie looking up at the trees, and the blossom floats down like—' She stopped the word in time, but she knew he'd guessed what she'd almost said.

Confetti.

He let it pass, but she was aware he'd quietly put a barrier up. On the Wednesday night of the third week, she got up at stupid o'clock, feeling queasy. It must, she thought, have been something she'd eaten. She sipped a glass of cold water, very slowly, and told herself she'd be fine in the morning.

Except she wasn't. The queasiness didn't pass during the day. And, worse still, it suddenly hit her that her period was late.

It couldn't be.

She was always regular, always twenty-eight days on the dot. A swift calculation told her she was three days late. And she hadn't noticed because she'd been rushing around between Kent and London.

She and Luke hadn't taken any risks—they'd always been scrupulous about using condoms—so she was pretty sure it was caused by stress, worrying about her parents and the orchard. But all the same she decided to take a pregnancy test. It was bound to be negative, but she knew that actually seeing a negative result would help to settle her fears.

Luckily Luke was in a meeting so she had time to buy it without him knowing. She didn't want to tell him because she knew how he felt about having children; although he seemed to have softened a bit since meeting her family, she knew that most of his barriers were still there and she wasn't going to take anything for granted.

She bought a digital test, read the instructions and headed for the bathroom. Once she'd done the test, she sat watching the window on the test stick. The window was flashing, showing that the test was working. Any minute now, the confirmation would come up: *Not Pregnant.* Any minute now.

And then the screen changed.

It really couldn't be any clearer.

*Pregnant.*

Sara stared at it, horrified. Pregnant? How on earth was she going to tell Luke? He had issues about families as it was; he still hadn't told her the whole story, but she guessed his problems lay with his experiences as a child.

And if she told him she was expecting their baby—that he

was going to be part of a family again, whether he liked it or not—how was he going to react? Would he be pleased? Would he be horrified? Would he retreat even further behind his barriers?

She had no idea.

She knew without having to ask that her family would be supportive. But the important one here was Luke. Would this be the one thing that pushed him away from her completely?

She couldn't think straight; her head felt fuzzy. And maybe it was the power of suggestion, but she was promptly sick.

'You look a bit pale,' Luke said when he returned to the office.

'I'm fine,' Sara said, giving him a smile that he thought was a little too bright.

He wasn't so sure. She'd been under a lot of strain lately, worrying about her parents and the orchard. 'Look, if you've got a headache, don't just sit there and struggle on. Take the afternoon off. Go upstairs and have a nap or something. There's some paracetamol in the medicine kit in the kitchen—it's the green box under the sink.'

'I'm fine. I don't need a nap.'

But, a few moments later, she bolted from the room, her hand over her mouth.

An autumn virus, maybe?

But Luke had a bad feeling about this. It was too reminiscent of the way Di had behaved in the early stages of her pregnancy: looking tired and pale, and then rushing from the room to be sick.

Could Sara be pregnant?

They'd always been careful. Always used a condom.

But supposing one had split and he hadn't noticed?

Then again, some couples spent months trying to make a baby. For Sara to be pregnant after just one accident, well, it was pretty unlikely.

Unlikely…but not impossible.

Was Sara expecting his baby?

His head spun. It was the worst possible thing that could happen.

He didn't want children. Never had, never would.

How could he possibly be a good father? His own had let him down. And, no matter how hard Luke tried to avoid it, he knew he'd end up following the pattern. It was inbuilt. He'd let his child down. Let Sara down.

And another deeper fear crept in. Would Sara let him down? If he took the risk and let her through his last barrier, let himself believe in families again…what if it went wrong?

He didn't think he could walk away intact this time.

Hell, hell, hell.

This was a nightmare.

But it was one he was going to have to face head-on.

Sara walked back into the office, and her face was even paler. He fetched her a glass of water.

'Thank you.' This time, her smile was slightly wobbly.

He stayed where he was, in front of her desk. 'I think we need to talk.' He folded his arms. 'Is there anything you want to tell me?'

'Such as?'

Might as well ask her straight. 'Were you throwing up just now?'

She closed her eyes. 'It's probably a virus.'

'Sara. Look at me.'

She did so, and sighed. 'All right. Yes. I'm pregnant. I don't know how pregnant—I only did the test today.'

The world spun and he felt sick. 'And you never even thought to tell me you suspected it?'

'I didn't. Not until today. When I started feeling sick and realised my period's a few days late. I thought it was stress, but I wanted to be sure.' She dragged in a breath. 'That test was meant to reassure me that I'm *not* pregnant.'

He knew he ought to be kind. That he ought to hold her and tell her he'd support her. But fear pushed him into snapping at her. 'How?'

'How do you think babies are made, Luke?' she sniped back.

'I know that. I meant how, when we were always careful to use a condom?'

'I don't know.' She looked wearily at him. 'I suppose I should be grateful that you're not questioning whether it's yours.' Her eyes narrowed. 'At least, I *hope* you're not.'

'Of course I'm not,' he snapped. It hadn't even occurred to him.

All he could focus on was the fact that he was going to be a father.

That he didn't know *how* to be a father.

That this was a monumental mess.

'I'll do the right thing by you,' he said, looking away.

'What?'

'Marry you.'

And then the phone rang. He stomped over to his desk, grateful for the diversion, and picked it up. 'Luke Holloway.'

Just what he needed. A problem with a contract that his solicitor needed to discuss with him. The timing couldn't have been better. 'OK. I'll be there. Twenty minutes.' He replaced the receiver. 'I have to go. Legal stuff. I'll be back later—we'll talk then. Leave a message on my mobile's voice mail if anything crops up.'

And then he walked out of the office. Into the fresh air. Where, just for a few seconds, he could breathe again.

Luke could see that Sara was spoiling for a fight the minute he walked back into the office. Her face was tight with tension, and she was slamming her fingers onto the keyboard instead of using her usual light touch.

'Hi,' he said.

She lifted her chin. 'Where the hell have you been?'

'Sorting out legal stuff. As you know.'

'And it didn't occur to you to call me or text me, let me know you were on your way back?'

It had. He'd decided against it; the kind of conversation he'd known he'd face was the sort that was much better conducted face to face. 'What's the problem?'

'What's the *problem*?' She shook her head in apparent disbelief. 'I tell you I'm pregnant, and you tell me you'll do the right thing by me.'

He spread his hands. 'What did you want me to do? Tell you that you were on your own?'

'It's the way you did it, Luke. You didn't even *look* at me when you talked about marriage. And you couldn't wait to get away. If I were the paranoid type, I'd say that you rigged that call from your solicitor. It couldn't have come at a more perfect time for you.'

'Apart from the fact I had no idea what you were going to tell me,' he reminded her, 'you're perfectly at liberty to call my solicitor and check where I've been. I don't have any reason to lie to you, Sara.' He tossed his mobile phone over to her. 'Here. Check the call list.'

'I don't need to check the call list!' She threw it back at him. Hard.

'Don't you think you're being a bit—' He stopped abruptly, seeing real anger in her face.

'Don't you *dare* accuse me of being hormonal, Luke Holloway. It's got nothing to do with that. It's the fact that you're so bloody compartmentalised. You're emotionally lacking.'

There wasn't anything he could say to that. Because he knew it was true.

'Luke, I'm pregnant. With our child. Doesn't that mean anything to you?'

'Of course it does. I told you I'd marry you. I'll put your name on the deeds of the flat along with mine. It's up to you whether you want to carry on working after the baby's born; if you don't want to, then that's fine—I'll add your name to my bank account and I'll make sure you're not short of money.' It was the perfect deal.

'It's got nothing to do with money! What about your time, Luke?'

'Time?'

'Time. Are you going to cut down your working hours to spend time with me and our baby?'

'I…' He faltered.

'I thought not. You can't run my life, or our child's, like the way you run a business. Life doesn't *work* like that. And if you can't see that…' She gave him a look of utter disgust, picked up her handbag and slammed the office door behind her. Hard.

Luke dropped into his chair. He'd give her a couple of days to calm down and see sense and then he'd go and fetch her. Talk it over rationally. Get her to see that he'd given her the perfect offer.

But in the meantime he needed a temp to keep things ticking over. Sighing, he picked up the phone and dialled the agency's number. Arranged for someone to come in, first thing in the morning.

Although he worked until his eyes ached, he couldn't settle that evening and he slept badly that night. It didn't feel right, not having Sara next to him. He missed the warmth of her body against his.

The kitchen didn't feel right, either.

Or the living room.

Everything felt very slightly out of shape. As if it didn't fit him any more.

Which was ridiculous.

He lasted three days before he called her again. Her mobile phone was switched off, the phone in Justin's flat seemed to be permanently on answering machine and she didn't return a single one of his texts. By the time Luke was meant to meet Karim on the Monday evening, he was in a seriously foul temper.

And then Karim said something that took the wind out of his sails completely.

'Guess what we did today?'

'Aired your flat after a month away in Harrat Salma?' Luke guessed.

'Nope.' Karim fished his wallet out of his pocket and drew something out of it. 'Look.'

It was a photograph. Most of it was black, but there was a triangular-shaped swathe showing the outline of a baby's head and curled-up body.

'It's the twenty-week scan of your honorary nephew-to-be,' Karim announced, beaming.

Luke couldn't help himself.

He flinched.

His best friend noticed immediately. 'Right. We're not playing squash. And I don't care if the court's booked or not. I think you need to talk.'

'I…' His protest died. 'Not here.' Not here, where they might be overheard.

Karim's eyes narrowed. 'When did you last eat?'

'Breakfast. I think.' Luke couldn't recall. And he didn't really care.

'Right.' Karim shepherded him out of the health club and into the small pizzeria round the corner. Being a Monday night, it was quiet and they managed to find a table right out of the way. Karim ordered for them both and kept the conversation light until they'd finished the pizza and were both drinking coffee. 'Now, talk,' he said.

'Can I ask you a weird question?'

Karim frowned but nodded. 'Sure.'

'When Lily told you she was pregnant…how did you feel?' Luke asked.

Karim's eyes widened. 'Are you saying…?'

'Don't answer a question with a question. I really need to know.' To know he wasn't the only one who felt that way, to know he wasn't going crazy. 'What was your first reaction—your very first reaction?'

'Shock, I suppose. Because we hadn't really been trying—and, to be honest, I'd wanted a bit more time with her just as a couple. But then it sank in.' Karim smiled. 'There's going to be someone else in this world like Lily—someone else I know I'm going to love from his very first second in this world.'

'So you were pleased?'

'And proud. And, I suppose, a bit scared. I haven't exactly spent a lot of time around babies. How will I know if I'm a good enough father?'

His best friend had the same doubts? But that was crazy. Karim would make a fabulous father. 'You'll be great. You've got the example of your own father,' Luke reminded him.

Karim looked thoughtful. 'So is Sara pregnant?'

Luke sighed heavily. 'Yes. And I reacted badly when she told me.'

'Ouch.'

Luke stared bleakly at his best friend. 'The way you said you felt—that's how I felt, too. Shocked. And scared.'

'And pleased?'

Luke shook his head. 'Right now, I still can't get past the fear.'

Karim paused. 'You've never told me the whole story, and I'm not going to pry. But the fact you were strong enough to walk away from your family…that tells me you're going to be strong enough to be a good father. That you'll be the father to your child that you never had yourself.'

'That very much depends,' Luke said dryly, 'on whether I get the chance to do that.'

'Sara's not speaking to you?'

'No. Her mobile's permanently switched off and she won't answer my calls. And, for the first time in my life, I honestly don't know how to fix this.'

Karim patted his shoulder. 'The only thing you can do is be yourself. Tell her how you really feel. Open up to her.'

Luke shook his head. 'I don't do open.'

'Neither did I—until Lily,' Karim replied. 'If Sara's the one, you'll know. Because it'll be much harder being without her than with her.'

'Without her, it feels as if the world's turned grey,' Luke admitted. 'Nothing fits any more.'

'Then she's the one,' Karim said. 'Talk to her. What's the worst that can happen?'

'She turns me down.' Luke gave a mirthless laugh. 'Well, she's already done that. I told her I'd do the right thing and marry her.'

'Because of the baby?'

'Yes.'

Karim sucked in a breath. 'Ouch. If I'd done that to Lily, she would've walked out on me. Sara needs to know that you want her—'

'—for herself,' Luke finished. 'Yeah. I just worked that out. I have a lot of humble pie to eat.' He drained his coffee. 'Thanks for the advice.'

'Let me know how it goes.'

'Yeah.' Luke wasn't even sure that Sara was going to talk to him. But he was prepared to do whatever it took to turn things around and make a real future with Sara and their baby.

But first he had to talk to her.

And he had to convince her that he was telling the truth.

Luke knew that if he turned up with a ring or a huge bouquet, Sara would reject them—and him. He needed to make her see that he meant it, that he really did want to be a family with her. Which meant giving her something that money couldn't buy.

On his way back to his flat, he walked past a mother-and-baby shop. In the middle of the window display was a baby book, its pages open; he glanced at it and realised it was meant to act as a book of memories.

That was when the idea hit him.

He'd give Sara proof that he loved her. Straight from the

heart. And not with artificial headings created by someone else. It would be all in his own words.

The shop was closed, but he knew a place that stayed open late. A place where, with any luck, he'd find what he wanted.

To his relief, he found the perfect notebook. One with handmade pages, marbled edges and a teal suede cover. And, back in his flat, he sat at the table overlooking the Thames and began to write.

# CHAPTER SIXTEEN

THE next morning at the crack of dawn, he walked up the stairs to Sara's flat. Rang the buzzer.

The intercom crackled. 'Yes?'

He recognised the voice instantly. 'Justin, it's Luke. I need to see Sara.'

'She doesn't need to see you.'

'Yes, she does.'

'If you hurt my sister you have me to deal with,' Justin warned.

Luke sighed. 'I'm not going to hurt Sara. I know I've screwed up—I'm here to fix it and make things right.' He took a gamble. 'I assume you know about the baby?'

'Yes.'

'And you know I asked her to marry me.'

'That's not quite how she sees it.'

'I screwed that up, too,' Luke admitted. 'There are a lot of things I need to say to her. A lot of things she needs to hear.'

'Only,' Justin said, 'if she wants to see you.'

'I'm not leaving until she sees me. If I have to, I'll camp on your doorstep,' Luke said.

'Ever heard of injunctions to stop stalkers?' Justin retorted.

'I'm not a stalker. I'm just an ordinary man who's made a mess of the most important thing that's ever happened to him. And I need a chance to put it right.'

'All right. Come up. But if she says no, you leave immediately,' Justin warned.

'Agreed. Thanks, Justin.'

Sara's brother didn't reply, but buzzed him up and met him outside the door. 'She's agreed to see you. So I'm giving you both space—but Sara has my number on speed dial.'

'She won't need it,' Luke promised.

'You look like hell,' Justin said, surprising him.

'I feel it,' Luke admitted. 'But it's no more than I deserve.'

He waited until Justin had left, then knocked on the door.

Sara opened it. She looked as bad as he felt; there were dark shadows under her eyes, her skin was pale and she looked as if she hadn't slept properly.

That made two of them. Except he'd been spared the morning sickness.

'Hi,' he said softly. 'Can I come in?'

She nodded and stepped aside.

'Thank you.' He dragged in a breath. 'I'm here to apologise—to tell you things I know I should've told you ages ago but…' He closed his eyes briefly. 'I don't find it easy to open up. But I know that's what it'll take to even start fixing things between us. And I'm prepared to do whatever it takes to make everything right again.'

'You'd better come through,' she said. 'Do you want something to drink?'

'No, thanks. Just to talk to you.' He followed her through to the living room; he wasn't surprised when she picked the chair, leaving him the sofa. He smiled wryly as he sat down. He had a long way to go. The only thing he could do was tell her the truth. Be honest. 'Nothing's seemed right since you left. Everything feels slightly out of shape, as if it doesn't fit. And it's made me realise that…' He dragged in a breath. 'I really hate having to admit this, but I need you.'

She said nothing, but he saw her eyes fill with tears.

'And I need to tell you something. About me. You once

asked me if I was part of a family business. Well, my family has a business. In the East End.'

She frowned. 'There's nothing wrong with the East End.'

'Most of it, I agree.' How could he explain? 'My family—they're what's known as…well, criminals.' Might as well tell her all of it. 'My dad's a thief, my grandad's a fraudster, my uncle's a fence. There's getaway drivers and muscle in the family, too. The kind of genes I didn't want to pass on.'

She went very still. 'So you're saying you want me to have a termination?'

'No. I said "didn't", not "don't". I'm trying to explain to you why I didn't want children. Remember I told you that my maths teacher spotted that I'd be good at economics?'

'Ye-es.'

'He told me at the police station—after I'd been arrested for shoplifting. He gave the police an assurance about me, and then started talking to me. He said I had a brain and, right then, I was wasting it. That if I carried on the way I was going, I'd end up so deep I'd never get out. That I could have a better life if I stayed on the right side of the law and used my natural talents.'

'So you took his advice?'

'I thought about it. Long and hard. And, yeah, I knew what he said made sense. It didn't go down well with the family, and it left me in a really awkward place. If I knew they were planning something and didn't try to stop them, that made me as bad as they were. An accomplice. But if I grassed them up to the police…'

'You were going against your own?' she guessed.

'Betraying my family.' He nodded. 'And that felt bad, too. For a while, I took the coward's way out and told them I'd keep quiet as long as I didn't know what they were doing.'

'The coward's way?'

'Because I should've shopped them.'

She frowned. 'Luke, how old were you when this happened?'

'Twelve.'

Her eyes widened. 'Luke, for pity's sake, you were still a child! There's nothing cowardly about what you did.'

'Hmm.' He wasn't so sure. 'Anyway. That teacher was the one who got me the market stall job and helped me keep straight. A few years later, I asked him why…and he said it was because he was like me once. Someone had helped him out, and he believed in…well, karma, I suppose. What goes around, comes around.'

'It does,' she said softly. 'So your family accepted it?'

He shook his head. 'It came to a head when I was fifteen. They wanted me to launder some money on the stall. I said no. It got messy. And in the end I gave them an ultimatum—accept that I wanted no part of what they did, or let me go.'

She bit her lip. 'And they let you go?'

'Even my mum turned her back on me.' It hurt to admit it.

'Your mum was a criminal, too?'

'No. She was…' He tried to think how best to explain. 'Fragile, I suppose. She found it easier to go with the flow. When Dad was inside, one of the family would come round and change fuses and fix leaks for her, that sort of thing. And they always made sure she was all right for money. I suppose they had a kind of honour—this thing about looking after your own.' He shrugged. 'The antidepressants took care of the rest of it. Dad would tell her what to say when the police came round, and she did it. So. That's why I don't—*didn't*—' he corrected himself swiftly '—do families.'

'I see.'

'And please don't get any rose-coloured-glasses ideas of getting me to make things up with them. I don't belong with them, and they don't belong with me. I don't want their kind of life—not for me, not for you and most definitely not for our baby.' He swallowed hard. 'But since I met you…I've learned something. I've realised that it doesn't matter where I came from. What matters is now. And I can make the family I want to be part of.' He looked at her. 'I want you, Sara. Being without you…it's like being back in those dark days, where I didn't believe in anything or anyone. When I kept everyone at a distance so they didn't have the chance to let me down.'

'I let you down, too,' she said. 'I walked out on you.'

'I pushed you into it. All I can say is that when you told me about the baby I panicked. And I swear I never meant to hurt you.'

'I saw all the walls go straight back up. And I didn't want to stay, drag you down until you resented me and the baby.'

'I'd never do that.'

'Wouldn't you?'

'No. Because I've learned the difference between what I thought I wanted, and what I really do want. I want a family, Sara. With you.'

'You offered me a business deal. A perfect contract,' she said. 'Not a family package.'

'And I was wrong. It isn't what I want, either.' There was nothing else for it. He was going to have to tell her. 'I won't blame you if you don't believe me, but I love you. And I can honestly say it's not just words for me. I've never said it to anyone else.'

And that was it. He'd given her all he had. Well, almost. He realised he was still clutching the paper carrier bag. He stood up and placed it in her lap. 'This isn't actually for you—it's for our baby, in years to come. But I'd like you to read it first.' He lifted a shoulder in a half-shrug. 'I'll see myself out. Call me if and when you want to talk.'

Sara didn't open the bag until after she'd heard the front door close behind him. She knew it had taken a lot for Luke to tell her the truth about his past. For a man who believed in straightforwardness and honour to admit that he'd grown up without either.

And the fact he'd said he loved her…

She believed that he hadn't said that to anyone else. That it had cost him a great deal to tell her. But could she let herself trust him? Could she believe that, if she went back to him, his barriers would stay down this time?

She opened the bag and took out the journal. Frowning, she opened the pages. It was hand-written, so he'd clearly taken the time to do this himself; he hadn't just dictated it for someone else to type up. So this was clearly important to him. Personal.

And he'd said it was for their baby.

She read on and realised he'd poured his heart out onto the pages. Telling their baby about her—what he loved about her, when he'd first realised that he loved her, how he felt when she was around. Admitting that part of him was scared to death that he wouldn't be a good enough father, but he was going to try because Sara had shown him what a family could be. How many things he was looking forward to—seeing their baby at the first scan, feeling the baby's first kicks, having that very first cuddle with a newborn. How he planned to spend time building sandcastles and paddling in the sea with their baby. Flying kites—the one good memory from his own childhood, one that he wanted to relive and share with their child—and having picnics at Greenwich. Being there to read a bedtime story; being there with a cuddle when their child woke in the night from a bad dream. And, most of all, being a family.

By the time she finished reading, Sara was bawling her eyes out. She rang Luke's mobile, but when he answered she was completely incoherent.

What seemed like seconds later, he was ringing the doorbell. She opened the door and just fell into his arms.

'I drove here as fast as I could. Are you all right? Is it the baby? Everything's going to be fine, honey. I'll call the ambulance. And I'm not going to leave you. Not now, not ever.'

He was halfway through punching in the emergency number when she stopped him. 'I don't need an ambulance,' she said shakily. 'The baby's fine.'

'Then why…?' He wiped her tears away gently with the pad of his thumb.

'I'm crying for you. For how much you missed out on as a child. But it's not going to be like that for our baby. We'll

be a family—a real family. Because I love you, Luke. I really
do love you.'

'Good. Because I love you all the way back. And it hurts
like hell.'

'It doesn't have to any more.'

And then she was in his arms. Held so tightly that she could
barely breathe—but she was holding Luke just as tightly. His
mouth over hers, his kiss hot and demanding.

She'd untucked his shirt when he released her and took a step
back.

'Luke?'

'I want you, Sara.' His voice had dropped an octave, and she
could see the hunger in his eyes. 'But not here. It feels wrong.'

Disappointment clogged her throat. 'So what do you suggest?'

'Come home with me to the flat. *Our* flat,' he emphasised,
'for now. But if you want somewhere with a garden, we'll go
house-hunting. Choose a place together.'

'But you love your flat. Your space.'

'It doesn't feel right without you. I need you, Sara.'

'And you'd really move, for me?'

'I'll do whatever it takes to make this right. To be a family
with you. Because you and our baby are more important to me
than anything else in the world.'

'Luke.' She kissed him hard.

It was less than twenty minutes before they were back at
Luke's flat.

Less than one minute later before there was a trail of their
clothes from the door to the bed.

And oh, it was good to feel his skin against hers, the warmth
of his mouth as it teased hers to fever-pitch.

'Luke, you're driving me crazy. I need…'

'Me, too,' he said softly. 'But this time I want more. I want
all the barriers gone. I want you and me, and nothing in between.'

'It's a bit late for contraception anyway,' she said shakily.

He kissed her and, as he eased into her, it felt like coming

home. Making love with the man she loved more than anything—
and who loved her all the way back.

She felt her body tightening round his, and his body
surged in answer.

'Sara,' he whispered, 'I love you.'

'I love you, too.' And when she opened her eyes to look at
him, she could see that his lashes were damp.

Afterwards she lay with her head on his shoulder, her hand
resting on his chest and his fingers laced through hers.

'You're going to have to marry me, you know,' he said.

'Because of the baby?' That still stung.

'Because of *me*,' he corrected. 'I want to spend the rest of
my days with you.'

'Luke, you're telling me. You're supposed to ask me properly.'

'I'm telling you because I don't want to risk you saying no.'

She smiled. 'What's that saying of yours? The one that
annoys the hell out of me? Live a little.'

'You want me to ask you to marry me?'

'Give the monkey a peanut.'

'I love it when you're sassy with me.' He laughed. 'You'd
better get dressed.'

'Why?'

'Because I'm not telling our children that I proposed to you
stark naked.'

She couldn't help laughing back, but she did as he'd asked
and got dressed. He pulled on his clothes and led her out to the
bank of the Thames. Heedless of the people walking round
them, he dropped down to one knee.

'Sara Fleet, I love you and you make my world a better
place. I want to make a family with you. Will you marry me?'

There was a huge lump in her throat. But she managed to say
the important word—the one she knew he was waiting for. 'Yes.'